Without a thought, Morgan kicked off her boat shoes, climbed onto the transom and dived into the water and clawed her way down into the blue. She swam deeper and deeper until the light was flickering in her head and the crushing pressure against her chest was unbearable, then swam deeper still, squinting into the blurry distance, into the blackwater depths where the sounding fish had disappeared, but she could make out nothing in the darkness of the cold currents.

Then out of those murky depths a trail of bubbles rose towards her, a ghostly silver cloud climbing fast, spreading out, surrounding her, tickling across her bare arms, her belly.

Andy Braswell's last breath.

# Blackwater Sound

'James Hall has been one of my favourite crime writers for a long time. He's great. Hall has the same concern for the Florida wetlands as Carl Hiaasen but doesn't try to be so wacky. And I think he does it better. This is a bodacious novel: cool and violent, but with an energy that's hard to resist. Top of the class.'

MARK TIMLIN, *Independent on Sunday*

'James Hall really pulls it all together in *Blackwater Sound*: the stun-gun shocks and the delicately orchestrated mayhem; the monstrous villains and their elegantly evil schemes; the noble hero and his savage defence of Florida's fragile marine ecology. If violence can be poetic, Hall has the lyric voice for it. Truly haunting.'          *New York Times Book Review*

'An enjoyably racy tale. The fallibility of his hero, Thorn, is part of his charm. With a pair of wonderfully over-the-top psychopathic siblings as villains, Hall has come up with another lively thriller.'       SUSANNA YAGER, *Sunday Telegraph*

'In combining deep-sea lore with paranoid conspiracy, Hall creates something wholly his own.'

MARK LAWSON, *Guardian*

'Alarming is the *mot juste* for James Hall's *Blackwater Sound*. The narrative is chillingly gripping and there is a humdinger of a final surprise.'       GERALD KAUFMAN, *The Scotsman*

'I believe no one has written more lyrically of the Gulf Stream since Ernest Hemingway. His fascinating characters and his obvious love of the natural world make this book a wonderful reading experience.'       JAMES LEE BURKE

# James Hall

For the last twenty-eight years James Hall has taught literature and creative writing at Florida International University. He is the author of eleven novels, including *Red Sky at Night*, *Under Cover of Daylight* and, most recently, *Body Language* and *Rough Draft*, both of which are available from HarperCollins.

'James Hall is the master of suspense . . . his writing runs as clear and fast as the Gulf Stream waters.'
*New York Times Book Review*

'Hall writes splendidly plotted tales which, largely inhabited by comic but terrifying psychopaths, delight as they dismay . . . Do not miss.'
GERALD KAUFMAN

'Hall delivers oddball fun at a rip of pace, without letting you forget that he is a literate, stylish writer. Like beer from the bottom of a bait well, Hall's books *psst* and bubble over as soon as you open them.'
*Los Angeles Times*

'Think Walter Mosley and James Lee Burke. Hall's writing is terse like Mosley's, but he can also nail a vivid metaphor and turn your head with a violent twist as well as Burke does. Multi-charactered, darkly comic . . . sharp laughs and heart-stopping thrills.'
*Houston Chronicle*

'Hall is the finest and most literate of thriller writers.'
*San Francisco Chronicle*

## By James Hall

NOVELS

*Under Cover of Daylight*
*Tropical Freeze*
*Bones of Coral*
*Hard Aground*
*Mean High Tide*
*Gone Wild*
*Buzz Cut*
*Red Sky at Night*
*Body Language*
*Rough Draft*
*Blackwater Sound*

POETRY

*False Statements*
*The Mating Reflex*
*The Lady From the Dark Green Hills*

SHORT STORIES

*Paper Products*

# JAMES HALL

# BLACKWATER SOUND

HarperCollins*Publishers*

HarperCollins*Publishers*
77–85 Fulham Palace Road,
Hammersmith, London W6 8JB

www.fireandwater.com

Special overseas edition 2002
This paperback edition 2003
1 3 5 7 9 8 6 4 2

First published in Great Britain by
HarperCollins*Publishers* 2002

First published in the USA by
St Martin's Press 2002

ISBN 0 00 711275 0

Typeset in Meridien by Palimpsest Book Production Limited,
Polmont, Stirlingshire

Printed and bound in Great Britain by
Clays Limited, St Ives plc

*For Peter Meinke,*
*great poet and teacher*
*and always good for a laugh*

## Acknowledgments

I'm deeply grateful to a host of people who assisted me in writing this novel. I absolutely could not have done it without their generosity and good cheer. I thank you each and all.

Mike Lemon, who unintentionally got this started. Joe Wisdom, my boon companion, always merry and bright. Charlie Meconis, for his excellent technical expertise. Dean Travis Clarke, who opened doors and allowed me to use his words. Clay and Kim Hensley, for their wonderful stories, without which I would never have seen the way to go. Garry Kravitz, for going above and beyond. Captain Johnny, James, and Mike for allowing me to bounce along. Les Standiford, who always steers me back on course. And Richard, who tells the truth every step of the way. And Charlie and Sally, the best readers and editors I could wish for.

And Evelyn, for her unfailing love, support, and wisdom.

Grief fills the room up of my absent child,
Lies in his bed, walks up and down with me,
Puts on his pretty looks, repeats his words,
Remembers me of all his gracious parts,
Stuffs out his vacant garments with his form.

—*King John*, WILLIAM SHAKESPEARE

# Prologue

The marlin was the color of the ocean at twenty fathoms, an iridescent blue, with eerie light smoldering within its silky flesh as if its electrons had become unstable by the cold friction of the sea. A ghostly phosphorescence, a gleaming flash, its large eyes unblinking as it slipped into a seam in the current, then rose toward the luminous surface where a school of tuna was pecking at the tiny larvae and crustaceans snagged on a weed line.

The marlin attacked from the rear of the school. An ambush. It accelerated from thirty knots to double that in only a few yards. A fusion of grace, efficiency, and blinding power. For a creature with the bulk of a bull, the marlin was as sleek as any missile and blazed through the water at a speed not even the most powerful torpedo could attain. When it crashed into the school, it stunned each fish with a blow from its three-foot bill, then swallowed it headfirst.

Morgan Braswell saw its dorsal fin and the curved arc of its tail. She saw its shadow just below the surface. Maybe it was simply the angle of the sun, but the fish looked twice the size of an ordinary marlin. Before she could utter a word, the marlin hit the trolled lure and the outrigger popped.

'Fish on!' Johnny yelled.

In the fighting chair Morgan lifted the rod and settled it into the leather holder that was belted around her waist. At the same moment the rod tip jerked and the hundred-pound monofilament began to scream off her reel. Nothing she could do for now except hold on and watch. They were twenty-two miles south of Key West, a marlin highway that ran along a drop-off in the ocean floor, an east-to-west ridge that plummeted from nine hundred feet to two thousand in less than a mile. Wood's Wall was its name, the beginning of the Straits of Florida.

Andy and Johnny stood beside her. Her two brothers. Andy was the older, curly blond hair and rangy like their dad. At seventeen, a major-league science whiz, chemistry, electronics. He spent long hours in the MicroDyne lab, tinkering with new materials, new fibers, new everything. He was movie-star handsome, funny. A gifted athlete, president of his high school class, perfect scores on his college boards, courted by Stanford, MIT. A golden boy. Everyone in awe of him, most of all Johnny. Johnny was the quiet kid who tracked his big brother's every move, stood in his shadow, said little.

Morgan was the second child, a year younger than Andy, with electric blue eyes, a sinuous figure, glossy black hair that she wore as short as Andy's. She was well aware of the effect she had on boys, but didn't give a damn about trading on her looks, scoring points in the Palm Beach social scene. She'd rather hang with Andy. The two of them endlessly tinkering in A.J.'s workshop or at the company lab. Metallurgy, ceramics, carbides. Morgan had the intense focus and scrupulously logical mind. Andy was the creative one, spontaneous and intuitive, a genius. She was the yin to his yang. The controlled left brain to his exuberant right. A neatly nestled fit.

Up on the flybridge, Darlene Braswell stood beside her husband, watching her daughter closely. A tall, black-haired woman with shadowy Italian eyes. A violinist with the Miami Symphony till she'd met and married A.J. Braswell. Now a vigilant mom. Too vigilant. She and Morgan hadn't spoken for days. A bitter standoff. Last week, coming into Morgan's room, staring at her for a full minute in prickly silence. Morgan knew what it was about, but didn't think her mother had the nerve. She held Morgan's eyes and finally spoke, voice neutral, asking if anything was going on she should know about. Going on? Morgan playing dumb. You know what I mean, Morgan. Is something happening between you and Andy?

Morgan said nothing, glaring into her mother's dark eyes. Okay, her mother said, if you won't discuss this, then I'll talk to Andy. One way or the other, I'm going to find out. You go ahead, Mom, talk to Andy, but if you do, I'll never speak to you again. Never. Now get out of my room. Morgan pointed at her door, kept pointing till her mother turned and walked to the door and stood there a moment waiting for Morgan to open up. But she didn't. She wasn't about to. Her mother wouldn't understand. Never. Not in a million years.

From up on the flybridge her father yelled at her to pay attention.

'A little more before you hit him. Ease off on your drag, this is a big girl.'

She picked her moment, then yanked back on the rod, sunk the hook, and in the next instant the fish showed itself. Forty yards behind them, its long bill broke through, then its silver head, holding there for several seconds, its wild eye staring back at Morgan as if taking her measure. The fish shook its head furiously and flopped on its side and was gone. Sounding, diving down and down and down, the reel shrieking, the rod jumping in her hands as if she'd hooked a stallion at full gallop.

On the bridge, A.J. was silenced by the sight.

Johnny stood at the transom transfixed, staring out at the blue water where the fish had disappeared. His blond hair hung limply down his back. A pudgy baby, a pudgy kid, and now a pudgy teenager. Smiling at the wrong times, always fidgeting, gnawing his fingernails to the quick.

Her dad stood with his butt to the console, reaching behind him to run the controls, doing it by feel, backing the thirty-one-foot Bertram toward the spot where the fish had disappeared. The Braswells worked as a unit. It required first-rate teamwork to catch these fish. No one could do it alone, not the big ones. Someone to handle the boat, keep it positioned; an angler strapped into the fighting chair; a wire man to grab the leader when the fish was finally brought close to the boat. Then a gaffer who nailed the fish in its bony jaw and helped haul it through the transom door. The five of them circulating the jobs.

'You okay, Morgan? You want some water?' Andy asked.

She was pumping the rod, then cranking on the downstroke. For every yard of line she won back the fish was taking out two. The reel was more than half-empty and Morgan had begun to sweat, her fingers throbbing already, back muscles aching. In only twenty minutes the fish was making her pant.

'Water, yes,' Morgan said.

He held the water bottle to her lips, tipped it up. With a towel he mopped her forehead. He gave her shoulders a rub, stayed with it for a while, a good massage, working his fingers in deep.

The line went out in screaming bursts and with grim focus she reeled it back in, inch by grueling inch. The fish stayed deep, two hundred yards of line, perhaps. A. J. cheering her on, giving her small instructions, though Morgan knew the drill as well as he did. She could hear it in his voice, a trace of envy. It should be him in the chair. It was his passion more than hers. He went to the tournaments. Mexico, Bahamas, Virgin Islands. He hung out with marlin men. Went fishing on the bigger boats of his rich friends. Boats with fulltime crews. Two million, three million dollars purchase price, a few hundred thousand a year to maintain and staff them. He lusted for one of those boats, a sixty-footer with four thousand horsepower rumbling belowdecks. At the rate MicroDyne was growing, it wouldn't be long before he could afford one.

Her dad should be the one in the chair hauling his fish to the surface. But that wasn't how it worked. The Braswells rotated the angling on a set routine. Morgan first thing in the morning, Andy next. After lunch A.J. took the chair. Then her mother had her shot, and finally in the last hours of the day, it was Johnny's turn. Johnny, who would rather work the wire, the close-in stuff. He didn't want the spotlight for hours at a time, didn't have the patience for that kind of labor. He liked the big, dramatic moments. Slipping on the heavy glove and taking a couple of quick wraps and then arm-wrestling that fish to the edge of the boat, gaffing it.

An hour passed. Andy gave her water, her father rooted her on. As Morgan pumped the reel, her mother watched silently. Morgan was dizzy. Despite

6

the fluids, she felt dehydrated. They'd not seen any sign of the fish again. It was down about nine hundred feet and was heading east out to deeper water. Her dad was quiet now, handling the boat. Wanting to be in the chair so much, but not a whiner, trying to be encouraging to his daughter.

'You want me to take over, Morgan?' Andy asked her.

She told him no, she wanted to see this to the end.

Her hands were numb. Her back muscles in spasm. She struggled to breathe. The fish was down there cruising east, towing them toward the horizon. She held on because that's what you did in this family. She held on because to give up would change things. She would lose something she couldn't name. Some part of her identity. Who she was, who she wanted to be. It was what her father would do, and what Andy would do. So she hung on. She pumped and cranked on the downstroke. She fought that goddamn fish.

Then it was two hours. A little after ten in the morning. She'd refilled the reel more than halfway. Bringing the fish up, winning the battle. She lifted the rod, then lowered it and pumped the reel. Lifted it, lowered it and pumped. The world was now a narrow slit through which she saw only a few square feet of water where the line disappeared. Her tongue was swollen. Her hands were knotted with pain, arm muscles quivering, but she cranked the reel.

It was almost noon when she felt the slack. A belly in the line. No pressure when she reeled. She realized what was happening and was about to call out to the others when the marlin rocketed the last few yards to the surface.

In a great geyser it exploded, silver and blue, its entire electric length, shimmering like polished chrome and the bluest blue, a scream erupting on the boat, from her mother, from the entire Braswell clan, a chilling collective roar, as the marlin launched itself high into the air and hung in all its colossal radiance, a terrible angel against the clouds and sun and sky, like some divine appearance, the embodiment of all fish, of all life in the sea, a giant long-billed, scythe-tailed deity, a monster, dreadful and magnificent. Broken loose from gravity, hanging there for longer than was possible.

Finally it dropped, splashing on its side, sending a cone of water as high as the flybridge.

Morgan reeled and reeled, cranking as fast as her muscles allowed.

It was the largest fish she'd ever seen. Larger than the blue marlin on the wall of her father's study. His was eight hundred pounds, caught in the Virgin Islands when he was twenty-eight. The fish that had started his obsession. But this one was half again as large. A giant. Bigger than anything in the magazines, anything on the endless videos A.J.'s friends brought back from the Great Barrier Reef or Kona. This was the mothership.

Her father was silent. Everyone was silent. Johnny turned to look at his older brother, and whatever he saw on Andy's face made Johnny's mouth go slack. This was not just a big fish. This was the fish that lurked in their dreams.

'Jesus,' Andy said quietly. 'Jesus.'

He came behind her and once again he massaged her shoulders while she cranked the last few yards of line and saw the wire leader emerge from the sea.

'It's given up,' her dad said. 'You beat it. It's given up, Morgan.'

But she didn't think so. Until just before the leap, the marlin's power seemed undiminished. The fish was still green. Still strong and alive. Unfazed by the fight. But the leader was only a few feet away, the fish lying slack a few feet below the surface. So maybe she was wrong. Maybe it had caved in after just one spectacular jump.

Andy let go of her shoulders, turned, and flung open a drawer in the supply case and grabbed a stainless steel cylinder a little larger than a cigar. It was one of Andy's inventions. A float on one end, a stubby aerial on the other. It was designed to be hooked beneath the marlin's second dorsal fin with a small surgical steel anchor, and was programmed to come alive for one week each year. On the appointed date, the electronic sending unit would begin to transmit all the information its microprocessor had collected that year, a day-by-day report on GPS locations, depth, water temperature, speed, distance traveled. By activating it only during that one-week window, Morgan estimated the unit would last for eight to ten years. Sometime during the crucial week when the transmitter came live, they had to get lucky and the marlin had to break the surface, either to sun itself or to attack schools of baitfish. Just a few seconds was all. When the antennae broke through, data would stream up to a satellite and a few seconds later the blue ping would pulse on the Braswells' receiving unit. The ping would mark the fish's present location and would continue to ping until the fish was submerged again or the week was over and the unit shut off.

Much better than conventional tagging methods. If it worked, it could revolutionize everything. You could track a fish's migration, begin to understand its life cycle, its mating habits. Steal a look into the secret life of that mysterious fish. But she and Andy weren't thinking of its commercial value when they designed and assembled it from salvaged computer parts. The pod was a gift to their dad, their attempt to take part in his consuming obsession.

Andy used a tiny ice pick to activate the unit, then clamped it just behind the sharp point of a customized harpoon.

Morgan hauled the fish closer and could see its blue shadow rising through the water. Listless, on its side. Either defeated or playing possum. It was impossible to tell.

Andy leaned over the transom, cocked the harpoon back, picking his spot.

Her mother called down to Andy. In her tense voice, telling him to be careful. Very careful.

Andy leaned another inch or two, then stood back up.

'It's too far, Dad! I'm going to have to wire it, bring it up closer.'

'Morgan,' A.J. called. 'Keep the line tight. Keep it close so Andy can work.'

Andy grabbed his glove from the back pocket of his shorts and pulled it on. Another of his creations. An ordinary blue denim work glove with a thick cowhide pad stitched across the palm and sides. Even a medium-sized fish could badly bruise a hand, or sometimes crush bones.

Johnny seized the biggest gaff from the holder.

'We're not gaffing it, Johnny,' A.J. called. 'We're just attaching the pod.'

'But this is a world record, Dad. This is the all-time big mother.'

All of them laughed, and from that moment Big Mother was her name.

'Tag and release, Johnny, that's what we're doing.'

Stubbornly, Johnny held on to the gaff, planting himself at the starboard side of the transom while Andy stood to port, the harpoon in his right hand. He was touching the metal leader wire with his left, stroking it lightly as if wanting to establish some connection with the giant.

Morgan had handled the wire on small sails and yellowfin tuna. It was dangerous, but thrilling. The saying went, 'One wrap, you lose the fish, three wraps you lose a finger.' Two wraps was right. You took two wraps of the leader wire around the gloved hand, no more, no less.

Andy took three.

Morgan wasn't sure if she'd seen right. Her mind so foggy. Her tongue so swollen, she could barely speak. Maybe he took one more wrap for extra measure, because the fish was huge, maybe he made a mistake, or she was simply wrong about what she thought she'd seen.

A.J. backed the boat slowly.

'Okay, Andy. Pick your spot, jab it in hard and true.'

Johnny edged closer to his brother, gaff at the ready.

Slowly the bill appeared as Andy hauled it up.

'Jeez, it's way over a thousand pounds. Maybe fifteen hundred.'

Andy had the fish at the transom. Its bill was longer than any she'd ever seen in photographs, on walls, anywhere.

Johnny leaned over the edge to touch the fish.

'No, Johnny. Let Andy do his work.'

The fish must have seen their shadows because it shied away. Andy braced his knees against the transom, leaned back, using all his weight to drag the fish back into place. Morgan could see the muscles straining in his back, in his arms and shoulders. A wiry boy, narrow-waisted, wide shoulders and rawhide-tough. But the fish was strong, very strong.

Andy cocked his arm, held it for a second, then plunged the point of the harpoon into the second dorsal.

'It's set, Dad! I felt it lock on.'

He shouldn't have done it. Shouldn't have turned his back on the fish to beam up at their father. With a fish that big, it was reckless. But he was so proud, so hungry for a morsel of their dad's approval. In that half second his back was turned, the fish swung back and made a slow pirouette, disappearing into the transparent blue.

Andy was jerked backwards, his hip banging against the transom. Johnny reached out for him but it was too late. Andy lurched overboard, his hand trapped in the wire. Morgan heard his scream, heard it stifled as he was dragged under, saw him moving quickly through two feet of water, three, four, five, saw him turning back toward the light, trying to swim one-handed toward the surface, a useless stroke against the horrific power of that fish. She saw his face, his blond hair pulsing like a jellyfish around his head, she saw his white flesh turning blue, blue as the water, blue as the fish.

'Reel, Morgan! Reel, goddamn it!' A.J. was screaming.

A second later he was beside her. He tore the rod from her hands, cranked the fish back up, cranked.

But the line continued to unspool, the sharp ratchet of the reel clicking faster than she'd ever heard it.

A.J. heaved back on the rod, tightening the drag as he did, pulling with all his weight, all his life and breath and muscle.

Morgan couldn't scream, couldn't breathe. A dull paralysis had taken hold of her. Shock and terror and utter exhaustion.

She rose from the fighting chair, watched the water, saw a flash of white. Andy's face, his shorts, something. Down in all that blue, his body dragged deeper and deeper into the airless depths. A bear hug crushed her chest, a pressure greater than bones and flesh could possibly withstand.

Her father was groaning as he reeled against the power of that fish, winning back a few feet, a few more. Johnny dropped to his knees, holding to the transom as if he were seasick, peering out at the water. From the flybridge Darlene screamed. Her boy, her precious son. Her wail ripped apart the air.

And then the crack of a rifle shot as the heavy monofilament snapped.

Her father crashed against the side of the chair and crumpled to the deck.

Without a thought, Morgan kicked off her boat shoes, climbed onto the transom and dived into the water and clawed her way down into the blue. She swam deeper and deeper until the light was flickering in her head and the crushing pressure against her chest was unbearable, then swam deeper still, squinting into the blurry distance, into the blackwater depths where the sounding fish had disappeared, but she could make out nothing in the darkness of the cold currents.

Then out of those murky depths a trail of bubbles rose toward her, a ghostly silver cloud climbing fast, spreading out, surrounding her, tickling across her bare arms, her belly.

Andy Braswell's last breath. Her brother. Her love.

# TEN YEARS LATER

# 1

Thorn had brought along the .357 magnum not because he was worried about being attacked by pirates, but because he wanted to give the pistol a long-overdue burial at sea. Maybe have a little ceremony, just he and Casey, say a few words, something short and funny, then sling the goddamn thing out into the water. Stand around afterwards and watch the ripples die out, have a sip of wine, put his arm around Casey and hold on.

She didn't know yet about the gun being aboard. He'd told her about some of the violent incidents in his past, but if he got too specific, she always winced and turned away. Casey had inherited her light and airy view of human nature from her hippie parents. Growing up in Islamorada in an apartment above the gift shop where they sold rolling papers and hookahs and conch shells and custom-made sandals. Now in her late thirties, after years of waiting tables, Casey had started a roadside business in Tavernier, selling life-sized manatees and alligators that she made from plaster casts, then painted in garish sunset colors. The manatees and alligators stood up on their hind legs and gripped US Postal Service mailboxes in their flippers and claws. She was doing well with the mailbox stands. You saw them on nearly every street in Key Largo and Tavernier. People dressed up their manatees with goggles and snorkels or straw hats, cocked fishing poles and scoop nets up against the gators. Put witches' hats on them at Halloween and white beards for Christmas. Lately, Casey had moved on to a few non-Keys animals. One of her new creations, a full-sized, neon pink buffalo, now stood like some crazed sentinel between Thorn's house and the water's edge, where it stared out at the sunsets.

The .357 was inside his tackle box that lay on the deck near where Casey was sunning. When he finally landed the sea trout on his line, he was going to let her know what he had in mind. He'd been holding on to the damn thing too long, and now that they were several hours out into the deserted Florida Bay, it seemed like the right time to dump it.

For the last two years a long string of wonder-fully unremarkable days had come and gone. Each night the breeze stirred the curtains and the cardinals trilled their evening song, each morning at first light the mourning doves lowed from the upper branches of the tamarind tree, and almost every hour of the day palm fronds tickled against the tin roof like the whispers of angels. Not even the weather seemed to vary, with steady tropical trade winds pouring up from the south, a constant cinnamon-scented flow.

But even amid that unceasing peace, Thorn often jerked awake in the middle of the night, sheened with sweat, thinking about the pistol wrapped in oily cloths, tucked in a bottom drawer of his desk across the room. He thought about its history, the dark karma that clung to it. More than once he'd taken it out of the desk and walked out to the end of his dock to pitch it into Blackwater Sound, where it would sink into the silt and begin its long chemical unraveling. But something in him had resisted. Some wary voice had murmured in his ear. You are not finished with it. A bad day is coming.

But now, by God, he was determined to heave the thing away. Far enough from shore where no one would ever stumble on it. Far enough away from home that Thorn would forever be beyond its magnetic field. Today he would officially and irrevocably lay down his arms and the voice would go still, the fist in his stomach would unclench, and the days would once more stretch out lazily ahead of him, and he'd take one easy breath after the next, savoring the juicy Florida Keys air for the rest of his stay on earth.

'You going to catch that fish, Thorn, or bore it to death?'

Casey squeezed more suntan lotion into her hand and slathered it across her bare breasts. She was stretched out on the forward deck, while Thorn stood on the platform perch above the outboard. In the four days they'd been out on the water, Casey had been nude most of the time and her bikini lines had vanished. She had a narrow face, bright green eyes, an easy smile. After all those hours in the sun, her shoulder-length hair was a few degrees blonder than when they left, and even the patch between her legs had lightened. Now when he lowered his face to it, he could smell the golden afterglow of the sun along with the faintly tart citrus scent that rose from Casey when her flesh was heated.

'It doesn't feel bored to me,' Thorn said. 'It feels kind of excited.'

Thorn cranked the reel, two careful turns. It was wrapped with three hundred yards of four-pound-test monofilament. Line so wispy, if you thought about it too long it would snap. He figured the sea trout probably went about ten pounds and it'd already stripped off two hundred and fifty yards. For the last ten minutes he'd cut the drag back to zero, letting the trout take all the line it wanted in ten-, fifteen-yard surges, then when the line went slack, the lunker taking a rest, Thorn would win back a yard or two.

Letting the water wear the fish down. Water and time and the weight of that three hundred yards of fragile monofilament.

'If you used ten-pound test, you'd have that fish filleted by now.'

'If it's too easy to catch,' Thorn said, 'it doesn't taste any good.'

Casey finished oiling her breasts. Head to toe, she was now as glossy as fresh varnish and her nipples had tightened into dark buds. Thorn could feel a tingle working its way down from his navel. Things shifting inside his cutoffs.

Thorn's skiff was pole-anchored in about two feet of water over some grassy beds where schools of silver sea trout had flickered past all morning. In the last few days they'd seen dozens of tarpon and permit and bones skimming the flats, lots of rays and more sharks than they could count. The sky had been clear all week and Thorn's eyes were dazzled and aching from staring into the shallows. A good ache.

On that April morning, Monday or Tuesday, he wasn't sure, the breeze had died off and the Florida Bay stretched out as flat and silver as a platter of mercury, running off toward the western horizon where it turned into a blur of blue chrome. The air and water were within a degree or two of his own body temperature. Dipping in and out of the bay, one element to the other, he hardly noticed.

A hundred yards east of their spot, the *Heart Pounder*, his thirty-foot Chris-Craft, was anchored in four feet of water on the edge of the flats. Their mothership. A couple of narrow bunks, a stove, a cooler full of fruit and cheese and a few bottles of a cut-rate Chardonnay. They'd towed the skiff behind the big boat to have some way to get into the skinny water, chase the fish.

The *Heart Pounder* was a teak and white oak beauty. Built before Thorn was born, it was low and slow, with the ancient grace of an era when getting from here to there as quickly as possible wasn't the point. Thorn had spent all of March and half of April replanking the hull. Tearing out a dozen rotting boards and fitting the new ones into place. Harder job than he'd anticipated. Made harder by the fact that he had absolutely no idea what the hell he was doing when he started. He'd torn out too many planks, used the wrong screws, applied the wrong caulk to the seams between the new boards, then wound up having to pull off his planks and begin over. Finally he'd found a boatwright in Islamorada who gave him a few lessons in carvel-planking, and the use of bunged screws and stealers, those triangular-shaped strakes that allowed Thorn to slightly alter the hull profile. For several weeks with the old man standing over him puffing on his pipe, Thorn managed to learn just enough to get the *Heart Pounder* watertight again. Skills he hoped he never had to use again.

'What's another word for blue?'

'Blue?' Thorn looked over at her. 'What're you, depressed?'

'No, that.' Casey lifted her hand and pointed lazily up at the cloudless expanse. She was propped on one elbow now, her breasts doing nicely against the pull of gravity. 'I'm thinking of doing a rhino in that color. I want the right word for its name. *Blue rhino* sounds dull.'

'A rhino?'

'I'm tired of manatees and alligators. I'm artistically restless.'

'Azure,' Thorn said. 'Cerulean.'

'Too hoity-toity.'

'Sapphire.'

To the west across the flats was a small mangrove island. Gulls dove into the shallow water rimming it. A great blue heron stood in the flats just a few yards from the snarl of mangrove roots. On the charts the island was unnamed, but he and Casey had been calling it Mosquito Junction. A dark haze of bloodsuckers that'd probably never tasted human flesh before hovered over it like an evil bloom of radiation. Last night the little bastards had followed the wisp of light from their kerosene lantern across a mile of motionless air right into the *Heart Pounder*'s cabin to dine on their exposed flesh. He and Casey had to decide whether to douse the lantern and stop reading, or put up with the itchy nuisance. They read. Swatted and read.

'Cobalt rhino,' Thorn said. 'Or navy.'

'Okay, you can stop. I'm sticking with blue. It's not great, but it'll do.'

'Turquoise.'

25

Casey gave him a quick, precise smile.

'You know too many words, Thorn.'

'Is that possible?'

'All those books you read, you're clogged with words.'

'I'm just a simple guy with a simple vocabulary.'

'Yeah, right. Sure you are, Thorn. You're so simple.'

'Indigo,' he said.

Casey aimed her chin at the sky.

'That,' she said. 'That color. Whatever it is.'

Casey stretched her arms, pointing both hands up at the unnameable heavens. Her breasts shimmered, taking the light and playing with it and sending it on its happy way.

'So what're we having for supper?'

'I was thinking fish,' he said. 'In fact, *that* fish. If it ever gives up.'

'Fish again?'

'You like fish.'

'Four days ago I liked fish. At the moment I'd kill for a hamburger.'

'You're a vegetarian.'

'My point, exactly.'

Thorn fished for a while and Casey basked. She was excellent at it. Basking seemed to be one of her gifts. She had such a remarkably even disposition, nothing seemed to rouse her to anger or even mild distress.

For the last couple of months they'd been sharing his small stilthouse and his monotonous days. She

26

went off to her roadside shack every morning to make her plaster animals while he tied bonefish flies. After work, he helped her unload her latest creation from the back of her ancient Chevy pickup and she set up her paints out near Blackwater Sound and spent the next few hours covering that dull gray plaster with the gaudiest colors she could swirl together.

While she painted, Thorn tied flies or crafted the wooden lures he carved for a few longtime clients who believed his handiwork had some kind of supernatural power to catch fish. God bless their superstitious butts. The lures Thorn made were torpedo-shaped pieces of gumbo-limbo or live oak ornamented with a few dabs of paint and glitter and glass bead eyeballs, nothing more or less. But if those fine folks wanted to give him cash money to carve them and sand them and fine-tune them with a little color, then fine. Go with Allah.

Last week after he'd finished replanking the hull, Thorn decided he needed a break from the routine. A shakedown cruise seemed just the thing, putter out into the backcountry, deep into the Florida Bay, and see if the dignified old lady still leaked.

It'd been a long while since Thorn had motored so far into those waters, and though he'd heard the backcountry was in bad shape, seeing it firsthand was something else entirely.

The Florida Bay was a flat, shallow basin that lay at the tip of the Florida peninsula. Bordered on the east by the upper Keys and running west to the other

27

side of the state where its waters merged with the Gulf of Mexico. For centuries the bay had received the freshwater outflow from the Everglades and had converted it gradually to saltwater by the time it reached the Keys and the coral reefs. The eelgrass had once grown in thick beds, covering most of the bay, providing the nutrition-rich nurseries for shrimp and the other lower-pecking-order creatures. When Thorn was a boy, exploring the nooks of the Florida Bay in his wooden skiff, he'd assumed such abundance would last forever. That the water would always be crystal, that the undersea kingdom would ceaselessly flourish.

But since those days Miami and its suburbs had quadrupled in size and were trying to quadruple again and the people up there were stacked butt-to-jowls twenty stories into the air without room to turn or bend over to tie their shoes, and now that the sugar growers had intimidated or paid off all their foes and were once again happily scattering phosphorus and mercury and a long list of other unpronounceable toxins across their vast acreage, the end result, a hundred miles downstream, was that the pristine Florida Bay was now teetering on collapse.

A never-ending flood of solvents and cleaning fluids and petroleum products and every other form of exotic contamination had been oozing out the rectum of the state, a spew of caustic wastewater and runoff and overflow and toilet flush, leaching into the bay, poisoning the shrimp with its acid, overheating the water with its super-mambo genetically indestructible fertilizer spillage, causing great blooms of algae that stole the oxygen right from the water, leaving the fish to writhe and float to the surface. Decades of abuse. An endless tonnage of disregard. All of which would've killed the bay long ago if it weren't for the steady string of hurricanes bringing in their million million gallons of diluting fresh water. Nature's irony, using one disaster to neutralize another.

Because of several busy hurricane seasons in a row, the bay water was not as salty or as acidic. You could see the bottom again. Patches of eelgrass were growing. Clusters of shrimp snapped by. But there was no cause for celebration. The rebirth was only temporary. The ever-sprawling masses up the road would win eventually. They'd kill the Keys. One day soon, one of those weekend visitors would snap off the last finger of coral, snatch up the final living conch. And no matter what anyone tried to do, you could absolutely count on the fact that those toxins would continue to pump into the Everglades and filter into the bay until it was all as bleached out as the whitened bones of a desert coyote ten years lying in the sun.

This was death-throes time. Time to bring your ear close to the lips of the dying creature and hear its final rasping words. Thorn couldn't help being gloomy about it. The only way not to be gloomy was not to know it was happening or not to give a rat's ass. He'd tried the rat's-ass approach, tried it and tried it.

So he and Casey had come out on a shakedown cruise and the new hull hadn't leaked. Thorn was pleased with the hull, and a little amazed. But he was deeply disheartened by what he saw beneath the glittery surface. Last night, after two rum drinks and a long dose of starlight, he'd proposed that the two of them take another trip. Cross the Gulf Stream, go over to the islands, poke around. He'd heard about a place near Andros, the blue holes, the wall. Go diving in the deep stuff. Fish on flats where the bonefish had never seen human shadows. Maybe search out some fresh place to set up shop. A new home where the tourist Huns had not yet arrived.

Casey said nothing, and Thorn dropped the subject.

Now in the fading daylight, Thorn started in on Andros again. And those other little islands where wild goats and rats and iguanas were the only residents. He'd been down there as a kid with the folks who'd raised him, Doctor Bill Truman and his wife, Kate. They'd crossed the Gulf Stream on the *Heart Pounder*. It'd been his first experience with deep-sea fishing, sailfish, marlin, and yellowfin tuna. Thorn was only ten, but he remembered it clearly. Great fishing, wild landscape.

'Leave the Keys?' Casey said. 'All this?'

She levered herself up to a sitting position. Naked and oiled and squinting at him through the harsh sun. He looked out at the water where his fish was taking a breather, hiding behind a rock, probably hoping this was all just a terrible dream.

'I'm ready for something new,' Thorn said. 'I've got an itch.'

He cranked the reel, brought the fish a foot closer to the boat. Then another foot.

'I think this is the end, Thorn.'

'The end?'

'Of you and me. Our romance.'

He gave her an uncertain smile.

'Because I want to go to the islands?'

'No,' Casey said. 'It's been coming for a while. It arrived just now.'

'What?'

'The end. The end of our affair.'

He cranked the fish closer. It seemed to have given up. Just a dull weight now.

Casey said, 'We're different. I thought it would work out, you being how you are and me being who I am. But it hasn't.'

'It's working for me.'

'You like me because I'm shallow, Thorn.'

'You're not shallow.'

'Hey, it's nothing to be ashamed of. It's who I am. How I was raised. I don't have a complicated view of the world. I don't have dark places. Brood over stuff, get all tangled up in my thoughts. You like me because I'm easy. A lick and a dash and you're on your way.'

Thorn looked out at the bright water. His eyes hurt and his shoulders were tired from hauling in the damn fish on such light tackle. Casey was right. There was no reason to be sporting when all you were doing was catching your supper. Just put ten-pound test on the reel and haul them in as efficiently as possible and be done with it.

'Are you listening to me, Thorn?'

'Oh, yes. I'm listening.'

'You've just been using me to relax. I knew that. My girlfriends told me from the beginning. All the women you've been with, what they were like. I'm not like any of them. But I thought I'd give it a try. And sure, it was fun most of the time. The sex was fine. But we're not the same. We're just not. It's pretty simple when you get down to it. We have fun, but we don't exalt each other.'

'Exalt each other?'

'Maybe it's not the right word. I don't know. But you know what I mean. We don't push each other up the incline. We're just hovering in the status quo.'

Thorn cranked the sea trout up to the side of the boat. He climbed down from the platform and used the scoop net to bring the fish aboard. It lay inert on the deck, all its fight gone. Thorn squatted down. He withdrew the barbless hook from its lip and eased the sea trout back over the side and washed it back and forth through the water till it was revived. When he let it go, the fish hesitated a moment, sinking several inches through the water, then with a couple of flutters of its tail it was gone.

Thorn looked out toward the small mangrove island, at the bright water stretching beyond it, the vast silvery plain that ran for miles up toward the mainland.

'You sure, Casey? I like you a whole lot. I'm very happy with you.'

'Happy isn't good enough, Thorn. Sorry.'

'It's not?'

'Happy is pretty low on the joy scale.'

She reached over and picked up her yellow blouse and slipped it on and buttoned it. She looked at him for a moment, then looked out at the water again.

'Tell me the right words. I'll say them.'

She smiled at him.

'At a time like this, one chance is all you get. It's over, Thorn. But don't worry. You'll find somebody else. That's how you are. A week, two weeks, you'll be on to the next thing. Making some other girl all swoony.'

As they motored south the western sky turned pale gold. Along the horizon it was shot full of purple streaks and eddies of red. To the north, out over the Everglades, the sky was bluish-black with thunderstorms – a late cold front stalled just north of Miami. Thorn guided the boat around the shallows and Casey sat in the fighting chair drinking wine and looking back at the froth of their wake.

They were maybe ten miles southwest of Flamingo, the primitive national park that covered the extreme southern tip of the state, about as far from civilization as it was possible to go and still be in Florida waters. Thorn pulled open the tackle box and drew out the .357. He held it in his right hand, steering with his left. Behind him Casey was still facing the wake, sipping her wine. Thorn gripped the pistol by the barrel, and without ceremony, he hurled it over their starboard bow. More heavy metal added to the seabed. An empty gesture. It proved nothing, ended nothing. If the bad shit started again, he could always go buy another gun. He'd tossed the thing away but felt not one bit better about anything. Still stuck in his own tight skin. Cramped by his own mulish ways.

Before him the water lay flat with a spreading scarlet sheen. The twilight air was mellow and seasoned with the tang of barnacles and muck clinging to mangrove roots. The red sun was a smudged thumbprint a few inches above the horizon. Maybe an hour of light left.

Thorn had his face in the wind, steering them around a small mangrove island rimmed with white sand, when he sensed something off to the northwest, and turned to see the silhouette of the jet, a black cutout against the crimson sky.

Casey felt it, too, and swiveled the fighting chair halfway round and stiffened. Thorn pulled back on the throttle. The plane was growing larger by the second.

'Please tell me that's a fighter jet going back to Homestead Air Base.'

Thorn shook his head.

'Wrong color, wrong shape.'

It was skimming very close to the water, headed in their direction, maybe a mile or two away. A 747 or 767, he wasn't sure. But big, very big, and closing fast. A great blue heron wading on a nearby sandbar squawked once and untangled into flight. To their south a large school of mullet splashed the surface and quickly disappeared.

'Hear that?' Thorn said.

'I don't hear anything.'

'Yeah,' he said. 'Engines are dead.'

'Shit!' Casey dropped her wineglass on the deck, stood up.

The *Heart Pounder* was too old and slow to dodge anything hurtling that fast. Anyway there was nowhere to hide, and no way to be sure he wasn't putting them even more squarely in the jet's path.

Thorn shifted the engine into neutral and watched it come.

# 2

Minutes after takeoff, Captain Kathy Dubois was still holding at three thousand feet, just passing beyond the southern tip of the state, when she felt the first jolt. No more than a hard buzz in her sinuses, then a quick double blip in her pulse. Miami Departure was keeping them at three thousand because of a jam-up of inbound traffic from the south at five thousand. The Departure controller was sending everyone south over the Everglades to dodge the line of level-five thunderstorms to the north. A dark, roiling mass parked over Fort Lauderdale, extending ten miles out to sea and halfway across the state.

'You feel that?'

Mark Hensley, the copilot, was staring down at the instrument panel.

'Just a fritz in the system,' he said. But he didn't sound so sure.

She glanced over at him.

'A fritz?'

'You know, some little hiccup, dirt in the fuel line. Like that.'

'Dirt in the fuel line?'

'It's from *Bonnie and Clyde*, the movie. Some auto mechanic is working on their car . . .'

Out the windscreen of the MD-11, Kathy could see the sun about to melt into the Gulf, splashes of purples and pinks rising up from the horizon. They had one hundred and forty-three aboard, seven crew. American, Flight 570. On their way to Rio.

Mark was still chattering about the movie scene when all the cathode ray screens went blank. Kathy stared down at them. Everything gone except the analog backup instruments.

Mark rapped a knuckle on one of the instrument display screens. All the panels were dead, even the overhead lights were off. They were down to four instruments: airspeed indicator, whiskey compass, altimeter, and the ADI, the artificial horizon. Bare essentials.

'Shit, we've lost the glass. Everything's dark.'

A second later the engines began to wind down, reverting to a preset power setting.

'Oh, man, oh, man.'

'We can still fly,' she said. 'We've got power. No ailerons, but the rudder's still there. Thank God for cables.'

'Jesus, what the hell is this?'

'Call the tower, tell them we're coming back.'

He tapped a fingernail against his microphone.

'Radio's gone,' he said. 'Everything's fried. Absolutely everything.'

Then she felt another jolt, an electrical stab in her belly, like the first wild kick of her only child.

That's when the artificial horizon indicator began to spin. At night or in clouds, the instrument showed their upright position, sky above, ground below. It was hooked to a dedicated battery. So whatever they'd just experienced was more than a general electrical failure; their backup systems had been zapped, too. Without the artificial horizon, she'd have to rely on her senses to keep their wings level, stay right side up. Senses that were already more than a little scrambled.

Then the yoke went loose in her hands.

'Oh, Jesus.'

'All three engines flamed out.' Mark tightened his shoulder harness. Took a quick look out the windscreen at the Florida Bay a half mile below.

The big jet slowed like a roller coaster reaching its steepest crest. She heard a single piercing scream from the cabin.

Kathy Dubois drew a long breath, tried the yoke again, but it was still dead. She swallowed hard, realigned her microphone, bent it close to her lips.

She whispered something for the black box. A few words to her daughter. Then as the plane began to

drop, she and Mark went to work, cycling the hydrau-
lic systems, the electrical panels, trying to crank the
auxiliary power unit.

'It's back,' she said. 'It's back.'

She wasn't sure what they'd done, but the yoke
was alive. And Kathy Dubois started to pull them
out of the free fall. Fifteen hundred feet, a thousand,
seven-fifty, five hundred, enough time left, drawing
up the nose, getting it level for a water landing. But no
time to make announcements, pull out the manual,
go over ditching procedure. She had to keep the
landing gear up, flaps down, that much she knew.

There was nothing on the Florida Bay. Calm seas. A
long silvery runway. She had to keep the wings level
with the water, not the horizon, she remembered
that. Get speed down. She was thinking of the flare
and touchdown, rotating ten degrees nose high, she
was thinking of the APU and engine fire handles
that she would have to override. Or would she? The
engines weren't turning. She stifled the half second
of panic, got her focus back.

Mark said something, but Kathy wasn't listening,
keeping the wings level, bringing it down, feeling the
ground effect, that aerodynamic cushion that kept the
plane skimming the surface of the sea like a pelican.

She was ditching the plane on the shallow bay.
A strange serenity flushing her, the yoke alive in
her hand. A single fishing boat appearing in the
distance.

The nose of the jetliner pitched up, transforming

speed into lift, but this couldn't go on forever. Kathy would have to get the speed as low as she could manage, then do what no other wide-body pilot had ever accomplished, make a successful water landing.

Thorn watched the jet scream out of the northwest, darken the sky, and pass so close overhead that its brutal tailwind lasted for half a minute, a hundred-mile-an-hour squall buffeting them broadside, nearly capsizing the *Heart Pounder*. The tidal surge that followed slammed them a second time. Casey was hurled backwards onto the deck and slid on her butt to the transom. Thorn managed to hang onto the wheel, trimming the engine down, and digging through the sudden surf, until he got the vessel back under control.

'You okay, Case?'

She lifted her head and squinted at him.

'Jesus,' she said. 'Jesus, Jesus, Jesus.'

A half mile to the east, the jet exploded. A greenish-red plume shot ten stories into the air and a few seconds later the blast-furnace *whoosh* swept over them. Casey ducked below the gunwale and began to weep.

A flock of egrets that had been hunched in the high branches of the nearby mangroves burst into the air, white and stalky and deathly silent. Thorn swung the wheel and mashed the throttle forward. He made a wide arc to the south, then cut back his speed and headed east toward the crash site. Through the dusk, he saw the flames dotting the water like the campfires of some ghostly, defeated army. Five-foot swells pounded their hull and all around them the twilight was tinted a sickly green.

'What the hell're you doing, Thorn!'

'Going to help.'

'Are you crazy? All that fire, we'll blow up.'

Casey staggered to his side, stood at the windshield looking out. Blurry ripples rose from the surface of the water like heat off a summer highway.

'I'll get a little closer, then I'll take the skiff. You can stay here.'

A caustic breeze flooded the cabin with the fumes of jet fuel and bitter smoke and the sweet, sickly reek of charred flesh.

'I want to go home, Thorn. I want to get the hell out of here.'

'So do I,' he said. 'But we can't. Not yet.'

He motored forward into the haze. Billows of smoke curled up from the surface of the bay; the water smoldered and fires flared to life as if spurts of volcanic gases were breaking through the earth's crust. As he worked closer, Thorn saw the outer edge of the debris field scattered several hundred yards from what he took to be the center of the crash site, a single wing that jutted up like some senseless monolith planted in the sandy bottom. Next to it, a twisted section of the aluminum fuselage glowed in the strange green light.

41

Mats of insulation floated on the surface, a stack of white Styrofoam cups bobbed past, life jackets and seat cushions, a black baseball hat and several blue passports. As the flotsam thickened, Thorn shut down the engine and while the boat coasted forward, he went to the stern, unknotted the rope from the cleats, and hauled in the skiff. Casey watched him, shivering, holding herself tightly.

'It's all right,' he said. 'Get on the radio, channel sixteen, make a distress call. I'm going to look for survivors.'

She opened her mouth but found no words and clamped her lips together and looked away.

Thorn climbed down into the skiff and popped loose the long white fiberglass pole, and he mounted the platform over the outboard. He planted one end of the pole against the soft bottom of the bay and leaned his weight against it and shoved the skiff forward. If there were in fact survivors floating out there, it was no time for a propeller.

He drew the pole out of the muck and planted it again and heaved the skiff ahead. The water was less than four feet deep. Shallow enough for an average adult to stand flat-footed with his head out of water. But Thorn saw no sign of life, no movement at all as he poled past a floating cockpit door, more seat cushions and drifting clothes and baby bottles and a blond-haired doll.

He was fifty yards from the jutting wing when he heard the first splashes and made out the whimpers and soft cries, and a low, wet snuffling like penned-up horses. He poled faster, sweating now, as the boat skimmed ahead, the last ticks of daylight dying in the west. Everything was coated with gold. The bay, the shadowy people floundering up ahead, the suitcases and duffels that hung like dark icebergs just an inch or two below the surface.

The first two he came upon were women. One in a blue business suit, another in a white sweatshirt. They thrashed over to the skiff and clambered aboard before he could get down from the platform to help. One was dark-haired with a bad gash across her forehead. The one in the white sweatshirt was a frail woman with weak blue eyes. A triangular chunk of flesh was missing from her cheek. The business suit thanked him and the other woman peered at him, then her face collapsed and she began to sob. The large woman took the small one in her arms and held her tightly as Thorn pushed on.

'There's a first-aid kit in the console.'

The woman looked back at him.

'Who are you?' she said.

'Nobody.'

'You wait out here for airplanes to crash?'

'You're my first,' he said. 'You should put something on those cuts. You're losing blood.'

She tightened her hug on the small woman.

'We're all right. Believe me, there's others who need it more.'

Behind the broken fuselage he heard voices, cries

43

and blubbering, the first moments of numbness and shock wearing off. He shoved the pole into the sucking mud, withdrew it, shoved it in again, and the skiff coasted forward.

'On your right,' Thorn called to the woman in the business suit. 'Coming up on your right.'

The woman looked out and saw the child's arm and let go of the delicate woman and leaned over to grab the elbow. She swung forward, then drew back with the arm in her hand. A bloody stump severed at the shoulder. She held it up for Thorn to see, then dropped it back in the poisoned water.

On that first pass, he filled the skiff with nine adults and two children and a small white poodle before he swung around and poled the sluggish boat over to the beach of the mangrove island. There was a nurse in that first group, and although her left arm was badly broken, she took the first-aid kit and was already bandaging the most badly hurt as Thorn headed back to the crash site through the last golden moments of twilight.

Thorn was hauling an elderly man aboard when the first Coast Guard helicopter arrived, followed almost immediately by a news chopper. Their searchlights held on him for a moment. Holding the man by his armpits, Thorn stared up into the brightness. The choppers moved on, sending a ghastly halo over the scene and illuminating another boat he hadn't noticed earlier.

It was only thirty or forty yards away, idling near

a half-submerged engine pod. At the helm of the twenty-foot Maverick was a woman with short black hair, and flanking her were two men. One was tall and lanky and wore a cowboy hat. The other man was stocky and short. As Thorn poled through the bloody waters searching for survivors, the Maverick shifted its position, inching along the perimeter of the wreckage. They were making no effort to save the injured, but seemed to be angling for the best view of the proceedings.

Thorn worked for another hour as helicopters filled the sky and the Coast Guard and marine patrol boats finally arrived. He brought four loads of passengers to the beach. Most were badly mangled, gibbering and torn, bones exposed, faces blackened with soot, flesh lacerated and scorched. Some were weeping, moaning, others struck dumb. On his last trip a young man in a blue track suit went into spasms on the foredeck. A middle-aged black woman scooped him into her arms and the young man stiffened, then went slack. The black woman continued to hold him, rocking him gently and crooning what sounded like a lullaby. The deck of his skiff sloshed with blood. Through the darkness, he watched the sharks move in, snatching down the easy meat, and he saw the gleaming snout of an alligator gliding through the wreckage.

Twice more he noticed the Maverick moving in and out of the shadows. And an hour later he saw the boat again, the three passengers at the docks at Flamingo. The men were straining to lift a large cooler from the boat up to the dock. Out in the large parking area dozens of medevac helicopters were landing and taking off, and the television cameras were set up. By then he was woozy with exhaustion, as numb and shaky as if he'd gone without sleep for a month.

He tied up his skiff near the tackle shop and came ashore. A few minutes later as he wandered amid the confusion, he caught sight of Casey staggering across the parking lot, supported by a man in a blue paramedic's jumpsuit. He jogged over to her and called her name and she swung around and watched him approach. Her mouth was rigid, eyes unlocked from the moment.

'Your boat's in the marina,' she said in a dead voice. 'Slip eighteen.'

'Are you all right?'

'No, I'm not all right. I'm not all right at all.'

Thorn looked at the paramedic. He had his arm around Casey's waist.

'This is José,' she said. 'He's looking after me.'

'I'm sorry,' Thorn said.

She reached out and smoothed a hand across his cheek, then cocked it back and gave him a sharp slap.

'You're a goddamn magnet, Thorn. You attract this shit. You're the baddest luck I've ever known.'

He watched her limp away, then he turned and went back to the docks. His daze had hardened into a cold shock that felt like it was rooted so deep in his tissues it might be with him forever. The sky was a black whirling mass overhead, and the earth rocked and wobbled beneath his feet. The roar of the choppers and sirens and the crowd was setting up a deep hum in his skull. Someone handed him a beer and he drained it and dropped the can on the sandy soil. A man in a fishing hat handed him another, and he meandered through the hallucinatory throng of reporters and medics and wild-eyed relatives of the passengers. A woman with a blond helmet of hair and perfect teeth, followed by a cameraman, jabbed a microphone in his face, and he shoved it away and kept on walking.

Gulping the beer, he followed the brightest lights to the pavilion near the boat ramps. Beside the pavilion were four concrete fish-cleaning tables the media were using as the local-color backdrop for their live shots.

He nudged into the crowd and jostled to the front. The woman from the Maverick was being interviewed. Her black hair gleamed in the lights and her blue eyes were achingly pale. She wore a long-sleeved white fishing shirt and khaki shorts. Her legs were sleek and deeply tanned and she stood with the gawky elegance Thorn associated with high-fashion models, back straight, hips and shoulders canted in slightly different directions as if to catch the most flattering light. There was a single spatter of blood on her right sleeve, but otherwise she seemed as cool and unruffled as if she'd just stepped from her dressing room.

'Bonefishing,' she was saying. 'Johnny and I were

out on the flats when it came down. Maybe a mile or two away.'

'And what did you hear, Miss Braswell? Were the engines running? We've heard reports that they were shut down.'

Her eyes roamed the crowd, then returned to the reporter.

'Yes, I believe the engines were silent. It was all very eerie.'

The reporter thanked her and turned back to the camera. He was excited, working a major story, a career boost. He sounded almost elated as he told the TV viewers that so far sixty survivors had been pulled from those remote waters. And that none other than Morgan Braswell, prominent local businesswoman, had been an eyewitness to these tragic events. According to Ms Braswell, the plane's engines were shut down at the time of the crash.

As the reporter continued to speak, the woman peered beyond the lights. Her eyes catching on Thorn's and holding. After a moment, she reached out and put a hand on the reporter's sleeve, silencing him mid-sentence.

'There's the man you want to interview.' She lifted a slender hand and pointed him out. 'Right there. He saved dozens of lives. Far more than we managed to. He's the hero of the hour.'

The cameraman swung around and spotlights glared in Thorn's eyes.

The reporter took a step his way, lifting his mike.

'Sir?' he said. 'Could we have a minute?'

Behind him the dark-haired woman motioned to someone in the crowd. And when she brought her pale blue eyes back to Thorn, a faint smile formed on her lips as if Thorn's uneasiness amused her.

'Sir? Sir?'

Thorn turned from the reporter and ducked into the shifting crowd.

As he emerged from the rear of the pack, a chunky man with stringy, shoulder-length blond hair blocked his way and pressed a cold can of Budweiser into his hand. Chubby cheeks, small gray eyes. He was in his mid-twenties and had on a fresh blue workshirt and white baggies and boat sandals. His flesh was stained the deep chestnut of someone who labored in the tropical sun.

'Beer's been at the bottom of the cooler all afternoon. Nice and icy.'

Thorn squinted out at the parking lot where the fire rescue vans were screaming away into the night. He fumbled with the tab on the beer can, got it at the wrong angle, and broke it off. He looked at the kid. A toothy grin flickered on the boy's lips as if he were trying to decide whether to laugh or take a bite from Thorn's neck.

'That was you on the Maverick.'

'Yeah? What if it was?'

The kid's grin grew blurry. The whole goddamn night had turned blurry. Though not yet blurry enough.

'And what's your name?'

The kid thought about it for a moment.

'"Don't your nose get sore, sticking it all the time in other people's business?"' The young man grinned. 'That's George Raft, from *Nocturne*, 1946. With Virginia Huston and Myrna Dell.'

Thorn peered at the kid for a moment, then shrugged and brought his attention back to the beer can. He tried prying at the broken tab with his thumbnail, but got nowhere.

The kid reached in the pocket of his shorts and came out with a knife and flicked out the blade. He took the can from Thorn's hand, dug the blade into the tab, and popped it open. The knife had holes in the grip and a blade that looked heavy enough to gut a moose.

'You admiring my shiv?'

'Not really.'

On the kid's thumb was a bandage with blood seeping through the gauze.

Thorn took a slow pull on the beer. The kid held the knife at his side.

'So how long were you out there?' the kid said. 'Before the crash.'

'Why?'

'Me and my sister were fishing over behind that island. We didn't see you. You just kind of popped up out of nowhere.'

'I didn't see you either. Not till after the crash.'

The kid smirked as if he'd tricked some vital detail out of Thorn.

'The three of you didn't seem to be getting your hands real dirty.'

'Two of us,' the kid said. 'Me and my sister.'

'I saw three,' Thorn said. 'You and her and a guy in a cowboy hat.'

'Yeah, well, I guess you're mistaken, crabcake.' The kid looked back toward the TV lights. 'And we pulled in a few survivors. Maybe not as many as you, but who's counting?'

'That's not how it looked from my seat.'

'What're you, the head Eagle Scout? Handing out the merit badges.'

'Your cooler looked pretty full. Must've caught a ton of fish.'

'We caught our share.'

'But you still got the creases in your shirt.'

'So?'

'So you weren't out there fishing. You weren't out there doing anything. You haven't broken a sweat.'

The boy's smile went sour. He peered into Thorn's eyes and his knife rose in what looked like a reflexive gesture. As if his first instinct was to slash the throat of anyone who called his bluff.

Then he halted and took a quick look around at all the potential witnesses and he lowered the blade. He stepped back and raked Thorn with a look.

'If you weren't fishing,' Thorn said, 'maybe you were bird-watching.'

A breeze drifted in off the bay, heavy with the sickening fumes. The kid snapped his knife shut and

51

slid it into his pocket. He glanced toward the TV lights, then turned back to Thorn. His fingers toyed with the lump in his pocket.

'You know what you need, asshole?'

'A better haircut?' Thorn said.

'You need a little negative reinforcement, that's what. Like maybe somebody should drop a tombstone on your head.'

The kid flashed Thorn an ugly sneer, then swung around and sauntered away into the bedlam.

Thorn drifted back to the docks and watched the Coast Guard and marine patrol bringing in the bodies on stretchers. Most of the living were already on their way to hospitals, and now it was time for the dead. The men worked quietly, with the grim efficiency of those who trained for just such disasters. For the next half hour Thorn nursed his beer and stayed in the shadows, watching the boats unload the charred and mangled remains. Getting glimpses of bodies so twisted and broken they might have been trampled by a stampede of buffalo.

When he could stomach it no more, he located the *Heart Pounder*, brought the skiff over, and lashed it to the cleats. He started the engine and headed out into the dark, staying away from the searchlights and rescue boats. He headed across the black bay, and when he was a half mile beyond the crash site, he opened up the engine, rising onto the smooth sea. Around him the moonlight coated the bay like a crisp film of ice.

With his running lights shut off, Thorn steered his phantom ship south, plowing across that murky void. A cold shiver whispered beneath his shirt. He took a last look behind him, north across the Everglades where the black sky pulsed with lightning. Then he turned his back on the mainland, gripped the wheel, and put his face in the wind, standing stiff and empty, blinded by starlight.

# 3

Thorn made it home by two that morning. Totally wiped out, but too wired to sleep, he sat out on the porch of his stilt-house and watched Blackwater Sound twinkle and listened to the distant rumbles of thunder. At dawn he went inside and took a shower. He got dressed and stood out on the porch for a while watching the water brighten. The mourning doves that roosted in the tamarind tree were coming and going in twos and threes, resettling briefly, then exploding from their perches in a panicked flailing of wings. A small boat muttered by and he watched the ripples work toward his coral and limestone dock.

He went back into the house, stared at his face in the bathroom mirror for a while, then stripped off his shorts and T-shirt and took another shower, scrubbing harder this time. His back muscles were sore. His fingers and arms ached. He toweled off, chose a fresh pair of shorts and another T-shirt, and put them on. Still, his skin felt strange. Too tight, too clammy.

At nine he was waiting outside the Key Largo Library when June Marcus, the tall, dark-haired librarian, unlocked the front door. She looked at him for a second or two as if she didn't recognize him, then said an uncertain hello and stepped back out of his way.

'You were at the crash,' she said. 'The airplane that went down.'

'How'd you know that?'

'Saw you on the news this morning,' she said. 'You were pulling somebody out of the water. An old man.'

He nodded.

'It must've been awful out there. I can't even imagine. All that carnage.'

In the reference section, June showed him how to run a computer search. It took only a minute or two. Morgan Braswell was on the cover of several magazines from a few years back. The library had hard copies of several of them. Business monthlies. Long articles. A couple of newspaper stories. Big turn-around at her father's company. She flashed a variety of smiles, arms crossed beneath her breasts, looking satisfied, in control, a woman full of bold confidence. From Tragedy to Triumph. That was the theme.

After the heartbreaking loss of her older brother in a boating accident, the family business floundered, disintegrated, but with courage and a maturity beyond her years, Morgan managed to pick up the pieces and rebuild her father's company into a major player in the technology sector.

June Marcus photocopied the articles and didn't ask why he wanted them. She patted him on the shoulder as he walked out of the library.

He took them back to his house and sat out at the picnic table. It was a hot morning, the breeze off the Atlantic shaving away a few degrees. Northeast above Miami, dark blue clouds hovered in the sky. The cold front was going nowhere. He read the articles, looked at Morgan Braswell's pictures. Read them again.

At noon he nagged his Volkswagen Beetle to life and drove out to US 1 and headed up the eighteen-mile strip to Miami. Thirty minutes later, at Cutler Ridge, the rain started and didn't let up till he was in Palm Beach. It was after three o'clock when he found the Braswells' neighborhood. They lived in a two-story Mediterranean villa three blocks from the ocean. Oak trees lined their street. Fancy lamps on brass poles were planted along the sidewalk. He drove past the house and parked half a block away. He sat for a while staring down the street toward the Atlantic. There was a pleasant lift to the breeze rushing in off the sea, cool and sweet, seasoned by money.

No traffic. No pedestrians on the sidewalk. Most of the wealthy snowbirds had already fled north to avoid the first upticks of the thermometer. A snowy egret stood on the snipped lawn next to his car and regarded him haughtily. Thorn wasn't sure why he'd driven all this way, wasted the day, fought I-95 traffic. The photocopies lay in the passenger seat. He picked them up, glanced through them, and dropped them back. These people weren't any of his business. He had things to do. Bonefish flies to tie, lunkers to catch. He didn't need this. He'd saved a bunch of people's lives. He should be feeling good this morning. He should be rejoicing. Not feeling so numb, so crazy.

He started the car and made a U-turn and drove back past the Braswells' house. Pink and purple bougainvillea climbed a trellis in the side yard. The cross-hatched wood had pulled loose from its posts and was sagging toward the house next door. The Braswells' grass was scraggy with yellow patches and weeds. Flakes of white paint curled off the window frames. In an upstairs window a broken pane was covered with what looked like a square of sandwich wrap. The mail slot in the front door was rimmed with rust. Somebody hadn't been paying much attention to maintenance.

He drove west beyond I-95 into the golf communities. Heron Glen, Willow Walk, The Banyans. Miles of red tile roofs and guardhouses and endlessly repeating franchise strips. He kept going till he was beyond the turnpike, beyond the last stucco wall, the last rigid row of royal palms. The land was scrubby and wet and of no use to anyone except alligators and woodstorks.

Only an occasional straggling 7-Eleven and a couple of industrial parks marked the desolate landscape.

Seven miles beyond the turnpike, Thorn pulled into a complex of low, windowless buildings. At the guardhouse a young woman with a yellow buzz cut stepped out with a clipboard in her hand. She wore a sidearm in a glossy leather holster and a tailored gray uniform that showed off her bulky shoulders and cinched waist. There were spikes in the road, tilted forward to rip the tread off tires. A yellow steel crossing arm striped with red closed off the entrance.

She bent to his open window and didn't smile. Didn't say a word. She looked at him, looked at the passenger seat, peered into the back.

'Am I in the right place?'

'I doubt it,' she said.

'MicroDyne?' said Thorn. 'Morgan Braswell.'

She shifted the clipboard to her left hand, freeing up her right to pump him full of lead.

'Is this MicroDyne?'

'You have business here, sir?'

'What do they manufacture?'

The blank look on her face got blanker.

'None of the news articles say. Government contractor, that's the phrase. What's that mean? Is that defense work? Military? Top-secret gizmos? What?'

She took a step back from the car. Her eyes were working. She was going over procedures in her head, making decisions about how to proceed. Memorizing his face, the car. On a better day Thorn might have trotted out the charm, tried to win her over, seduce a fact or two. But today he was shit out of charm. It was all he could do to press the accelerator, turn the wheel. Hold one thought for more than a few seconds.

Thorn put the VW in reverse and backed slowly out of the short drive.

The security guard stood in front of the steel barricade with her legs spread, right hand close to her holster. Annie Oakley about to shoot the hearts out of silver dollars flung high into the air.

Thorn took the turnpike south.

He hit rush hour in Miami. Fifty miles of raging incivility.

'Did he give you his name?'

Morgan Braswell was looking at her computer screen, the freeze-frame of the surveillance tape from the front gate. The man from last night at the crash site, the big hero who'd pulled thirty, forty people from the water. Lanky, blue-eyed, tan, tousled sandy hair.

'No, ma'am. He didn't say his name.'

'But he mentioned me? By name.'

'That's correct.'

Morgan ran her tongue along her upper lip. She leaned back in the leather chair. Behind her desk was a large window that looked down into the testing lab. A quiet, sterile space where dozens of men and women in white lab coats spent their days peering into computers, monitoring the sintering furnaces that were located behind layers of tempered steel in a distant section of the plant.

'Did you get a license number?'

'Yes, ma'am. I'm running it through DMV. But there might be a problem. It looked like it was an expired tag.'

Johnny was standing at the window looking down into the lab. It was empty now. Everyone gone home for the day.

Johnny wore navy blue shorts and a white polo shirt with their boat name embroidered on the left breast. His long hair was clenched back in a ponytail.

'He probably wanted a date,' said Johnny. 'A little cootchie-coo.'

'Joyce,' Morgan said.

'Yes, ma'am?'

'Print out the best frames of that video. His face from the front, profile. As many angles as you can get. Enhance them, sharpen the focus.'

Joyce nodded.

'The pictures and whatever you get from DMV on my desk in the morning.'

'Yes, ma'am.'

'He was a smart-ass,' Johnny said. 'He said he saw three of us on the boat. You, me, and a guy in a cowboy hat. I should've iced him right then. Filled him full of daylight.'

Morgan swiveled her chair around and looked at her brother.

'Joyce,' she said, keeping her eyes on Johnny until he finally turned and read her expression, then quickly looked away. 'You can go now. But I want those items first thing.'

When Joyce shut the door, Morgan said, 'Johnny?'

He was staring down at the test lab and wouldn't look at her.

'Johnny?'

He swallowed and stepped back.

'Come over here, Johnny.'

He shook his head, mouth clenched, eyes dodging hers. A four-year-old doing his willful routine. Her tone was delicate, coaxing.

'I just want to talk to you, Johnny, that's all.'

He tipped his head back and looked at the ceiling as if conferring with his personal savior.

'Johnny.'

He blinked, then stepped over to the side of her desk, bowing his head.

'Look at me, Johnny. Lift your head and look at me.'

He drew a breath and met her eyes.

'What did you do wrong just now?'

'I don't know,' he said.

'Yes, you do, Johnny. You know what you did.'

'I spoke out of turn.' His eyes were half-shut. Shoulders slumped.

'That's right. You spoke out of turn. You made a

61

threatening remark in front of one of our security officers. You mentioned a man in a cowboy hat.'

'I'm sorry.'

'Is anyone supposed to know about Roy besides you and me?'

Johnny shook his head.

'Is even Dad supposed to know? Or Jeb Shine?'

'No. Roy's a secret. Just between us.'

'So why did you do that, Johnny?'

He took a breath and his hand went into his pocket.

'You need to think, Johnny. You have to organize your thoughts, deliberate before you say or do things.'

'I'm too reckless,' he said. 'I have low impulse control.'

'Johnny, listen to me. You're a fine brother. I'm proud of you. You've been a great help to me lately. But we're at a crucial juncture. No rashness allowed. Self-discipline, restraint. We have to be very careful, Johnny. Very very careful with everything we say or do.'

'I'm sorry,' he said. 'I let you down.'

He drew the knife out of his pocket and opened it. His mouth was crimped. He blinked his damp eyes.

'No, Johnny, wait. You don't need to do that.'

Morgan stood up, came quickly around her desk. But he'd already peeled the bandage off the thumb of his left hand. The cap of his thumb was scabbed over.

Morgan made a grab for his hand, but Johnny swung his back to her.

He hunched over and pressed the blade against the tip of his thumb. He gritted his teeth, then clamped his eyes and balled his hand into a fist. With a low growl, he shaved off the scab and a layer of bloody flesh beneath it. Blood washed down his hand.

Morgan groaned and looked away. She took a full breath, then snatched up a wad of tissues from her desk and took hold of his hand, pressing the tissues to the wound.

'It hurts,' he said.

'I know, I know.' Morgan put her arm around his shoulder. 'I wish you wouldn't do these things, Johnny. It's not necessary. Really, it's not.'

'I need negative reinforcement,' he said. 'That's the only way I'm ever going to learn.'

She kept her arm around his shoulder until he stopped trembling. When he grew still, she gripped his chin and turned his face to hers. She leaned close and kissed both his teary eyes, then smoothed a hand across his cheek and stepped back.

'Now you're better. Aren't you? The pain is all gone.'

He looked at her and nodded.

'Some of it.'

'I want you to stay here,' she said. 'Pull yourself together. I'll be back in a minute and we'll go home. You can choose what you want for dinner. Burger King, pizza, anything you want, Johnny.'

\*     \*     \*

As Morgan approached her father's office, Jeb Shine stepped from his doorway and peered at her over the frames of his reading glasses. He was a tall, hump-shouldered man. Bald, with a half-assed ponytail he plaited together from his stringy fringe hair. He was wearing a blue Hawaiian shirt printed with yellow hula girls and pink flamingoes. His khaki shorts were rumpled and he wore his usual pair of rubber sandals. Same age as her father, but dressed like a college kid on perpetual spring break.

'Got a minute, Morgan?'

'Not really.'

'It's important. Quite important.' He stepped aside, bowed at the waist, and motioned her into his office. But she held her place in the hallway.

'If it's about payroll,' she said, 'we don't need to cover that again. Just find another creative solution, stretch us out a little longer. A week, ten days, that's all we need. Things'll be fine.'

'I'm fresh out of creative solutions, Morgan. There isn't a bank left in South Florida that hasn't turned us down. We've depleted our rainy-day fund. We're a dime away from being flat broke. Short of a bag of money showing up on my desk by next Friday, all the payroll checks are going to bounce.'

'One week, Jeb. That's all I need. Seven days. You'll see. I have a deal working.'

'What kind of deal?'

'Don't worry about it, Jeb. Have I let you down yet?'

He looked at her for several moments. When he spoke, his voice was as gloomy as the haze in his eyes.

'It's more than the payroll, Morgan. And I think you know that.'

He walked over to his desk and pushed aside a pile of folders and took a perch. His thick, white, hairless legs dangling. Despite his island-boy clothes, Jeb was as pasty as a hibernating mole.

'On top of everything else the spark plasma furnace went down again.'

She sighed and came into his office and shut the door behind her. Lately, Jeb had developed a nodding habit, as if he were constantly consulting some inner voice. He nodded now as he stared down at the weave of the carpet.

'It was working fine, DC voltage pulses steady. We were getting excellent results. Better than the liquid phase sintering oven, all that microgravity stuff. This is much better. Good deflection temperatures, dimensional tolerance, the tensile elongation modules all running fine. Ran perfectly for the last few weeks, no sign of anything wrong. Then suddenly it shut down. We're trying to track down the problem now. Should have it back on-line by morning.'

'And that's what you wanted to tell me.'

He looked up at her and nodded to himself.

'You know, Morgan, I was never much of an accountant. This CFO thing, it's always been a joke. Me and A.J. were just a couple of tech guys, lab rats.

We didn't give a shit about money. Only reason I got stuck taking care of the books was because A.J. was so damn bad at it. But it's never been something I relished.'

She kept her tone relaxed, working up a little smile.

'But you do it so well, Jeb.'

He scratched at his bare knee, avoiding her eyes.

'So today, I was going over the quarterlies, looking for expenses to trim, some way to get beyond this crisis.' He nodded at the far wall. 'It's been a while since I took a good look at the books. I've been a little lax, letting you and the real accountants run the show. I've been so involved with setting up the new furnaces.'

'Is there a point here, Jeb? I'm really very tired.'

Jeb closed his eyes and nodded gravely.

'I found an item I couldn't explain, Morgan. A distressingly large item tucked away in the fine print.'

She felt the air harden in her lungs.

'What exactly is a TP3 hybrid fuel cell, Morgan? Could you explain that to me? Could you tell why in the last six months we've devoted almost half a million dollars of research and development money to a battery?'

He lifted his eyes and settled his gaze on hers. The nodding had ceased.

'Are we in the battery business, Morgan? Because if we are, I think somebody should explain why that is.'

'We're not in the battery business, Jeb.'

His eyes drifted up, holding onto a spot a few inches above her head.

'Well, maybe we should be. I tracked down the specs, looked over the tests you've been running on this TP3. I must say, Morgan, it's got a very impressive performance history. Packs one hell of a wallop.'

Morgan strained to keep the smile on her lips.

'I'm going home now, Jeb. If there's anything else, it can wait till tomorrow.'

'So, if we're not going to manufacture these batteries, why're we doing all this fuel cell R and D, at a time when our resources are strained to the limit? You mind telling me?'

'Good night, Jeb.'

'Is this another one of Andy's ideas? Something else you found in his notebooks?'

Morgan felt the smile die on her lips. She drew a calming breath.

'No, it's not Andy's idea. It's mine. All mine. Is that so hard to believe? That I would have an idea once in a while.'

'Nothing personal, Morgan, but it's been my observation that your strength lies in marketing products, not creating them.'

She turned to go but Jeb Shine slid off his desk, angled in front of her, and blocked her way.

She kept her tone relaxed.

'Maybe it's time you started thinking about retirement, Jeb. Take up golf, shuffleboard. Maybe a nice long cruise around Polynesia. You've served your time in the salt mines. What you need to do is kick back a little, take a few deep breaths, you know, before it's too late.'

He squinted at her.

'Too late?'

She reached out and touched the point of her fingernail to one of the hula girls on the belly of his shirt.

'Good night, Jeb. We'll talk again soon, I promise.'


When she opened the door to his office, her dad was at his desk staring into his computer screen. He wore a green polo shirt and a pair of khakis, leather sandals. Gray was creeping into his sandy hair, but otherwise he was still trim and youthful. His office walls were bare except for a single photograph that hung across from his desk. Andy and A.J. stood by a seven-hundred-pound blue on the docks in Venezuela, her dad with his arm over Andy's shoulder. A golden light suffusing the sky behind them. Eleven years ago, back when beautiful sunsets were still possible.

On her dad's computer screen she saw the wavy blue lines, the circles and swirls of a tidal chart.

A.J. was running the program he'd written that attempted to plot the movements of Big Mother. Using her last known position, two hundred miles southeast of St Thomas in the Virgin Islands, he was computing the effects of tidal shifts on her migratory pattern.

Her last appearance on the global positioning satellite was on April fifteenth of the previous year. So the computer program had to sift through a year's worth of data to make its current calculation. Tidal shifts were only one of dozens of variables influencing her direction. The ever-changing temperature variants, the snaky course changes of the Gulf Stream and the dozen other tidal currents, the effects of storms, lunar cycles, even the presence of a fishing fleet in a particular zone had to be factored in. And, of course, there were forces he had no way of reckoning. It was, as Morgan had known from the start, a hopeless enterprise. A futile task that nevertheless consumed most of his waking hours. And she was fairly certain it consumed most of the others as well.

'Where is she, Dad?'

'Still off the Abacos. South and east. Thirty, forty miles. I'm beginning to think it's her mating grounds.'

He continued to click his mouse, adding data, correcting.

'It's time to move the boat,' he said. 'Marsh Harbor, that's our best bet. Only a few days before the pod switches on. We have to be ready.'

'I know, Dad. Only a few more days.'

'This is the year, Morgan. This is the year we nail her.'

'Yeah, Dad. This is the year.'

But she didn't believe it. No matter how sophisticated his program was, it just wasn't possible to calculate exactly where the fish would surface next. Too many variables, too much chance. Marlin were the least understood fish in the ocean. They'd never been raised in captivity, never studied up close. Placed in an aquarium at any age, they died in hours. Even the top scientists with the national marine fisheries who spent their careers investigating marlin had been unable to track their migration patterns or understand something as basic as their spawning habits. They were loners, these fish. Mysterious and baffling. Otherworldly.

Big Mother might reappear anywhere on the globe. No way to be sure. Math couldn't do it. Black magic wouldn't either. For all they knew, the transmitter might have broken loose this year somewhere in the marlin's travels. Or the fish might have died since last year's ping – caught by a long-liner, or maybe attacked by its only enemy in the ocean, a great white.

In the weeks following Andy's death, Morgan and her dad had created a duplicate pod, programmed identically, so they'd have an idea of the life span of the pod hooked to Big Mother. The duplicate hung on the wall across from A.J.'s desk, its battery still chugging. Morgan's calculations said it had a ten-year life, but there was no way to predict such a thing with total accuracy. So far, so good. Each spring for the last nine years, the duplicate unit came alive right on schedule and beeped steadily for seven days.

'I'm going home, Dad. I'll pick up something for supper.'

'I'll be along in a while.'

'All right.'

'Tell Johnny he needs to get his gear together. Tomorrow we're heading to Abaco. We have to be close by when she surfaces.'

'All right, Dad.'

'And you're coming, right? To Marsh Harbor?'

'I don't know. There's a lot of work around here.'

He let go of the mouse and swiveled his chair around to face her.

'This could be our last shot,' he said. 'That battery's about to give out. It's now or never, Morgan.'

'It's a busy time, Dad. A lot of things around here need my attention.'

He reached out and took her hand in his. His palm was roughened from boat work and fishing, the hand of a laborer.

'Family, Morgan. It's more important than business.'

'Is it, Dad?'

His dark eyes took her in and he gave her a quick boyish smile. The smile her mother must have fallen in love with. This man who had once been so easy and fun-loving, brimming with dreams and self-confidence. Nothing like the dark set of his mouth that dominated his appearance these last few years as his attention to the world dwindled to a fine point. Until all his energy, all his time and intelligence was

71

focused on that one thing, a blue marlin swimming somewhere in the oceans of the world. Big Mother.

'Family,' he said, a brief light filling his smile. 'It's everything, Morgan. The whole ball of wax.'

She nodded and said okay, yes, she would go along this one last time.

'Good. Maybe you'll be like your mother. She always brought us luck.'

'Yeah,' Morgan said. 'A lot of luck.'

'It wouldn't be right if you weren't there.'

'But when the battery dies, it's over. No more trips. No more chasing.'

His smile drifted away, eyes blurring.

'And you'll come back to work. Start minding the store again.'

He blinked and returned from somewhere far off.

'I know this has been hard on you, Morgan. I'm very proud of you, the way you stepped in and took charge. I couldn't have managed without your help.'

'So you'll come back and everything will be like it was.'

'Someday, sure,' he said. 'This can't go on forever.'

'No,' she said. 'It can't.'

He took her hand and gave it a squeeze, then swung back to his work.

Morgan stood behind him for another moment and watched her father shift through the screens. Entering new data, studying the small mutations that this fresh information made on the global model.

She watched him type, watched him click the

mouse. She reached out and laid a hand on his shoulder but he did not register her presence. He simply continued to type, to move from screen to screen, entering the latest information, then switching back to the global chart to see what effect his new data had on Big Mother's position.

Morgan closed her eyes and tried to focus all her being on the palm of her hand. Tried to feel the energy that resonated from her father. But all she could sense were the tiny adjustments of muscle and sinew as he typed, as he clicked, as he peered at the cold, bright, deathless screen.

# 4

The bar at Sundowners was quiet. Willie Nelson crooning softly from the overhead speakers, the bald, heavyset bartender whistling along. Only Thorn and a couple of schoolteachers on spring break from Chicago staring at each other across the bar. A short, blocky blonde and a tall redhead with a piercing laugh. They talked to him for a while. Told him what they did for a living, where they were from. Going home tomorrow, back to the grind. All those papers to grade. After ten minutes of flirting, they bought him a round, then came around the bar, took the stools on either side of him to watch him drink it. The redhead giggled. They were drunker than he was. Having a lot more fun.

They leaned behind his back and whispered to each other. The blonde whooped with laughter. Thorn poured the Bilge Burner down his throat and stared straight ahead at their reflections in the dark glass that looked out on the canal. The alcohol wasn't working. The smell of scorched flesh still lingered and he could hear whimpers echoing from the shadows of the bar.

The blonde cupped her hand around Thorn's ear and leaned close.

'Can I interest you in an orgasm,' she whispered. 'Two-for-one special.'

The redhead scratched a message on his wrist with her fingernail.

'Sorry,' he said.

'Sorry?' the blonde said. 'What's that mean? Sorry.'

'It means I'm not that kind of guy. At least not tonight.'

'Every guy is that kind of guy,' said the blonde.

'He's telling us he's gay, Charlotte.'

'He won't be gay after we get through with him,' Charlotte said.

'You're drunk,' said her friend.

'Well, of course I am. This is the Keys, isn't it? That's the law down here. Get drunk, stay drunk. Isn't that the law, Mr Scruffy Keys Man?'

'Thanks for the drink,' Thorn said, and got up and moved around the semicircular bar.

For the next fifteen minutes the two schoolteachers glared at him and murmured to each other till finally Sugarman showed up.

'Friends of yours?' he said, nodding hello to the schoolteachers.

'They think I'm gay.'

'You don't look gay,' said Sugarman. 'You look morose.'

Sugar was his oldest, closest friend. Jamaican father, Norwegian mother. From that odd mix, he'd inherited a quirky nature, a blend of hot-blooded and serene, sexy island rhythms and cool detachment, a jovial nature, a dissecting mind. He was strikingly handsome with short, dark, curly hair and a thin, straight nose and shrewd dark eyes. His mouth was supple and he had half a dozen different grins at his disposal. His skin was silky and its color was two shades lighter than Thorn's tan. Wherever he went, Sugar got second looks. Once down in Key West, while walking along Duval, two breathless adolescents mistook him for some TV star and pestered Sugar for his autograph, making such a fuss that finally he signed their napkins to make them go away.

A few years back Sugarman resigned his job as a Monroe County sheriff's deputy and opened a private investigation firm down in Tavernier. Since then he'd been scratching by on runaway kid cases and occasional security work. Enough to pay the mortgage and buy groceries, but no frills. Then last summer Jeannie, his wife since high school, decided she'd had enough of flirting with poverty. She filed for divorce. 'Irreconcilable economic aspirations,' is how Sugarman put it. Somehow, she won custody of

Janey and Jackie, their twin girls. Jeannie carted the five-year-olds and the rest of her possessions up to Miami, where a few months later she moved in with some charlatan who was pocketing large sums by guiding weak-minded souls to their previous lives. Jeannie always had a soft spot for gurus.

'You realize you're a TV star, Thorn?'

'I heard.'

'They been running the same footage over and over. You're in your skiff pulling some old guy out of the water. I've seen it half a dozen times already. An unidentified Good Samaritan. How's it feel to be famous?'

'Shitty,' he said. 'Very shitty.'

Sugarman ordered a Corona. The schoolteachers were arguing. The blonde wanted to move on to another bar. Her friend wanted to go to bed.

'Thanks for coming, Sugar.'

'Hey, you call, I come. That's how it works.'

'Something's strange.'

'Strange?'

'About the crash.'

Sugarman took a longer look at him, and shook his head sadly.

'Oh, no. Here we go.'

Sugar's beer arrived and he removed the wedge of lime and took a sip.

Thorn told him about the boat he'd seen, the three people aboard.

'So they didn't want to get involved,' Sugar said.

'Nothing weird about that. A lot of people freeze up in emergencies.'

'Afterwards, at Flamingo the kid came over to me. He was trying to be cagey, but it was clear he wanted to see if I'd noticed them before the crash. Like he was worried I had something on him. He had a weird knife and real dodgy eyes. Talked like some half-assed gangster.'

'A weird knife and dodgy eyes,' Sugar said. 'Hell, let's go arrest the son of a bitch, toss him in solitary.'

Thorn told him about going to the library, about the articles on Morgan Braswell, her father, A.J., about driving to Palm Beach, the run-down mansion, the tight security at the plant.

Sugarman had a sip of his beer. He squeezed some lime into the bottle and had another sip.

'You've been so good lately, Thorn. Everything's coasting along so nice and easy.'

'You think I'm making this up?'

'I was wondering how long it would last. This stretch of tranquillity.'

The schoolteachers paid their bill and got up. They walked behind Thorn and Sugarman. The blonde leaned close and hissed and flashed her claws.

'The world springs from your mind, Thorn, and sinks again into your mind. That's what the Buddhists say. And if you ask me, there's something to it. You see what you want to see.'

'That goddamn airplane didn't spring from my mind, Sugar.'

They sat in silence for a while, watched the bartender wash the teachers' glasses. Thorn pushed his drink away. He was wasting good alcohol, pouring it into a bottomless cavity.

A couple of guys with long hair and Hawaiian shirts came into the bar. The schoolteachers were with them. Everyone laughing. On the same boozy wavelength.

'There's nothing weird about this, Sugar? You sure?'

'Nothing you told me sounds weird, no. Some rich assholes from Palm Beach didn't want to scuff their manicures. That's all. I think what it is, you're shell-shocked. An airplane crashes in your lap, it's only natural you get a little case of post-trauma. And the way you're dealing with it, being Thorn, you rush out and start sniffing around, thinking you gotta fix things.'

Thorn looked over at the schoolteachers and their new friends. Bilge Burners all around.

'You're right,' he said. 'I'm full of shit.'

'I didn't say that.'

'Yeah, you did. Not in those words, but it's the same thing.'

The bartender came over and asked if they wanted another round. Sugar said no. Thorn shook his head.

'I think the NTSB might want to talk to you. Transportation Safety Board. You've heard of them, right? The people that investigate these things.'

'I've heard of them.'

'They'd probably like to debrief you. You being an eyewitness and all.'

'What am I going to tell them? I saw the plane crash. It nearly capsized my boat. I don't know anything else.'

'You should call. It's your civic duty.'

'Sure,' Thorn said. 'Soon as I get a phone installed.'

Sugarman finished his beer and slid it to the edge of the bar. He picked up the tab and kept it out of Thorn's reach.

'You want me to, I'll call them for you.'

'No,' he said. 'I'm going to stay the hell out of this.'

Sugar got down from his stool and rested his hand on Thorn's shoulder.

'You get some sleep, buddy. You'll feel better tomorrow.'

'Yeah,' Thorn said. 'Some sleep. That'd be nice.'


Morgan put the leftover Chinese in the refrigerator. Six white boxes. Shrimp fried rice, garlic chicken, the usual. Enough for dinner tomorrow. She wiped off the table, rinsed the plates and silverware, put them in the dishwasher. She corked the Pinot Noir and set it on the shelf. Set up the coffee machine for the morning.

Johnny was upstairs in his bedroom. Her dad was in his study. Leaving her the woman's work. Just like they'd treated her mother.

Morgan turned off the kitchen light and went upstairs and stopped on the landing outside Johnny's room. Marlon Brando was lecturing one of his thugs, using his muffled Godfather voice, as though his cheeks were stuffed with dental cotton. She stood for a moment listening to the familiar dialogue. Johnny watched them every night, gangster movies. Said it relaxed him. Cagney, Bogart, Pacino, Mitchum. Gunfire coming from his room, sirens, swelling music, fuck this, fuck that. For years she tried making fun of the movies, tried bullying him. Neither worked, so finally she gave up. She wasn't his mother. If he wanted to wallow in that trash, fantasize an alternate life, it was his own choice. She was only his sister. That's all she was, a sister and a daughter. Her brother and her father were mature adults. She had to keep reminding herself.

She went down the narrow hallway and opened the attic door, took a deep breath, and climbed the narrow stairs into the dark, airless heat. It'd been months since she'd been up there. That long since she'd needed to make the journey. But it was coming up on Easter, the anniversary of all the bad shit. And then there was the stuff from work, the pressures, the desperate come-from-behind finish she was trying to pull off.

A wedge of light angled across the dusty floor of the attic. Passing into the shadows, Morgan bumped her shin against a footlocker. She winced, sucked down a breath, and kept on going, slipping past a broken rocking chair, a stack of old records, a baby bassinet. The cane-back chair was still there. Standing upright now.

She held on to the back of the chair and stepped onto it, teetering for a second. When she had her balance, she reached overhead into the darkness and found the rafter, and ran her hand down the smooth wood until she came to the nylon rope that her mother had knotted there.

She touched a fingertip to the bristly end where Johnny's knife blade had sawed through the strands. She closed her eyes and gripped that stub of rope and held on until the blood ran out of her arm and it began to grow heavy and numb.


Morgan lay in the dark, her head on Andy's pillow. His room was the same. Untouched in ten years. His clothes ironed, hanging neatly in his closet. His shelves lined with novels and science texts. His trophies from high school, a photograph of Albert Einstein, a bust of Beethoven. His notes organized in colored folders. His careful script. A treasure trove. Notations, pages of math, detailed technical drawings, his storehouse of ideas. Like some young Leonardo da Vinci, his engineering designs and scientific observations, his experiments light-years ahead of his time. Morgan had managed to decode only one of his ideas so far and it alone had managed to steer MicroDyne back to profitability. There were hundreds of pages of other formulas, detailed drawings of machines and microcircuitry he'd conceived. And there were the anatomical doodles of women with boyish hips and small breasts. Dozens of them. All with Morgan's shape.

Morgan could no longer smell his scent on the pillowcase. She had long ago inhaled all those leftover particles. Absorbed them, taken them into her bloodstream. Now there were only the invisible molecules, charged atoms, the last traces of his fairy dust lingering in the air. She breathed them in, let them out. Breathed them in again.

Then she was drifting into a dream: Andy was writing on a chalkboard, Morgan sitting in the front row of an empty classroom. Andy was walking her through a formula, the numbers hazy in her dream. She squinted at them but couldn't make them out. She raised her hand, and was waiting for him to turn from the chalkboard and call on her when the phone shook her awake.

She fumbled in the dark and got it on the third ring. Her hello was deep-throated and groggy.

'Morgan Braswell?'

'Yes?'

'My name is Julie Jamison.'

'All right.'

'I'm sorry to disturb you so late, Miss Braswell.'

'Is this a sales call?'

'I'm a writer,' the woman said. 'I'm calling to confirm a few facts on a story I'm doing.'

'About me?'

'Your family,' the woman said. 'Do you have a minute? Somebody's made some pretty serious accusations. We'd like to hear your side of things before we go ahead with this.'

It was nearly two in the morning when Morgan parked the six-year-old Mercedes in their space at Hobe Bay Marina. Johnny shuffled along behind her, head bowed, mumbling. Morgan marched down the dock. It was breezy and the halyards were jingling and dark water sloshed against the pilings.

'My thumb aches,' Johnny said. 'I think I nicked the bone. It really hurts.'

'Not now, Johnny. Not now.'

Their Hatteras was moored in the last slip on A dock. The yellow security lights gleamed against the sleek hull.

Morgan halted ten feet from the slip and raised her hand. Johnny stopped behind her and started to speak but Morgan shushed him.

On the side dock that bordered their Hatteras, Jonas Mills, their night security guard, was asleep in a canvas-backed chair. His head propped against a piling. He was Jamaican, father of five. He'd been with the Braswells for over a year. No complaints. At least not till now.

Morgan stepped over to him. She raised her right foot and planted the bottom of her tennis shoe against the arm of the chair and threw her weight against it. Jonas's eyes came open and he yelped once and kicked his legs out straight, then tumbled backwards. His skull whacked against the rub rail of the yacht and he dropped ten feet into the glistening water of the harbor.

She and Johnny peered over the dock and watched him bob to the surface, gasp several times, then begin to thrash.

'He can't swim,' Johnny said.

'It's time he learned.'

Jonas reached out for a ladder mounted against the piling, and yowled as his hands shredded against the barnacles.

'Jesus,' Johnny said. 'You just going to leave him down there?'

'Unless you want to shoot him. Fill him full of daylight.'

Gasping, Jonas grabbed hold of the ladder and hauled himself up to the bottom rung.

She stepped aboard their boat and Johnny followed silently.

She opened the cabin with her key and switched on the lights in the salon. She went down the narrow gangway to her stateroom. Flung open the door and stalked to her wardrobe and shoved aside the panel.

'That's where you hid it, in your closet?'

'Right there.'

There were a pair of sandals on the floor. That was all.

'You're sure?' Johnny said. 'Right there on the floor? Blueprints, too?'

'That cocksucker.'

Johnny stared into the closet.

'Which cocksucker?'

'Who do you think, Johnny?'

'I don't know.'

'Who else could it be? Who else had access? No one would question him. No one would think to tell us he'd even come aboard. Everybody's big buddy.'

'Arnold?'

Morgan slammed the closet door shut.

'That cocksucker,' she said. 'That goddamn son of a bitch.'

# 5

'I thought we were going fishing,' said Lawton Collins.

'Soon as we're done here, Lawton. Another minute or two.' Arnold gave him a pat on his bare knee.

They sat side by side in the high-backed leather booth, Lawton Collins and Arnold Peretti. Both of them seventy-two years old. Longtime buddies.

Lawton had on his yellow Bermudas with a blue sleeveless T-shirt, nicely weathered by paint specks from projects over the years. His daughter, Alex, said that outfit made him look like a trailer park derelict and tried to dress him better. But the clothes were comfortable and they reminded him of things from the past. Things he couldn't name, but he could still sense them when he put on those clothes. So he wore them as often as Alexandra would allow.

Lawton Collins held the box on his lap like Arnold had told him. Everybody at the table was aware of it, like the thing was glowing. Lawton didn't know what was inside it, but it was as heavy as a goddamn box of rocks.

Across the booth from them were a couple in their late twenties, early thirties, Charlie and Brandy. Good-looking young folks. Especially the girl. Charlie had a two-day beard, the shadow of dark bristles covering his cheeks.

The four of them had been sitting there quietly since the food arrived. Waiting for somebody to break the ice.

So Lawton said, 'You know what Harry Houdini's real name was?'

The two young people stared at him.

'It was Erik Weisz,' Lawton told them. 'Houdini's family came from Hungary. He did his first trick at six years of age. Made a dried pea appear in any one of three overturned cups.'

The young man gave Lawton a careful look.

'What's wrong with this guy?' Charlie said.

'Nothing's wrong with him. He's getting old. Same as me.'

'What's this shit about Houdini?'

'I like Houdini,' Lawton said.

'He likes Houdini,' Arnold said. 'So there.'

Lawton smiled at the young woman. Brandy was her name. She had a large smile and even larger breasts.

'Me and Arnold go way back,' Lawton said. 'In the old days I used to bust him about twice a year. Didn't I, Arnold?'

'Like clockwork,' Arnold said.

'You're kidding me. This guy's a cop?'

'Used to be,' said Arnold. 'A good one, too.'

'Yes, sir, I was a cop and now I've got a daughter in law enforcement. She's a photographer for the City of Miami Police Department. Crime scenes, corpses, bullet wounds, blood spatters, gore. You name it, she snaps it.'

Charlie frowned.

'I don't like this, Peretti. Some fruitcake listening in.'

'Hey,' Lawton said. 'I may be retired, but I still got full arrest powers.'

'Yeah, right,' Charlie said. 'Cardiac arrest.'

Brandy giggled, then caught herself and tried to look serious.

'Look, Charlie, not that it's any of your business,' Arnold said, 'but after we're done here, me and Lawton are going fishing. I'm looking after him today.'

Charlie closed his mouth and shook his head. The shit he had to endure.

'I think he's cute,' the girl said. 'You hear, Lawton? I think you're cute.'

Lawton let go of the box and extended his left hand across the narrow table and cupped the girl's right breast, lightly feeling its contour. Lawton knew how to touch a woman. He'd never been rough, even when he was young and full of fever. Her breast was round as a honeydew and just as solid.

'Hey!' Charlie said. 'Watch it, asshole!'

Brandy drew back carefully, easing out of Lawton's grasp. She flattened herself against the leather seat, trying to keep her smile together.

Charlie Harrison leaned halfway across the table.

'Touch her again, old man, you're dead meat. You hear me?'

'Relax,' Arnold said. 'He's confused, that's all. He makes mistakes.'

'I'm cracked,' Lawton said. 'That's what they say. Loopy doopy. There's a name for it, but I forget.'

'Jesus,' Charlie said. 'You okay, Brandy?'

'I'm fine, I'm fine. Leave him alone, Charlie. He's okay.'

'Cracked,' Lawton said. 'But still full of beans.'

Everyone was quiet for a minute, eyes wandering the room, trying to put the moment behind them.

Truth was, even in his heyday, Lawton Collins's brain had never been what you'd call razor sharp. For one thing, he'd always been lousy with time stuff. Most of his life, you could ask him the day of the week, he'd have to puzzle on it a while. Season of the year was the same thing. But that was partly Miami's fault. Anywhere else in the world, somebody asked you what month it was, you looked out the window, you could tell. Leaves turning gold, snow on the ground, jonquils blooming. But in Miami, windows were useless. January looked exactly like June and August was the same as November.

Back in his police days, faces were Lawton's strength. Faces and the names attached to them. But that other stuff, time and dates, chronologies, what happened when, he was never good with that. Like he'd gotten a head start on old age. So when all the rest of the stuff started evaporating in his head, like the fizz going out of a soft drink, it took Lawton and everybody else, even his daughter Alexandra, a good while to notice anything strange was happening.

Right then it was lunchtime, Wednesday. Easter coming up. Beyond the curtained windows the sky was full of juicy spring light, while the interior of Neon Leon's Riverside Café was as murky as an underwater cave, most of the light coming from one big-screen TV that was tuned in to a pro wrestling match.

Charlie had another tug on his beer, wiped his mouth, and fixed his glare on the box in Lawton's lap like he was cranking up his X-ray vision.

'So that's it?' Charlie said. 'You got it.'

'Like I promised,' Arnold said. 'My word's my bond.'

'So what do you want from me, Arnold? Credit report? Take a polygraph, what?'

Arnold said nothing. Just eyed the young man in that leisurely way he had.

The boy was wearing khaki slacks and a blue button-down. A long way from the scruffy crowd around the rest of the bar. Tattoos and pierced eyelids everywhere you looked. Ratty T-shirts and torn jeans.

Brandy was silent, smiling nervously at Lawton. Brandy had on a shapeless shirt of pale green and baggy jeans. But the clothes didn't conceal her. Already several of the guys at the bar had quit watching the wrestling match, swiveling their stools around to give Brandy their total attention.

'Always in a hurry, this generation. Can't wait to get to the end of the story, find out what happened. Lost the ability to savor. Isn't that right, Lawton? Not like us old guys, sitting back, swishing the wine around in our mouths before we swallow it, enjoying every tick of the clock.'

'True,' Lawton said. 'But I gotta say, this young lady certainly has nice bosoms. Firm and round. They'll come in very handy for suckling her young.'

'All right, that's it,' Harrison said. 'Come on, Brandy, we're out of here.'

Arnold reached out and thumped his knuckles on the manila envelope.

'Keep your ass planted right there, Charlie. You'll get what you want, but first I got to get what I want. *Quid pro quo.* You know your Latin, right?'

Charlie stared down at the baskets of fried food that sat in front of him and resettled himself in his seat.

For thirty years Arnold and Lawton had been friends and in all that time Arnold hadn't changed a bit. Still master of ceremonies wherever he went. For five decades he'd run a sports book out of his

92

condo up in Hallandale. Anybody that was anybody in South Florida knew Peretti.

Seventy-two and still commanded respect. Didn't matter he was silver-haired with a short, stocky build. Didn't matter he dressed like a dork. Like today in his lemon-yellow shirt, black shorts, and sandals with white knee-high socks. Big square glasses with gold frames. Behind the thick lenses his eyes were watery and dark. Everywhere he and Lawton went, people knew Arnold. The right people. They were always happy to see him, slapping him on the back, buying him drinks, lighting his cigars.

'I think it's me,' Brandy said. 'I think I'm the problem, Charlie. Your friend doesn't want to do business with a woman present.'

Arnold glanced her way, then looked at Lawton, gave him a small, disappointed shake of the head.

'What're you going to do with this generation? Never had a decent war or a good Depression to give them any depth of character. Minute they were born, they thought they were entitled to the first-class seat without doing a damn thing to earn it.'

Brandy scooted to the edge of the booth.

'Would you gentlemen excuse me? This lady needs a potty break.'

She stood up and ambled across the room, with Arnold and the gang at the bar following her movements reverently. As she passed by the last stool and turned into the murky back room, a rack of pool balls exploded.

'Nice girl,' Peretti said. 'At least we know that much about you, Charlie. You got good taste in broads.'

Someone cheered at the bar, and Lawton turned in time to see a big guy on the TV with long hair and a beard toss a guy who looked just like him over the ropes into the first row of the crowd. A murmur passed along the bar. A couple of guys talking on cell phones pulled them away from their ears to watch.

'I can't tell which ones are the bad guys,' Lawton said. 'Used to be, you could tell.'

'They're all bad these days,' Arnold said. 'That's what sells.'

'Bad against bad? Where's the fun in that?'

Out on the river a Haitian freighter piled high with mattresses and bicycles moved slowly downstream. Along the dock Arnold Peretti's big Bertram bumped lightly against the pilings in the swell of the freighter's wake.

Arnold selected a fried shrimp, dunked it in the cocktail sauce, sucked it down. He patted his lips with the napkin and smiled at Charlie.

'Look, kid, I like to have a feel for the people I'm doing business with. Especially a thing like this, the likely repercussions.'

'I'm an average guy. Let's just leave it at that.'

Arnold settled a sharp look on Charlie. He tapped the manila envelope.

'When you write this exposé, you're going to piss some people off. You ready for that, Mr Average Guy? You ready to go into hiding for a while?'

Charlie pushed his Heineken aside. His eyes settled on the envelope.

'Don't worry, kid. It's all there. Everything I promised. Blueprints, schematics, the whole deal.'

Charlie swallowed.

'How'd you get hold of it, Arnold? Tell me that.'

'Not to worry, kid. It came into my possession, now it's about to pass into yours. And this thing, it's a prototype. You know, a scale model. I don't know if the goddamn thing even works, but there it is.'

'It seems damn small for what it's supposed to do,' Charlie said.

'Like I told you, all I know is what I overheard. Sounds to me like it's a contraband weapon. Somebody's doing a little arms dealing on the side. I thought somebody with some investigative training should look into it, expose the bastards.'

Arnold helped himself to another onion ring.

'I need to know if you stole this stuff, Arnold.'

'What? You think they said, Hey, Arnold, why don't you take this thing out for a test drive? Damn right I stole it.'

'So my article would be based on information acquired illegally.'

Arnold waved the thought away with his big paw.

'Tell me something, Charlie. All this time I been talking to you, not once have you asked me why I'm exposing this guy.'

Charlie closed his eyes and opened them again, like Peretti was trying his patience.

95

'All right, Arnold. So tell me. Why're you exposing him?'

Arnold smiled. Showed his big teeth.

'Long and short of it, I want to save his ass, set him back on the right course.'

'Save him?'

'Yeah,' Arnold said. 'I've known him a long time. There's a loyalty factor at work. But I still got to expose him. For his own damn good.'

Arnold swiveled his head and stared at his smoky reflection in the mirror.

'Why not go to the cops, the FBI?'

'Like I got such a good working relationship with the law enforcement community. They're going to jump up and salute when I walk in the door.'

Charlie picked up a limp onion ring, inspected it for a second, then let it drop back in the basket.

Arnold said, 'Next thing you should've asked me but didn't is, how come I chose you. Why the hell didn't I call up the *New York Times*, *Washington Post*? Shit, anybody would kill to get this story.' Arnold took off his glasses, wiped his eyes, put them back on.

'You like how I write.'

'Fuck, no. What do I know about writing?'

'So why?'

''Cause of that Sugar Bowl, ten years ago. Way you played that night.'

'Aw, Christ.'

With a corner of his paper napkin Arnold blotted the catsup from his lips.

'Yeah, I know,' Arnold said. 'People bring it up all the time, you're sick of hearing it. But that's the truth. I remember that game fondly. Then like I say, one of my people showed me your byline in that piece-of-shit paper you write for, what's it called?'

'The *Miami Weekly*.'

'Yeah, yeah. But it was basically the Sugar Bowl. Jesus, that was a classic. Smallest guy on the field, but every fucking play, there you were batting down a pass, squirting through the line with all those corn-fed linemen trying to crush your ass. Man, it hurts my ribs just thinking about it.'

'So you called me up. And here we are.'

Arnold selected another onion ring, held it in front of his lips and said, 'So let's hear what you know about him, kid. Tell me.'

'Oh, come on. A pop quiz?'

'I need to know if I'm talking to a schmuck or what.'

Charlie Harrison shook his head, closed his eyes again. Lawton had to hold himself back from reaching over and smacking a little common courtesy into him. The young man leaned back in the booth, got a bored sound in his voice.

'He lives in Palm Beach, runs MicroDyne Corporation. Used to manufacture computer hardware, silicon chips, all that shit. But six, seven years ago they were losing their asses to the California heavyweights, profits slipping, so his sexy daughter drops out of MIT, swoops in and saves the day.'

'Sexy?' Arnold said.

The kid rolled his eyes.

'Yeah, Arnold. How you think she got on the cover of *Forbes, Fortune*?'

'By being smart.'

'There's lots of smart girls. Except most of them have thick ankles and thicker glasses. Morgan Braswell's a babe. Photogenic as hell. Don't tell me you haven't noticed.'

'She didn't save the company with her looks.'

'She comes swishing into a room full of five-star generals, I bet she makes an impression.'

'She's a smart girl. It's not about her appearance.'

'Hey, Arnold. You want to know if I've done my homework. Well, okay. The fact is, yeah, I've invested some time in this already. One thing I found out, MicroDyne doesn't actually manufacture anything. What they do is coat stuff with some hot-shit enamel or metallic powder or something. It's all classified. Some kind of glaze that goes onto the chips and microcircuitry modules that run the telemetry systems and onboard computers for military weapons and fighter jets. All that hardware comes in the front door, they zap it with their coating and send it back to McDonnell Douglas or whoever, and those other guys build the planes and missiles.'

'And that's what you know. The sum total.'

Charlie frowned. He reached into his shirt pocket, came out with a little notebook, and flipped through the pages until he found the one he wanted.

'F-22 Raptor, the Bell V-22 Osprey helicopter, AIM-120 C missile guidance systems. The ALQ-99 jammer carried by the F/A-18F Super Hornet, and the Sanders situation awareness integrated system that regulates all deception countermeasures for the Hornet, the expendable decoys and signal and frequency emission systems. Those are a few of the systems coated with this shit.'

He flipped the notebook closed and put it back in his shirt pocket.

'Satisfied, Arnold? Do I get an A?'

Arnold was staring down at his thick hands spread out on the tabletop.

'That's good, Charlie. That's good stuff. Very specific.'

'I'm pleased you're pleased.'

'But you still got some more digging to do.'

'I'm aware of that. I just got started.'

'You study up on the rest of the family?'

Charlie sighed.

'Braswell's wife was a suicide, ten, eleven years ago. That what you mean? Went into a funk after her son died and jumped off a chair with a rope around her neck. Not very creative.'

Arnold swallowed and looked across at the television.

'So you know the story about the son, Andy Braswell, how he died.'

'A fucking marlin ate him, that's what I read.'

Arnold turned his head and looked at the kid.

'It didn't eat him,' he said. 'It drowned him.'

'Okay, okay. So, what's your point, Arnold? You think all this personal bullshit goes into the piece? What? Like Braswell's son dies, that's supposed to excuse the bad shit he's gotten into?'

Arnold popped the onion ring into his mouth, then reached out and thumped a solid finger on Charlie's forearm, munching while he spoke.

'Braswell's a decent guy. He got derailed from all the suffering he's been through. I think that's the slant you take.'

'I'll figure out my own goddamn slant.'

Charlie put his elbows on the table and leaned forward.

'What is it, Arnold? You change your mind? Decide you don't want to do business with me? All right, fine. So just take your goddamn envelope and your prototype and slither back under your rock. I got other stories. But don't jerk me around.'

Arnold topped up his beer mug from the pitcher, then leaned forward quickly to suck away the overflowing foam.

Eyes on the wrestling match, Arnold said, 'That was some kind of fucking night, that Sugar Bowl. Unassisted tackle record still on the books. You were golden, kid. You were ten feet tall and you fucking glowed.'

'We lost the game, that's what I remember.'

'Yeah, yeah,' Arnold said. 'But you gotta keep in mind, kid, like they say, it's not whether you win or lose, it's whether you cover the spread. And you did, Charlie. You covered it just fine.'

'I made you some money.'

'You made me a shitload, Charlie. But that's not why I'm here. Reason I'm here is 'cause I like guys with grit, tenacious little pricks like you.'

'Thanks.'

'I like 'em, mainly 'cause I can trust 'em not to give up their sources. I got a feeling about you, Charlie. A guy puts a gun to your head, you're not going to let somebody's name slip out. That's real important to me, to stay the hell out of this thing.'

'Okay, I'm a tenacious little prick. I don't give up my sources. Yeah, you picked the right guy.'

'Because what I haven't told you yet, Charlie, I'm a member of the family.'

'What? The Braswells?'

'A.J. married my daughter. Her name was Darlene. She's the one jumped off the chair with the rope around her neck. Not very creative.'

'Hey, I'm sorry. I didn't realize.'

'Well, now you do.'

'You're Braswell's father-in-law?'

Arnold nodded solemnly.

'I got an interest in this turning out right, Charlie. I want this exposed, but I don't want you disemboweling these people. Is that clear?'

Charlie searched Arnold's eyes for a moment or two, then nodded. It was clear. He didn't much like it, but yeah, it was clear.

Brandy reappeared, crossing the room through the gauntlet of hungry eyes, and she eased back into her seat.

'I miss anything?'

Lawton leaned forward, inhaling deeply.

'Nice perfume,' he said.

'Thanks.'

'Like fresh-cut clover with a rainstorm approaching.'

Lawton sat back, basking in Brandy's smile.

Charlie Harrison grumbled and pushed his beer bottle out of the way and stared at Arnold.

'All right, Arnold. You gonna give me this or what?'

Arnold took one more look at the young man, then nudged the envelope across the table. Charlie peeled back the tabs and pulled out the papers and started glancing through them.

'So how you gonna make out on the story, Charlie?' Peretti gave Brandy a wink. 'Gonna be a good payday, I bet.'

Harrison was studying the blueprint.

'Just my regular salary.' Mumbling, not even looking up.

'Charlie doesn't care about money,' Brandy said. 'It's one of his virtues.'

'Whoa!' Arnold peered at the boy. 'Say that again.'

Charlie glanced up from the page. Gave Arnold a cute smile.

'I get a weekly wage, Arnold. That's how it works in the real world.'

'You telling me you're just going to give the story to this *Miami Weekly*?'

'That's right.'

'What're you, crazy? Only reason anybody looks at that pissant rag is for those sleazy personal ads. Bunch of perverts trying to find each other.'

'That pissant rag has been buying my groceries the last five years.'

'What about *Time, Newsweek*, one of those big guys? This isn't some little local story. It's national. Bigger than that, even. You take this story, peddle it to one of the big guys, I bet they'd pay you more than your biweekly salary. Ten thousand, fifteen at least.'

'Twenty-five,' Brandy said.

Arnold blinked, then swiveled his head slowly and peered at her.

'I have a friend.' Brandy smiled at Charlie. 'Her name's Julie Jamison, she's an editor at *Rolling Stone*.'

'You didn't,' Charlie said. He let the blueprint flutter to the table.

Brandy closed her eyes and opened them, trying to be patient with him.

'I was very discreet. I told Julie about the story and she thought about it and called me back to say they'd probably do it as a three-parter, pay fifteen up front and ten more when the last section was printed.'

'Jesus Christ,' Arnold said. 'When'd you do this?'

'A couple of days ago. Why?'

'When?' Arnold said. 'What day?'

'I don't know, Monday, Tuesday. Hey, it's a big

103

story. You said so yourself, Arnold, it should have major circulation. Charlie should get some financial benefit from it. A career boost.'

Arnold took off his glasses, rubbed his eyes. Then he put them back on and peered around the bar as if these men had suddenly become dangerous.

Lawton shifted in his seat. He lifted the lid of the box and looked inside, then dropped the lid back into place.

'Can I press it now, Arnold?' he asked. 'Can I press the button?'

'No, Lawton. Just sit there, okay? Let me think.'

'Christ, Arnold,' Charlie said. 'Don't get paranoid on me. Relax, everything's cool.'

Arnold leaned forward against the table, raised his hand and flagged their waitress, flicked his hand for the check. Then he looked across at Charlie and lowered his voice. 'Is that what you think? It's cool?'

'Julie won't mention it to anyone,' Brandy said. 'I told her to keep it on the q.t. The secret's safe, Arnold.'

Lawton opened the lid of the box and peeked down at the contraption inside. It was a wild tangle of wires and a stack of circuit boards connected to several cylinders filled with blue fluid. The contraption reminded him of something. He wasn't sure what.

'The q.t., huh? This Julie, she's real tight-lipped, is she? Like maybe she got that figure, twenty-five thousand, it just came out of her head? She didn't have to go to her boss, run it by anybody else. She's not sitting around right now with the magazine's lawyers, discussing the possible libel case? Maybe calling up Braswell, trying to confirm a few items of interest. Nothing like that.'

Charlie leaned forward and laid a hand on Peretti's. '*Tranquilo*, Arnold.'

Arnold jerked his hand away.

Lawton was staring down at the device. There was a blue button and a green one beside it. On one side of the contraption there was a small cone like a megaphone, or the speaker on an old Victrola, and behind the cone a bird's nest of wires, and those tubes connected to the circuit boards.

Lawton remembered what it reminded him of. The microwave oven he'd taken apart, trying to repair. There on his workbench in the garage, all those circuit boards and wires and transistors. He had no idea what any of it was. Never even got the thing put back together.

Lawton snuck his right hand into the box and pressed the blue button but nothing happened.

Beside him Arnold was staring out the window muttering to himself. Lawton tried pressing the green button and still nothing.

'Look,' Brandy said. 'I don't know why you're getting worked up. Julie's professional. They do big stories all the time without leaking anything.'

She pouted at Arnold. Then turned the pout on Charlie.

Lawton could feel the box humming on his lap.

It hadn't been humming before. So at least he'd gotten it started. Revving a little. Maybe what he should do now, he should press both buttons at once.

'How about my name?' Arnold said. 'You happen to let that slip?'

Brandy pressed her lips together, fluttering her lashes. It was probably how she'd gotten out of trouble in the past. But it wasn't working with Arnold.

'You did, didn't you? You told them my fucking name.'

Brandy gave a guilty nod.

'Jesus God,' Arnold said. 'You fucking idiots.'

Lawton slid his hand inside the box and pressed both buttons at once. The hum deepened. It sounded like a tuning fork held close to the ear. Lawton could feel his knee joints buzzing.

Across the room the television made a pop and went black.

At the bar, the two men with cell phones jerked them away from their ears. One man tapped his phone against his palm, then pressed it against his ear again. He shrugged and set the thing on the bar. The bartender was fiddling with the remote, trying to get the TV on again. The Christmas lights twinkling along the top shelf of liquor bottles had gone out.

Arnold grabbed Lawton's wrist and pulled his hand out of the box.

'Aw, shit, Lawton, what'd you do?'

'Nothing.'

Arnold looked across the room at the dead television.

Then he snatched the blueprint off the table and slid it into the envelope. He prodded Lawton with his knee and the old man slid out of the booth, and Arnold got out after him.

'Wait a minute,' the kid said. 'Let's talk about this like adults. Nothing's changed. Not really.'

'The fuck it hasn't.'

Brandy was looking at the blank television.

'That's what it does? It turns off televisions?'

Arnold stood there a moment staring at the two of them.

'Peretti, you're overreacting, man.'

Arnold headed for the door. Lawton padded behind him, lugging the box.

Outside in the daylight, Arnold halted and took the box out of Lawton's hands. Overhead a jetliner was roaring into a thin spray of clouds, lifting off, heading east out toward the Atlantic.

Lawton said, 'So what is this thing, some kind of ray gun?'

Arnold looked at him for a second or two.

'Yeah, I guess that's what it is. Yeah, a ray gun.'

'What's the range on this baby?'

'Now that's the question, isn't it? That's the million-dollar question.'

Lawton glanced up at the rumbling sky, then back at his friend.

'All right,' Arnold said. 'Come on, old buddy. I need to get you home.'

'You said we were going fishing.'

'Plans've changed,' Arnold said. 'You and I, we're going to have to keep our heads down for a while, Lawton. Not have any contact.'

Lawton followed Arnold over to the Bertram. Printed in gold letters across the stern was the boat's name: *You Bet Your Ass*.

Arnold climbed aboard and Lawton loosened the lines from the dock cleats and tossed them over the rail to Arnold. Arnold grabbed them and let them fall at his feet. He didn't coil them like he usually did. He just let them lie there, in a mad tangle on the deck.

# 6

Arnold slipped the box into the cockpit storage locker. He dug out the ignition keys and handed them to Lawton, then turned and lifted his eyes and watched the laughing gulls spinning over Neon Leon's, a few of them diving down at the roof shrieking as though whatever had turned off the television had also driven them insane.

'I got to use the head, get rid of this beer. I'll be up top in a minute.'

'It's true, isn't it, Arnold? I used to arrest you?'

'Yes, it's true.'

'Why was that? You a dope peddler?'

'No, it wasn't dope, Lawton. I never dabbled in dope.'

He turned and gave Arnold a long look. 'Don't tell me you were a professional killer.'

Arnold patted him on the shoulder. 'You get us a little downstream, I'll be right up.'

'We going fishing, catch some dolphin?'

'Not today, Lawton. I need to get you back, safe and sound. I'll stick around till Alexandra gets home, then I got a couple of things I gotta attend to. We'll go fishing soon as this thing gets cleared up. I promise.'

'Don't worry about your boat. Go on, take a piss. You can trust me.'

'I know I can.'

'Hey, Arnold, is this guy Braswell trying to kill us?'

'No, Lawton. Braswell went over to the Bahamas. He's hanging out in Marsh Harbor, trying to locate a blue marlin. No, we're fine. We're just dandy.'

'He's after that fish you told me about? One with the transmitter on it? Looks like a cigar?'

'That's right, Lawton. He's chasing that fish. He doesn't have time for a couple of old farts like us.'

Arnold gave his shoulder another pat, then headed for the cabin.

Lawton climbed the ladder to the flybridge and started the big engines. Nudging the right throttle, then the left, twisting the wheel, he eased the Bertram away from the dock and out into the dark, oily center of the Miami River.

A hundred yards away, a squat, thick-necked tugboat was chugging toward them like some kind of irritable bulldog, so Lawton edged Arnold's sleek white yacht over to the right half of the river.

110

He kept the Bertram idling forward, two knots, three, inhaling the river scents, industrial smells of kerosene and turpentine and a burnt coffee odor, all of it riding the sugary breeze.

Lawton Collins always had an easy hand with boats. As close to a natural gift as he could claim. He wasn't a certified captain, hadn't taken the Coast Guard courses, and he didn't know all the niceties of radar and GPS and Loran, and he knew next to nothing about the big turbo-charged diesels belowdecks, but Lawton could still handle a boat with charmed certainty. Didn't matter how big or small the craft was. Give him a target on a nautical chart, set him behind the controls, and he'd roll through fifteen foot seas or search out the twisting channels through treacherous shallows and get to his destination every time. It was one of the few skills he still possessed. Almost the only talent that hadn't deserted him these last years as his limbs were crabbed by arthritis and his brain hollowed out.

Soon as his hands were on the controls of a boat, he was rejuvenated. Muscles springy, heart alert. Mind of a twenty-year-old.

As the big boat grumbled ahead, Lawton's mind whisked back to the days when he used to steer his small wood skiff with the forty-horse Evinrude through the chaotic chop outside of Key West Harbor, into the rush of open water and the sloppy convergence of tides and currents across the reefs, on and on, south by southwest, finally into the blue-green sand flats of the Marquesa Islands, volcanic and remote and crackling with fish, the Marquesas where he and his buddies built a little fishing shack tucked among the mangroves, a place to camp under the unsullied heavens, far from the dogs barking, the guns cocking and brakes squealing on dark, bloody streets, just him and his buddies lying on the wood planks he'd nailed into place, lying on a blanket or a nylon sleeping bag, shutting off the kerosene lantern, and gazing up at the dense speckle of stars and the dark birds circling against the moon, all that splendor to feast on, simply because he could handle a boat, wasn't afraid of the markerless waters, could guide his way through the shoals and the narrow limestone channels, following a simple compass heading, reading the stars, or else doing it by a blind man's intuition, and even to this day he had all those same skills, even though his brain was as leaky as the spongy earth beneath the Florida topsoil, and he damn well could still recall every patch of water he'd ever crossed, had a freeze-frame of each acre of blue water in crystal-sharp focus, just like the day he'd crossed them the first time, as if every boat he'd ever steered, every wake he'd ever thrown was still there, white foamy trails across the transparent surface of the world, all the pathways he'd taken to get to this day, to this narrow, greasy river, to this boat, *You Bet Your Ass*.

Lawton eased back on the throttle. The tug still hogged the middle of the river, a freighter looming behind it, big rusty-red hull, deckhands scurrying about on the foredeck, chattering, full of bustle. And other boats were strung out farther back, a fishing trawler, a small open fisherman, a Hatteras yacht. A regular parade coming up the river for repairs or gas or to deliver their loads.

As Lawton steered the boat, a scene from long ago flashed before him. A night in the Marquesas when the mosquitoes were so bad Alex and her mother and Lawton had to climb down the wooden ladder and submerge themselves in the water for a little relief. He saw that moment. Black water, glossy with moonlight. Alexandra's mother in her bathing suit with the flowered skirt. What was her name? The woman he'd married. The woman he'd lived with for nearly forty years. He remembered the swimsuit she'd worn that night. It had flowers. Pink flowers. He remembered that. Hibiscus.


Arnold Peretti took one step into the Bertram's main salon and stopped. Sitting in a leather chair was Johnny Braswell. He had his elbows on the dining table, a sheet of paper lying in front of him. Johnny looked up from the paper and smiled at Arnold. The kid wore the same straw hat he always wore when he was out fishing, wide-brimmed sombrero with the top cut out like he was letting his skull breathe. Dark blue shorts and a white polo shirt with *ByteMe* embroidered over the left breast. The name of the Braswells' yacht.

Arnold stayed in the doorway, one foot in the cabin, the other still on the rear deck.

'Hey, Johnny.'

'Hey, Arnold, What it *is*, man?'

Johnny Braswell had a chirpy voice, smiled too much. Lying on the table beside the sheet of paper was one of Johnny's knives, blade open. The kid loved knives, always had.

'Come on in, Arnold, shut the door, relax, man. I need to talk to you. Pick your brains a little.'

Arnold held his ground, trying to keep cool but running a quick movie in his head: slam the door, take two quick steps, throw himself over the gunwale into the river. Workable, except for one minor detail. He didn't swim a stroke.

Still, as he took another look at that knife, today might be the day to learn.

'You like this blade, Arnold? It's an AK 430. Customized version of one the Special Forces used in Desert Storm. Slices through solid bone like it was mayonnaise. Lot better than packing iron. Don't you think? I mean, sure, there's a higher spatter factor, but then what's a little gore, right? Just the cost of doing business.'

Arnold looked at the knife with its glittery blade, some kind of pygmy machete, a sugarcane cutter or something.

Johnny was thick-waisted, with a bulky chest and a baby face. Always flushed from the sun, and squinting, even when he was indoors. Arnold had seen the kid work the wire on a few giant marlin and knew the blubber under Johnny's shirt wasn't blubber at all.

'I believe I invited you inside, Grandpa. Didn't I?'

Arnold took a step backwards onto the deck. The door still open. If he was going to get cut, he wanted witnesses.

Johnny grinned at the old man's cockiness.

'Okay, sure, Arnold, outside's cool. Wherever you want.'

Johnny got up from the table. He came across the cabin and stepped onto the aft deck, holding his knife down by his leg. He took a perch on the starboard gunwale and watched Arnold grip the back of the fighting chair.

'We got a stowaway,' Arnold called up to Lawton.

Lawton turned and looked down.

'Hey, Arnold? You remember my wife's name? I was trying to recall.'

'Her name was Grace, Lawton.'

'Yeah, yeah, that's right. Grace. Grace Collins.'

'Lawton, you just keep us going downriver, me and my friend are going to socialize a bit. Okay?'

'Grace is a pretty name,' Lawton said. 'I like that. Grace. It's got kind of a religious connotation to it.'

Arnold nodded.

'That's some captain you got,' said Johnny. He smiled at Arnold in that bleary hey-this-is-great-shit way he had. 'What's wrong with the dude?'

'He lived too long,' Arnold said. 'That's all.'

'Yeah, that seems to be going around.'

'Johnny, listen. You got some problem with me, fine, we'll handle that however we can. But that old man up there, he's got no part in my business. Get that straight. He's an innocent bystander, that's all.'

'Whatever you say, Arnold. You're the head goomba. At least for the time being anyway.'

Arnold shook his head, got the fighting chair between him and the boy.

'You know, Arnold, I'm disappointed in you. Old fuck like you, you shoulda known you couldn't break the omerta. Finger your own people and we'd sit still for it. And here all this time I thought you were a stand-up guy.'

'Johnny, Johnny, Johnny. I told you once, I told you a million fucking times, I'm not in the Mob. I'm not a fucking Godfather. All I am is a bookie, for Christsakes. I take bets. Football, basketball, the ponies. Nothing more than that.'

'Sure, Arnold. However you want to play it.'

Up on the flybridge, Lawton kept the boat idling along. He glanced back, showed Arnold a worried look, then turned back to the river.

'"In Italy, for thirty years under the Borgias,"' Johnny said, '"they had warfare, terror, murder, and bloodshed, but they produced Michelangelo, Leonardo da Vinci and the Renaissance. In Switzerland, they had brotherly love; they had five hundred years of democracy and peace – and what did that produce? The cuckoo clock."'

'Yeah, yeah, I know,' Arnold said. 'Orson Welles, *The Third Man*.'

'Good, Arnold. You remembered.'

'Listen to me, Johnny. Let's put the knife away, we'll have a cocktail, talk this thing through, take a little boat ride, enjoy the sun. When we're done, we swing by the Jockey Club, pick up a couple of girls I know. You'd like that, wouldn't you? A couple of girls.'

They were passing beneath the Brickell Avenue drawbridge, cars backed up in both directions. Moving along slowly, almost to the mouth of the river.

'What girls, Arnold? What kind of girls could an old brontosaurus like you show me?'

Johnny smiled but there was nothing behind it. He pushed himself up from the gunwale and took a step toward Arnold and stopped.

'I like you, Arnold. I like your boat, I like how you live. I always thought you were a classy guy. For a goomba, you got refinement. You have that John Gotti thing going. Dapper don, old Moustache Pete.'

'That's movie bullshit, Johnny. You lie there and you watch Edward G. Robinson and Robert Mitchum all the fucking day and night and your brains are turned to mush, boy. That's not how the world is. It just isn't, son.'

The boat passed beyond the no-wake zones, and Lawton Collins pushed the throttle forward and got them up on plane. The big mirrored windows of the office buildings slipping away to the north. Behind them a jet ski bounced across their wake, crisscrossing back and forth, searching out the best bumps.

Arnold looked out at the watery blue dazzle. He wasn't sure why he'd never learned to swim. Probably too busy running errands for guys on Miami Beach, getting his start in the business.

Arnold took off his glasses and wiped the salt spray off the lenses with his shirt tail. When he put them back on, Johnny had moved a step closer to him, watching the jet ski cutting back and forth over their wake.

Peretti looked ahead at the big Rickenbacker Causeway coming up, all the joggers and skaters and bicyclers pedaling across it. Everybody out enjoying the weather, the sun. Staying young and healthy, gonna live forever, this generation.

'Now look, Johnny, if your dad or Morgan has a beef with me, then I'm going to talk directly to them. A family meeting, fine. But I'm not doing this with you. You could wave the biggest fucking knife in the world, I'm not saying another word. A.J. wants to hear my side of things, we do it face to face.'

Eyes drowsy, Johnny said, 'We're out on this boat, Arnold, nice sunny day, know what I'd like? I'd like to catch a fish, put some meat on the deck.'

'What?'

Johnny tucked the knife in his belt, grabbed one of the rods out of the rod holder, opened the bailer on the reel, reached up to the tip of the rod and pinched the big stainless steel hook and pulled out some line.

'You got any bait around here, Arnold?'

'What're you doing, Johnny? What is this?'

'You should always carry bait. You got all these rods, you need fresh bait.'

'I got some frozen squid down below. Take a minute to thaw it out.'

'What I want, Arnold, I want some fresh bait. Something still alive, full of blood, you know what I mean. Maybe about the size and shape of a finger. You see anything like that around here?'

'Johnny, listen. Don't push this thing where it doesn't have to go.'

'Live bait, Arnold. You got any idea where we could rustle some up?'

'Hey, come on, Johnny. You're not like this. You're no gangster. You're a rich kid, runs his father's fishing yacht, keeps the reels filled with line, the drag set right. That's who you are. You're my grandson, my sweet little boy. Not some thug out of the movies.'

Johnny's smile hardened. He set the rod in the holder and drew out the knife.

'You been fucking with my family, Arnold. We don't stand still for that.'

Arnold felt his legs freezing up. The time to jump was past.

'Am I right? You been fucking with the family, Arnold?'

Arnold raised a hand. 'It's not like that, Johnny. I swear it's not.'

Johnny moved across the six feet of deck quicker

than seemed possible. He grabbed Arnold's right wrist, and held it in his iron grip.

'Sooner or later, always comes a time,' Johnny said. 'Castellano whacks Gambino, Gotti clips Castellano. It's how it happens, the baton pass, old man, one generation stepping up, taking over. That's what time it is here. So no more yapping. You'll just stand there and take your medicine, and learn to like it.'

'Stop it, son. This isn't you. This isn't who you are. You're a good kid.'

'You don't know me, Arnold.'

'Sure I do. I knew you since the day you were born. Held you in my lap, changed your fucking diapers, kid. You're a good boy. You're not like this.'

Johnny's eyes lost their focus for a moment. Working out this problem. Not the brightest bulb. Not somebody you'd send alone to do a job unless you were spread thin and there was no one else. Arnold watched as the boy's eyes cleared. And his grip tightened. He twisted Arnold's arm back against his elbow joint. The air blew out of the old man's lungs.

'You should always keep live bait aboard your boat, old man. You never know when you might need to catch your supper. Live bait, that's the number-one rule of the sea.'

Johnny wrenched Arnold around and bent his hand toward the wooden step plate on the starboard gunwale. He pressed Arnold's palm flat to the step plate and laid the edge of the blade against the base of his little finger.

'Johnny! No.'

Lawton slowed the boat and said, 'Hey, you. What's going on down there? What're you up to?'

Johnny eased his face close to Arnold's. Holding him in that arm lock.

'Johnny,' Arnold said. 'You can't do this to your own flesh and blood.'

'What flesh and blood? You're not my granddad anymore. My granddad wouldn't betray his own family. You lost your union card, old man. My sister and my dad, that's my family.'

'Johnny, I'm pleading with you.'

'Sorry, Gramps. Your time's come.'

He gave Arnold a sad smile, then leaned into his work, pressing down with all his weight, and sliced through the first knuckle of Arnold's little finger.

The old man howled and dropped to his knees. A cold spike hammered through his heart and he collapsed against the transom. He was still conscious, but the daylight was thickening to a yellow haze. Blood spilled onto the deck.

'Jesus, Granddad. You got some porky digits on you.'

Johnny held up the finger and grimaced as he curled the sharp point of the hook through the meat. Then he opened the bail on the reel, whipped the rod back, and cast the plug of flesh out into the wake. He put the rod in the holder on the arm of the fighting chair and watched the finger skip across the bay.

'Now I got your full attention, Arnold, I want to

know where you put it, that thing you stole from my family.'

Hunched against the transom, Arnold was trying to draw a breath. He pressed the stump of his finger against his thigh and a jolt of current ripped through him.

He opened his mouth to speak but found no air to fill his words. Johnny was letting out line, trolling with Arnold's little finger.

'And the second thing is,' Johnny said, lifting his head, looking off like he was struggling to summon up his orders, 'I want to hear the name of every asshole you been sharing our private affairs with. And once I hear that, we'll get onto our main business. Baton pass time.'

Lawton Collins could see it wasn't right, the things happening on the deck behind him. He could see the old man getting cut. The old man with white hair and a thick neck. Blood spilling on his yellow shirt. Lawton knew the thing on the deck below was all wrong, probably illegal. But the problem was, he wasn't sure whose side he was on.

He tried to remember these men's names. That was always the place to start. The name led to the other things. That was what worked in the past. Once you remembered their names, the other things started to flow back.

There was the old man down there and there was

a young one. He had long blond hair and looked like a punk. Though these days, it wasn't easy to tell. He could be a rock star or own a restaurant, be a CEO. Hell, these days everyone was trying hard as they could to look like a criminal.

The old man gripped his bloody hand. Pressing it against his shirt. His glasses had come off and were lying on the deck. Lawton kept the boat going along the channel, glancing behind him to check on the activities down below.

He thought the old man looked familiar. The other one didn't. He'd never seen him before. He was pretty sure of that. He was usually good with names. Names and faces, that was his strength. But this old guy's name was hanging out there in the mist, in the half light. A name he knew. A name he'd said a hundred times. He knew that guy, that much he was sure of. He looked at him and something felt good inside him, warm and easy.

And that's all he needed. The old guy had to be a friend. He didn't need to know the guy's name. All he needed to know was that the guy was his friend and this punk was cutting him.

Lawton swung the wheel hard and the Bertram swerved toward a piling that marked the Intracoastal Waterway. The old man sprawled onto his back and stared up at Lawton. The kid with the bloody knife and topless sombrero rode the lurch of the boat like it hadn't happened. An old hand on deck.

Aiming the point of the bow for the piling, Lawton

pressed the throttle forward, then swerved at the last second so they took a glancing blow. Still, it banged Lawton's ribs against the chrome rail and nearly knocked him off the flybridge.

Behind him the marker pole was bent cockeyed and another boat coming up the channel cut hard to starboard to get out of Lawton's path. The old man with the bloody hand was crouched in the corner, his back against the transom. He was grimacing at Lawton. The old man he recognized but couldn't name. And the punk, the one in the sombrero, had vanished. Lawton was looking back into the wake to find him, when the kid's blond hair and stupid hat appeared on the ladder. The guy was peering up at Lawton, using one hand to hold the ladder, the other gripping his knife.

Lawton spun the wheel all the way to starboard, accelerating again, heading for the seawall. Ram it hard, sink the goddamn boat if he had to. Anything to shake the bastard loose from that ladder. The baby-faced kid with a dull smile, coming up that ladder one step, then the next, then the next, till his face was even with the flybridge deck.

Lawton swung around and aimed a kick at the boy's teeth, but the boy ducked to the side in time. Lawton tried another kick and missed again. Down on the deck, the old man was on his feet. The old man's name was starting to appear out of the fog. He watched it take shape a letter at a time. And then there it was. Of course, Arnold, old Arnold Peretti.

124

Now he remembered. The bookie. His fishing buddy from way back.

Arnold was up on his feet, clawing at the blond boy's ankles, trying to drag him down, slinging blood across the deck.

Lawton turned back to the wheel and saw the seawall coming up fast. Rocks along the bank, boulders big enough to gash a serious hole in that Bertram's hull. Lawton mashed the throttles flat, milking the last trickle of power. Roaring at the seawall. Going to shake that bastard loose. Sink the goddamn boat if he had to. Arnold had plenty enough money to buy another one. No problem there.

Lawton Collins snatched the end of the red coiled line attached to the kill switch, and snapped the free end to his belt loop. Now if he was thrown overboard, the kill switch would activate and the boat would shut down and no one would be able to get it started unless they pulled him out of the water first.

Lawton pressed hard on the throttle. That yacht was turbocharged, a hotdog of a boat, a drag racer. Tuned that way so it could fly from one fishing spot to another. They had to be doing over forty knots.

Sitting on the seawall, a young black man with a cane fishing pole lifted his head and saw the Bertram and he looked at it for a couple of seconds, then he dropped his rod and scrambled to his feet and screamed at Lawton. Then the man swung around and galloped through the tall grass of the vacant lot. Another hundred yards, that's all it was before they'd crash.

The boy in the sombrero was kicking his leg at Arnold Peretti, and he must've got Arnold in the face because Lawton saw the boy grin and the old bookie stumble backwards, lose his balance, and grab for the outriggers. He missed them by a few inches, then staggered to his left and smacked into the gunwale and tumbled headfirst over the side.

A second later the kid was on the last step of the ladder, drawing back his knife, looking up, and for the first time seeing where they were headed, how close they were to crashing. The kid cocked his knife, took aim at Lawton's back and that's when Lawton swung the wheel hard to port, slammed the gears into reverse and held on for all he was worth.

# 7

'I know this guy,' Lt Romano said.

He peered over Alexandra Collins's shoulder as she videotaped the body, then gently raised the camera to record the alley, the overturned garbage cans, moving in on the young woman, her long blond hair tangled with candy wrappers and gummy with blood. Early thirties for the guy, while the young woman was maybe late twenties. The male was wearing khaki trousers, a blue button-down shirt. The woman's outfit was also casual but classier. Green silk blouse, designer jeans. Paying big bucks to look laid-back.

There were three bullet holes in the man's chest, two more in his forehead. Somebody making damn sure. Very damn sure.

Alexandra eased down the alley, zooming in on the

man's wounds, holding there, then slowly zooming out and lifting the camera to show the narrow space between those two warehouses, a freeway for rats. The remains of a cardboard refrigerator box lay on its side down below the fire escape stairs. An army blanket and some fast-food boxes spilling out of the opening. Someone's campsite.

Then Alexandra slid her viewfinder to the right and taped the young woman. She was on her back, staring up at the narrow slot of sky. A blue heavenly day. Her arms were flung out to her sides as if she were about to embrace her lover, lowering himself above her. She had a smile.

Alex didn't see many of those on the people she recorded. Usually it was some kind of grimace, scowling at the pain and unfairness of it all. Every once in a while she saw a flash of serenity on their lips, blessed relief as they fled this mortal plane, abandoned their hungering and impossible search for money or cocaine or love. Lots of grimaces, but hardly ever a smile.

This one was small, just a Mona Lisa hint, as if some big secret had broken into view at the moment of death. One bullet hole in her temple, a second in her left breast. Her shirt had been ripped open by the killer or some passerby, exposing the shapely contour of her bosom, the bullet hole centered perfectly in her nipple as though her killer hadn't been able to draw his aim away from that beautiful target.

But that wasn't Alexandra's concern. Speculating

about motives or indulging in suspicions was for the detectives. She was merely an ID technician, a crime scene jock specializing in photography. Her only issues were with light and shadows, keeping her hands steady so she could document the stark authenticity of the moment. She didn't care what explosion of emotion put this handsome couple in this narrow alley. She didn't care how these two young people had wound up together. It was Alexandra's job to remain detached, float above the scene, a single all-seeing eye. Occupied only with the exposure settings on her thirty-five-millimeter or the Sony recorder, framing each shot, slow panning, lingering on their facial expressions, trying in her way to do justice to these people who had only Alexandra Collins to speak their last words, send their dying signals to the world. That's how she thought of it, those final looks and gestures were like notes in bottles, quick desperate communiqués frozen on their faces and in the arrangements of their bodies and their clothes – a last message flung out into the departing tide.

Alexandra was thirty-one years old and had been doing this work for a decade. A third of the way to retirement, wearing the same cheap blue jumpsuit for eight hours every day, the same routine back at the office as she processed her film and precisely organized the photos or videotape. A job that could be grueling and soul-draining, though she couldn't imagine finding work that suited her better. Walking down these narrow alleys, or into the stifling, lurid apartments, or the spacious mansions of the grotesquely rich and freshly dead, always with the prickle of excitement, always the fresh rush, absorbing these places, these limp bodies, taking her pictures, bleak documents, graphic and obscene. For much of her eight-hour shift she did just this, circling corpses, staying vigilant, heedful of every angle, every item. The hairbrush on the dresser, the slash of lipstick on the mirror, an overturned bottle of perfume. You never knew which seemingly insignificant detail was going to pay off.

And she always took her shots quietly, with a reverential hush. The other officers chattered in the background, making their jokes, planning their after-hours drinking, but Alexandra Collins stayed quiet, always with that deep ache of awe. Recording one after another of these grim scenes.

'Yeah, yeah,' Romano said. 'This is the smart-ass who's always nosing around the department, stopping people in the hall, chatting 'em up, trying to wheedle some dirt. Same fucker who wrote that piece on Karen Curtis over in vice. About her and that nineteen-year-old stud going to that sex club. You remember that, Alex, two, three years back. Got Curtis relieved of duty. Just a little friendly hanky-panky with the hot-oil and rubber-sheet crowd and bang, that's the end of her career. Busted for debauchery.'

'I remember.'

'That's him,' Romano said. 'The shit apparently stuck his nose too far into something this time.'

'Charlie Harrison,' Alex said.

'Yeah, that's his name. Writes for the *Miami Weekly*.'

'Wrote,' she said, moving down the alley, getting a couple of footprints, flat-soled shoes with tiny creases, like boat shoes, made to grip slippery decks. The boat shoe killer, that's what Charlie Harrison would tag him. The yachtsman assassin, something like that, smug and self-conscious, trivializing the horror of it. One of the things that seemed to come so easily to journalists.

Alexandra would have to take the shoe impressions later, make sure none of the detectives stumbled into that area close to the side of the corrugated aluminum warehouse.

Romano squatted down beside the girl. For the last month he'd been on a diet, cutting back on his doughnuts and coffee, down to only a fifth of rum a night, although it hadn't worked worth a damn. He was still fifty pounds overweight, and his face was always flushed and the scalp showing through his thinning white hair fired up to a bright crimson at the least upward bump in his blood pressure.

'I don't recognize the hotty,' he said. He tugged her shirt back across her breast. Gruff Dan Romano, the prude. 'Could be it's his mistress. Like maybe Charlie's wife is spying on him, finally catches him with the broad, and she goes ballistic, like in a literal sense. Takes them both out. Bing, bang, bong.'

'Maybe.'

131

'Which would make it the third one of those in the last week. Jealous rage. If I can't have you, no one can. Man, I'm getting sick of that shit. You know, Alex, my personal creed when it comes to being rejected by women – if I can't have you, then fine, to hell with you.'

Alexandra switched off the sound on the video recorder. It would be too distracting later as she was reviewing the scene to hear all this irrelevant byplay.

'They were shot somewhere else, dumped here.' She motioned at the twin set of parallel grooves in the mud where the victims' heels had dragged. One of the girl's leather sandals lay ten feet away at the opening of the alley. 'You would've noticed eventually.'

Romano stood up and coughed. He reached into his breast pocket, got his pack, tapped out a cigarette, lit it, took a quick, deep drag, then immediately stubbed it out on the side of his silver Zippo. He put the dead cigarette in his jacket pocket, which was bulging with its brothers.

'Harrison is the same guy did that piece on the Gator football team. A couple years ago, maybe three. Some female alumnae sneaking into the locker room before games, sticking hundred-dollar bills down some random jockstraps. Hell, that one article got three assistant coaches fired, half their offensive line thrown off the team. Wrecked Florida's season. Put them on probation. So my guess is, our man Charlie was a guy without too many friends. A professional asshole like that, you want to know where to look for someone with a motive to kill him, you flip open the phone book, close your eyes, and put your finger on a name.'

The other detectives had arrived and were talking and smoking at the end of the alley. Billy McCabe, a young patrolman, looped the yellow crime scene tape from one gutter drainpipe to another, blocking off the far end of the alley. The white City of Miami crime scene van pulled up behind a couple of the green-and-white patrol cars, and Stanley Fitzhugh, the other ID tech working the day shift, got out, followed by their new crime scene trainee, a young black woman named Lisa Roberts.

'Reinforcements,' Alex said.

Romano lit another cigarette, took a quick hit, then stubbed it out on the Zippo. He went through close to three packs a day like that. Dan's way of cutting back. He liked to call it 'going warm turkey.'

'Maybe I'm crazy,' he said, 'but sometimes I find myself longing for the bad old days. Cocaine cowboys running amok, Marielito ex-cons killing each other off. Five homicides before midnight, running our asses all over town fast as we could just to stay even. Stretched so thin, Christ, we were in a hyper-drive the entire shift. All that *café Cubano*, all that adrenaline. Now look at us, we got our feet up on the desk half the day, we finally get out to a scene and we got so many extra personnel we're walking all over each other.'

'That's sick, Dan.'

'It is?'

'Nostalgic for a higher murder rate? Yeah, I think we could call that an unhealthy view.'

Dan rubbed his chin and took a meditative look up at the sky, as if struggling to see the error of his ways. She could see some smart-ass remark forming on his lips when his cell phone squawked. He glanced back at Alex and shrugged. 'Hey, I'm just saying the job used to be more stimulating when those idiots were shooting up the town. Now it's all this pathetic back-alley shit. Boyfriends shooting girlfriends. The glamour days are long gone.'

He scowled at the dead couple, then plucked the phone out of the leather holster on his belt, listened for a second or two, then said, 'Yeah, yeah, I got it. Northeast side of Rickenbacker Causeway. Yeah, yeah, we're rolling.'

He clicked off, put the cell phone away, and shook his head at Alex.

'Be careful what you wish for.'

'Let me guess,' Alex said. 'Murder rate just took a bump.'

'One dead, maybe more. They're waiting for us before they haul the body out of the bay.'

Alex sighed, lifted her video camera and switched it on, and took a last look through the lens at the young woman with the bullet through her breast, running the camera up and down her body, then panning carefully left and right.

'Floaters,' Dan said. 'Jesus, I hate floaters.'

'New or old?'

'Fresh,' he said. 'Some kind of boating accident.'

Alex lingered on Charlie Harrison's scowling face. A bitterly impatient look, as if he'd just gotten the juiciest scoop of his career and now was forced to deal with this annoying interruption before he could rush it into print.

'You about through?'

She switched off the video recorder and capped the lens.

'Sure,' she said. 'Let me brief Fitzhugh, and I'll follow you over there.'

Dan fingered his pack of Marlboros, debating another quick hit.

'Hey,' he said. 'Wasn't your dad going out on a boat today?'

Alex raised her eyes and studied Romano for several seconds.

'You had to say that, didn't you? You had to go and say that.'


The body was twenty yards offshore of Rickenbacker Causeway. A Canadian family picnicking in the shade of a coconut palm had spotted it and called police. Now the young Canadian father was taking snapshots, angling around behind the cops to get a better view of the body rising and falling in the light chop. His two blond daughters and blond wife stayed on their picnic blanket, staring off at the distant city skyline.

Dan Romano had gone down to the shoreline to talk to the cops while Alexandra stayed in her van to use her cell phone. She dialed her dad's number twice more, but got only the 'customer is unavailable' message. She snapped the phone shut and sat there a moment longer, looking out at the glare of blue water. Either Lawton had switched off his phone or he and Arnold were out in the Gulf Stream by now, beyond cell range. That had to be it. Had to be.

Nine days out of ten at this hour Lawton Collins could be found at Harbor House, an adult care facility out in Kendall. Basket weaving, a rousing game of checkers, a light aerobic workout, a fairly nutritious lunch followed by a nap. The staff-to-client ratio was good, the facility was clean, and they didn't allow the patrons to languish in front of the television all day. Lawton enjoyed the place, mainly because he was the darling of half a dozen different widows who vied for his attention with a constant onslaught of cookies and pies. Much to Alexandra's relief, every morning he showered and shaved, doused himself with Aqua Velva, and got dressed without any prompting.

For a couple of years now Lawton had been taking a day off from Harbor House twice a month for an excursion with Arnold Peretti. Fishing mostly, or sometimes just cruising around the bay, having a couple of beers, reminiscing. Now and then Arnold drove them up to Gulfstream to bet the daily double. Arnold and Lawton had been friends since before Alex was born, and he was one of only a few of her father's buddies who hadn't deserted him when he started his decline. The fact that Arnold Peretti had spent his entire professional life as a bookie only mildly disturbed Alex. His friendship with Lawton had given her dad a boost that Alexandra, as hard as she tried, hadn't been able to accomplish.

Alex zipped the phone back in her purse and got out of the van. She unloaded the video camera from the rear and hoisted it on her shoulder and began to tape the scene as she slogged through the thick sand down to the shoreline. A sweep from south to north to place the scene in context, from the arching Rickenbacker Causeway, to the skyscrapers of downtown Miami, and finally the rainbow-tinted high-rise condos along Brickell. As Alexandra worked forward to the water's edge, the cops made way for her. She taped the two Miami PD divers in their wetsuits wading into the shallow water. No tanks, no masks, no flippers, sloshing out to the waist-deep water where the body floated face down. She couldn't tell much about how he was dressed, but she saw he had white hair.

A dark buzz began to burn in the back of her head. Alexandra stepped forward, following the divers into the water, rolling videotape, the bay water warm against her flesh, rising to her knees, then her crotch, Dan Romano calling to her from dry land, telling her there was no need for that, no need to get wet, telling her to stay on the beach, let the divers bring the body in, but she followed them out, focusing on their backs, inching deeper across the smooth, silty bottom, until the water was at her navel, and Alex followed the divers, until they reached out for the body, and she stepped around him so she could witness it all, so she could tape this victim, seeing through her lens the man with white hair, long and wispy, that floated around his head like the delicate roots of some rare flower, and the diver said something to Alexandra, asked her a question, but she didn't register his words, taping as she was, focused with all her being on the lens, on what she was seeing through the glass eyepiece, and then Dan Romano called from shore again, yelling for her to get the hell back in there, what did she think she was doing out in the middle of the goddamn ocean, that equipment was expensive for Godsakes, but Alex didn't flinch, kept her finger tight against the switch, taping this floating man, this man with white hair whom the diver was turning in his arms, turning and lifting, cradling up from the water, holding him like a sleeping child, the man's right cheek resting against the diver's chest, and Alexandra moved the camera to the man's face, the man's familiar face, that face that was not her father's, not Lawton Collins.

'You okay?' the diver asked her.

Alexandra lowered the camera and stared at the dead man's features.

'No,' she said. 'Not okay.'

'What is it? You know this guy?'

'I know him, yes.'

The diver trudged through the water back to shore with Arnold Peretti's head bumping against his chest and the old man's sightless eyes gazing up at the flawless span of blue.

# 8

Thorn was outside in the dark tying flies. A dim, moonless night. He'd never done this in the pitch-black before, working blind with tweezers, glue, silver beads from a key chain, mounting those shiny eyeballs on one of the triangular epoxy bases he'd created last winter. Dark Avenger. That's what he'd call this one. Maybe wrap it in black Mylar thread, use the dark boar bristles for its body, those short, brittle hairs one of his clients plucked from a wild hog he'd gunned down on some fenced-in hunting ranch.

Dark Avenger. Yeah, it had the right quixotic tone for the half dozen bonefish guides who were his biggest customers. A bunch of romantics. Priests of the flats with hair-trigger muscles and supernatural vision. On misty days or in the full blast of sun, those guys could detect the gray shadow of a bonefish ghosting the shallows from fifty yards away, or the imperceptible riffle on the surface of the water that marked the bone's wary passing. They prayed to that silver god, worshiped at the altar of tail and dorsal fin. They devoted their lives to stalking a fish so elusive that weeks could pass without sighting even one of its kind.

Thorn squeezed out a micro-dot of glue and tweezered the silver eye into place. In the dark like this, he was probably bungling the job, creating some kind of misshapen monster, something that would spook the bonefish back into hiding for months. But he didn't care. At the moment he needed to keep his hands busy, needed to keep his focus short. Doing this purely by touch on that gloomy night, nothing to break his concentration but the occasional boat passing on Blackwater Sound, and the light breeze moaning in the wispy Australian pine.

Deep in his inner ear there was a sharp pinging, probably from the bottle of cheap Chardonnay he'd guzzled at sunset, the last shrill cries of dying brain cells. He was feeling sorry for himself, and for the dozens of people who'd died in the airplane crash, and for the Florida Bay and for every other damn thing that crossed his mind.

Thirty yards to the east, Sugarman's car crunched down his gravel drive. Thorn recognized the chuff and sputter of the old Ford V-8. Sugar killed his lights and got out and came up the stairs. Thorn didn't look up. He glued the other eye into place. Maybe what this fly needed was three eyes, or four, maybe a dozen. Dark Avenger, all-seeing, all-knowing. A sinker that would drop down through the clear water into the silt and mud and turtle grass and stare straight into the gray eyes of those ravenous bonefish.

Sugar climbed the steps and took a seat across from Thorn. On the table between them he set a glass pitcher that rattled with ice.

'Green tea,' Sugar said. 'Thought you might need a pick-me-up.'

'I'm fine,' he said. 'Never better.'

'Oh, yeah, Thorn. You've got such a happy glow.'

Sugar lifted the pitcher and filled Thorn's empty wineglass. Ice sparkled in the faint moonlight. Thorn caught a whiff of the tea. He stared at the glass, then set down the glue, lifted the drink, saluted Sugar's health and took a sip.

'Casey not here?'

'She left.'

'Left?'

'Came by this afternoon. Packed her stuff and split.'

'For good?'

'Looks that way.'

'You try to stop her?'

'I asked her not to go.'

'That's all?'

'Did I block the door, try to use force? No.'

'You tell her you love her?'

Thorn glanced across at his friend.

'I would've told her if it was true.'

Thorn lifted his eyes and watched the channel marker in Blackwater Sound blink like the secret pulse of the world. Slow and steady, unfazed by the disastrous affairs of humankind. He tried to time his heartbeat to it, but it was no use. He was hopelessly out of synch.

'She take the pink buffalo?'

Sugarman was peering out into the dark.

'No,' he said. 'She wanted me to have a memento of our good times.'

'I don't know why, but I like those stupid things. I'm thinking of getting one for my lawn. Maybe a whole herd. To perk up the neighborhood.'

A thin scum of clouds dulled the moon and blotted out the stars. Night birds cut swaths through the haze of insects that floated in humming clouds out in the darkness.

Thorn had another sip and Sugarman topped up the glass.

'You feel bereft?' Sugarman said.

'Bereft?'

'You know, bereaved, dispossessed.'

'I feel sad,' Thorn said. 'Not as bad as bereft.'

'Bereft is about as bad as it gets.'

'Casey said I liked her because she was shallow. I wanted someone simple and uncomplicated.'

'An insightful observation.'

'No, it's not. I liked her.'

'You liked her because she was easy. Because she didn't have a lot of baggage, or seething conflicts. There's nothing wrong with that. You deserve to coast a little, all the shit you've been through.'

'I was coasting? That's what Casey was about?'

'You want a bunch of lies, you should get a new friend.'

Thorn turned his head, squinted through the dark at Sugarman.

'You've been reading those self-help books again, haven't you?'

'Go on, make a joke. But it's true, Thorn. You need people to smack you in the head sometimes. Tell you the truth. How else you going to figure things out?'

There was a boat out on the sound. A big one, going full-bore along the dark channel toward the mouth of Dusenberry Creek, that narrow passage through the mangroves over to Tarpon Basin. The vessel was a fifty-footer, maybe sixty. A rarity that time of night. Usually the traffic died out after sunset, just a shrimper or two or some midnight yellowtailers heading out to the reef.

'What you need, Thorn, is a woman who likes to dance on tables. Somebody in full celebratory mode. *Joie de vivre.*'

'A wild woman.'

'Wild, yeah. Fun. Able to let go. Somebody that makes you laugh.'

'Thanks, Sugar. I'll keep my eyes open.'

'You'll find somebody,' Sugar said. 'You always do. But this time, you should hold out a little longer, be picky. You deserve the real thing, Thorn.'

'I've had the real thing. I've had it a few times.'

'And it hurt so bad when they left, you chose Casey this time. Someone that wouldn't hurt.'

'Okay, okay. Enough.'

Without slowing down, the boat took a hard left out of the channel and headed toward shore. Thorn peered out through the dark. None of his neighbors had boats that big. No one he knew.

'Did you throw your pistol away like you were planning?'

'Yeah,' Thorn said. 'Just before the plane came down.'

'You stay close to home today?'

Sugar topped up his glass again.

'You mean did I go poking around anymore in the Braswells' business? No. I'm finished with that. I don't give a shit who they are, what they're up to. I did my good deed for the month. I'm back in retirement.'

'Good,' Sugar said. 'Very mature. Very level-headed.'

The yacht was less than half a mile from shore, its running lights on, all its deck lights, too, a big, sleek, white boat, Hatteras, Bertram, one of those. It was just after high tide, so there was four feet of water about twenty yards from shore. Then it got shallow very fast, except for the one channel that ran due west from his dock. That boat was on a heading that took it just south of Thorn's house.

'What's that dumbshit doing?' Sugar stared out at the dark water.

'Just some drunk.'

'Yeah,' Sugar said. 'One of our own.'

'Well, here's to the brotherhood of drunks,' Thorn said and raised his glass. 'Another of our clan, lost at sea.'

The yacht had slowed to an idle a few hundred yards south of Thorn's. He heard voices calling back and forth from the boat to someone on the land. Sounded like the boater was lost, asking one of Thorn's neighbors for directions.

'Okay, so yeah, I've been reading all these books,' Sugar said, 'trying to figure out what I did wrong with Jeannie. Maybe there's some way I can patch things up, get the girls back. But every time I finish one, I think I've got the answer. I loved too much. I was overly enmeshed. Then I read another one, and I think, no, I was too distracted, too caught up in my own world and didn't see how depressed Jeannie was. I'm reading a new book every week and every week I discover I got a different neurosis.'

'Maybe some people are just meant to live alone.'

Thorn was watching the yacht head out to deeper water, then make a sweeping turn to the north. By the time it got out to the channel it was doing at least thirty knots, throwing a giant bow wake.

'Isolation isn't healthy, Thorn. You gotta be around people, socialize a little, or you'll turn into an ape man. You know, reverse the evolutionary process, slide back down the greased pole of civilization. Before you know it, you aren't bathing anymore, forgotten your table manners, stopped brushing your teeth, shaving your beard. Next thing happens, you've lost your motor skills. You're nothing, just some blob, sitting there, half-alive.'

'Doesn't sound so bad.'

The big boat's spotlight swept back and forth across the shoreline. Now the yacht was on a heading for the dock where the *Heart Pounder* was tied up. The spotlight stopped moving and held tight on the old Chris-Craft.

Slowly Thorn stood up, watching the yacht coming fast across the basin, along the channel that led to Thorn's deck.

'You expecting somebody?'

Sugarman rose beside him. The boat was plowing ahead, thirty yards from the dock, going way too fast to stop in time. The *Heart Pounder* and his skiff were already beginning to shift against the pilings like horses sensing some approaching calamity.

'Jesus, look at that asshole!'

Thorn hustled down the stairs and sprinted across the yard with Sugarman close behind. Thorn yelled into the darkness, waved his arms above his head.

The dark water curled away from the bow of the big yacht as it headed directly toward the dock with the throttles firewalled. Up in the flybridge the captain was hidden behind the glare of the spotlight.

The cylinder of light found Thorn, and froze for a second on his outraged face, then blinked off. A second later the captain yanked the throttles back to idle, slammed the gears into reverse and ran the throttles back up to full. The big engines slowly spooled upward as the wake caught up with the transom and started to shove the boat forward as if it were surfing on the crest of a tidal wave. Finally the turbos started to whine with boost and the props grabbed, and in a wild overstraining of gears and pistons, the huge boat, somewhere near a hundred thousand pounds of ungodly momentum, shuddered and shook and was suddenly quiet, only the faint hollow bubble of diesel exhaust announcing its arrival.

Thorn rubbed at his blinded eyes. By the time he could see again, the rest of the boat's wake was rolling ashore, coming several feet up his sloping yard. Not even four solid hours of Hurricane Mitch had moved that much water that far inland. The boat itself had run aground, its big bow lodged in the sandy muck two scant yards to the north of his dock. By some miracle of physics he didn't comprehend, his dock was still intact and both his skiff and the *Heart Pounder* were bobbing peacefully, still lashed to their cleats.

'Now there's one hell of an impressive entrance,' Sugarman said.

'Oh, man,' Thorn said. 'I knew it was a mistake.'

148

'What was a mistake?'

'Throwing away that damn .357.'

Thorn stepped beyond the harsh glare of the spot-light and watched as a man climbed down the port ladder and stepped carefully off onto the dock. Sugar and Thorn waited in the grass at the end of the dock, watching the man come toward them. He tottered with an uncertain limp or drunken wobble.

'You armed?'

Sugar said no, he wasn't.

The man stepped off the end of the dock into the damp grass. He halted a couple of yards away. He was white-haired, wearing Bermuda shorts and a sleeveless T-shirt. His hands were empty. And from what Thorn could make out, he had spindly legs and a pronounced potbelly.

'You better have a pretty damn good story,' Thorn said.

'Are you Dr William Truman?'

'What?'

The old man stepped closer, peering into Thorn's face.

'You Dr Truman?'

'No, I'm not,' Thorn said. 'Dr Bill Truman was the man who raised me. He died twenty years ago. My name is Thorn.'

'But this is his place?'

'It used to be. It's mine now.'

'Well, good, I'm in the right spot then. I've had one hell of a time finding you, Dr Truman.'

'My name is Thorn. The man you're looking for died a long time ago.'

'Well, look here, buddy, like it or not, you're next on the list. I came down here to warn you to take cover.'

'Take cover?' Thorn said. 'From what?'

'And I wanted to hear what you know about this ray gun thing.'

'Ray gun?' Sugar gave Thorn a quick eye-roll.

'Yeah, yeah. Some kind of secret ray gun. I had the damn thing right in my lap and I fiddled with it and it blew out the television at Neon Leon's. And that's why Arnold Peretti was killed. The blond kid cut his hand and then Arnold got knocked overboard. I went back for him but he was gone.'

'You've made a mistake, sir. I'm not Dr Bill.'

'I wasn't sure where I was,' the old man said. 'It got dark and I thought I was lost, then I found Jewfish Creek, Gilbert's Marina. It's been a long time since I was down here in the Keys. But when I saw the Jewfish Bridge I knew it was just a little way longer. Thank the good lord, I've still got a pretty good memory some of the time. That's how it goes. I recall some of it real well and the rest of it kind of evaporates when I go looking for it. That ever happen to you? If it hasn't yet, it will soon, I can promise you that.'

Sugarman took a turn. 'This man is named Thorn, sir. He's not Dr Truman. Bill Truman died some years back.'

'You don't have to yell. I'm not deaf. I hear just fine.'

The old man stepped past them, walking up the sloping yard toward the house. He lifted both arms and swung them toward the branches of the trees.

'Nice place you got here. Rustic and remote. Always did like the Keys.'

Thorn watched as he swung around and came marching back.

'Did I tell you, my name is Lawton Collins?'

The old man put out his hand.

Thorn smiled and took hold of the man's hand. It was dry and light, boneless in Thorn's grip.

'Nice to meet you, sir.'

'So, like I said, my friend Arnold drowned this afternoon. Do you know Arnold Peretti, the bookie?'

Thorn said no, he didn't.

'Well, anyway,' Lawton said, 'it's not about gambling. It's all about this ray gun thing. You should know that in case something happens to me.'

'Ray gun,' Sugarman said. 'What kind of ray gun?'

'That's what the kid wanted,' said Lawton. 'He knew Arnold had it and he wanted it back. That's all I know. Oh, yeah, and there's another guy, he's in the Bahamas right now. He's involved in this somehow. That's what Arnold said. This other guy was some kind of friend of Arnold's. He's gone over to Marsh Harbor fishing for marlin. After I'm finished with you, I'm headed there. Give him a good old-fashioned third degree. I been over there a dozen times. It's a piece

151

of cake getting across the Gulf Stream. Piece of angel food cake.'

The old man wobbled over to the pink buffalo and leaned against it.

Thorn went over to him and laid a hand on the old man's arm.

'You all right?'

'Oh, it hurt at first. I about passed out. But I'm mostly numbed up now.'

'You're injured?'

'What kind of doctor are you, anyway? It just so happens, I might need a stitch or two.'

'I'm not a doctor,' Thorn said. 'But we can take you to the hospital if you're hurt.'

'No, sir. They'll find me at the hospital. You can bet on that. They have their ways, these people. No, siree. No hospitals.'

'What's wrong with you, Lawton?'

Lawton laid a hand on the buffalo's mane, gave it an inquisitive stroke.

'Look, son, you're second on the list. Arnold was first and we know what happened to him. After it happened and I'd had a minute to calm down, I was out there in the middle of Biscayne Bay, trying to work out what the hell to do next. That's when I found the list. Sitting there on the table in the salon. And I knew I had to investigate this thing. That's my profession, I investigate things.'

'You're a cop?'

'Retired,' he said. 'My daughter Alexandra's the cop

152

in the family these days. Like father, like daughter. She does crime scene photos. Not a real cop, but close. Me, I'm retired.'

'Maybe we should call your daughter. She's probably looking for you.'

'I'm retired, but to tell you the honest truth, I miss the police business. It might sound like bragging, but I think I still got a pretty good nose for crime.'

'What list are you talking about? This list I'm on.'

'Arnold was number one. You're number two. There's even a nautical chart or else I wouldn't have found you at all.'

'Could I see this list?'

'You don't look much like a doctor. You look like a ragamuffin.'

Sugarman chuckled.

'Though I realize things have changed. Wrestlers are all bad guys now. Nobody looks the way they're supposed to anymore.'

Lawton Collins reached into the pocket of his shorts and came out with a folded sheet of paper. He opened it and handed it to Thorn.

Thorn stepped over to the edge of the spotlight's beam and tipped the paper to the light. Sugar looked over his shoulder. It was a page torn from a standard nautical chart, showing Blackwater Sound and an arrow pointing to Thorn's land. In the upper corner of the page someone had printed:

1. ARNOLD
2. DR WILLIAM TRUMAN (FT112)

At the bottom of the page was what looked like a bloody smudge.

Thorn handed the sheet to Sugarman, and he stepped into the light and studied the document. Sugar made a noise in his throat, looked at Thorn, then walked away into the dark, over toward the house, stood there a moment, then turned around and came back.

'What is it, Sugar?'

'Your license.'

'License?'

'FT112. That's your tag number.'

'You know my license number?'

'Hell, I been looking at that damn thing for twenty years. That tag's been expired forever.'

'What the hell?'

'If my memory serves, that plate was on the VW when Dr Bill was still driving it,' Sugar said. 'Some day you should probably get around to renewing the registration. That's what normal people do.'

Thorn stared out at the dark bay. Dull moonlight sheening its surface.

'What kind of person has to draw up a list to remember two names?'

'We're not dealing with a genius,' Sugar said. 'But then it wouldn't be the first time I've run across a lawbreaker who was a little dim.'

'What I think,' Lawton said, 'this punk kid had two jobs. When he was done with Arnold, he was going to commandeer this boat, come down here, and take you out. What he didn't bargain for was running into an old goat like me.'

'How'd you get away from him?'

'Knocked the little turd overboard. Rammed Arnold's yacht into a seawall and sent that kid flying.'

'You're lucky you didn't sink.'

'I'm a lucky guy,' Lawton said. 'Always have been. I'm Irish.'

He stroked the buffalo's big face.

'You got a gun, son? Some way to protect yourself?'

'No,' Thorn said. 'I'm unarmed.'

Lawton moaned softly, his face tightening into a sudden grimace.

'You okay, Lawton?'

'Little twinge is all.'

'Let's have a look.'

'It's nothing,' he said. 'A scratch.'

'Show us,' Thorn said.

Lawton Collins huffed, then executed a military about-face and lifted his shirt, presenting his back to Thorn. And there, buried in the love-handle at his waist, its wicked glitter catching the edge of the spotlight, was the long, narrow handle of a knife. A wide swipe of blood had leaked from the puncture wound and had dried along his beltline.

'Christ, we gotta get him to the hospital, Thorn.'

'No hospitals,' Lawton said. 'They'll find me in a hospital.'

'Who'll find you, Lawton? Who did this?'

'That young punk. I don't know his name. That's why I gotta go to the Bahamas, talk to this guy down there. Get in his face, ask him some questions. He's the logical next step in my investigation.'

'What guy in the Bahamas, Lawton?'

The old man dropped his shirt tail and turned around. He rested his weight against the buffalo.

'Man by the name of Braswell. He's down there marlin fishing.'

Thorn turned slowly and looked at Sugarman.

Sugar said, 'Would that be A.J. Braswell, by any chance?'

'You know him?'

Sugarman shook his head at Thorn.

'Good God, Thorn, how the hell do you do it?'

'It's the magnet on my back. Big goddamn magnet.'

# 9

'You sure you haven't seen him?'

'Not for weeks, Alex. He doesn't come in here that much anymore.'

Alexandra eased her grip on the phone. Across the room a Toyota commercial played on the black-and-white TV, just a minute remaining till the eleven o'clock news. Alex wore jeans and a plain white T-shirt, running shoes. After work she'd unpinned her black hair and it was loose, draping across her shoulders. An inch behind her eyes, a headache clanged. She tapped her foot, every nerve burning. As taut as a sprinter in the blocks, waiting for the starting pistol to fire, waiting and waiting.

'You tried Captain's Tavern? He used to hang out there.'

'They haven't seen him either,' Alex said.

'How about Fox's?'

'Fox's, Duffy's, Gil's Piano Bar. No one's seen him.'

'You been busy.'

Benny Stuart had been one of Lawton's closest friends. They'd partnered on the streets when Lawton first started out. And for the next twenty years they'd orbited the same cop bars, regularly lifting a few brews after work. Not a serious drinker, Lawton might still consider one of those old places a safe haven.

Benny said, 'Hey, how about Mikey's out in Sweetwater?'

'It's Cuban now. They haven't seen an Anglo in months.'

'Well, that's the whole list, Alex. Sorry. Wish I could help.'

'Thanks anyway, Benny. Sorry to call you so late.'

'I was up,' he said. 'So he's lost, huh?'

'Lost, yeah. I guess you could call it that.'

'You try that place he goes in the daytime, what is it, a nursing home?'

'Harbor House,' Alex said. 'Yeah, I tried there. And I called all his lady friends. No one's heard from him.'

'Does he remember phone numbers?'

'Some of the time, yeah. He's got all my numbers in his wallet.'

'Well, he'll turn up. And when he does, tell him I asked about him. He can find me at Captain's Tavern from six to nine most weekdays. Tell him to stop in, we'll shoot the shit. Tuesday is still lobster night. Great food. Our old bartender, Jeff, still works there.'

'I'll tell him, Benny. Thanks.'

She clicked off. Holding the portable phone in her lap, she sat down on the foot of her father's bed and watched the old Sylvania perched on the cherry dresser, the same TV set Lawton and Grace Collins had shared all their married life. The commercials had ended and the lead story was still the crash of Flight 570. The female pilot still in a coma. A couple more survivors had died. Then they moved on to the double homicide of Charlie Harrison and Brandy Perkins. Alex listened, tapping her foot, as the slender blonde stood just beyond the alleyway and described the ghastly scene. In less than three minutes she managed to get three or four facts wrong, then after a little byplay with the anchor about the tragedy of losing such a dedicated young journalist, they cut to the third piece. The TV people were calling it 'Mayhem at Sea.' One passenger dead, one other missing, while the captain of the vessel was sought by Miami Police and the US Coast Guard.

The reporter was tall with wild, curly hair blown wilder by the late-night sea breeze. He was positioned on the beach near Rickenbacker Causeway, near the same spot where that afternoon Alex had waded into the water. With the smugly amused tone they reserved for the more outlandish stories, the reporter summarized the facts the police had released so far. According to an eyewitness who'd been windsurfing in the area, the boat was traveling at a high rate of speed and in an erratic manner for over a mile. Two men were thought to have been thrown overboard as the yacht rammed at least three channel markers and the seawall along the Intracoastal Waterway, and finally slammed the structure of the Rickenbacker Causeway itself.

The reporter paused to invite the eyewitness forward and the camera angle widened to include the wiry young man. His name was Tim Corash. He was shaggy-haired and wore a long-sleeved white T-shirt, and he seemed confused, squinting into the television lights, not sure where to make eye contact.

'Well, I mean, it looked like the captain or pilot or whatever you call it, he was trying to throw those guys off.'

'Intentionally knock them off the boat?'

The young man looked at the reporter, then back at the camera. 'Well, yeah, that's how it seemed.'

'Is it possible he might simply have lost control of the vessel?'

'Maybe. But to me, it looked like he was steering that way on purpose.'

'Did you get a good look at this man who was piloting the boat?'

'An old guy. White hair, he was kind of short. He was coming right for me at one point, but you know, I was on a good tack with a solid breeze, so I was out of the way in time. I still got a pretty good view of him. He had this crazy look like he was high on something.'

They filled the screen with the photo of Lawton Collins, a snapshot Alex had provided the TV stations late in the afternoon. It was a few years old but still caught his present-day features. Intense blue eyes, sharp cheekbones, the unruly mane of white hair. Alex had taken the snapshot one afternoon at a picnic for the Police Benevolent Association. A sunny day with lots of beer and hot dogs and children and silly games. Being among old friends all afternoon had cheered Lawton, but still when she looked at the image on the screen she saw the desolate traces of melancholy that had taken root there after Grace's death. From the day of her funeral, he'd never been the same. Grace and Lawton were childhood sweethearts – a sixty-year romance. Losing her had hastened Lawton's decline, put a dull glaze where once there'd been such sparkle. Although an array of medications and herbal remedies had slowed the process somewhat, giving him lucid stretches, still, the deterioration seemed inexorable, as each day more of his memories moved just beyond his grasp.

The reporter thanked the windsurfer, then turned back to the camera and began to summarize the high-lights of the story. According to the county medical examiner, the drowning victim had sustained broken bones and other serious injuries before being thrown into the bay and may have been unconscious when he entered the water. He was identified as Arnold Peretti, a longtime Miami resident with ties to organized crime. The yacht was registered to Mr Peretti and was dubbed *You Bet Your Ass*, no doubt a reference to Mr Peretti's alleged association with the underworld. The second man thrown overboard remained unidentified.

When he finished, the newsman handed off to the studio and the evening anchor bounced it back with another question.

'So is Mr Collins a suspect in these deaths?'

'Well, right now, Willie, he's just being sought for questioning and for leaving the scene of an accident. If anyone has information concerning either the whereabouts of the fifty-five-foot Bertram sportfisherman or of Lawton Collins, you are asked to notify either Miami police or Crime Stoppers immediately. We've also been informed that Mr Collins, who is a retired City of Miami police officer, suffers from occasional memory lapses, so he might appear to be dazed or bewildered.'

'Is he considered dangerous, Andy?'

'Willie, at this time, the police aren't using those words. But as I've reported, one man has died and one other is missing, and since Mr Collins has not yet come forward to explain his role in the events, it appears at this moment that he is the main target of an intense police investigation. So I suppose it would be safe to say that anyone spotting Mr Collins should proceed with extreme caution.'

They flashed Lawton's photo one more time. Shuddering with rage, Alex reached out and snapped off the TV. As usual the news guys were pumping up the volume, wringing every last drop of melodrama they could from the situation. Managing to turn a frail old man into a desperado. If Lawton happened to see the TV news, it would only drive him deeper into hiding.

Taking careful sips of air, Alex tried for a moment to ease the pounding in her skull, but it was no use. Heart working double-time, veins about to rupture.

She stood up and began to roam his bedroom, searching again for any hint of whom Lawton might have called or where he might have fled, anything at all that might get him back.

One wall was covered with photos, black-and-whites mainly, some from his war years, Lawton kneeling in profile in his uniform with a German castle in the background. There were courting pictures with Lawton and Grace standing beside various automobiles in suits and hats decades out of fashion, and another with Lawton in his cop's uniform posing at parade rest, and one of him wearing madras Bermudas and a long-billed hat, holding up a wahoo he'd caught down in the Keys with one of his old buddies. Then there was the one of Lawton and Alexandra on the beach up in the Panhandle. Alex was ten years old, sunburned and happy, crouched behind the four-foot-high sand castle she'd labored on all summer vacation. Lawton clowned behind her with Alexandra's red pail balanced upside down on his head, while he saluted the camera with the matching shovel Alex had used to construct her fortress.

On the other wall his bookcase was full of knick-knacks, old beer steins and some wood carvings he'd done in his youth, mostly fish and a few fanciful creatures of his own design. His holster from the Miami PD lay next to a couple of framed citations for excellence on the job. On a middle shelf was a collection of trinkets Alex had given him for birthdays and Christmases over the years. A brass trout rising from a brass pond she'd found in an antique store. Some bottles of fancy cologne he'd never opened. A mahogany plaque she'd made in high school shop that said TO THE WORLD'S COOLEST DAD. And from her one summer at camp, there was a lanyard she'd woven in shades of blue to match his police uniform. In the last few months Lawton began asking her to remind him of the stories behind the knickknacks. And she would dutifully repeat the same things over and over while he stood with a vague smile as if listening to some bedtime story he never grew tired of.

The only book on the shelves was a tattered paper-back he'd discovered at Harbor House a month or two earlier and had gotten permission to bring home. *The Secrets of Houdini*. She picked it up, paged through it, examining some of the ink sketches.

Lawton had taken to studying the book for hours at a time. He'd all but abandoned television, which suited Alex just fine. Sitting in his favorite recliner in

164

the living room with a yellow legal pad on his lap, he meticulously copied the pen-and-ink drawings from the book. Houdini's never-before-revealed methods for extricating himself from iron boxes, straitjackets, and submerged packing cases. Lawton had no interest in the card tricks or mind reading or the sleight of hand deceptions. He focused entirely on the escape techniques. As if by analyzing some of the great magician's stratagems, Lawton might discover a way to wriggle free of the bondage that was tightening around his own life.

It crushed her heart to watch him practicing with such grim patience, using an old pair of handcuffs he'd carried for thirty years on the job. Locking them on his wrists, then repeatedly whacking the steel manacles against the edge of a marble bookend, trying to find the exact place on the steel cuffs that would spring open the mechanism. In a month's time Lawton had managed to duplicate Houdini's handcuff escape only once, releasing the catch with a single sharp rap. But that one success lifted his spirits so dramatically that Alexandra had given up trying to steer him away from this new fascination.

She set the book back on the shelf and walked into his bathroom. She stared at her image in the mirror, mouth tense, eyes haggard. For the hundredth time she cursed herself for being so goddamned negligent as to let a man like Arnold Peretti take charge of her dad. A man whose ties to the criminal world had obviously caught up with him. Some botched business deal, some vendetta or unpaid debt had placed her father in the line of fire. She was sure of it. And when the violence began, Lawton was panic-stricken. The tottering pedestal on which he managed to hold his fragile balance had collapsed beneath him. And now there was no way to guess what shape his terror was taking. Which direction he was headed, what logic was guiding his decisions.

A search of the nighttime waters was out of the question. At dawn the Coast Guard boats and helicopters would begin to sweep Biscayne Bay, starting from his last known location. By then, in a vessel as fast as Peretti's, Lawton could be anywhere from east of the Bahamas to midway into the Gulf. He could be as far away as Jacksonville, or holed up in one of the thousand marinas dotting the coast. Or it was equally possible that he had docked the boat somewhere in South Florida, then wandered off, searching for his way home.

With the phone in one hand, Alex touched a finger to the bristles of his shaving brush. And as the first tears she'd allowed herself stung her eyes, the front doorbell rang.

She gasped, whirled around, bumped her shoulder against the doorway, then rushed down the hall to the front door. Wiping her eyes, she caught a glimpse of white hair through the eye-level window and tore open the door.

'Got anything to drink?' Dan Romano said. 'I mean drink-drink. The real stuff. 'Cause I'm off duty.'

Beside him was a tall, dark-haired man who was giving Alexandra a pained smile, as if to apologize for Dan's lack of grace.

She leaned out the doorway and glanced behind them. No one.

'Did you find him?'

'Not yet, not yet.' Dan stepped past her into the house. 'Whiskey if you've got it. But rum'll do.'

'You haven't heard anything?'

'Nothing.' Then he gestured at the other man and said, 'Wingo, introduce yourself. This is Alexandra Collins.'

The tall man nodded with that same embarrassed half smile. He shut the door behind him and stepped into the foyer. He wore khaki slacks and a white polo shirt. His arms were deeply tanned.

'Good evening, Ms Collins. I'm Jamie Wingo.'

She swung away from his outstretched hand and marched into the dining room.

'Dan, what the hell's going on? Something's happened, hasn't it? Talk to me, goddamn it, talk to me.'

Romano plucked a bottle of Bacardi from the liquor cabinet, uncapped it, and poured himself a shot in an old-fashioned glass. He had a taste, then set the glass on the table before him.

'Take it easy, Alex. No, we didn't find him. He's still missing.'

'And who's this?' She slashed a hand at the tall man.

'Okay, okay, you're upset. I should've called first. But this thing came up, it's kind of weird, nothing I wanted to discuss on the phone, so I drove over.'

From next door the Morrisons' beagle began to howl. Probably picking up the jittery vibes radiating from Alexandra's house.

The slim man stepped into the doorway. Dan shrugged at him and waved his hand – take it away, it's all yours.

Wingo closed his eyes and opened them. He stood silently for a moment as if gathering his dignity.

'I apologize for the intrusion, Ms Collins, especially at such a traumatic time. And I'm very sorry about your father's disappearance.'

Dan poured himself another sip of rum and took a seat at the head of the dining table. Lawton's place. He fumbled in the pocket of his yellow sports coat and drew out his pack of Marlboros and shook a cigarette loose.

'Not in here,' Alex said. 'You want to suck on that poison, go outside.'

Dan studied her briefly, then replaced the cigarette and slid the pack into his jacket pocket.

Wingo said, 'There are indications, Ms Collins, that the case I'm investigating might overlap with your father's disappearance. So I have a few questions I need to ask you.'

Alex stared at the man. His black hair was thick and slicked back. He had a coppery complexion and a raven's inky, impenetrable eyes. His forehead was broad and high and his nose mildly hooked, the faintly aristocratic profile of a Cherokee brave.

'I'm listening,' she said.

'May I sit?'

She shrugged and Wingo took a seat on one side of the dining table. He rested his wrists on the edge of the table and gazed across at the far wall. There was a stillness about the man that was unnerving. Alex stayed on her feet, too wired to sit. The Morrisons' beagle continued to bay with delirious abandon.

'It's connected to those kids in the alley,' Romano said. 'This afternoon, the newspaper guy.'

'Charlie Harrison?' Alex stared at Dan. 'What does Dad have to do with Charlie Harrison?'

'There's a link,' Dan said.

She peered at Dan, then gripped the back of one of the chairs. She eased herself down and looked across at Wingo.

'I've seen you somewhere. What are you, FBI?'

'Ms Collins,' he said, 'vice chair for the NTSB, National Transportation Safety Board.'

'Airplane crashes,' Dan said, and gulped down the rest of his rum. 'Railroads, buses, the whole gamut.'

She nodded. Feeling the fog begin to rise inside her head, a drifty sensation as if gravity had suddenly lost its hold on her. Blinking, trying to focus, keep it all clear.

'Airplane crashes,' she said. 'Charlie Harrison's murder. What the hell is going on?'

'Ms Collins, I'm working the American 570 crash.'

Wingo shot her a quick look as if to appraise her reaction. Alex gave him nothing and finally he moved on. 'You're familiar with it, of course.'

The haziness that had been clouding her thoughts vanished. She was suddenly flushed with anger, eyes clear, blood singing. She drew a long breath and counted to three before releasing it.

'Okay, so let me get this straight. My dad not only killed his closest friend this afternoon, he's also mixed up in this airline crash? What is he now, a saboteur?'

Wingo gave her a bruised smile and directed his eyes to the far wall.

'Hear him out, Alex,' Dan said. 'Something weird's going down. If what Wingo thinks is true, Lawton may have stumbled into something.'

'Into what?'

Dan picked up his empty glass and stared into it.

'Right now it looks like he stepped into a major-league pile of shit.'

# 10

'Talk to me, goddamn it,' Alex said.

Wingo reset his wrists against the table. When he spoke, his voice was smooth and neutral, professionally aloof. A federal official taking charge.

'Perhaps the lieutenant should bring you up to date on his side of the investigation, Ms Collins, then I'll fill in the rest.'

'I'm about two seconds from throwing both of you out of my house. So you better make this good, Dan, damn good.'

'Okay, okay,' he said. 'Here's how it is, Alex. This afternoon right after we notified next of kin in the Harrison case, we get a call from the kid's editor at the *Miami Weekly*. He wants to help with the investigation, so I hear him out. Seems Charlie was working on a story about some kind of secret military gizmo that might've fallen into the wrong hands. Around noon today, he was supposed to meet his contact at Neon Leon's on the river. You know that place, a bunch of scuzzballs. So I bop over to Leon's, pass the kid's picture around. And yeah, sure enough, they remembered him. Him and his hotty girlfriend. I get five solid IDs. They agreed it was Harrison sitting in a booth. Him and his girlfriend and two other guys. Two senior citizens. One of them turns out to be Peretti and the other one, well, you can figure that out.'

'Dad was at Neon Leon's?'

'I put him there roughly forty-five minutes to an hour before the shit hit the fan at the Rickenbacker, which is more or less the length of time it would take a boat like Peretti's to get from a little way up the river to the causeway.'

Dan lifted the bottle of rum, then thought better of it and set it down.

Wingo tilted his chin up and gazed at the molding that edged the ceiling.

'Look, Alex. It's pretty much speculation at this point, but here's the story I see taking shape. Somebody smacked Harrison and the girl right after they left their meeting at the bar with your dad and Peretti, and at about the same time they were being tapped, there was some serious havoc aboard Peretti's yacht. Seems to me these two events might just be intertwined. Like someone wanted to keep certain clandestine activities from appearing in the newspaper, say, and they wanted it real real bad. So they sent their people to put out the lights on everybody involved.'

'You're saying someone tried to kill my father because of some military secret Arnold was going to give to the newspapers? Arnold Peretti, the bookie?'

Dan nodded.

'And tell me, Dan. How the hell does a retired gambler get hold of military secrets?'

Romano stared down into his glass.

'This is nuts, Dan, horseshit. Complete and total horseshit.'

Romano shook his head, then cut a hard look at Wingo. 'This is where you take over.'

Wingo took a leisurely look around the room as if running an inventory on Alexandra's taste and tendencies. There wasn't much in the dining room that revealed either, a little family silver displayed on the sideboard, an unexceptional painting of a mountain meadow that had been her mother's favorite. But when Wingo finally brought his eyes to hers, he looked at her with guarded approval.

'Again, I apologize for barging in at such an hour. And I certainly hesitate to involve you in these matters, Ms Collins. This is a case in which the less you know, the safer you might be.'

'Involved! Christ, my father is wandering around in the dark right now, probably scared out of his mind. I *am* involved. I'm big-time involved! And I'm a police officer, so if you have some information concerning my father's whereabouts, then just cut the coy bullshit and tell me what's going on.'

'Ms Collins, I'm sorry about your father's disappearance. If the results of my inquiries lead us to your father, then I will certainly be pleased. However, my focus is on another issue entirely, the deaths of dozens of innocent people.'

Alex glared at the man.

'This isn't protocol,' Alex said. 'If you've got knowledge of criminal activity in an airplane crash, the FBI is supposed to take over. NTSB doesn't do criminal work. You're supposed to handle safety issues, investigate the causes of the crash. But that's all.'

'You're absolutely correct.'

'So where are they? The FBI.'

Wingo looked down at the table.

Dan said, 'FBI took a pass. They don't share Wingo's suspicions. In fact, I think the word they used was *kook*. Isn't that right, Wingo?'

'Kook, yes. That was one of the milder terms, I believe.'

Dan poured another finger of rum into his glass, tossed it back, and pushed the glass aside.

'It's something called a HERF gun,' said Dan. 'H-E-R-F. Stands for High Energy Radio Frequency. But the Feds don't believe the thing exists. After Wingo came around yesterday to brief Miami PD about the progress of the NTSB investigations, we started talking in the hall and he mentioned the HERF gun. After he left I was curious, so I got on the phone, talked to a couple of FBI computer nerds at the Miami field office. I even called Washington, spoke to some of their upper-echelon whiz kids. It's the same thing up and down the line. Wingo is full of shit. There is no HERF gun. It's some kind of urban myth. Been batting around the Internet for years, a sci-fi weapon you solder together from Radio Shack parts. Generates a ton of energy, electromagnetic radiation, like what a nuclear explosion puts out, only this thing costs only a few hundred dollars to construct, small enough to fit in a backpack, and blammo, you stand outside an office building, zap all their hard drives. Shut down Florida Power and Light, the whole world goes back to the Stone Age.

'So when this thing happened today with your dad, I thought of Wingo and his HERF gun thing and I gave him a call.'

'This is ridiculous, Dan. It's some kind of bad joke.'

'Well, yes, what Romano says is true,' said Wingo. 'I don't have a great deal of support for my theory. Ridicule has been the most frequent response. Nevertheless, I believe there is substantial evidence on Flight 570's cockpit data recorder and in the pre-liminary investigation that is entirely consistent with the use of a device like the one Lieutenant Romano describes. However, so far, despite that evidence and my best efforts, my colleagues at NTSB seem deter-mined to find some other explanation, an internal flaw in the onboard electronics that could account for the situation, or some kind of mega-short.

'You see, Ms Collins, if the pilot's account is accurate, what happened on that jetliner was an electrical failure more cataclysmic than any we've ever encountered. The radio was destroyed. All backup systems were fried. Auxiliary batteries, redundant wiring, everything. Some of the silicon barriers on the computer chips were fused. Only a small segment of the electrical system aboard that plane was unscathed. Fortunately, some of that was crucial wiring and gave the captain just enough power to regain control of the plane and set it down on the ocean and save some lives.

'But what I'm trying to tell you is that there are absolutely no precedents for an electrical malfunction of this magnitude in the history of aviation disasters. Not even multiple direct hits by lightning, not even the bombers exposed to nuclear explosions have shown such total and complete power failure. I hope I'm wrong, Ms Collins. I hope it turns out that I am a crackpot and the meltdown on board that MD-11 has some other explanation. Because I would hate for it to be true. For a cheap, portable weapon of this sort to exist would be bad news. Everyone who depends on electrical power would be vulnerable. And by my reckoning, that's everyone in this society, Ms Collins. Everyone.'

Alexandra sat back in her chair. The Morrisons' beagle had gone quiet. A few frogs chirped and warbled in her backyard goldfish pond. A motorcycle rumbled by on the adjacent street.

Romano said, 'He gave me that same speech. So I brought him over.'

Alex took a careful breath. Her hands were trembling. There was a scream building in her chest.

'So what is it you want from me?'

Wingo brought his eyes to hers.

'For starters, how well did you know Arnold Peretti?'

'Not as well as I thought I did.'

'Do you have the names of any of Mr Peretti's associates?'

She looked over at Dan. He was tapping his fingers on the table-top, playing scales up and down a silent octave.

'I don't know any of Arnold's friends, no. We don't travel in the same circles. My dad might know one or two. When we find him, we'll ask.'

Wingo acknowledged her sarcasm with a small nod.

'Would you know where Mr Peretti was on the first of March, last month?'

'And how the hell would I know that?'

'How about your father? Do you know his whereabouts on Wednesday, March the first?'

'He was in the same place he always is. At Harbor House adult care facility out in Kendall or at home, right here.'

'You mean he's there when he's not consorting with Mr Peretti.'

'Consorting!' Alex looked back and forth between the two men, her fury coming back to a boil. 'Look, my dad's been fishing with Arnold three or four times. Day trips, out and back. They caught fish, he came back happy, so I naturally assumed everything was all right. They're old buddies, but I assure you, Lawton Collins is not involved in any shady business deals with Arnold Peretti. My father is ill.'

Wingo nodded. 'I understand that,' he said. 'So you're absolutely certain your father was not on Mr Peretti's boat on March first?'

Alexandra ran the dates in her head. It'd been only a week since their last fishing trip. Before that they'd gone out in February, the day before Valentine's. She remembered because Lawton spent the day at Harbor House cutting red hearts out of construction paper and gluing them onto white sheets of typing paper. Cards for all his sweethearts. He brought one home for Grace and was angry at Alex when she told him Grace was no longer alive. She'd been dead for years. Lawton didn't believe it. He threw a tantrum and cursed her and locked himself in his room. The next day he and Arnold went fishing and Lawton seemed to remember none of the previous night's hysterics, kissing her good-bye with the same warmth he usually did.

'I'm sure of it,' Alex said. 'Now what's this about?'

Wingo looked across the table at Dan; a look passed between them that she couldn't read.

Alex came to her feet and pointed at Wingo.

'Listen. If my dad is mixed up in this, I want to know about it. And I want to know right now. Do you hear me? Every detail, everything you know.'

Dan shrugged at Wingo.

'What difference does it make? She knows the rest already.'

'I don't want her mixed up in this.'

Dan shook his head.

'Yeah, well, looks to me like she already is.' He gave her a quick smile. 'See, on March first, another plane crashed up in Palm Beach. Two people died, pilot survived. It was on the news, but no big deal. Small plane, Piper Cub flying out of Palm Beach International. Plane got out over the water and experienced electrical difficulties, circled back to the airport, crash-landed on the runway.'

Wingo gave her his profile and dusted his palms together.

'As long as we're confiding in you, Ms Collins,' Wingo said, 'you might be interested to know that some of the features of that crash are strikingly similar to the American 570 event over Florida Bay.'

She felt something tumble in her chest.

'This is preposterous. Tell him, Dan. My father's sick. His memory is failing. He's a retired cop, for Godsakes. He's not capable of committing a crime, even if he wanted to.'

Wingo turned his head and held her eyes calmly.

'Earlier this afternoon,' he said, 'Lawton Collins was sitting in a booth with Arnold Peretti. We have eyewitnesses who are absolutely certain he was holding a large box in his lap.'

'A box. What box?'

179

'Your father was holding this box . . .'

Alex slashed a hand through the air.

'What's that supposed to mean? Because my dad's got a box sitting in his lap, that means he and Arnold are shooting down airplanes? That's outrageous. Get up right now, both of you, and get the hell out of my house!'

Dan stood up. His mouth was tight. In ten years working alongside him, she'd never seen him so bleak.

'Look, Alex, you have a right to be angry. We barge in, all these accusations flying around. But the fact is, something happened at Neon Leon's when Peretti and Lawton were there. We think it was a demonstration of this device.'

'What kind of demonstration?'

'The TV went off, Alex. TV, cash register. Three cell phones. Everything electrical in that room blew out. Power went out all up and down the street. A half a block away.'

'It was a power outage. It happens all the time.'

'No, Alex. It was cell phones, too. An old guy in a warehouse next door collapsed and almost died 'cause his pacemaker shut down for half a minute. We're not talking about a power outage. No, we're not.'

'And Dad?'

'Well, right after the lights blew, Lawton got up with that box and he and Peretti left in a big hurry.'

Wingo pushed back his chair and came slowly to his feet.

She said it quietly, not quite believing the words as they left her mouth.

'You're crazy, both of you. You're absolutely insane.'

Morgan was in Johnny's cabin drinking wine. Way past drunk.

Sitting in the leather chair, feeling the rumble of the big diesels, the vibration working into her bones, setting up some kind of harmonic resonance with the tremble that was already there. She lifted the glass for another sip and the Cabernet slopped over the brim, spattering on the lap of her white shorts. She looked down and touched the stain with her fingertip, smelling blood again, and felt a queasy wobble in her gut.

'Johnny, please!' She shook her head at him. 'My head's splitting.'

Johnny was propped up against his pillows, lying on the top of his navy blue bedspread. The Damascus carbon throwing blade was in his hand. It pissed her off that she even knew its name. Like a parent who'd had to learn all the cartoon characters her kids watched on television to understand what the hell they were talking about. Knives were Johnny's fantasy buddies. He discussed their features, their virtues. Like she cared. Like it was part of her job to participate in his fixation.

'I'm just relieving a little stress,' he said. 'I'm not hurting anybody.'

He pinched the throwing blade by the point, drew it back over his shoulder, picked a spot just above his dresser, and flicked it at the far wall. It stuck in the paneling with a thunk and shivered in place.

Dozens of knives were fixed in the maple paneling. Some Johnny had thrown, some he'd jabbed, then drawn out and slammed into the wall again. She'd watched him do it. His entire collection, close to a hundred. Each one lodged at its own crazy angle. Steel blades glittering, leather grips, handles of rubber, ivory, ironwood, carbon fiber, mother-of-pearl. Sheep-skinning knives, fillet knives, super liners, Swiss precision, bear claws, switchblades, hybrid tactical folders. Every knife he owned was stabbed helter-skelter into the stateroom walls. Bare patches of the maple paneling were butchered with old gouges where Johnny had pried one loose to throw again.

'You're drunk,' he said.

'Damn right.'

Johnny rolled off the bed and went over to the wall and wiggled a couple of the blades loose.

'What'd you do with the gun?'

'Keep your voice down.'

'He's up on the goddamn flybridge. How's he going to hear anything? We're in the middle of the fucking Gulf Stream, it's almost midnight. You think somebody's outside the window listening?'

'I pitched it in the Miami River,' she said.

'Cool.'

He lay down on the bed again, spread out the knives beside him.

'How'd you lure them into the car?'

'I don't want to talk about it, Johnny.'

She slugged down the rest of the glass of Cabernet, reached over to the bottle, uncorked it, and poured herself another.

'You whacked them in the car? Inside the Mercedes?'

'I said, I don't want to talk about it.'

She gulped down half the glass. Rubbed a finger at the stain on her shorts.

'Dad's not pushing very fast. We're not doing more than twenty knots.'

He slung the Bowie knife at the wall and it hit butt-first and sailed a few feet to the left and stuck in the carpet.

'When they were walking to their car, I rolled down the window and said, "I understand you wanted to talk to me."'

'Yeah? That's pretty bold. Anybody see you?'

He flicked another blade at the wall and it stuck just above his dresser. Side by side with a long fillet knife.

'The guy, Charlie Harrison, he didn't recognize me. I said, "I'm Morgan Braswell. I understand you wanted to talk to me."'

'He must've shit.'

'He got in the front. The girl got in back. I drove them around. I didn't even have a plan. I didn't know what I was doing. I'm not like that. I never go out without a plan. But this time I had no idea what I was going to do. It happened so fast. I'd hardly had any sleep. We had to do something and we had to do it right away. So I just started talking and he was quiet. Listening to me. I was looking at his girlfriend in the rearview mirror. She was squirming around back there. She knew something wasn't right. But the newspaper guy didn't pick up on it. He just sat there listening, taking it all in. I'm yammering away, I'm telling him about the Cold War, disarmament.'

'Cold War?'

'About the Defense Department cutbacks, Johnny. The contraction in demand. The way it trickles down. The impact it has on people.'

'How many times you shoot them?'

Morgan took another sip of wine. She stood up and walked over to the wall of knives. She touched the Vaquero Grande, the AR 5. Turned around and faced him. Let him throw. Let him sink one in her left ventricle. She didn't care. She wanted it to be over. Wanted the trembling to cease.

'I was lost. I was driving around that neighborhood by the bar and I got farther and farther away from anything I recognized. That part of town, I've never even been there before. I could still see a couple of the downtown skyscrapers off in the distance, but I was totally turned around. Disoriented.'

'So which one did you do first? I'd've done the guy.

You should always do the guy first, get him out of the way. The girl starts screaming, then you got to do her quick or you draw attention.'

Morgan went back to her chair and poured more wine. The last of the bottle. Feeling the deck shudder beneath her feet, the vibration working up her legs.

'There were warehouses all around. I didn't see anybody. But there could've been people all over the place, for all I knew. Winos, workmen, whoever. I wasn't even looking anymore. I was so out of it. I parked the car near an alley. And the guy, Charlie, he goes, "You're in some serious trouble, lady." And I go, "Yeah, I know. But this is how I'm getting out of that trouble."'

'And you pull the gun out. And you bumped them off.'

'I turned around and shot the girl first. I don't know why. I guess I didn't want her to see what was happening. Like she couldn't handle it, seeing her boyfriend die and knowing she was next. Her terror, I didn't want to see that in her eyes. Like I was afraid I wouldn't have the nerve to go through with it. I'd let her go or something. So I shot her twice.'

'*Blam, blam,*' Johnny said and threw another knife, which ricocheted off the wall and clattered onto the dresser.

'But the guy didn't grab for the pistol like I thought. He didn't struggle or anything. He could've done it. He could've defended himself. He was a strong-looking guy. I expected him to. I pointed it at his face. And he looked right into the barrel and didn't say anything for a few seconds.'

'He was shitting his pants.'

'He was calm,' she said. 'He was calm as hell.'

'If it had been me, I would've stuck you with a blade. I would've whipped out the AR 5 and, *splat*, sliced your hand off.'

'I didn't shoot and at that point, I didn't even know if I was going to shoot. The noise from the first two was so loud. I was thinking no, the whole thing was over. I was going to hand him the gun, turn myself in, it's all over.'

Johnny was staring at her, head tilted like a dog hearing a high whistle.

'He looked at me and he said, "I had a bad feeling about this whole deal. It's why I wore my good underwear today."'

'His good underwear? He said that?'

She sat back in the chair, had another sip of the Cabernet.

'Joking with me. Gallows humor. Trying to win me over, I guess. I shot him in the chest. Three times. Then twice in the forehead. I came around and opened the door and I dragged them down this alley and I left them there side by side. I don't know if anybody saw me.'

'Mercedes must be torn to shit. Blood all over it. That was supposed to be my car some day.'

'Now we're going marlin fishing,' she said. 'Now we're going down to Abaco and get some sun and try to catch the fish that killed my brother. Like nothing ever happened. Just on to the next thing.'

'"You've got an honest woman's conscience in a murderer's body."' Johnny smiled at her. 'That's from *Fear in the Night*, De Forrest Kelley said it.'

He flicked another knife at the wall.

'You want to hear about Arnold? How I cut off his finger? I said I wanted some live bait. I was pretty funny. I didn't plan it out either. But it all went okay. Except having to swim back to shore. That sucked. But the rest of it was okay.'

She looked over at him. 'But you didn't get the HERF. And you didn't get down to Key Largo, to do your other job.'

'No, but the rest of it went okay.'

'The rest of it? You were supposed to get the HERF, Johnny.'

'Yeah, well. I asked him about it. But things got crazy.' Johnny took a grip on another knife. 'But there's one thing I'm not sure about. I mean, Arnold is dead, and I was there when it happened, but I didn't actually rub him out. You know, I didn't actually do the deed. So does that count? What do you think, Morgan? I need a ruling. Am I a made guy now?'

She looked at him for a moment and closed her eyes.

'We're fucked,' she said. 'We need that HERF or it's all over.'

'I thought that was your boyfriend's job,' Johnny said. 'Mr What's-his-fuck.'

'Yeah, my boyfriend,' Morgan said. 'Our last, best hope.'

# 11

They sat out on the porch till well after midnight. Lawton Collins's gash was now sterilized with Mercurochrome and bandaged with gauze and adhesive. The old man steadfastly refused to go to the hospital, even threatened to jump back aboard his boat and head out to sea if the two of them tried to dragoon him off to some emergency room. No, sir, the people trying to murder him would sure as hell make quick work of it if he showed up at some goddamn emergency room.

The blade had gone deep into the fleshy saddlebag at his waist but the wound looked relatively benign. While Lawton was in the john, Thorn and Sugar had a quick whispered exchange.

'Let's wait till tomorrow,' Thorn said. 'See how he is.'

'We need to call the police right now, Thorn. The guy's dotty.'

'He's also scared silly,' Thorn said. 'We can't just turn him over to the cops. That's cruel. The old guy would freak.'

'It's the right thing, Thorn.'

The toilet flushed and Lawton came whistling through the living room.

'No,' Thorn said. 'In the morning he'll be calm. We'll deal with it then. Police, hospital, next of kin, whatever seems right. But not now, the state he's in.'

Lawton stepped out through the screen door.

'You boys got any rope around here?'

'Rope? What do you want with rope?'

Lawton sat down at the picnic table.

'I'll show you a couple of tricks. Knot me up tight as you can, I'll be free two seconds later. I've been studying the legendary Houdini's methods of escape. There wasn't a lock that man couldn't pick, a set of manacles that would hold him. Either of you have any handcuffs?'

'No handcuffs,' Thorn said. 'How about you, Sugar?'

Sugarman said no, his handcuff days were long gone.

'Sugar used to be a cop.'

'Yeah? Do you still have full arrest powers?'

'Not really,' said Sugar.

'Not even cardiac arrest?'

Thorn smiled uneasily. A little worried he was starting to enjoy Lawton's careening logic. Like maybe he was on his way to joining the old guy in the paradise of lost thoughts.

'Okay, then, this'll have to do.'

Lawton reached into the pocket of his shorts and drew out a length of heavy twine. He made a quick loop around one wrist, knotted it, then took a couple of turns around the other wrist and stuck his hands out in front of Thorn.

'Best knot you got. And tie it tight. Don't go easy on me.'

Thorn looked at Sugarman. Sugar shrugged. Go ahead, humor the guy.

Thorn reached out and tied a half hitch around the old man's right wrist.

'Tighter,' Lawton said.

Thorn tugged the knot snug. Nothing to cut off Lawton's circulation, but a serious test.

'One trick, then I got to leave.' Lawton drew back his hands and slid them under the table. He peered at Thorn with a mischievous glitter in his eyes.

'Leave for where?'

'I told you,' Lawton said. 'Marsh Harbor on Great Abaco. Go talk to this Braswell fellow. He's down there chasing a blue marlin fish. It's got a little silver transmitter attached to it. Like a cigar with an antenna on one end. When the marlin surfaces, this thing sends messages to the satellites and those people follow the fish. Arnold told me all about it. That's why I'm going down there to the Bahamas to talk to him. He's our only lead.'

Lawton brought his hands out from beneath the table. He held up the rope by one end.

'Far out,' Sugarman said. He smiled at Thorn. 'The guy's good.'

Lawton dropped the rope on the table and took a nip of his tea.

Thorn turned his face again to the dark water. Something had splashed near shore like a handful of gravel peppering the still surface, probably a school of pinfish, chased by something dark and fast, a barracuda, a jack. He listened to the feathery scrape of the tamarind branches against his roof, to the mutter of traffic making its ceaseless rounds up and down the Overseas Highway. He smelled the ocean breeze coming from the east and the deeper, richer fragrance rising off the bay, the reek of barnacles exposed by the low tide, the sewery scent given off by that mat of seaweed that was trapped in his neighbor's lagoon, rotting all day and night. He looked across at the old man who was now regaling Sugarman with another story, some yarn from his cop days, about a bank robber he'd put away by the name of Frank Sinatra.

Thorn half listened to the story, but his mind was drifting. It'd been a long while since he'd thought about Dr Bill Truman and his wife, Kate. The good-hearted couple who'd raised him as their own flesh and blood. While Lawton talked, Thorn summoned what he could of Dr Bill. A square-jawed man with pale blue eyes, a Clark Gable mustache that came and went according to whims that Thorn never fully understood. Dr Bill was not quite average height, gaunt and hard-muscled, with a Puritan's discipline and a heart surgeon's rules of order. A place for everything and everything in its place. Keep your tools oiled, your rod and reel thoroughly rinsed with fresh water, your hooks and knife blades filed sharp. Hands always busy, brain working overtime, Dr Bill never rested, never simply sat and gazed off at the distance.

Though he was stern to a fault and no great talker and certainly not a hell-raiser of any kind, Dr Bill had more loyal friends than anyone Thorn had ever known. Up and down the Keys, up and down the social register. When they held his funeral on the high school football field, more people attended than were in the stands when Thorn's team played for the district championship.

All in all, Thorn had enjoyed a damn lucky childhood. Schooled by a man who was thoroughly versed in fish and boats and weather and stars and every crucial thing about the outdoor life. A man who traveled the world every year to cast his lures into exotic waters, who took along his moody daughter and his shy adopted son and his wife, Kate, who was every bit his equal with rod and tackle. Those summer trips had given Thorn his best education, his only claim on a worldly view, having spent a month here and there around the world, on boats and in rough-and-tumble fishing camps. Sleeping in a nylon bag beside Dr Bill and Kate, watching them stoke fires and broil fish from the waters of Mexico and South America and Alaska and the Caribbean, listening to them talk, watching the powerful shape and heft of their love.

Sugarman was laughing now at the punch line of the Frank Sinatra escapade.

'That was his real name?'

'Sure was. Not the singer. Just some punk who liked to give out his phone number to the pretty clerks he was robbing. Like he thought they'd call him later, go out on a date, spend some of the bank's money. Sure made my job easier, having the guy's phone number.'

Sugarman laughed again and turned to Thorn.

'Well, buddy, sorry to say, but I got an early day tomorrow. You going to be okay, or you want me to stay around, help you handle this?'

'I'll be fine,' Thorn said. 'Thanks for dropping over.'

Sugar rose and picked up his glass pitcher, empty now.

'I should be going, too,' Lawton said. 'Got a long trip ahead.'

'You're not going anywhere, Lawton. You need your rest. You lost some blood today. In the morning we'll talk it over, see where we go from here.'

'Hey, this is my job. I just came to warn you, is all, and see if you knew anything relevant to the case. I'm not asking for any help.'

'But you wouldn't mind if I came along, right? Just to observe a seasoned investigator at work?'

Lawton squinted at him for a long moment. 'Okay,' he said finally. 'But one condition.'

'What's that?'

'Things start to heat up, get a little dangerous, you gotta take cover, let the professional handle it.'

'It's a deal,' Thorn said.

Sugarman stood there a moment more, smiling at Thorn, shaking his head and smiling.

After Thorn checked the old man's dressing and found the bleeding had stopped and the bandage was holding fine, he got him settled in bed. He left Lawton drowsing beneath the sheets and went back out into the yard and climbed into the hammock and for a while he stared up at the cold pinpricks of light in the endless sky.

For half an hour he battled a mosquito nagging in his ear until finally he crushed the little bastard against his cheek. Then a heavy sleep drew him down into a warm stream of images, and he was assaulted by more dreams than he'd had in years. In one he stood beside Kate and Dr Bill, knee-deep in a frigid mountain stream, laying a dry fly near a boulder, feeling the first shy tug on the line, then the smack of a hungry salmon. A host of other dreams came and went, flickering images of those two tough, generous people who'd raised him as their own son.

For much of the night he fished again in streams he'd long forgotten, witnessed the marvelous doings of the dead, all the while feeling the smoldering ache of their absence. Then Casey, and Monica Sampson and Darcy Richards and Sarah Ryan appeared, the four women who'd given his life what warmth he'd known in these last dozen years. They stood shoulder to shoulder and spoke to him in a chorus, but he couldn't decipher a thing they said. Then each one took her turn, trying to explain to Thorn about the careless shape his life had taken. The vast wisdom of women, there for the harvesting. But he simply smiled idiotically at their stream of speech, nodding and nodding, hearing only garble.

Then he was swimming in a clear blue sea beside an old man with a snorkel and mask, a spindly codger with spear in hand, who was stabbing at a school of sharks that was closing in on the man and Thorn, their rows of white dagger teeth slashing and snapping, taking big ripping gulps of water, while with supernatural grace the old man fended them off, thrusts and parries of his spear, shielding Thorn with his body. And there were more dreams, underwater and in dazzling sunlight, and one particularly vivid scene in which Thorn rode across Blackwater Sound in the rumbling cockpit of a big cabin cruiser.

All through that dark and breezy night, held aloft by the woven strands of rope, Thorn floated above the earth, dreamed of people and places so excruciatingly dear to him that he'd found no other way to deal with their absence than to force them to the subterranean depths where they cruised endlessly just beneath the hard crust of his ordinary life. And now suddenly they were back. All of them, a lava flow of images, these people he had once loved, one by one parading past in all their aching reality.

He woke with a jerk in full sunlight and peered up into the brightness at a man in a glossy black helmet and goggles and a black flak jacket who was aiming a pistol at his forehead.

On the other side of the hammock another man dressed in the same costume pressed a shotgun tight against his shoulder. Thorn closed his eyes and willed the hallucination away, but when he opened them again the men were still there, the pistol barrel hovering only inches from Thorn's nose.

'Ah, yes,' Thorn said. 'Room service.'

'Take it easy, buddy. No sudden moves.'

'I'll have two over easy with a side of bacon,' said Thorn. 'Crispier the better. Big mug of coffee.'

'Sit up, do it slow, and keep your hands in view.' It was the man with the Glock automatic. Thorn could see his coarse black beard showing around his chin strap, his Adam's apple jumping to a fast tune. From high in the gumbo-limbo a cardinal chirped, and a mile away out on the sound a fast boat cruised past. The world proceeding with surreal normalcy.

'Where is he?' a woman asked from the rear of the group. 'What have you done with him?'

Thorn sat up as slowly as his muscles would allow. The men in flak jackets tightened their stances, a half dozen gun sights trained on his vital organs. Thorn showed them his hands. He tried a smile but no one was impressed.

'Where is who?'

Then Thorn heard Sugarman's car rolling down the drive. Two of the SWAT guys peeled off from the rear of the group and jogged over to deal with the interloper.

'Scratch the coffee,' Thorn said. 'Don't think I'm going to require any caffeine today. Nothing like a few guns in your face to get the blood buzzing.'

It was hard to read their expressions behind the goggles, but he was fairly sure he hadn't won them over yet. A hard crowd.

'Feet on the ground, then lower yourself, face in the grass.'

'Maybe I should see some ID first,' Thorn said. 'Or did they cancel the Constitution while I was asleep?'

'We're looking for Lawton Collins,' the woman said. 'We received information that he was here.' She appeared to be the only one not armed.

'What'd he do, rob Fort Knox?'

'Where is he?' The woman wasn't wearing flak gear. Her black hair hung free. She wore a loose-fitting gray shirt tucked into blue jeans. She was tall and rangy, with the sinewy arms Thorn associated with long-distance runners and hardcore vegetarians. Her eyes were an intense blue, indigo perhaps. All at once he saw the resemblance around the slant of her cheekbones and in her wide, thin-lipped mouth.

'You're Lawton's daughter. Alexandra.'

She flinched, but made a quick recovery.

'Where is he? What have you done with him?'

'About midnight I put him to bed up there.' He pointed toward the house.

She stung him with a final look, then swung around and led two of the goggle-eyed warlocks up the flight of stairs to the porch. But Thorn already knew they'd be back in a few seconds, this time with tougher, nastier questions. He was staring out at his dock. The *Heart Pounder* rested calmly beside his skiff, but the big white yacht had vanished.

# 12

The last of the SWAT guys climbed into the white van and the van pulled out of Thorn's drive. Alexandra Collins and a white-haired police lieutenant named Romano and another man who looked like a professional golfer were inside Thorn's house. They were talking quietly. They'd been in there for ten minutes now. The most company he'd had in years.

Sugarman was staring up at the tree limbs. Thorn sat across from him at the picnic table. Sugar had been quiet, poker-faced, since they'd finished interrogating him and let him come back outside. Humiliated, pissed off, Thorn couldn't tell.

'Sugar, why the hell didn't you let me know what was going on?'

Sugarman kept his eyes on the tree limbs.

'If you had a goddamn telephone, Thorn.'

'You're five minutes away, you could've driven over.'

'Look, they were showing the old guy's photo on the morning news, I called in, told them what I knew, then I took a quick shower, gulped a bowl of Wheaties, got in the car, drove over, and bang, they were already here. I sure as hell didn't think they'd show up so fast. Or in such force.'

Thorn craned to the right and looked into the kitchen window. It looked like Alexandra was getting a lecture from Romano. She was staring up at Thorn's corkboard collection of bonefish flies with a defiant clench in her jaw. The other man, Wingo, was still prowling Thorn's living room, opening drawers, poking in the broom closet.

'Why send a SWAT team for an old guy like that? He wandered off, got lost. That the usual police response, eight hot dogs with automatic weapons?'

Sugarman fixed his gaze on the bay. It was a gloomy morning, low dismal clouds sneaking in from the northwest, like somebody up in Miami had set a mountain of rubber tires ablaze. The bay was a dull, tarnished silver, nothing moving out there, no birds, no boats, not even the riffle of wind.

'This isn't just a missing-person case. Lawton was in some kind of boating accident. Somebody died. Knocked overboard. Witness said Lawton might've been trying to throw these people off his boat. So we're talking possible homicide.'

'That old guy? No way.'

Sugarman shook his head. Out of answers.

'You tell them the stuff he said? The ray gun thing. Braswell.'

Sugarman shook his head.

'Why not?'

'They didn't ask the right questions.'

'So we're being dodgy with them?'

'I just answered what they asked. I'm biding my time, trying to see what's going on.'

'How come they don't want to interrogate me?'

'I don't think these guys are into irony. They pegged you as a smart-ass.'

'They're pretty perceptive, for cops.'

'That attitude isn't getting us anywhere, Thorn.'

'Hey, I thought I did pretty well, waking up with all that goddamn artillery in my face.'

'I think they'll be getting around to you. A minute or two.'

'How about the knife? You tell them he was wounded?'

'Yeah,' Sugar said. 'It pissed the girl off even more than she already was. She wanted to know why we didn't take him to a hospital.'

'We should have.'

'I know, but he was freaking out, and the wound didn't look all that bad.'

'You told her that?'

He nodded.

'She didn't buy it, did she?'

'She asked me how long I've been practicing medicine.'

'She's a hard-ass.'

'Her father's missing. She's distraught.'

'Okay, she's a distraught hard-ass.'

Thorn looked back at the window and Alexandra was staring out at him through the screen. Four feet away, easy earshot. In that light the black hair framing her face looked like a nun's cowl. A hard-ass nun.

Wingo pushed the screen door open and stepped outside, followed by Romano. A moment later Lawton's daughter stepped out behind him.

'Apparently we owe you an apology, Mr Thorn,' Wingo said. 'We were under the impression you were holding Mr Collins hostage. Obviously we were mistaken.'

'Don't worry,' Thorn said. 'I'm not going to sue anybody.'

Wingo had on a blue button-down shirt and khaki pants and white tennis shoes. He had exotic good looks and was slim enough to be a catalogue model. Selling blue button-down shirts and khakis.

'Apology accepted,' said Thorn. 'Now what about the explanation?'

Alexandra's mouth hardened and she turned away, staring into the house.

'Mr Collins was involved in a boating incident yesterday,' Romano said. 'There was a fatality.'

'But come on, Uzis and flak jackets? What's that about?'

Alexandra turned to the table and lowered herself onto the bench, shoulder to shoulder with Sugarman. Staring across at Thorn.

'As for me,' she said, 'I'm not feeling real apologetic.' She gave Thorn a dead-on look. 'The second my dad showed up here, you clowns should've picked up the phone and called the authorities. But no, you treat it like it's a big goof. An old man wanders up, lost, confused, a knife in his back, and you have a few laughs with him and put him to bed. He had phone numbers in his wallet. There were a dozen things you could have done. But you chose to do nothing.'

'That's not how it was,' Thorn said.

'You're a big joker, aren't you, Mr Thorn?'

'Calm down, Alex,' Romano said. 'Take it easy.'

'Where's the knife, Thorn? The weapon you pulled out of my father.'

'Like I told you, I put it next to the kitchen sink.'

'It's not there.'

'Well, maybe he took it with him.'

Beyond the screen door, Thorn's ancient refrigerator rumbled to life.

Alexandra shook her head with sad contempt. 'What's your form of employment, Mr Thorn?'

'Is that relevant?'

'Your friend here says you tie fishing flies for a living. Is that true?'

'And a meager living it is.'

'Or maybe you have some other source of income.'

'What? Now I'm a drug dealer, a pimp, what?'

204

'I look around here,' she said, 'what I see is some middle-aged beach bum. Mister march-to-the-beat-of-a-different-drummer, making his cute jokes, not taking anything seriously. That's who I see, someone who had a chance to do the right thing by an old man who was in serious trouble but no, you decided instead to stick a Band-Aid on him, tuck him in bed. Then somehow you don't even manage to wake up when he starts his boat, big twin diesels, thirty, forty yards away from where you were sleeping. Or more likely stoned.'

'I heard the boat pull away, but I turned it into a dream.'

Alexandra kept boring in on him with those dark, unflinching eyes. Her mouth was twisted out of shape, working hard to hold back another spew of outrage.

Her hair was thick and loose. It hung just beyond her shoulder blades, with bangs that grazed the middle of her forehead. Her nose was a little crooked across the bridge and it was maybe a half millimeter longer than fashion allowed and her lips were thin. It was a wide, agile mouth, one that seemed to expose a lot more emotion than her eyes revealed. Her face was pale, but not the pasty stuff you saw on the potato people just arriving from Minnesota and Wisconsin. Hers had a healthy flush, a Florida girl with Celtic genes. Creamy skin passed down from generations of hardy folks who stalked the desolate moors where the sun was never more than a dull silver presence behind layers of fog.

She had the straight-ahead, no-nonsense bearing of a cop, but she wasn't armed, which, all in all, was probably a stroke of good luck for both of them.

'First, I don't sell drugs,' Thorn said. 'If I did, I'd live in a nicer place than this. And second, there aren't any beaches in the Keys, not any real ones.'

'What's that supposed to mean?'

'You called me a beach bum.'

Romano cleared his throat, laid a hand on Alexandra's wrist.

'So why'd he come here?' Romano asked. 'You have any idea?'

'He was confused,' Thorn said. 'When we saw his wound, we tried to get him to go to the emergency room, but he was afraid.'

'Afraid of what?' Alexandra's mouth clenched.

'He wouldn't say.'

'So who stabbed him?'

'He wouldn't talk about any of that.'

'Well, what the hell did you talk about?'

'So, Thorn.' Romano shot a cool-it look at Alexandra. 'What about where he might be headed next? He happen to let anything slip about that?'

'The Bahamas,' Thorn said. 'Great Abaco Island.'

Alexandra craned forward. 'The Bahamas!'

Thorn was having trouble opening up, telling these people the whole story. It had something to do with waking up with all those guns in his face, and it also had something to do with the guy Wingo, sitting there silently, unmoving. He struck Thorn as a guy with a lot of high-priced, state-of-the-art training and a global view. Over the years Thorn had met a few guys like that, peacetime soldiers with too much time on their hands, out-of-work mercenaries who thought in big, sweeping terms. More often than not, guys like that didn't give a particular shit about individuals, their pain, their sacrifices, their deaths. If your ends were grand enough, you could justify almost any means. And Wingo fit the picture, staying aloof, staring down at the table, listening, taking that silent, internal dictation. Like a guy with perfect recall who could trip you up later with a half dozen inconsistencies in your story. Thorn kept looking at him but the guy wasn't giving off anything. No emotion, no body language, just that irritating, untouchable calm.

'He was planning on going to the Bahamas,' said Romano. 'How? In Peretti's boat?'

'He didn't say. In a boat like that, if you knew what you were doing, you could leave at dawn, be there for an early lunch.'

'Why the Bahamas?' Wingo said. But there was no curiosity in his voice. Almost a yawn.

Thorn leaned his way. 'And who pays your salary?'

Alexandra looked off at the dense stand of hardwoods. Romano closed his mouth and smoothed his palm across his inflamed cheek. Wingo just kept staring at a dot about five feet up in the air.

'He's with the NTSB,' Sugarman said. 'I've seen

him on TV at the news briefings this week. He's the vice chairman, lead investigator for the American 570 crash.'

Thorn turned his head and looked at the shoreline, watching an egret poke in the shallows along the rocks, while twenty yards south a heron stood at rigid attention, head cocked back, eyes riveted on activity only it could see.

'Does this have something to do with a ray gun?'

Thorn looked back at the cop and Alexandra and the government man. He'd hit a funny bone with all three. The air trembled.

'Talk to us, Thorn,' Romano said, his red face glowing. 'We're all ears.'

'No, it's your turn. I'm shutting up unless there's some fair exchange.'

'Maybe we should run him in, Dan. Put him in a room, give him time to consider his civic duty.'

'Hey, you're Miami PD, right?'

'That's correct,' Romano said.

'Aren't you a little beyond your jurisdiction? They haven't expanded the city limits this far yet, have they?'

'We're here with the full knowledge and cooper-ation of the sheriff of Monroe County.'

'Well, good. I'd hate to think you violated my rights in any way.'

'Talk to us, Mr Thorn,' Wingo said. 'Let's hear about this ray gun.'

'Way I see it,' Thorn said, 'you talk a little, then I

talk a little. I mean, I don't expect you to tell me the whole truth. I know you guys never do that. I just want to get a glimpse of what's going on here. That's all, just a peek.'

Sugar said, 'Thorn promised Lawton he'd help. They kind of forged a bond.'

Alexandra lifted her eyes and settled them on Thorn's face. They were still burning, but the heat had backed off a few degrees.

'Help him how?' she said.

'Whatever he wanted me to do. I said I'd go along.'

'How do you know about this ray gun?' Wingo said.

'Lawton mentioned it in passing, that's all.'

'What did he want in the Bahamas?'

'To see somebody, some guy he thought might have some information.'

'He thinks he's still a detective,' Alexandra said. 'He's investigating a crime, the death of his friend.'

'Who'd he want to see in the Bahamas?' Romano said.

'No, it's your turn,' Thorn said. 'We're at that place, I've given you a couple of fairly significant things, but you're still sitting there with your assholes sewn shut. Now let's start playing fair.'

'Did he have something with him, a large box?' Wingo's voice was still disengaged, but his poker face was starting to crumble. A little eagerness showing, that flare of nostril, widening of pupil, like some damn bloodhound getting the first grain of scent.

209

'Oh, the box,' Thorn said. 'You mean where he kept the ray gun.'

Wingo straightened. 'He had it with him? You saw it?'

'Hell, no. He didn't have any box. You see any box, Sugar?'

'No box, no.'

Wingo looked at Thorn for several seconds, then blew out a breath.

'Hey, guys, if you won't answer my questions,' Thorn said, 'we'll keep dancing around, playing these stupid games. I try to trick something out of you, you do the same with me. You want that?'

'What do you want to know?' Romano said.

'Here's a question,' Sugarman said, turning to Wingo. 'You're investigating the 570 crash, so what's the deal? You think that old man is involved? Like a terrorist or something?'

Alexandra said, 'That's what he thinks, yeah.'

Sugarman gave his head a small shake as if his ears were ringing.

'Look, I mean no offense, Mr Wingo, and hey, I'm not a big-time government investigator or anything, but I'd have to say that's pretty much a crock of shit. And no offense to you either, Ms Collins, but your dad didn't strike me as having the mental acuity for a fast game of darts, much less a terrorist plot.'

Wingo sighed. 'No one's claiming Mr Collins is the mastermind behind this scheme.'

'If there even *is* a scheme,' Romano said, looking

across at Wingo. Then he turned to Thorn. 'It's called a HERF gun.'

'Romano!' Wingo warned.

'Hey, don't try to bully me, Wingo. We've played it your way and come up with shit. I'm giving Mr Thorn a little glimpse, then he's going to give us a little in return. Aren't you, Mr Thorn?'

Thorn tried for an affable smile.

While Wingo sat stiffly on the picnic bench staring out at the dense gray sky, the lieutenant explained what Wingo believed to be true. A small, cheap weapon that could blow out electrical circuits, shut down power plants, knock airplanes from the sky.

'Well, well,' Thorn said when he finished. 'Buck Rogers flies again.'

Alexandra said, 'Now why did Dad want to go to the Bahamas?'

'To see a man named Braswell.'

Wingo's upper lip twitched but that was all. It might have been a tic of some kind, but Thorn doubted it. Guys like that didn't have tics. Masters of self-control.

'Braswell?' Romano said. 'Who the hell is he?'

'Lawton didn't go into a lot of detail,' Thorn said. 'He said this guy was fishing for marlin.'

Wingo's face was drained of expression.

'And why did Lawton have a hard-on for this guy?' Romano took a cigarette from his shirt pocket and began to fiddle with it. 'Did he say?'

'Not really. He wasn't real logical in his explanations.'

'We've got to go over there, Dan.'

'Well, the Bahamas *are* a little beyond our jurisdiction. They kind of frown on us barging in, flashing our badges over there.'

'Screw jurisdiction,' Alexandra said.

'Let's don't get ahead of ourselves,' Romano said. 'My bet is, Lawton's going to show up in the next few hours, some marina somewhere nearby, in the Keys, Miami. He'll call Alex, ask you to come get him, like nothing's wrong, just a typical day. That's what's going to happen, you watch.'

Alexandra reached across and touched Romano's arm.

'Do we have enough to bring in the FBI?'

'We got squat,' Romano said. 'Less than squat. We got some hocus-pocus weapon. We got an old-man wandering around telling stories, maybe they're true, maybe they're hokum. He may be in the Bahamas, he may be out shopping for a loaf of bread. We got diddly.'

'Dad's a fugitive. He's wanted in connection with an accidental death, leaving the scene. That should be enough to get some assistance from the Bahamians. Pass his photo around, hold him for questioning if he shows up.'

'Sure, sure. We'll do that, and we'll do whatever else we can,' Romano said. 'But if he does somehow get over there and keeps his head down, I don't see there's much we can do. People go to the Bahamas to evaporate. It's a national industry. Authorities over there aren't about to put a damper on their economy by tracking our runaways.'

'I'm going, goddamn it,' Alex said. 'Officially or not.'

'Whoa,' Romano said. 'Think about it. Even if for some reason Lawton got it in his mind to go to the Bahamas, is he sharp enough to read charts, get himself across the Stream?'

'Put him on a boat,' Alex said, 'he's sharp as a twenty-year-old.'

'Two hundred miles of open water?' Romano said. 'I don't see it.'

'He's taken boats over to the islands dozens of times,' said Alexandra. 'In heavy weather, at night. He's got a sixth sense about navigation.'

'Even in his current condition?'

'Most of his skills are still there,' Alex said. 'It's his short-term memory that's bad.'

Romano shook his head, still not buying it.

'You're underestimating him,' Thorn said. 'He may be a bit confused, but he sure as hell was energized.'

Alexandra gave Thorn some careful scrutiny, then turned to Romano.

'Look, Dan,' she said. 'I've got vacation time coming.'

'No one's going anywhere,' Wingo said. He brought his gaze back from the middle distance and gave each of them a taste of his glossy black eyes. 'This is my investigation. I won't have you endangering it.'

'Wingo, I don't give two shits about your make-believe weapon. All I want is to get my father back.'

'Look, this is a great deal more serious than you know.'

'Bullshit,' Alex said.

'All right, look,' said Wingo. 'There's something I didn't tell you.'

'Great,' Romano said. 'More fairy tales.'

Wingo stared vacantly at the horizon. He drew a breath.

'Back in March, on the Piper Cub flight, their electronics were damaged. Fuses, some wiring. But still they managed to circle back to the airport and they would have made it safely except the pilot was so rattled, he set the plane down too fast and steep. Then a month later, on Flight 570, the complete electrical system went down, but once again the captain managed to regain enough control of the aircraft to save significant life.'

'Yeah?' Romano said. 'And this is supposed to mean something?'

'What it says to this aeronautical engineer is that they haven't achieved sufficient power in the electromagnetic pulse. Not enough to totally obliterate all electrical systems.'

'So this fantasy weapon doesn't even work?' Thorn said.

'That's not what I'm saying.' Wingo gave Thorn a sharp look, then turned his eyes back to the gray blur of the horizon. 'Between the March event and

214

this most recent one, they've clearly made progress. A lot of progress in a very short time. The damage to the American flight was far greater than to the Piper Cub. What that says to me is that they're still evolving. And at this rate of increase in their power gain, it might only be a short time before the thing is fully operational and could start bringing down planes anywhere in the world.'

At the edge of the porch a sluggish breeze sifted through the coconut palm's big fronds. A rattle and hiss that sounded like a dying man's final gasps.

'So what's the plan?' Thorn said.

'Forget it.' Alexandra stood up. 'Get back to your different drummer. Forget any of this happened. We'll take it from here. But if my dad shows up again, by God, you damn well better hold on to him this time, and call us right away. Is that clear?'

Thorn managed a smile. 'Happy to oblige.'

'Come on, Dan, we have to move.'

The three of them rose from the picnic table and headed for the stairs.

'And oh, yeah,' Thorn said. 'Feel free to stop in anytime. Bring your friends. Maybe next time they can take off their goggles, we'll have a party.'

Thorn tagged along down the stairs. The two cops in the lead, Wingo lagging. In the yard Thorn caught up with him, matched his stride, leaned in and said in a hushed voice, 'This guy Braswell, he's the one that built the ray gun, huh?'

Wingo halted, his lips twisting into a nasty frown.

Thorn watched as Wingo slowly regained control and the look melted back into the bland countenance he'd maintained before.

'Why do you say that?'

'Oh, just a wild guess.'

Wingo brought a smile to his lips but there wasn't any fun in his voice.

'You'd do well to keep tying your little flies, Mr Thorn. And stay out of deeper waters.'

# 13

Sugar and Thorn shared a pot of coffee, watching the low clouds dissolve, some ragged patches of blue beginning to appear. A heron drifted in and touched down along the shore and began its slow, regal prowl.

Thorn put down his mug and reached into the pocket of his shorts and drew out a plastic baggie with a knife inside.

'Christ, Thorn, that's withholding evidence. A felony, man.'

'Hey, I found it after they left.'

'Yeah, sure you did.'

'Those people didn't inspire a lot of confidence in me.'

Sugarman shook his head sadly.

'You know anything about knives, Sugar?'

He took another sip from his mug. 'I know a jackknife from a Bowie. That's about my limit.'

'Mine, too. But this one. It looks familiar to me.'

'Yeah?'

'That long-haired creep I was telling you about. Johnny Braswell. Very close to the one he had.'

'You sure?'

'Not positive, no. Maybe it's just wishful thinking.'

'That was stupid, Thorn. Just plain stupid hiding that knife.'

'I didn't care for Wingo. Something isn't right with his eyes.'

'But you liked the girl. I could see that.'

He smiled at Sugar.

'For a hard-ass she wasn't bad. But I like her father more.'

'I don't know,' Sugar said. 'This ray gun thing sounds like a bunch of hooey.'

At the shoreline the heron was peering up at them as if requesting quiet.

'Oh, God, you got that look, Thorn. You got that goddamn look.'

'Hey, I liked Lawton, what can I say? We connected.'

'Where's that sheet of paper, the nautical chart? Might be fingerprints on it.'

Thorn shook his head.

'Lawton must've taken it with him.'

Sugar looked out at the heron. It was stalking

toward the neighbor's property, giving up on this noisy spot.

'Well, hell,' Sugar said. 'I guess it wouldn't hurt to poke around a little. I mean, purely as an intellectual exercise. To satisfy our curiosities. But that's it.'

Thorn smiled.

'I was thinking about Cappy Adams.'

Sugarman hummed his approval.

'Smart,' he said.

Thorn watched a flats boat hotdogging across Blackwater Sound, putting a white seam across the flat silver surface. Everyone had them now. The new fad. Fast little skimmers that could take their owners way up onto the fragile flats where they could do more damage in a few seconds than could be undone in years.

'All right then,' Sugarman said. 'But just to satisfy our curiosity, nothing more.'

'I have to take a quick shower first, put on a fresh T-shirt. I don't want to go out looking like some beach bum.'

Cappy Adams lived on the ocean side of Lower Matecumbe in an orange-and-blue A-frame that looked across a narrow canal at a tangle of mangroves. The second Sugarman and Thorn stepped out of the Chevrolet, a whining cloud of mosquitoes engulfed them and the swarm grew thicker as they mounted the metal stairway. While Sugar fanned and swatted, Thorn rapped on the frame of the screen door.

'Friend or foe!' Cappy yelled from somewhere deep in the house.

'Two friends,' Thorn called back. 'No foes.'

'Enter!'

The house consisted of one large room and a small loft. A half dozen skylights provided the lighting. Cappy was at the far end of the room, smoking a pipe, hunched over one of his battlefields. He was shirtless and barefoot, wearing only a pair of old blue overalls, his thick mat of white chest hair coiling over the edge of the denim. He wore his gray hair in a braided ponytail that hung to the middle of his back. On the upper side of his left forearm the tattoo of a red-haired bombshell had faded to flesh tones.

He looked up at them and smiled, puffed on his pipe, and bent back to his work.

The kitchen area was neat and gleaming and in one corner of the room a recliner was aimed at a small TV set, while the rest of the open area was crammed with a dozen tables made of plywood sheets lying atop stacks of concrete blocks. Spread out on each of them was a miniature scene of war. Sand tables, they were called. Half-inch tall soldiers with muskets, others with swords or rapiers, and still others with M-16s or long rifles with fixed bayonets. Cappy used papier-mâché and balsa wood, pipe cleaners and duct tape to build his own mountains and boulders and bridges and form his own trees and shrubs and bombed-out buildings.

From years of crafting fishing flies, Cappy had mastered lifelike reproductions. He molded the rifles and swords and cannons out of bits of modeling clay, whittled muskets and shields from wood or scraps of plastic. Everything was perfectly in scale, and every last belt buckle and helmet cover and uniform was excruciatingly accurate. Near the corner of each table was a brass plate with the name of each scene: THE BATTLE OF CULLODEN, THE BATTLE OF STIRLING BRIDGE, MASSACRE IN THE PASSES, THE ATTACK ON TARANTO, FREDERICKSBURG, and ANTIETAM. The room reeked of glue and mineral spirits and acrylic paint.

Though he'd long admired Cappy's skill and liked him personally, Thorn always felt uneasy in this room. Maybe it was because the grim tableaux struck him as even more grim for their absence of wounds or even a dot of imitation blood. This was war without penalty, an elaborate exercise in intellectual sport.

'Gentlemen, come in. See my latest.'

Cappy was using a pair of tweezers to position a miniature Confederate flag on the grass near the outstretched arms of a fallen rebel soldier. Bodies were strewn three and four deep along the rocky banks of a stream that formed the border between a wide green meadow and a dense woods. Peeking out from behind almost every tree and several boulders were the Union troops, rifles aimed at the growing pile of dead.

'Battle of Peachtree Creek,' Cappy said. 'Just out-side Atlanta in July 1864. The rebs threw a brigade at Pap Thomas's fifty thousand troops that were part of the force surrounding Atlanta. This is the right flank of one regiment that was destroyed. Seven men were killed in this little battle alone while trying to raise their flag. Color-bearers. Those were the true believers. Wave the flag, get everyone charged up. So they're out there, unarmed, easy targets, drawing a lot of fire, because if they go down, the fighting spirit of the rest of the troops gets dampened. On this particular day, seven men were slaughtered just trying to wave their flag.'

Thorn and Sugar gave the seven a moment of silence.

Cappy drew on his pipe and let loose the smoke, which hung above the battlefield like the fog of departing spirits.

Cappy Adams had been fresh out of military school when he took his first command, a tank brigade that was ordered to mop up the straggling German resist-ance after D day. Turned out to be a lot more resist-ance than anyone expected, a hell of a lot more mop-ping up. Cappy rarely spoke of his military exploits, but whatever he'd done in those few months after D day had bumped him up from lieutenant to major. When he retired at forty-five, he was a full bird colonel.

'Normally what I do, I try to think my way back to the day of each of these battles, put myself in the place of the commander, and see if there's something I could've done differently with the information available to him at the time. I'm playing Monday-morning quarterback, yeah, but I try to stay disciplined, pretend I don't know the things the commander would've had no way of knowing. But with this battle, Christ, I can't find a goddamn thing I would've done differently except to turn tail and get the hell back to my cotton plantation. It was suicide, plain and simple.'

'Fifty thousand, that's a lot of men in one place,' Thorn said.

Cappy blew another cloud of smoke.

'Armies weren't always that large,' he said. 'Thirteen hundred years ago the king of Wessex had it all broken down. One to seven men were considered simple thieves. Seven to thirty-five was a band – you know, Robin Hood and his merry bunch, that sort of thing. Thirty-six and above, now that was all it took to qualify as an army. But that was seven hundred AD, before we got so civilized and could put fifty thousand men in the same uniform in the same meadow on the same July afternoon.'

Cappy nudged the miniature Confederate flag an inch closer to the fallen soldier. Just beyond his grasp.

'And check this one out.'

Cappy led them to another table that was heavily forested; a steep hill reared up in the center of the table. Dozens of tiny tanks and other military vehicles were distributed around the base of the hill.

'Here's one I'm still wrestling with. Hitler sends the entire Forty-eighth Panzer Corps to chop off Patton's neck after the breakout. But the Krauts can't take Hill 314 at Mortain. Old Hickory – that's the US Thirtieth Infantry Division – only has one battalion on that hill, without any anti-tank weapons.'

Cappy pointed out the array of lightly armored troops hiding among the trees on the top of the hill.

'Now, *Kampfgruppe* Ullrich does its job and takes the steep southwestern quadrant of the hill here in hand-to-hand combat at two in the morning. But *Kampfgruppe* Fick doesn't launch a coordinated attack up the road on the shallow east face. It just sits there. Now why'd they do that? The experts think Fick was afraid to go up that road because of the heavy fog. Afraid of an ambush, they say. But I'm thinking, no, would the SS be afraid of a little fog? I don't think so. But let's say their attached armor support got lost in the haze and didn't make it on time, then I can see those panzer grenadiers waiting for daylight. But of course, by then it was too late. It's just another forgotten battlefield in Normandy, but that fog changed a lot of lives. It may have even had a small effect on the eventual outcome of the war. A little thing like that. Moisture in the air. Disastrous dew point.'

Thorn stared at the elaborate replica, imagining that small hilltop swarming with troops, men full of righteous belief in their gods and their leaders, considering for a few seconds the absurd sequences of luck and accident that so often nudged the human race in some new direction.

'So you boys stop over for a history lesson or just want to bum a beer?'

'Beer would be nice,' Sugarman said.

'Two would be better,' said Thorn.

They followed Cappy over to the kitchen. He set the tweezers down on the counter, got out three Budweisers and twisted off the caps. Thorn took a deep pull and set it down beside the tweezers.

'I get the feeling beer isn't what you came for either.'

Thorn drew a squiggly line through the sweat on his bottle.

'You ever hear of something called a HERF gun?'

Cappy eyed him for a moment. He lifted his beer and had a long swallow. He put it down and eyed Thorn some more.

'God almighty, what the hell have you boys gotten yourselves into now?'

'I don't know yet, that's why we're here.'

'A HERF gun, huh? High Energy Radio Frequency, is that what you're talking about?'

'That's it,' Sugar said. 'You know about it?'

'I know enough to say with reasonable certainty that it's a lot of snake oil. Right up there with that rubber that never wears out, cars that run on seawater.'

'Reasonable certainty?'

Cappy's eyes were painfully pale, bleached by the

sun. Too many years on the water tracking the never-ending travels of tarpon, that silver monster he'd specialized in for the twenty years he'd guided out of Islamorada.

'Anything you know would be helpful, Cappy.'

'I live to serve,' he said.

He gave Thorn a thoughtful look. Then gazed down at Hill 314.

'It's also called EMP, electromagnetic pulse. People have been aware of it, at least conceptually, for at least fifty years, ever since the first nuclear tests. Our boys at Livermore and Sandia labs realized the power of the electromagnetic pulse given off by the explosions and they've been working on ways to harden facilities against an EMP attack for decades.

'I seem to remember reading about the Sandia boys building a giant wooden platform in the desert near Luke Air Force Base in Arizona. Thing looked like a huge train trestle. They propped a B-52 bomber on it and blasted it with EMP to see what it would take to protect its electrical systems. I never heard how that one turned out, but you can bet that these days our vital nuclear weapon systems and command sites have been hardened. Jet fighters, naval equipment, everything necessary to fight a war.'

'So it does exist?'

'EMP exists, sure. But what a HERF gun is supposed to do, well, that's another story.'

Sugarman was studying a Zulu battlefield. Row upon row of near-naked warriors with shields and axes marched headlong into row upon row of other warriors with much larger shields and spears. The guys with the smaller shields and axes were clearly winning. Shaka Zulu's tactic was to let his troops take the first barrage of spears on their shields, suffer some casualties, then race in for close combat. Because they'd abandoned the clumsy sandals of other African warriors and had hardened their soles by running over rough terrain, they were more maneuverable in close quarters. Smaller shields, smaller hand weapons, no shoes. Those three things had led Shaka Zulu to control more land and resources than Napoleon at the height of his power.

Cappy took a slug of beer and said, 'HERF supposedly works by beaming a huge burst of radio noise at its target. Fifteen to twenty megawatts. Backpack size, buy the stuff from your local Radio Shack. Any hacker or Electronics 101 student can do it. At least that's the fantasy. Now on the official side, I know NSA has a classified program called TEMPEST that is testing the technologies in this area, but there are two big, bad problems with HERF guns. One, there's no portable energy source powerful enough to create that kind of pulse. Oh, yeah, in the last ten years we've made serious advances in non-nuclear power sources, what's called Air-Independent Propulsion. The main application is for non-nuclear submarines, to enable them to move underwater without needing to suck in air by a snorkel that pokes above the surface – and is easy to detect. The big advances are in fuel-cell technology. We're talking enough power to propel a two-thousand-ton submarine underwater at bursts up to twenty knots per hour. Enough power perhaps to operate a HERF weapon. Main problem is size. To make a weapon like that work with current technology, you'd have to have enough fuel cells to stuff the largest moving van on the road, not a backpack.

'And the second problem is, it's pretty damn hard to focus a pulse of that magnitude. So if you set it off, the thing would be likely to kill the person operating it and everyone in the immediate proximity. Now that would be considered a fairly serious drawback from a military perspective.'

'From almost any perspective,' Thorn said.

Sugarman said, 'What if you put the gun somewhere real isolated? And you triggered it by remote control, would that work?'

'Isolated,' Thorn said. 'Like out in the middle of the Everglades.'

'I don't see why not,' Cappy said.

'So it is possible?' Thorn said.

Cappy had a sip of beer. His eyes strayed off to his sand tables, all those plastic heroes. Victory and defeat so dependent on chance. Not right or might, but just a little fog, an hour's delay.

'Back in '62,' he said, 'when the US exploded Test Shot Starfish over the mid-Pacific, it was a one-point-four-megaton nuclear blast and its electromagnetic pulse destroyed satellite equipment and blocked

228

high-frequency radio transmission for hours all across the Pacific. Ever since then, people have been speculating about generating the pulse without setting off the explosion. Is it possible? Well, I'm no physicist, but if it was doable, then it would sure as hell change a whole lot of what we accept as reality right now. Very possibly it might alter the very nature of warfare. All the sophisticated electronics we depend on, radar, supersonic jet fighters, laser-guided missiles, that would all be useless. A bunch of strategically placed HERF guns out in the field could knock everything out and we'd be walking around in the dark. We'd be back to Shaka Zulu and his shortened ax.'

'All in all,' Thorn said, 'that might not be so bad.'

Cappy gave a rueful smile.

'Don't be so sure, Thorn. Take away the nuclear arsenal, supersonic fighter jets, the radar, the smart bombs, yeah, I know it sounds like an improvement, but think about it. If the rules changed all of a sudden, things could get awful goddamn bloody before the power structure got sorted out again. A clear pecking order is what keeps the status quo, and the status quo is what keeps things stable, orderly, and peaceful.'

Everyone considered that for a moment. Then Thorn reached into the pocket of his shorts and brought out the plastic baggie. He handed it to Cappy without comment.

Cappy held it up and inspected it through the clear plastic.

'Intriguing tool,' Cappy said. 'We're definitely not talking about an instrument to clean your fingernails. No, sir, this is obviously a man-killer.'

'Anything you could find out would be interesting,' Thorn said. 'But you probably shouldn't touch it. Might smudge the fingerprints.'

'I know a few guys into knives. I'll dig around.'

'So the bottom line on this HERF thing, Cappy, you think it's bullshit.'

Cappy had a sip of beer and stared at Thorn.

'There's a lot of science going on these days,' Cappy said. 'Who can say for sure? To make something like that portable, someone'd have to come up with a new-generation battery. Some breakthrough in fuel-cell technology. Then yeah, I guess it could happen. But I hope to hell I'm not alive to see it.'

Two beers and a half hour of gossip later, Sugar and Thorn were back in the car, killing a few stray mosquitoes as they headed back up the Overseas Highway.

'So what do you think?'

'I think it's a damn good thing you're out of the loop on this one, Thorn. This is some heavy shit.'

'Fairly heavy, yeah.'

''Cause if this HERF thing exists, you're dealing with something that's way, way out of your league. And if it doesn't exist, then you're dealing with some world-class loonies. Either way, it's no-win.'

As they passed by Vacation Island, the pager on Sugarman's belt began to pulse. He pulled it off, checked the screen, and gave Thorn a quick, unhappy look.

'I gotta take this,' he said.

A mile up the road, he pulled off at a Circle K and while Thorn went inside for a jar of chunky peanut butter and a six-pack, Sugar used the pay phone.

Sugarman was behind the wheel by the time Thorn climbed back inside.

'So who was it?'

'Professional courtesy call. Our new friend in Miami.'

'The hard-ass?'

'No, Romano.'

'So?'

'So the boat turned up. Peretti's boat.'

'Let me guess.'

Sugar said, 'It ran ashore on a remote beach on Treasure Cay.'

'That's Abaco. North end of the island. He made good time.'

'Yeah, but still a long walk from Marsh Harbor.'

'Oh, he'll make it,' Thorn said. 'I don't doubt it for a second.'

'He's a tough old coot, all right.'

'Yeah,' Thorn said. 'Made it across the Gulf Stream, found the island. Ditched the boat before anyone could arrest him for stealing it. He's not as loony as he seems.'

'Romano says they're sending somebody over there from Miami PD to do the crime scene stuff on the boat, locate Lawton, and bring him home. So they don't need your help.'

'I'm sure they don't.'

Sugarman studied him for a long moment. Thorn gave him a sober look.

'This HERF thing has looney tunes written all over it. I'd stay well clear of this one.'

Sugarman started the car and put it in reverse and backed out of the space. He halted at the edge of US 1, waiting for an opening in the traffic. He glanced across at Thorn.

Thorn had tilted his head to the side. His eyes were shut and he had a rapturous look as if he were communing with his long-dead loved ones.

'All right. What the hell're you doing now?'

Thorn kept his eyes closed.

'Just trying to pick up the beat,' he said, 'of that different drummer.'

# 14

Her father opened Morgan's cabin door and stood there for a moment until she'd blinked and stretched herself awake.

'It's pinging,' he said. 'Started a couple of minutes ago.'

'How close?'

'Twenty, twenty-five miles south.'

'Well, congratulations, Dad. Your calculations were accurate. You must be pleased.'

He nodded, but he didn't look happy. Not at all.

'Come on, Morgan. We have to move.'

'All right, all right. Give me a minute.'

But A.J. stayed in the doorway, arms loose at his sides. Eyes downcast, mouth warped with anguish, his throat working as if he were struggling to swallow some dry crumb of food.

'No, Dad, come on. Don't do this.'

Her father closed his eyes, bowed his head, and shook it hard as if trying to silence a host of whispering voices.

'This is my goddamn fault. All of it.'

Morgan sighed. Veins and sinews showed in his throat. Dark voltage radiated from his flesh.

'It's okay. You did all you could, Dad.'

He lifted his head and looked at her carefully.

'Did I?'

'You did everything possible.'

'Goddamn it, Morgan. I could see Andy just a few feet away. It was my one chance. He was so goddamn close. His hand reaching out. He was alive, looking at me, eyes wide open, waving that hand.'

'The line broke, Dad. You couldn't do anything about that. You fell, you busted a rib. Remember?'

'I could've jumped into the water like you did. Held my breath.'

'It was too late by then, Dad. He was too far down. A second after the line broke, I couldn't see him anymore. He was gone.'

'This is my fault, all of it.'

Morgan let go of another long breath. She rubbed at the ache sprouting behind her temples. Ten years later, it was still the same, like all the clocks had broken, the galaxies had stopped spinning on the day Andy died. The same exchange they'd had back then, the same one they'd had every year since. Her father's ritual week of self-loathing. Morgan reciting her useless refrains.

'I grabbed the rod out of your hands, then I set the goddamn drag too tight. I knew better. But I panicked. I wanted to reel him back to the boat, so I pushed the drag too far and the line couldn't handle the strain and it broke.'

'It's over, Dad. Now we're going to catch her. We're going to set it right.'

'I screwed up. I lost your brother and I lost Darlene. Oh, I don't blame her for what she did. No mother should witness such a thing. I never should have taken you all along in the first place. It was my passion, not anyone else's. I dragged everyone out there, exposed my family to that danger. For what?'

A.J. stared fiercely at the beige carpet, as if he could penetrate the hull of the boat, see down into the awful depths.

'I had that rod in my hand and I panicked. The one time I needed to apply my skills. The one time when everything I knew about the art of fishing really and truly mattered, and I blew it. I lost my son. And look at this, where we are. What I did to us. We're what's left, Morgan, you and me and Johnny, the sad remains.'

A.J. peered at her through the fog of his heartache. He blinked. His eyes were damp and filled with fluttery light.

'It's pinging, Dad. We shouldn't be wasting time.'

He looked up, swallowed. The light rose in his eyes.

'All right, Morgan. Get up. Come on now. Let's move. Let's kill this son of a bitch.'

'Yeah,' Morgan said. 'Okay, Dad. Okay.'


It was Good Friday, the twenty-first of April. A coolish morning, low humidity, only a few patchy clouds along the horizon, slick seas spread in all directions, a vast blue mirror. A.J. had them running south, the big yacht hauling ass, close to forty knots. Morgan stood beside him on the flybridge while Johnny fussed with the lures down in the cockpit.

As they churned across the calm seas, the GPS screen in front of A.J. pulsed with a bright blue dot a few inches due east of the *ByteMe*'s location. A sharp ping sounded on each beat.

'How far away?'

'Five miles, maybe less,' A.J. said. 'At least she was when that last ping came in half an hour ago. She's submerged again. She's moved by now.'

'In half an hour,' Morgan said, 'she could've gone ten miles in any direction.'

She knew her father didn't want to hear it, but it was true. A marlin that size could sustain speeds as fast as the Hatteras's top end. And it could hit bursts of almost twice theirs.

'She's damn close,' A.J. said. 'Closer than she's been since the day we saw her.'

'That big an area, it'd still be a miracle if we could raise her.'

A.J. gave Morgan a sharp look.

'Don't be a doubter, Morgan. You have to believe, you have to trust your passion.'

Morgan looked out at the spreading sea.

'You know this is what we have to do, Morgan. This is our job, to set things right. We don't have a choice in the matter. When this is done, there'll be time to turn ourselves to other tasks.'

'If we can remember how to do anything else.'

Morgan looked off to the west. A couple of other sport fishing boats were roaring south toward the Mushroom and Jurassic Park, the marlin fishing grounds most of the captains preferred. They were going to fish the bottom contours and current confluences or else they'd work the deep water as close to the hundred-fathom curve as they could. Just like the Braswells would've done if they'd still been fishing for blues, truly fishing. But that was all finished. They were following the ping. That was it. Just the ping.

A.J. turned the wheel a few degrees to the north.

On the console another light began to blink, this one green.

'We're getting a fax,' A.J. said. 'Go check it, Morgan.'

Morgan climbed down the ladder and went into the salon. The fax was printing out. When it was done she pulled it from the machine and carried it out into the sunlight. Just a single sentence from Jeb Shine. One sentence.

Morgan closed her eyes and stood there a minute just breathing.

When she'd gotten herself together, she climbed up the ladder, took her place beside her father. A.J. glanced at her.

'What is it?'

Morgan shook her head.

'It's from Jeb Shine.'

'Go on.'

'At eight-seventeen this morning, the duplicate pod died. It's gone.'

A.J. flinched. He looked out at the stretch of blue sea, took a long breath, then resumed his watch of the GPS screen. He nudged the throttle forward. Steering the boat one-handed, he sank away again into his bottomless trance.

A while later as the *ByteMe* entered the target zone, A.J. cut the engines back to trolling speed. Down in the cockpit, Johnny lowered the outriggers to their gull-wing position, clipped each line to their tips, and let out the baits, free-spooling each rod until he had the baits where he wanted them, about two hundred eighty yards back, the exact same spacing they'd been using ten years ago when they jumped Big Mother.

He stood there a moment watching as the baits skipped along the flat sea just outside the foamy wake. Ducking into each wave, then coming out the other side. No natural baits for the Braswells, slimy mackerel or tuna, all that cutting open and hiding the hooks and lacing the fish back together.

238

No, they used soft-sided lures with chisel heads, a hydrodynamic design meant to imitate flying fish. Those were on lines one and four, while two and three had purple and black Mega Billfish lures that were supposed to resemble small black fin or skipjack tuna striking at the surface. Same rigging they'd used the day Andy died.

Morgan looked at her father. The old man was staring out at the water, scanning the surface. Willing Big Mother to rise. To show herself one more time.

Down in the cockpit Johnny took a seat in the padded angler's chair. He drew one of his knives from its leather sheath. Then he slid his whetstone from the pocket of his baggies, spit a dot of saliva on it, and began a slow, soft, circular grind of steel against stone.

Ten hours later, on their way back to shore, Morgan handled the boat and her father sat in the fighting chair and stared out at the foamy wake as the daylight died. The ping was quiet now. It might stay quiet forever, or it might switch on again tonight or tomorrow. No way to know.

They'd dragged bait all day, covered every inch of the target zone, and they'd raised nothing, not even a dolphin or sail. A.J. sat motionless, staring out at the last desolate traces of sunlight.

By seven-thirty they were back in the main channel. Morgan worked the boat across the marina toward their private dock. As she rounded the last turn and their slip came into view, she saw a man in a blue sleeveless T-shirt and yellow shorts standing stiffly at the end of the dock. He had white hair and a potbelly and seemed to be watching their approach.

'Somebody we know?' Johnny reached below the console for a pair of binoculars and popped off the caps.

Morgan squinted through the half light but couldn't make him out.

She picked up the radio and hailed Maurice Black, their security man, one of the two they brought along on these outings. She asked Maurice whom he'd let out on the dock.

'I thought you'd want to see him, Ms Braswell. It's an older gentleman.'

Morgan held the mike close to her lips.

'We know a lot of older gentlemen, Maurice.'

'I don't know his real name, Miss Morgan,' Maurice said. 'But I suspect you might want to meet with him since he says his name is Mr Arnold Peretti.'

'Fucking-A.' Johnny lowered the binoculars. 'He came to us. The old guy on Peretti's boat, he fucking came to us.'

'Well, well.'

'Did I do all right, Ms Braswell?' Maurice said.

Morgan's grip on the microphone relaxed.

'You did fine, Maurice. Just fine.'


Not two minutes after they'd gotten the old man into Johnny's stateroom, gagged him and trussed him up,

240

Roy Givens came clomping down the wooden planks in his white cowboy hat, those red boots, pearl buttons on his green-and-white checked shirt. Blue jeans cut tight to his lanky frame. Just showed up without warning. No hello, just, 'It's time to talk.'

Morgan made him a bourbon and water and they sat in the salon chitchatting, waiting until A.J. finally emerged from his stateroom and wandered off to dinner at the resort restaurant.

When he was gone, she swung around and faced the Texan.

'I told you it was next Saturday, the twenty-ninth.'

'I know what you told me, darling,' Roy said. 'But some of my associates, they've got a bad case of the heebie-jeebies.'

'About what?'

'Heard you'd gone and lost the item. Put it somewhere and can't find it.'

'Look, I don't have time for this bullshit. You need to get back on your horse and ride on home, Roy.'

Roy was leaning back against the tan leather couch. He spread his arms out across the top cushion. Very relaxed, settling in, going to stay as long as he liked.

Morgan was in her white terry-cloth robe. Her hair wet from the shower.

'You heard wrong, Roy. There's no problem. We're going on as planned. Demo next week, right on schedule.'

'You have the device then, it's in your possession?'

'That's right, we have it, Roy. We have the device.'

'Funny. We heard an old man had it. Some crazy old coot got hold of it and run off and you were chasing after him.'

Morgan sat down on the couch next to Roy. She flicked some lint off the knee of his jeans.

'Where'd you hear that, Roy? A crazy story like that?'

'Business I'm in, you gotta have good sources. And I do, pretty lady, best that money can buy. Police, FBI, we got people everywhere.'

'Get a refund, Roy, because your sources suck. We've got the device and we're going to put on a major show next Saturday, week from tomorrow. Now you get up and drag your carcass on back where you came from and sweet-talk your people. You hear?'

'And the blueprints?'

'Saturday after the show, you'll get everything you need, the complete starter kit. You can go into full-scale production, Roy, just mass-produce the ever-loving shit out of this thing.'

Roy gave Johnny a long look.

'Where can I find me a hat like that, boy? One of them convertible jobs.'

Johnny kept his lips pressed together.

Roy gave him a big smile, then turned back to Morgan.

'See, what it is, little lady, some of my folks are just flat out of patience.'

'Screw them,' Morgan said.

'Well, now, that's one approach, I suppose. But it's an attitude that might just come back to bite you in the ass. 'Cause just between you and me and the fat boy over there, you don't want to get us riled up. My people, we got enough demolitions in our back pockets to blow up . . . hell, I don't know. Enough to blow up this whole damn island, I'd guess.'

Morgan sat back against the cushions.

'Are you saying something to me, Roy? Is that bullshit coming out of your mouth supposed to be a threat of some sort?'

'No, missy, ain't no threat. No threat at all. But see, you got to understand the people you're in business with. We get a little idea in our heads, an idea like maybe you're playing games with us, not being totally straight, well, we get all flummoxed. We don't know how to react like normal folks, ball up our fist and punch a hole in a wall, something civilized like that. No, sir, folks like us, we're used to doing our responding with gunpowder and dynamite. It's sad but true.

'And what we think is, we're being conned. We've given you a satchel of money, half a million dollars upfront, the other half when you deliver our brand-new shiny toy. But the second half doesn't happen. Planes crash, yeah, but not the way they're supposed to. The weapon's not up to snuff, that's how it seems. And then we hear this other thing, about some old man running off with the device, so now you don't even have the goldarned thing you promised us in the first place. And then we find out you're down here big-game fishing like nothing's going on. Like maybe you're just spending our half mil without any intention of delivering our goods.

'Well, that just damn near pushes us over the edge. So some of my associates, they're pulling out their Zippos and they're flicking them and flicking them again, and they're getting out their fuses and their dynamite sticks and they're talking all squeaky and strange and wanting to come down here to this pretty little island and make a statement. That's what I'm telling you, missy. You're dealing with some high-octane kooks here. World-class ding-a-lings. Pawing the ground, snorting and hissing.'

Morgan closed her eyes and listened to the blood thump in her ears.

'But now, I expect if I came back and told my boys I'd actually laid my eyes on the device, that just might be sufficient to satisfy them. Anything less than that, I don't know, missy, you might be in for a volatile situation.'

Morgan looked over at Johnny, then back at the Texan.

'It's not here,' she said. 'Finishing touches are being put on it. We're bringing it up to full power this time. But it's not here, Roy.'

'That's too bad.'

'You think I carry something like that around on the boat?'

'My people ain't going to like this,' he said. 'Not even a little bit.'

Johnny stepped forward, tried to make his voice sound hard.

'Who the hell are your people anyway?'

Roy eyed him with a hint of a smile.

'We're American citizens, is who. Land of the free, home of the brave.'

'Who're you against?'

Morgan shook her head sadly.

'Johnny, shut the fuck up, okay? Stay out of this.'

'No, I want to know. I'm curious. Come on, Roy, tell us. Who is it you hate? Who're you going to destroy?'

Roy smiled at him, probably the same cornpone, shit-kicking grin he used on his wife just before he started smacking her around.

'You just wait,' Roy said quietly. 'Once we get what we ordered you'll know who it is soon enough.'

'Well, whoever it is,' Morgan said, 'it gives me a warm feeling, Roy, knowing you're going to make the world a better place.'

'Damn right we will. Damn right. You just stand back and watch.'

'"Hating is always the same,"' Johnny said. '"One day it kills Irish Catholics, the next day Jews, the next day Protestants, the next day Quakers. It's hard to stop. It can end up killing men who wear striped neckties."'

Roy stared at him.

'Robert Young said that in *Crossfire*, 1947.'

'Johnny's a movie buff,' said Morgan.

'I see that.'

'Okay, listen to me, Roy,' she said. 'You go back and tell your brethren they'll get what I promised, and when they get it, they'll be the most dangerous people that ever walked this dirtball planet. There's never been anything like this. It isn't some stupid, fucking, overgrown firecracker that knocks down buildings. This thing is the ultimate kill switch. It flips every switch to off. Wherever you point it, lights out. Meltdown. Blink, it's gone. It's over. Stand outside a bank, blow out their security, their computers, every fucking electrical circuit in the building. Walk right in, fill your pockets. That's what we're talking about, Roy. Not some truck full of fertilizer, a cast-iron pipe crammed with gunpowder and rusty nails. Roy, this is a fucking miracle weapon. When this turns off the lights, they don't come on again. You tell them that, Roy. A week from today, I'll show them what it can do.'

Roy kept looking at her a few seconds, face empty. Then a smile curled across his lips and he shook his head.

'I don't know, missy. You make a deadline, break it. Give us your word, then change your mind. You said that little plane in Palm Beach would prove it. Then you said a passenger jet out of Miami would prove it. But they were busts. Now it's "wait till next Saturday." You're holding a half a million of our nice fresh dollar bills, and we haven't seen shit in return.'

Roy looked around the salon, at the tan furniture, the shiny walls, the bar with all the sparkling glasses and bottles, then he looked at the two of them sitting there, Johnny and Morgan. All the light gone from his eyes now.

'I'll do what I can,' he said. 'But I'll tell you one thing. We don't like to be taken lightly. We don't like that at all.'

# 15

On Thorn's nautical chart, Marsh Harbor bore an eerie likeness to a marlin's head. Its bill was the long spike of land pointing east into the perfect blue of the Atlantic. That narrow rapier was where the public docks were located. The outline of its sleekly tapering head was formed by Old House Point and Pond Bay. The marlin's neat circular eye was a perfectly round, perfectly placed lagoon a few degrees inland from the harbor itself. Even the marlin's flaring dorsal fin was in the anatomically correct position, a roughly triangular jut of land known as Pelican Beach.

Or maybe Thorn was just loopy from lack of sleep, those hours of constant pounding across the Gulf Stream rollers. But damn it, what was it, if it wasn't

248

a marlin there on the nautical charts, staring at him right in the eyes as he motored in off the twilight waters.

There were two places to dock in Marsh Harbor. Two that Thorn knew about. Marsh Harbor Marina was tucked inside a protective horseshoe cove, a small port consisting of three long floating docks with maybe sixty boats. Trawlers and live-aboard sailboats, boaters on limited budgets. The Jib Room was there, perched on the steep hill overlooking the marina, a yellow-and-white bar and restaurant where Thorn had spent a few memorable evenings back in his twenties.

Around the point from there on the Atlantic side was Boat Harbour, which acted as the private marina for the Abaco Beach Resort. Boat Harbour was the home port for a fleet of million-dollar yachts, row after row of gleaming sixty-footers, the marlin fishing fleet with young, sun-darkened crews. And then there were the big ocean cruisers owned by oilmen and computer men and movie stars, boats that cost more money to operate every week than Thorn had made in his entire life. The bar at the Abaco Beach Resort was far fancier than the Jib Room. You could sit on concrete stools half-submerged in the pool and guzzle Rum Runners all afternoon in the sun. Or you could hang out in the tiki bar and sip Mango Fizzes serenaded by a reggae band that jingled and jangled, binged and bonged in the shade of gracefully arching coconut palms.

Blue-collar Jib Room, or silk-collar Abaco Beach Resort.

If Thorn were there for a holiday, there'd be no contest. It would be the pit barbecue and the Bilge Burners of the Jib Room, the maudlin stories of burned-out Americans who'd sailed down to the Bahamas twenty years ago and never found their way home. But this wasn't a holiday. He would have to find an open slip among the sleek, full-race marlin boats, try to mingle his way into the world of the Braswells. In the empty hours crossing the Gulf Stream he had developed an idea about how to manage that, but it depended on locating an old friend from two decades back. An iffy proposition in this rootless age.

After two hundred thirty miles of dark ocean, dodging freighters and cruise ships, thirteen hours of bumpy seas, including one passing squall that severely tested both Thorn's navigational skills and the *Heart Pounder*'s new hull planking, Thorn was ready for a good long nap. But as he rounded Outer Point Cay and headed into the harbor in the gathering darkness of that Saturday evening, he had a sneaking suspicion that rest would be a long time coming.

Miracle of miracles, Thorn found an open slip in the far western edge of the marina for a mere two hundred a night that included water hookup and all the electricity he cared to consume. On either side of his slip were marlin boats dressed out in full regalia of glittery outriggers and dozens of matched custom rods mounted in rocket launchers along the rim of the flybridge, each heavy rod with its five-thousand-dollar gold reel. All the decks were scrubbed spotless, the chrome freshly polished, new varnish shined the teak, everything buffed to perfection. The big Davis on his left was running its air-conditioning full bore, and rock and roll music thumped inside its lustrous hull. Below decks on the sixty-foot Davis to his right, peals of girlish laughter broke out every few seconds followed by deep male guffaws. Another night in consumer paradise. Men who had played their cards right, then played them right again and again. Proving themselves all day against the ultimate gamefish and all night against what sounded like even tougher odds.

At the dockmaster's shack, Thorn counted out the correct number of fives and tens and rumpled ones for his first night's stay and handed them to the assistant dockmaster, a tall, smiley Bahamian named Bailey James who spoke his personal brand of English with such musical relish it seemed he was just a hair-breadth away from song.

'You be staying for the season then?'

'A few days,' Thorn told him. 'Depends on the fishing.'

'Plenty of fishes out there, yes sir, that much is for certain. Depends on you finding them, is what it depends on.'

Thorn peeled off another ten from his roll and held

it out to the young man. Bailey skimmed it from Thorn's palm with well-oiled dexterity. A couple of sunburned men in khaki shorts and white T-shirts with boat names printed on them passed by and nodded their helloes. Bailey James came to mock attention and threw them a spiffy salute.

'So they catching any blues?' Thorn asked when the men had passed.

Bailey gave him a studied wink.

'Oh, yes, fishing is good. Marlin fish out there in great abundance. You just got to be knowing where you must look. And which bait they be hitting.'

'And I bet you know both.'

'I know a few things, yes sir. You live on this island your whole life long, you learn one or two things about those fish, yes, you do. Whether you spend a single day on a boat, or all your lifetime right here on land, you get to know about them wayward creatures, where they go and what they do. Yes, sir, you get an education growing up in this place, you certainly do.'

Bailey James looked down at the wad of sweaty bills in his hand and fingered them with a certain wariness as if he wasn't used to anything but the freshly minted green of the ultra-rich.

'While I'm here, I wanted to look up a couple of folks. Marlin people.'

'If they anchored here, I know them.'

'A.J. Braswell,' Thorn said.

Bailey's squint tightened.

'They here, all right. Yes, sir, the entire Braswell family. Their Hatteras yacht is down there on A dock, last slip. They just come back in a while ago.'

'They doing any good?'

Bailey James looked out at an overpowered dinghy skimming across his harbor.

'Thought you knew Mr Braswell.'

'Why do you say that?'

'You ask if they're doing any good, but that phrase don't truly apply to those folks, I don't believe.'

'I don't know them that well, but I thought they were marlin people.'

'They marlin people, all right. They big marlin people. But they don't go fishing like you and me go fishing.'

'More intense, huh?'

'You could say that. You could say more intense, I expect.'

Thorn looked off at the collection of white yachts, the end-of-day rituals. Crews hosing everything down, cocktails served on the aft decks, tanned women in long flowered dresses, marlin widows, showing off their lean bodies for the crew and the other marlin widows. Thorn tried to keep his voice neutral. Just shooting the shit, that's all.

'Sounds to me like there's something else about the Braswells you're not telling me.'

Thorn looked back at Bailey. The man had cocked his head, sharpened his squint. Thorn's attempt at casualness hadn't worked.

'You picking my brains, mister?'

Thorn smiled.

'How's a guy supposed to learn anything?'

Bailey James looked pointedly down at the sheaf of bills in his hand, Thorn's meager contribution to his retirement fund. Then looked at Thorn with an expectant lift of an eyebrow. But Thorn just shook his head. Ten dollars was all the gratuity he could manage. Around a place like that, it might take his remaining four hundred dollars to buy a cheeseburger. If he wasn't careful, he'd be starving by tomorrow night.

Bailey shrugged and closed his hand tightly around Thorn's cash.

'There's only one blue marlin those people want. All the other fishes of the seven seas could jump right onto their deck and those people wouldn't be one bit impressed, no sir, they wouldn't. Not one bit.'

'One fish?'

'Yes, sir, there's one fish they looking for and only one fish in the whole wide ocean blue that'll make those folks happy. The fish that killed their boy. That's what I hear. That's the story gets told about them. The fish that dragged their beautiful boy overboard and swam off with him, they're after that fish and that fish alone.'

Thorn looked out at the last pink tatters of daylight lying on the horizon back toward America. A throng of gulls followed a trawler into the harbor, a child on its deck tossing scraps of the catch up to the screaming horde.

254

'The Braswells hang out with anyone around the marina?'

'No, sir, those people stay tight to themselves. Unless there's something they might want from you, you just better stay back and keep your distance. They bring along their own security. Those big fellows in blue you see walking around with the radios and fancy pistols in their pants. They go where the Braswells go. If your name ain't on their clipboard, you don't get past. Far as I can tell, ain't nobody's name on that clipboard.'

'I see,' Thorn said.

'I bet it's the girl you're wanting to meet up with.'

'The girl,' Thorn repeated. 'You mean Morgan.'

'Oh, my, yes.' Bailey James smiled dreamily. 'I see a lot of women coming and going around here, wearing their teensy bikinis, showing off their fannies and their big store-bought bosoms. But there isn't but one Morgan Braswell. That woman's a double handful, yes, she most certainly is.'

Bailey disappeared inside his reverie, then a second or two later his eyes resurfaced and when he saw Thorn standing before him, he grimaced as if it were Thorn who had dragged him back.

'No offense, sir,' Bailey James said. 'But just looking at you and your raggedy boat and all, I'd have to say you're not exactly Miss Morgan's type. She tilts toward the more well-groomed gentlemen.'

'Yeah, it's true. My grooming's not my best feature.'

'And the other thing is,' said Bailey James, touching the roll of bills, 'don't look to me like you got a single thing those people might want.'

'You're right, I don't,' he said. 'But I'm working on it.'

Thorn rented a bicycle from the hotel office, put it on the tab for his slip, and he pedaled down the resort's long boulevard, waved at the uniformed officers in the guardhouse, and headed on out to the narrow public highway. It was less than a mile to the center of town, a straggling row of shops, a drugstore, a market, and some tourist stores that sold the usual T-shirts and island geegaws. He turned down Stede Bonnett Road and pedaled around the gaping potholes past some block houses with chickens and diapered two-year-olds lurching about in their dirt yards, squawking and screaming with terror and delight. One step up from a shanty town, this section was filled with flat-roofed, cement block houses painted in gaudy Kool-Aid shades. As if they'd splashed their concrete walls with paint as whimsical as they could afford to ease some of the dreary weight of their lives.

Though it had been twenty years, he imagined he would have no trouble recognizing the house, so vivid was it in his memory. But after winding aimlessly up and down the same set of streets for twenty minutes without success, he halted in front of an orange house with purple shutters, the only place he'd found that looked even remotely familiar. An old woman in a faded blue dress sat on the porch. From her cramped aluminum chair she'd watched Thorn pedal by her house several times, following his passages with candid curiosity.

In the yard next door, a half dozen kids were playing a screaming game of tag. They ignored Thorn as he climbed off his bike and rolled it into the woman's yard. She was a big lady with gray in her hair and she eyed him with a hint of droll disbelief. He gave her his best hello and apologized for disturbing her on such a fine night, and asked if she might happen to know the whereabouts of one Jelly Boissont.

Inside the house there came the heavy chime of steel against steel. Thorn recognized the sound from his high school days, all those tedious hours in the weight room. The unmistakable clang of twenty-pound plates sliding on and off the heavy bar.

The old woman took a breath, then another one. Studying Thorn, then surveying her yard and the surrounding darkness. As amused by this blond-haired white man who'd appeared in her front yard as she might have been by a talking pig. She fingered the handle of the aluminum cane that lay across her lap.

'I thought he lived nearby, though it's been a long time since I was last here. Maybe I'm lost.'

'Maybe you are,' she said. 'Maybe you aren't.'

'Is that name familiar, Jelly Boissont?'

'What if it is?'

'I have a proposition for Jelly. I was hoping he could help me with something.'

She gripped the cane and raised it into the air as if she meant to challenge him to a duel. Then she swung it to the side and pounded it against the frame of the screen door.

'Farley, get out here. They's a white boy here says he's got business with Jelly.'

'Are you Mrs Boissont?' Thorn said, edging closer.

'Not anymore I ain't,' she said.

A young man came to the doorway and filled it with his shoulders. He was shirtless and wore red-and-black striped bikini briefs that were cut so low a couple of inches of pubic hair spilled over the brim. Otherwise, his body was hairless and slick with sweat. His wide, solid chest tapered to an almost girlish waistline with ridged muscles in his arms and stomach that churned like oily snakes just below the surface of his gleaming skin even as he stood at rest. He wore his hair in Rastafarian dreadlocks that were tinted a brick red. He examined Thorn for several moments with wide-set, sulky eyes, all the while chewing on a wad of something large and leathery.

'I'm looking for Jelly,' Thorn said.

A flash of dark light passed through the man's gaze.

'No jelly around here, all we got is jam.'

The old woman chuckled quietly and stared down at her cane. It must've been an old refrain.

'He doesn't live here anymore?'

'Not here, not anywhere,' the young man said.

'He died?'

The young man pushed open the door and stepped outside. In the neighbor's yard the game of tag ceased abruptly, and the kids turned to feast their gazes on the young man's brawny body. They probably saw him every day of their lives, but he had the kind of body you could never quite absorb, brutish and graceful. A physique that probably filled them with never-ending awe. That one of their own could build himself to such stature and proportion must have seemed nearly miraculous. To Thorn such bodies always struck him as a little sad and pointless, like stuffing a six-hundred-horsepower engine under the hood of a family car.

The boy got a little closer to Thorn than he needed to.

'I'm sorry,' Thorn said. 'I didn't know he'd died.'

'He didn't,' the young man said. 'He's just waiting. We're all waiting.'

'What you want with Jelly?' the woman asked.

'He used to take me and my mother and dad fishing. He was the best.'

'He used to take a lot of rich white men fishing,' the old woman said. 'That don't make you special.'

Thorn looked back and forth between the two of them.

'Is he here?'

The woman chuckled, gave him a scoffing look.

259

'Now there's a good question. Is he here, Farley? Is your daddy here?'

The young man did an about-face and marched back inside the house.

'Go on, take a look,' the old woman said. 'But he ain't going to do you no good. Jelly ain't caught no fishes lately.'

Thorn went into the house. In the living room the big-screen TV was tuned to the weather channel. The tattered couch had once been a green-and-red plaid, the chairs covered in moth-eaten purple satin. Two white kittens were battling around the metal legs of a kitchen stool and the rest of the litter had taken up residence in a straw basket on the kitchen floor.

Thorn walked down the narrow hallway and stopped at the door of the first bedroom. Jelly Boissont was slumped in an ancient wheelchair that was positioned beside an open window that gave him a view of the neighbor's backyard, that is, if he could pull his chin off his chest and see. His hair was uncombed and looked like it had gone uncut for months, a wispy tangle of white. Clumps of wiry white hair curled from his chin and cheeks. He seemed to be dozing. A shiny ribbon of spittle coiled from his lips and hung like a silver thread from his chin.

Pressed against one wall was a tiny single bed. Against the other stood a wooden chair and a chest of drawers. The room smelled of urine and the sour reek of mildew and decaying flesh. An unemptied bedpan sat atop the dresser. The only sign of life in the room was the photographs that crammed the gray walls.

Thorn made a quick tour of the gallery. Hundreds of blue marlins hung from hundreds of weigh stations throughout the Caribbean. Jelly stood tall and straight and smiling beside an endless assortment of well-fed anglers. Sunburned and more often than not gripping beer bottles, these big white men grinned for the camera, full of bluster and macho high spirits, that afterglow that came from hauling those blue monsters to the surface. The photos seemed to cover Jelly's entire career, five or six decades. The clothes were different, the hats, the sunglasses, but neither Jelly nor his clients seemed to age.

Not until the handful of photos that hung beside Jelly's wheelchair. In those, the anglers were still the same big-bellied men in baseball caps, their sunglasses hanging on cords around their necks. One of the group always holding out the dorsal fin of the dead fish for display while the others kneeled or held their drinks up in a celebratory salute. The men were all middle-aged with a similar aura of vigor and bully-boy assurance, but Jelly was now shriveled and hunched in the shoulders. His smile no longer rooted deep. He looked out at the camera wistfully, a slight confusion in his eyes as if he could not remember the point of this ceremony.

On the opposite wall Thorn discovered a picture of Dr Bill and Kate Truman and a skinny twenty-year-old kid who bore a hazy resemblance to himself.

Someone had painted in white letters the weight of the marlin across its midsection: 896 pounds. A record at that time for those waters. A five-hour battle that Kate had won without complaint or jubilation. She'd beaten the fish and brought it to the boat, and as was the custom of the time, they'd killed that magnificent creature and hauled it back for weighing and display, its meat distributed later to the waiting dock kids.

Kate had her arm around Jelly's waist. Over several fishing seasons the two of them had become fast friends, an alliance built on their respect for each other's blend of tenderness and gristle. Dr Bill stood apart, looking out to sea. And standing just behind the fish was a scrawny black kid wearing only a pair of baggy shorts. He was stroking the flesh of that giant fish as one might touch the secret skin of a lover, looking out at the camera with the same sulky eyes he'd focused on Thorn a minute earlier.

'He's not going to be guiding you to no fish anymore,' Farley said.

Thorn took a last look at Kate and Dr Bill, then turned to the behemoth in the doorway. He'd put on a loose-fitting flowered shirt and yellow surfer shorts. But plenty of bulges were still exposed, his bull neck and his swollen forearms and calves.

'I'm not looking for fish,' Thorn said. 'I'm looking for an old man who lost his way.'

'Well, they's a lot of those,' Farley said. 'You come to the right place.'

'His name is Lawton Collins. He's about your father's

age, a retired Miami cop who still thinks he's carrying his badge. He's come down here looking for the people who killed one of his friends. Their name is Braswell.'

Farley blinked.

'You know them?'

'What the hell do you want, mister?'

Thorn mulled it for a second. To trust or not to trust, that was always the gamble. He glanced again at the scrawny boy touching the giant blue, then looked back at Farley.

'I need to find some way to get inside the Braswells' world.'

'You're white, you're already in their world.'

'I want to get closer. Real close.'

'Yeah? And who is this man, Lawton? He your daddy or something?'

'Not exactly,' Thorn said. 'But he's about as close to one as I have.'

'And you thought Jelly was going to help you buddy up to these people?'

'Jelly was catching blues before you or I were born. There isn't anyone who fishes down here who doesn't know him. And there isn't anyone who doesn't respect him. I thought he might know a way to open some doors.'

'All that's over with,' he said. 'All that's long ago finished and done.'

'What about you?'

The boy smoothed his right hand across the engorged

muscle in his left forearm. There was a faraway look in his eyes as if he were caressing someone else's body, some stranger who was inhabiting his same skin.

'What about me?'

'Are you a part of that world? The marlin world?'

Farley gave him a sour face.

'You mean, do I take the white man's money to lead him to the biggest, baddest fish in the sea? Do I show him the secret places it took my daddy his whole life to find? A hundred dollars in my pocket so some asshole banker that can't tie his shoes without help can take a glossy photo back home to Chicago, Illinois, or maybe even take that fish itself and hang it on his basement wall so he can look at it all the day long and pretend he's some big Ernest Hemingway with balls like oranges. You think I do that? You think I want to be like Jelly some day and sit in a wheelchair and all the people used to love him, used to buy him rum drinks, slap him on the back, introduce him to all their pretty blond wives, those people don't even know his name anymore, they don't pay his hospital bills, they don't come calling, say, Hi, Jelly, how's it going, old man, how's your wife and boy? Is there anything I can do for you, old Jellyroll, my buddy, any way I can pay you back for giving me the best goddamn hours of my life, the ones I'll remember when I'm lying on my bed, sucking down my last breaths. Is that what you think, white boy? I want to be a part of that world?'

Thorn turned and took a last look at the photo of

Kate and Dr Bill and the scrawny boy. He reached over and wiped the thread of spit off Jelly's cheek and dried his hands on his shorts. Jelly lifted his chin an inch from his chest, pried open his left eye, and peered up at Thorn. His lips twitched but he achieved only a faint gurgle. Thorn was turning away when Jelly lifted a crabbed hand off the arm of his wheelchair and reached out in Thorn's direction. Thorn took hold of the crippled hand, the bones as weightless as spun glass. He held the old man's hand for several moments until that one eye drifted closed again and Jelly's chin dropped back to his chest. Thorn replaced his hand on the wheelchair's arm and headed for the door.

He got only as far as the living room before Farley slapped a hand on his shoulder and wrenched him halfway round.

'Come here, white boy, take a look.'

Farley led him back down the hallway, past Jelly's room to a small cubicle at the rear of the house. In the center of the room was a weight bench. A bar with at least five hundred pounds was mounted in the cradle. On the far wall past the bench there was a shelf full of gold trophies and a scattering of photos.

Thorn walked across the room for a better look.

They weren't bodybuilding awards or photos of Farley clenching his biceps on some dais. They were marlin trophies. Firsts and seconds in some of the biggest tournaments in the Caribbean. Photos of Farley standing beside the same men his father had once worked for.

'You took over,' Thorn said.

'Nobody takes over for Jelly. That old man knows more about that fish than any human being ever walked this planet.'

'But you're good.'

'I'm not Jelly.'

'You're still good.'

The scrawny boy on the dock stared at Thorn.

'After Jelly, there's me. He's the man. I'm just a distant second.'

'And people know it. Marlin people know it.'

'The ones that matter do.'

'What do you know about the Braswells?'

'They're sons of bitches. Like all the rest of them. Only a little worse.'

'Anything else?'

'They don't fish by the same rules.'

'I hear they're after a particular fish, one that killed Braswell's boy.'

'Like Ahab,' Farley said. 'With about the same luck.'

'I want to get close to them. Buddy up.'

Farley shook his head.

'They're a family. No outsiders allowed. They got rent-a-cops to keep people like you away, twenty-four hours, seven days a week.'

'What if we could help them get to the fish they're after?'

Farley snorted with disdain and sat down on the end of the weight bench. For all his bulk he could look small sometimes, small and lonely.

'What I hear is, they got some electronic thing attached to the fish they're chasing. That's how the boy got killed, putting that electronic thing on. When that blue marlin surfaces, they can see it on a screen. They don't need a guide.'

Thorn looked at the weight bench, at Farley, at the trophies and the photos of sunburned men in T-shirts and baseball hats.

'What if someone was going after the same fish they're after? Trying to beat them to the fish they want so bad.'

Farley turned his head slowly and gave Thorn a suspicious scowl.

'And why the hell would someone do that?'

'Oh, I don't know. To get their attention. To piss them off.'

Farley lay back along the bench and fit his hands to the steel bar and drew a deep breath and lifted the five hundred pounds an inch or two out of the cradle. Thorn thought he felt the floor shift beneath his feet.

Farley held the weight there for the count of ten, his massive arms just beginning to tremble when he decided to ease it back down.

Pinpoints of sweat had broken out on Farley's forehead but he wasn't breathing hard. He lay flat on the bench for several seconds, considering the cracked and peeling ceiling overhead. Then he turned his eyes to Thorn.

'Exactly who the hell are you, mister?'

'Just some little boy,' Thorn said, 'your daddy used to take fishing.'

# 16

Saturday night an hour after sunset, two nattily dressed Bahamian police officers met Alexandra's chartered Cessna, saluted her with exaggerated respect, accompanied her through passport control, then hurried her to their open-air Jeep. They roared away into the night and in a few minutes were hurtling along a twisting road with only the moon for light. Alex got a series of quick, stomach-flipping views down into shadowy ravines, while her hair was snarled by blasts of wind from passing cars that careened by, only inches away.

The air was no cooler or drier, but somehow more refreshing than Miami's. Only two hundred miles away, but another century, another planetary system. Here, the sea scents flooded in from every direction and the long shadowy distances expanded everywhere into the boundless Atlantic. And though the sky was littered with stars and the moon was nearly full, the darkness on that remote road was more profound than any Alex could recall.

She could barely decipher the British burr of her driver, who had found no end of reasons to swivel around and shoot glances between her knees. He spoke in rapid bursts as he maneuvered them one-handed around the hairpins. He was a tall, narrow fellow with clever eyes and bright white teeth that he showed at every opportunity. His partner was small and glum, his compact body tightly filling his uniform, a blue suit adorned with gold buttons and epaulets. The glum one was named Darrell, while his chatty partner, their driver, introduced himself as Granger. Both had shaved heads that gleamed with starlight.

At the airport Granger informed her that it was a short drive, no more than twenty kilometers to the beach where the yacht had run aground. But after half an hour of being flung about without a seat belt in the rear of that speeding vehicle driven by a man more interested in looking up her skirt than in keeping them on the narrow band of asphalt, Alex was ready to revolt. She'd decided she'd rather hitchhike, walk, anything but this.

But as she leaned forward to make her demands, Granger slammed the shifter into a lower gear and cut the wheel sharply, and the Jeep launched three feet into the air over a sandy hump at the shoulder, then slammed through a stand of sea oats and whippy saplings and slewed down a steep embankment for thirty feet, spraying marl as they rode the face of a formidable dune and came finally to a stop on the hard-packed sand of a tiny beach.

And there, glowing in the golden light, tipping slightly to one side with its prow buried deep in the sand, was Arnold Peretti's two-million-dollar fishing boat. Apparently the tide had retreated since the boat rammed into the shore because now only a few feet of her stern was still brushed by the listless waves.

For a moment Alexandra studied the boat's enormous bulk, then she turned and drew her police flashlight from her duffel and climbed down from the Jeep.

'Do you require our assistance in any manner, Lieutenant?'

Though he'd made the same error at the airport, Alex had not corrected him. If being a lieutenant gained her any advantage, then by God, she was going to preserve the misunderstanding as long as possible.

'It's a crime scene,' she said. 'The less people tramping around, the better.'

Granger smiled and looked around until he spotted a wide, flat rock that looked inviting and told Alex that she was very welcome to take all the time she required, that he and Darrell would just rest for a while from their day's labors and perhaps indulge in a smoke.

Alex watched them walk away, then turned and began to circle the boat. The soft sand was tricky and walking was an effort. The hull was badly dented in several places near the bow, scuffed and banged along the keel. But it still looked seaworthy. After a minute or two of trudging, she found a place on the starboard side that looked promising. She got a foothold on a small chrome plate and chinned herself up onto the boat.

On the gunwale she sat for a moment to catch her breath. Wafting up from Granger's and Darrell's position near some scrubby vegetation was the unmistakable pungent spice of marijuana. She saw the glow of their spliff and heard their faint chuckling and the elegant cadence of their patois. These two fortunate souls, stranded so far from the messy back alleys of urban life, stretching out in this isolated cove lit by the moon, their air freshened by unceasing ocean breezes, these cops who laughed with the easiness of children.

Alexandra pushed herself to her feet. She wore a knee-length denim skirt and a long-sleeved white jersey. Unsure of local fashion, she'd dressed as blandly as possible, trying to strike a balance between casual and professional. Her leather sandals had rubber soles that squeaked faintly when she crossed the deck.

As she looked around, deciding where to begin, she tried to clear her mind. Stay positive, even though she was certain Lawton was long gone by now, off on the next phase of his inexplicable odyssey. But she couldn't let her expectations cloud her sight. She had to see what was here, not what she hoped or expected.

Usually she didn't have to summon such discipline. After ten years on the job, exercising a rigorous detachment in every kind of circumstance, grim and chaotic, risky or routine, Alexandra liked to believe she'd absorbed into her very marrow the lessons of her work. In those ten years she had purified her senses. Learned to see without the interference of ego or bias, to strip away her own point of view and become sublimely neutral. A tough, scientific mind recording in precise detail the bedrooms and alleys and backyards where rage and frenzy had torn apart lives and left behind wild montages of blood and gray matter, body parts and mangled corpses.

But tonight there was a shiver in her blood. Just as there had been a faint tremolo in her voice when she'd spoken to Granger a few moments ago. For this was not just another crime scene. As far as anyone could tell this boat was the last place her father had been seen. Dispassion was out of the question.

She looked over at the two cops trading their joint. Beyond them, moonlight quivered on the lapping waves. And in the heights of the sky, the million stars trembled like the glittering eyes of soldiers on the nervous eve of their first battle.

Alex drew a breath and clicked on the flashlight, held it near her right cheek, and fanned its light slowly across the cockpit deck. She stiffened and the air clenched in her lungs. For a second such a powerful wave of wooziness passed over her, she thought she might faint.

Before her, coating nearly every foot of the deck, were spatters of blood and fine red cobwebs and bloody footprints, large and small. Like some appalling work of extemporaneous art, with blood slung randomly here and there, loops and swirls, dots and smears, more blood coating the chrome rail and ladder up to the flybridge.

She swung the flashlight away from the deck and shined its beam out into the dark, where it was swallowed by the gloom. And held it there till she managed to bring her pulse back under control.

When she was ready, she turned back, steadied her light, and washed it again over that gory canvas. She kept her teeth clamped, breathed through her nose, managing a cold, bitter calm. There would be time in the daylight to photograph and study the patterns of the blood, to draw orderly conclusions.

The night was clear, no sign of a thunderstorm that might destroy this evidence. She could simply stay on board for the rest of the night, safeguard what was here. There was no hurry, nothing driving her to decode this mess right now.

She found a bloodless path to the door of the main cabin, turned the handle, and stepped into the living area. In the faint moonglow the leather upholstery was yellow and the barstools had legs of gleaming chrome. There was a flowery chemical taste in the cabin, some air-freshening device that Arnold must have used to combat the inevitable mustiness.

She stood for a moment in the center of the room and passed her light over the furniture, holding briefly on a shelf of mementos that Arnold had accumulated. Photos of a young, dashing Peretti standing alongside a variety of sleek and sporty women. On the bar she found a ceramic ashtray and a matchbook from Churchill Downs. And a wadded bar towel from the Doral Hotel, a couple of glass trophies from marlin tournaments, both of them fastened tightly to the shelves behind the bar. She scanned the room methodically, working as she'd been trained, breaking down the space into quadrants, exploring with her flashlight every surface, every crevice.

The décor was understated but classy. Cherry-wood cabinetry and mahogany trim, a light tan wall covering. Full-length tinted windows running down either side, an L-shaped coffee table with silk flower arrangement fixed neatly in its center. Pale yellow leather settees surrounded the table. She found some broken glass behind the bar, old-fashioned and martini glasses shattered on the parquet. No doubt flung from their shelves during Lawton's wild ride across Biscayne Bay.

She held the flashlight beam on the sparkling shards, then kneeled down and pinched up the edge of a small square bar napkin with an advertising logo. A blue dolphin rising from the waves to smile up at a bright golden stylized sun. ABACO BEACH RESORT was printed in blue below the surface of the sea.

She tucked the napkin in her skirt pocket and stood back up. She glanced around the room a moment or two more, but nothing struck her as the slightest bit out of the ordinary. Then she angled over to the window for a peek at her guardians. Their joint no longer glowed and both Granger and Darrell seemed to have dropped off to sleep on the flat rock. She was about to turn away when a blur of movement caught her attention. A shadow within the shadows moving along the sand halfway between the boat and the rock on which the two cops reclined.

She cupped a hand around her eyes and pressed her nose to the glass. But whatever had moved out there was motionless now. She shifted her gaze back to the sleeping cops. She could see the shine of Granger's forehead, and a couple of the gold buttons on his uniform. Sprawled beside him, Darrell was on his back, both arms flung over his head like a man trying to backstroke across solid stone.

She walked to the door and stepped outside, and held up the flashlight, pressed the button and trained it on the two men, first Granger, then Darrell. The beam was beginning to fade. Old batteries, rarely used.

Alexandra was about to call their names when she spotted the dark shimmer on Granger's neck. She focused the failing light on Granger, squinted through the dark, and made out a ragged gleam beneath his chin. Something that looked a great deal like the slow ooze of blood.

# 17

Alexandra staggered sideways, a gasp catching in her throat. She cut off the light and swung around to the side where she'd come aboard. But as she was lifting her foot to mount the gunwale, she heard the scuff of a clumsy step in the grasses nearby.

She stepped back, took a tight grip on the base of the flashlight. Black aluminum with four full-size batteries, heavy enough to serve as a nightstick for Miami patrolmen. She edged to the starboard rail, drew a breath, and peered over the side.

A man in a white shirt was smiling up at her. His hair was long and blond. His right arm hung casually at his side, the dark shine of a blade in his hand.

'Boo,' he said.

She cocked the flashlight back out of the man's sight.

'Drop the knife,' she said. 'Right now. Don't think about it, just do it.'

'Hey, lady. Who are you and what're you doing on my goddamn boat?'

'This isn't your boat.'

'Yeah, it is. See, here's my certificate of title.'

He raised the knife, and thrust it at her face. Alexandra ducked to her side, then lunged forward and clubbed him above the ear with the flashlight. He yelped and jumped back, then stumbled backwards into the shadows. She stood at the rail and aimed the flashlight into the darkness but could see no movement. She was passing the beam across a clump of bushes when behind her she heard a loud huffing, and whirled in time to see the man scaling the transom. Got just a fleeting glimpse of his round face and the blond hair swinging wildly as he hauled his bulk over the side.

By the time she was inside the cabin, he was on the cockpit deck, gliding past the fighting chair, heading her way. In his right hand was the long blade. Fumbling with the door handle, Alex watched him approach. She was trying to find a deadbolt, a lock of any kind, but there was nothing.

She swung away and sprinted across the living room, slipped into the narrow hall and slammed the mahogany door behind her. Next to the lever she found a small chrome bolt and shot it home.

Hardware too flimsy to hold back the heavyset guy, but it would slow him down, give her time to find a more potent weapon. Give her time to hide. Trapped now. No way out except through that door. A stupid move going inside, bad instincts. But it had happened so goddamn fast.

She flung open the first stateroom door. Scanned the space but saw only the twin bunks and a small locker. Nothing in the head. Even the medicine chest was empty. Arnold Peretti's spartan life at sea.

There was a knock at the door she'd locked. A polite tapping, four raps, then four more as if she might not have heard. As if she were napping and he was apologetically but insistently waking her.

She fled across the corridor to the next stateroom, threw open the door. A larger cabin than the first one. Probably the master suite. A king-sized bed with a red satin cover. Red pillowcases. A photograph on one wall of three racehorses in full gallop, one of them finishing a nose ahead. But what seized her attention was the couch.

The black leather sofa appeared to be molded into the cabin wall. Its seat was tilted up on hinges to reveal a narrow passage down into the bowels of the ship. She shined her light down the narrow tube on the chrome ladder that ran eight or nine steps to a fiberglass tunnel. Some kind of storage area or crawl space for working on the engines or air-conditioning.

Alex peered into the passage but didn't move. She wasn't claustrophobic, but she doubted she'd gain any advantage by squeezing down that ladder. It might be better to stand and fight, take her chances right here. Hope that her years of karate training would still be alive in her muscle memory, even though she'd neglected it these last few years, going soft and lazy as her spare time was consumed more and more by the care of her dad.

Down the hallway the knocking had ceased. A moment of silence, then the door exploded. It sounded like it had splintered in half. She heard the man's heavy tread in the corridor.

Without another thought Alex tucked the flashlight into the waistband of her skirt and ducked inside the passage, took three quick steps down the ladder, and shut the hatch above her. There was no locking mechanism on the underside of the lid. She had to hope her pursuer wasn't familiar with this aspect of Arnold's boat. Perhaps it was a custom feature. Something that could take hours to discover. That was her best chance, that Granger's and Darrell's disappearance would set off alarms and a posse would be dispatched. Though from the little exposure she'd had to the Bahamian police so far, such hope seemed a bit far-fetched.

She tried to keep her breathing quiet as she eased to the bottom of the tunnel. She switched on her flashlight, trained it on the wall beside her, but the dim light faded and was finally gone.

She patted down the wall on both sides of the ladder, searching for a light switch. Almost at the base of the ladder she located a small toggle. She had to hope the tunnel was thoroughly sealed and no light would escape above deck. But her choice seemed clear, either take the chance of being seen or try to find her way through the total darkness. She drew a slow breath, then flipped it on.

A few feet away a single fluorescent bulb sputtered. The light was so dim, there seemed little chance it would leak beyond that narrow space.

She settled herself on the floor and got her bearings. The passageway seemed to run the entire length of the boat. It was about six feet wide, but the ceiling was so low she had to kneel. There were open niches on either side where she saw insulated duct work for the air-conditioning and PVC plumbing pipes. There were other open areas that appeared to be storage bins filled with rudders, bilge pumps, an array of electronics parts sealed in plastic. Down the center ramp, the fiberglass floor was smooth and finished to a high gloss.

A ribbon of sweat tickled down her cheek and fell from the tip of her chin. Alexandra wiped it away, then dropped into a crouch and crawled toward the stern, listening to the tromp of the big man's feet on the deck above. It sounded like he was working his way down the starboard side, searching the two rooms opposite from the master stateroom. Only a few seconds away from entering Arnold's cabin.

At the third open compartment she found a set of wrenches clipped to the wall. She unsnapped the largest one, gripped it, swung it, but it didn't even have the heft of her flashlight so she put it back on the rack and scooted on down the tunnel.

As she was approaching the solid bulkhead, the fluorescent bulb fluttered and went out. Darkness thickened around her. A pang of dread fired through her chest. Why in God's name had she crawled into this place, this burrow, this mummy's tomb?

A silent scream grew inside her. She shut her eyes tightly, made a fist, ground her knuckles against the cool fiberglass floor, felt small grains of grit break her flesh.

And then the anger swelled. A sharp blast in her lungs. She opened her eyes and looked around her. Face hot, fury trembling in her muscles. More sweat slid down her temples, across her cheeks. She licked her salty lips and blew out a breath.

That thug was more than likely the same man who'd stabbed her father, sent him fleeing for his life. And here she was running from him, scuttling around in the absolute dark, flustered, confused, teetering on the edge of panic.

On her knees, she lifted her head, straightened up. Goddamn if she was going to keep running. She was going back and face the bastard, no more of this cowering bullshit.

But as she was turning, her sleeve snagged on the bulkhead and she halted, then swung back, smoothed her hand across its surface from one end to the other until she came to a straight seam in the fiberglass.

She ran her fingertip along it, tracing the cutout of a narrow hatch, no wider than an ironing board. She patted the wall until she located a simple lever recessed in the door.

Alex cocked the lever open, then put her shoulder against the fiberglass and nudged the hatch inward until it swung open onto an even darker space, fragrant with engine oils and gasoline and the thick fumes of stagnant bilge water.

She duckwalked sideways into the dark engine compartment. Warm water sloshed over her feet, her sandals soaked. She halted and listened but could hear nothing in that soundproofed room. She shut the hatch behind her and moved forward blindly, her hand outstretched. Her knee bumped hard against an unforgiving angle of steel. She stifled a cry and then, moving more carefully, she discovered a narrow aisle between the two giant engines, a gangway that led to the rear of the ship.

This had to be another exit. She'd been aboard enough boats to remember seeing engine room access hatches up on the deck of the cockpit. She clicked on the flashlight, tapped it hard on the side, focused its feeble beam on the overhead shadows, but the batteries gave her only a second of useless light.

As she was edging back toward the tunnel-hatch, she heard a voice through the hull, then a subtle shift in the boat as if the big guy had jumped back down to the ground.

Alex inched sideways along the narrow path between

the engines, her feet soaked now, sandals squeaking. When she reached the tunnel-hatch, she patted down the walls on either side of it, and yes, there was another ladder fixed to the wall.

Peering up at the underside of the deck, she thought she saw the dim outline of the cockpit access door. There were no more voices outside, no vibrations through the deck. Maybe the big man was mystified by Alexandra's disappearance and had abandoned his search. Or maybe he was outside with his knife cocked, simply waiting for her to pop into view.

She climbed the ladder and turned the silver knob and lifted the hatch an inch. Felt the night air rush across her face.

'We meet again,' the big man said.

She caught the quickest glimpse of him, kneeling at the edge of the hatch, peering through the narrow opening, stringy blond hair framing his round face. She slammed the lid shut and fumbled with the latch until she had it locked.

Alex stared up at the door.

'I don't want to hurt you,' the man said. 'I just need to find something on this boat. It belongs to me. I gotta check it over completely and you're down there where I need to search.'

'So we have a problem,' Alexandra said.

The man was silent for a moment.

Alex shifted the flashlight to her right hand, got the grip she wanted, maximum leverage, wiggled her arm to keep it loose, relaxed, get that extra whip and snap in her motion when the moment came.

'Who are you?' Alex said.

'I'm nobody.'

She stared up at the hatch.

'You're an employee, a hired hand.'

'Not exactly.'

'Who do you work for?'

She could feel him shift his weight on his haunches.

'I need to search down there,' he said. The hardness coming back into his voice. 'One way or the other I got to search.'

'Is it so important that you'd hurt me? Stab me if I'm in the way?'

'"Do what I tell you and don't make no fast moves – there's a lot of dead heroes back there."'

'What?'

'A crazed killer said that in *The Hitch-Hiker*, 1953.'

'Is that what you are, a crazed killer?'

Alex shifted on the ladder. She eyed the latch. It was possible the guy was lulled by now, standing too close to the lid. If she exploded out, surprised him, she might have one good shot. Then again, the angles were awkward. She didn't have much leverage on the top rung of the ladder. It would take two seconds, maybe three or four to get all the way onto the deck, find her balance, and be ready to fight. By then he'd have time to recover, maybe take a quick swipe or two with his blade.

No, she'd work the talk some more, see where it led.

'You like movies?' she said.

This time his silence lasted so long, she thought he might've left his post.

Then she heard a harsh rasping and peered up at the hatch cover.

She blinked, not believing her eyes. She shrank back, teetered on the ladder, had to snap a hand out to catch hold and regain her balance.

The silver tip of his blade was poking through the lip of fiberglass that held the hatch cover in place. He was sawing through the woven plastic as though it were paper. Even with an extremely sharp blade it would require phenomenal hand strength. But there it was, the weirdly serrated blade working around the lid, following the grooved seat of the hatch cover. Curls of shredded plastic fell into her hair like confetti. He was a quarter-way around. A little more and he could simply stomp on the hatch and it would explode in her face.

She raised the flashlight, shifted her grip, took aim with the butt, and hammered the blade. The first blow knocked it free of his hand, then she smashed it again and a third time and a fourth.

'Shit,' he said. 'Shit, what'd you do that for?'

She'd bent the blade at such a severe angle he couldn't pull it free. She nailed it one more time.

'Hey! That's a good knife. What the hell're you doing? You just ruined the Vaquero Grande.'

Alex pounded the blade twice more.

'Okay, okay, you made your point.'

'You stabbed that old man, didn't you? That was your knife sticking in his back. The old man driving this boat.'

The guy was quiet. She heard him resetting his feet. Less than an inch of fiberglass separating them.

'How the hell do you know about that?'

'The old man you stabbed is sick and confused. He's losing his memory. He might not know where he is or why he's there. I'm here to bring him home. That's all I want. I don't care about anything you might have on this boat. I'll get out of your way. But I want to get that old man back.'

'I can't help you there, lady.'

'But you know where he is, don't you?'

He hesitated a half second too long.

'Hell, no, I don't know where he is. I don't know what the fuck you're talking about.'

Alexandra could feel him moving around overhead, hear the grind of his boat shoes against the roughened deck as if he were pacing back and forth, trying to devise a strategy.

A truck blew past on the highway, tires squealing.

Alex twisted the lock open. She moved to a higher step, huddling into a crouch. Resetting her feet on the ladder, she cocked her weight against the hatch cover. She lowered her voice, tried to perfume it with a hint of erotic eagerness.

'Maybe there's another way to work this out.'

His movement halted.

She brought her voice down to a whisper.

'Do you know what I mean?'

'No,' he said. 'I don't.'

His voice moved nearer as though perhaps he were squatting close by.

With a throaty purr, she murmured something deliberately unintelligible.

'I can't hear you,' he said.

She let a second pass, time for him to lower himself still closer. Then she set her hands flat against the underside of the hatch, sucked down a quick breath, and uncoiled her legs, heaving upwards. She took two quick steps up the ladder, the fiberglass door slamming into some solid part of him. His skull perhaps, or knee. Whatever it was it sent him tumbling backwards and broke a sharp yelp from his throat.

She lurched onto the deck, swung the heavy flashlight against his shadowy shape, glanced off his wrist. He was sprawled on his butt, hands upraised to fend off her blows. She risked another shot and cracked him this time across the forearm and he cursed and scooted backwards out of range.

She blinked the focus back in her eyes and caught a glimpse of the silver glitter of a blade. A second knife. He was worming backwards past the fighting chair. The skin prickled on Alexandra's shoulders and neck. She'd vacillated a second too long, lost the momentum of her assault and her advantage. She swung around and scrambled over the edge of the transom, dropped down into the darkness. But she didn't gauge the distance well, twisting her right knee and crumpling hard against the sandy ground.

She hauled herself up, struggled into a clumsy trot, taking a quick look back at the beached yacht. If the blond man was pursuing her, he was staying well inside the shadows. She scaled one powdery dune and scuttled down the other side. Halfway down she caught her ankle on a hidden vine, floundered for a moment onto her knees, tipping forward, tottering, then lost her balance completely. She managed to tuck her head, lower her right shoulder and somersault the last ten feet down the steep hill of fine white sand.

She came to a halt in a grassy ditch. Dizzy and out of breath. Above her the dune glowed with golden moonlight. Somewhere in her tumble, she'd lost her flashlight. She lay still and listened for the squeak of his tread against the fine white grains, the chuff of his approach. But all she heard was the dry whisper of a breeze through the heavy fronds of a coconut palm like some bashful voice murmuring from the sky.

She got to her feet, staggered across another low dune till she located the Jeep. She climbed aboard, started it, shoved the lever into first, and tried to follow Granger's tracks back up the steep dune. The engine roared, sand flying behind her, the wheels slewing, but the Jeep plowed doggedly up the hill and crested the dune a few feet from the highway. She bumped onto the asphalt and slammed through the gears. Twenty yards ahead a white Toyota was parked on the shoulder of the road. Alex gave it a quick look, then revved the Jeep and hauled ass up the narrow highway.

# 18

A half mile down from Treasure Cay beach, Alex backed the Jeep into a narrow lane and waited for almost an hour before the white Toyota pulled onto the road and headed her way. She stayed put until it disappeared around the first sharp turn, then she cranked the balky engine to life. Grinding the gears, she lurched onto the road, got it into second, wound it to thirty, and slammed it into third.

She kept the lights off, staying well back of the Toyota. Then after a quick hairpin, suddenly a pair of headlights was bearing down on her.

The lights flashed and flashed again. Finally Alex realized her mistake and yanked the wheel left, fishtailing out of the path of a jitney bus, its horn honking wildly as it passed.

Heart hammering, she stayed in the left lane, switched on the lights, pushed the Jeep to forty, then forty-five, and watched as the Toyota's tail lights came back into view. She kept them in sight as she passed through a small settlement, a few shops, a brightly lit restaurant, then the road was swallowed by darkness again, snaking along the coastline, up and down a succession of gentle hills.

A good half hour later, after passing through two more small villages, the white Toyota wheeled off the road, making a hard right into the lighted entrance of a hotel complex. Alex drove past, shot a look at the lighted sign out front. Abaco Beach Resort. In a driveway half a mile farther on, she turned around and went slowly back up the highway and cut into the entrance. The Toyota had already passed the guard's gate and was headed toward the main buildings.

Alex eased up to the gate, ready to sweet-talk the guard, flash her police ID, whatever it took, when the chunky woman in a white uniform and white pith helmet saluted her and simply raised the gate. Nodding back, Alex let out a long breath and rolled into the compound.

She parked in a densely shadowed corner of the lot and sat there for a few moments trying to relax the clench in her jaw. She listened to a night bird calling from the high pines and the ocean breeze stirring their needles into an eerie whine. In the distance there was a band playing, and the sound of riotous voices, people high on the night air, on their immense good fortune, partying under the intoxicating tropical skies and a moon as ripe and golden as a fresh peach.

Two men lay dead on Treasure Cay Beach. She went over it slowly, tried to absorb the facts, measure the weight of her guilt. As she stared blankly through the windshield, an owl fluttered out of the darkness and landed on the hood. It hopped twice until it was facing in her direction, staring through the windshield with large, unflinching eyes. It was wide-shouldered and wore a long gray shawl like a monk's cloak.

She stared back, tempted to take the owl as a sign, a display of godly forgiveness sent down in feathery form. She gazed at the dignified bird for another moment, trying to believe, hoping to feel some small rush of comfort. But it just didn't wash.

Those two cops, Darrell and Granger. She'd dragged those innocents into harm's way without fair warning. Keeping them uninformed because her own mission seemed too critical to jeopardize with such petty worries. She betrayed her training, misled fellow police officers, put them in mortal danger. Two innocent men lay dead. No goddamn owl was going to absolve her of that.

Behind the hotel office Alex found an outdoor pay phone and managed to get through to the local outpost for the Bahamian police. Without preamble, she gave her name to the man who answered, described the events at Treasure Cay Beach, and told him her present location. The dispatcher was an older gentleman and he seemed bewildered by this grim flood of information.

'I have the officers' Jeep,' she said. 'I'm following one of the suspects now. I'm at the Abaco Beach Resort in Marsh Harbour.'

'You are a police officer from the United States?'

'That's correct. Alexandra Collins is the name. Miami Police Department. Except I'm not an officer. I'm just an ID technician.'

'A technician?'

'Crime scene specialist,' she said. 'Photos, finger-prints, like that.'

She could hear the scratch of his pencil as he crossed out words, added others.

'And there are two dead police officers?'

'Yes, their names are Granger and Darrell.'

'Granger McAdoo?'

'Granger is all I know,' Alex said. 'Granger and Darrell.'

'And this happened at the beach resort?'

'No, at Treasure Cay Beach. I'm at Abaco Beach Resort now.'

'And where is Granger McAdoo?'

'He's dead. Lying on a rock at Treasure Cay Beach. His throat was cut.'

The pencil stopped scratching.

'Hold on, missus, I must speak to the captain.'

The phone clattered onto a table and she heard him walk away, calling out in a shrill voice for his superior. Alex kept the phone pressed to her ear. From her position she could see most of the marina, row upon row of yachts sparkling in the moonlight. As she scanned the grounds, a husky man with stringy blond hair marched along the sidewalk heading toward the far dock. She wheeled around, slapped the phone back on the hook, and started after him. The police had enough for now, enough to find the bodies, locate the Jeep. She'd call them later, face the consequences.

She trailed the stocky man to the last dock. He was twenty or thirty yards ahead, returning helloes from some of the late-night revelers who'd spilled out onto the decks of a few of the boats. He wore dark shorts and a white T-shirt, boat shoes, the standard uniform from what she could tell. Alex hung back, strolling now, trying for a casual self-assurance she didn't feel. Her clothes were wrong, too citified, too dowdy for this brightly flowered, low-cut, strapless crowd. What she really wanted to do was run the chunky guy down, cuff him, slam him up against a wall, throttle him, then slam him again and again until he spilled his guts, revealed every last twist of the whole dirty mess.

Instead, she found a piling to lean on halfway down the dock, no one on the adjacent boats. Her hands were trembling but she pretended to gaze out at the moonlit water, with an eye on the blond guy, watching as a tall, muscular man in a uniform stepped out of the shadows and spoke to the stocky man, then moved aside and let him pass. Alex watched as he climbed aboard the white yacht moored at the very end of the dock.

'His name is Johnny Braswell.'

She swung around, bumped a shoulder into Thorn's chest.

'His boat is the *ByteMe*. B-y-t-e. Cute, huh?'

'What're you doing here?'

'Same thing you're doing, I imagine,' Thorn said.

He had on a blue denim shirt, sleeves rolled to his elbows, khaki shorts, and leather thongs.

'That's the Braswells' security guard down there. Guy by the name of Maurice. Nice enough fellow, but he doesn't have a very highly evolved sense of humor. I chatted him up earlier this evening and the guy didn't crack a single smile. Just stood there grinding his teeth, like what he really wanted to do was chew my nose off. So if you were planning to hop aboard the Braswells' boat to see if Lawton's inside, I'd think again. Looks to me like it's going to require a more creative approach.'

'Sometimes he used a fake finger,' Lawton said. 'Nobody ever noticed either, a little hollow finger that he gripped between his other fingers. And he could hide a key in there or a small knife, whatever he needed for a particular trick.'

'Houdini again,' Morgan said to Johnny. 'He's been talking about Houdini since he came on board.'

'The magician?'

'You know another Houdini, brainchild?'

'He hasn't said anything about the HERF?'

'Isn't that what I just said, Johnny? It's Houdini this and Houdini that.'

'Well, it wasn't on Peretti's boat. I checked from top to bottom. Zip.'

'Who was the woman, Johnny?'

'I don't know. She was just there with the cops. Maybe she was a cop, too, I don't know. "The work of the police, like that of women, is never over."'

'And what's that from, Johnny?'

'*He Walked by Night*, 1949. It's a semi-documentary.'

She angled close to Johnny, gave his eyes a careful look, trying to keep the anger out of her voice.

'And how'd she get away, Johnny? This woman.'

'She attacked me. Almost knocked me out. You want to feel the lump? It's like an ostrich egg.'

'No, Johnny. I don't want to feel your lump.'

Johnny stared at the stateroom wall.

'I send you out to do things and what happens, Johnny? What always happens?'

'I fuck up.'

'That's right. You fuck up. Always. Every time.'

Lawton was watching them. He was sitting on Morgan's bed. His wrists were clasped together with a plastic handcuff, ankles bound the same way. Just a simple self-locking cable tie that electricians used to bundle wires. Worked great as handcuffs, like what the cops used nowadays in riot situations, though Lawton didn't think much of them. A flick of a sharp knife and the cuffs were off. All that disposable stuff seemed unprofessional to him. Give him a good pair of steel manacles any day, shackles, irons, something with a little heft.

The young woman, Morgan, was wearing a white robe. She had short black hair, parted on the side like a man's, and her eyes were a bluish-white color like a welder's flame, the kind you can't look at long or you go blind. Lawton wasn't looking at her eyes or any of the rest of her, at least trying not to. He couldn't help himself now and then because her robe kept falling open and one of her breasts peeked out. Lawton had a soft spot for breasts. Even a woman like this, an obvious felon, it gave him a jolt of pleasure to glimpse that pink tip.

He wasn't sure why he was here. Wasn't even sure where he was. He'd known earlier but now he was tired and the reason for his being here had faded. It would come back though. He wasn't worried about that. All he needed was a reasonable night's sleep, and he'd remember everything again, and get on with whatever it was he was doing, probably an investigation of some kind. That's what he did. Lawton Collins was a cop. And a damn good one if he didn't mind saying so himself.

'You'd think someone would notice a man with six fingers,' Lawton said. 'But no, they didn't. Not once in his long career did anyone ever notice.'

Johnny stepped up to the old man, drew back his right hand, and whacked Lawton across the cheek. Red shards flashed in his head. Lawton blinked. His eyes watered and the room went muddy.

'Johnny, what the hell are you doing?'

'I'm hitting the man who walked off with the HERF and won't tell us where he hid it.'

He slapped him again on the other cheek. The room got muddier, starting to spin a little. Lawton blinked to slow it down.

'Stop it. The old man can't remember his own name, how's he going to remember where he put the HERF?'

'Early in his career,' Lawton said, 'Houdini used to let people from the audience tie him up, use whatever knots they wanted, tie 'em as tight as they liked. Then he'd go into a cabinet onstage. And if he couldn't untie the knots, he'd cut them with a knife he'd hidden in the cabinet, then he'd hide the cut-up pieces of rope in that same compartment and step out, holding up a new length of rope that he'd stashed inside the box. But later on, when he got really good, he'd sit right out in the middle of the naked stage, all the lights on full-blast, no funny business. Just do it with skill. Kind of skill that only comes with a lifetime of practice.'

Morgan sat down on the edge of the bed.

'This is what I've been listening to all night. Houdini bullshit.'

Johnny reached into his pocket and came out with his three-inch Ka-Bar.

'It was never magic, it was always skill,' Lawton said. 'That's my point. Something might look like magic, but it never is, it's always just talent. And it works the other way, too, somebody with a big talent, when they do that thing they've learned how to do, it looks so amazing, it's like magic. You stand there looking, shaking your head, not believing what you just saw. So it goes both ways. That's my point. Magic is skill and skill is magic.'

He'd gotten their attention. Morgan and Johnny were both staring at him. The woman with the welding-torch eyes, the boy still gripping the knife, a little sweat showing on his forehead.

'I'm going to cut him.'

'No, you're not.'

'I'm going to give him some reinforcement of the negative kind.'

'I said no, Johnny. We're not cutting on him.'

'What're you, getting soft?'

'Yeah,' she said. 'Maybe that's it. Maybe I'm getting soft.'

'Fuck soft,' Johnny said. 'We need that thing back, right? This geezer knows where it is. It's simple. We cut it out of him.'

'No, Johnny.'

'You just sit there and be soft, Morgan. Watch how it works.'

'This isn't a movie, Johnny. We're not mobsters. Leave the old man alone. I've had enough of this.'

Johnny stepped over to Lawton and gripped his right ear. Tugged hard on his earlobe, stretching it out. Then Lawton felt the cold burn of the blade against his flesh, and a hard sting like a hornet. It hurt, but Lawton had felt worse. That time he'd snagged his wedding ring on the railing of a boat when he jumped ashore. It almost tore his finger off. That was worse. Or passing the kidney stone. But this was bad. It hurt in the pit of his stomach and it hurt in his teeth. The room was woozy.

Johnny stepped away and held up the morsel of skin.

Blood flowed down Lawton's shoulder, warm and gluey.

'Where'd you hide the HERF, old man? You tell us right now, or we're going to keep cutting off little pieces till there's nothing left but the stump of your dick.'

Lawton blinked. The hornet sting was spreading its poison juices down his throat, numb and aching at once.

'You think I could have some water?' Lawton said. 'All this talking, I've worked up a thirst. And some ice if you've got it.' He looked down at his hands. They were swollen and turning purple. He flexed his

302

jaw. It was starting to ache, too. He looked back up at them, these people he couldn't quite place. His hosts. 'A squeeze of lime would be nice, too. But don't go to any trouble.'

# 19

Alex ordered a bottle of Kalik and Thorn told Julius, the bartender, to make it two. When she turned her head away, Julius gave her a quick inspection and shot Thorn an approving wink. Thorn shrugged. Yeah, she was better than he deserved, but sometimes a guy got lucky.

'Lawton showed up around sunset,' Thorn said.

She swung around and gave him her complete attention.

'He's here? You're sure?'

'Still wearing the same blue T-shirt and yellow shorts. I asked around, you know, very quietly, and found a couple of people who'd seen him. A maid and a yard guy. Dressed like that, he stood out around a place like this.'

'He's on that boat. The Braswells have him.'

'Probably, but we don't know that for sure.'

'The kid, Johnny Braswell, I followed him here from Treasure Cay. He was there to search Arnold Peretti's boat. There's something on it they wanted. Dad came here to confront the Braswells. That's how they must have known where the boat was. He told them.'

'And what do they want?'

'You know what, Thorn. Arnold had the HERF at Neon Leon's. He was about to show it to Charlie Harrison, with the *Miami Weekly*. He was going to expose the Braswells, but something happened. They had to make a run for it. But someone was hiding aboard Arnold's boat with a knife. The same guy I confronted tonight. This man cut off Arnold's finger and he stabbed Dad in the back. Dad and Arnold tried to fight him off. Dad apparently was at the wheel. Arnold got thrown overboard, the other guy, too. Dad wound up with the HERF. And the Braswells know that and they have him on board their boat.'

'Maybe,' Thorn said. 'Or maybe he's curled up in the shrubs, catching a nap.'

She slid off the stool, started away, but Thorn grabbed her shoulder and she halted.

'What're you going to do, throw a choke hold on Maurice, storm the ship?'

She swung around, snapped her right arm up, and broke his grip with a stunning whack.

Thorn rocked backwards, almost went off his stool.

His right hand numb. Several drinkers at the bar turned to watch.

'Jesus,' he said. 'What the hell was that?'

'Don't put your hands on me again.'

He showed her his palms.

'Was that karate?'

'Rudimentary,' she said. 'First lesson, first night.'

'I assume you went to more than one class.'

'Thorn,' she said. 'I could break every bone in your wrist. Then work my way up your arm.'

'Pleasant thought.'

'A thought you should consider before you try strong-arming me again.'

'Well, I'll know who to call when I need a bone broken.'

'You're not funny, Thorn. Whoever gave you that impression misinformed you.'

'Hey, look,' he said. 'We want the same thing. It's a question of strategy. You go running down the dock right now, sure, it's how you feel, you're going to do whatever's necessary to get your dad back, but the impulse is wrong. Think about it. If he *is* onboard and those people get wind somebody's onto them, they'll throw off their lines, be gone in a minute. Where'll we be then?'

'There is no we,' she said.

'Jesus, go ahead, then. Be a goddamn idiot, get it out of your system. But if you go rushing down there right now, believe me, you're not ever going to see that old man alive again.'

The veins rose in her throat.

'You're a prick, you know that?'

'You're not the first to notice.'

Julius was back with the beers. He set them on the counter, polished it with his rag, gave Thorn a commiserating smile. This one was a handful.

'Take a second, Alex. Cool off, think about it.'

Another vein had surfaced in her temple.

'All right, goddamn it,' she said. 'I'll give it a second. I'll think about it.'

She took her stool again and Julius raised his eyebrows. Just confirmed the bartender wisdom he'd volunteered earlier in the evening. You never knew what a woman was going to do. They were complicated biological creatures, driven by more mysterious forces than men. So you made allowances.

Alex had a sip of her beer, then another.

Thorn looked at her left arm, the dusting of black hair against that white flesh. He looked at her knobby wrist bone, at the web of veins crossing the back of her hand. She didn't wear nail polish. Her fingers were long and slender. Long enough to palm a soccer ball. Remarkably large. A feature he'd always liked in women. Don't ask him why, probably some terrible repressed disorder, a hand fixation.

Alexandra set the beer down and picked it back up immediately and had another sip. He liked that, too. That was a good way to drink beer. One sip and then another one right after. He was warming to her. Warming to her moves, to her arms and hands. Maybe if her hostility quotient dropped into the single digits, he could warm to the rest of her.

'I could call Romano, try to finagle a warrant,' Alex said. 'But that could take days, all the bureaucracy.'

'I'm working on something,' Thorn said. 'A plan I hatched tonight.'

She swung around, studied him a moment.

'What the hell are you anyway? Some kind of amateur vigilante?'

Thorn looked her in her eyes. They were powder blue, edged with a darker shade, and all that blueness stood out vividly against the white skin and black eyebrows. There was nothing to read into any of that. People exercised no volition in the choice of their eye color or the shade of their skin. It revealed nothing about who they were, what values they held, their tendency toward altruism or greed. The best you could say about such a combination of shade and tone was that it was pleasant to look at. In this case, exceedingly pleasant. Beyond that, Thorn was still reserving judgment.

'You drop everything and come over to the islands, hatching plans. I'm asking you a question, Thorn. What are you?'

'I'm an interested party.'

'You have one brief encounter with my dad and you drop everything and come running to his aid.'

'Yeah, I know, it seems a little reckless. But your dad is a compelling fellow. And then there's the airplane crash. I was out there when it came down. I was the first person on the scene. I pulled some people out of the water and took them over to a little beach and then went back and got some others. If you're asking why I'm here, it's because of those people who died in that crash. And because of your dad. Is that enough for you?'

She moved her eyes over his face.

'That was you on the news? The man in the skiff?'

He looked back at her and said nothing.

'You know, I looked you up, Thorn. I brought you up on the computer.'

He smiled, dropped his eyes to his beer.

'I'm flattered.'

'We have pretty fair resources, the police department. But you seem to have done a good job staying off the radar.'

'I'm a retiring kind of guy.'

'Bullshit. Just because you haven't got a driver's license or a social security card or ever paid income tax, that doesn't make you retiring.'

'Well, I try,' he said. 'But things happen.'

'Looks like a lot of things happen to you. Last few years you and your buddy Sugarman have been front-row-center at the scene of the crime quite a few times. Like you specialize in these things.'

'We're usually on the right side.'

'Point is, you're not a retiring guy at all. This is a way of life for you.'

'I keep getting dragged into things. People show up, they need help.'

309

'Like my father.'

'Like him, yeah.'

'You don't go looking for this stuff? Stick your nose in things. Like some kind of hobby.'

'Look, I tie my bonefish flies. I fish for my supper. I try to watch the sun set every night it's not raining. I read library books before I fall asleep. It's a simple life. I'm not looking for trouble.'

'I don't know what to make of you, Thorn.'

'You're not alone.'

She was definitely a hard-ass. But he was starting to get glimpses of another side, not soft exactly, but sensitive, aware, thoughtful. Something a little less brittle than what her voice suggested.

'You grab my arm, keep me from running off and acting impulsively, but from what I can tell, that's just what you've done on several occasions. You've acted impulsive as hell. Gotten yourself into some ugly situations.'

'I'm trying to do better. Learn from my mistakes.'

They each had a sip of beer. He watched a couple across the bar who were wearing matching flowered shirts and were necking openly. Both were blond and both were burned a bright crimson. Newlyweds, probably. The moon was full. It was having its effect on them, just as it was stimulating the fish that lived fathoms below the surface of the sea. Making everyone a little edgy.

On the stool next to the honeymooners, Jelly Boissont's son, Farley, was chatting with a tanned man in a baseball cap. There was a blue marlin on the breast of his shirt and under it was stitched the name of his boat. Another couple of guys were leaning over Farley's broad shoulders to listen in. Blue marlins were embroidered on their caps. Farley must've felt Thorn's gaze, because he looked up, glanced across the bar, nodded ever so slightly and got back to work. Spreading the word. Dropping little specks of meat and blood and gristle into the water. Chumming it up.

'I don't trust you, Thorn.'

He nodded. 'That's understandable. You barely know me.'

She touched the lip of her beer bottle with a fingertip. Her long, slender fingers. Her wrists, that sprinkle of black hair.

'I'm trying to find something about you to like.'

He looked at her eyes again.

'Some people find my boyish grin appealing,' he said. 'And of course, there's my snappy repartee.'

She pressed her lips together as if stifling a smile. Then she lifted her beer, had a long pull, set it down, and pushed the empty bottle forward onto the bar. Julius was there in a second with another.

'Well, if you discover anything appealing,' Thorn said, 'let me know. I could use a boost.'

A tiny smile made its way to her lips. Not much, but enough to turn the tingle he'd been feeling into a full-blown quiver.

'Let's hear this plan,' she said. 'I'm not saying I'm

going along with anything, but I'm prepared to listen. That's all.'

'You see that guy across the bar, one in the pink hibiscus shirt? Muscles everywhere? Don't worry about staring, everybody does.'

Alex tipped to her right and peered through the crowd.

'Dreadlocks? Sad eyes?'

'That's the one.'

'So?'

But before he could tell her about Farley Boissont and their scheme, two Bahamian police officers appeared across the bar. They were scanning the faces of the drinkers, moving down the bar methodically. Behind them, by the lighted swimming pool, four more officers worked their way around the deck, asking questions, taking careful looks at each of the guests.

Alexandra slid off her stool.

Thorn glanced at her, then looked back at the cops circling the bar, coming closer. The bar patrons pulling out their wallets, showing IDs.

'Shit,' she said. 'Shit, shit.'

'Is there something I should know?'

Her eyes were skimming the grounds, looking for a way out.

'Where are you staying?' she said.

'On my boat.'

'Room for me?'

'Two bunks, yeah. It's no yacht, but it's comfortable.'

'Don't get any ideas, Thorn.'

He showed her his palms again.

'I like the bones in my wrist just like they are.'

'Let's go,' she said. 'But keep it casual.'

He got down off the stool and they eased through the crowd, moving nonchalantly, taking the long way back to his boat, walking shoulder-to-shoulder through the shadows and across the well-tended lawn.

# 20

Sugarman found a parking spot on Ocean Drive just south of Fifth and walked the two blocks to the Palm Air Towers. The condo had no tower and only one scrawny palm, but there *was* a little air coming in off the Atlantic. The building was a pale pink three-story with blue and green neon swirls around the name and a couple of other halfhearted Art Deco flourishes. Not the kind of place Sugar would've pictured. A guy who spent his life as a Miami Beach bookie should've had a penthouse in one of the thirty-story monstrosities up near Fortieth. A place he could walk across the street to the Bal Harbor shops and buy a fifty-thousand-dollar tie pin.

Saturday night, getting close to midnight, and the South Beach cruisers were out in force, a solid line of stalled traffic from Penrod's to the north end of the strip, a lot of woofers and tweeters shaking the air, muscle cars and rental convertibles and some hundred-thousand-dollar jobs, midlife-crisis mobiles from the Gables and the Grove, stockbrokers and realtors showing off their new hair transplants and anorexic wives.

It was a two-birds-with-one-stone trip to Miami. Sugarman had to make the trip anyway for a case he was working. His only job at the moment, if you could call it a job, was tracking down a deadbeat father whose ex-wife and four kids lived a couple of doors down from Sugarman in Key Largo. The ex-wife worked three jobs and the two oldest kids worked as well, but it wasn't enough to pay the bills for the youngest, who had cerebral palsy and needed a full-time nurse. The father was an optometrist. For years he'd examined Sugarman's eyes. Nice enough guy, Chamber of Commerce, Rotary, upstanding. But when he divorced his wife and moved up to Miami with his Cuban sweetheart, all communication ceased. His ex-wife knew he was up there, but didn't know exactly where or how to force him to pay the court-ordered child support. For a few weeks Sugarman tried the regular channels. But nobody in child welfare had enough time to drive out and serve the guy papers. So Sugar went up to Miami and located the eye doctor's garden apartment on a lake near the community college. Just after suppertime, his Hispanic girlfriend answered the door in a see-through nightie with fluff around the collar. At Sugarman's ankles a little white dog flew into a frenzy, yipping and snapping at the air. The eye doctor came out of the bedroom, stumbling, all smiles, until he got close enough to see who it was. Then his eyes went cold. He was reeking of booze and marijuana. Across the room a giant aquarium covered the wall. It was swarming with a colorful array of exotics. Sugarman stood for a moment staring at the collection. There were enough high-priced creatures in that giant tank to pay for a full-time nurse for a couple of years.

Sugar slid past the girlfriend, put a hand on the eye doctor's chest, and backed him into a corner, knocked over a table lamp doing it, while his girlfriend pounded on Sugar's back every step. He got into the doctor's face and told him what he was going to do. Nothing tonight. But next time, he was bringing a baseball bat and sharp stick and one of them was going into the doctor's eye and the other was going up his rear. Unless, of course, the doctor did the right thing and started sending the checks. The guy was all bark at first, threatening, going to call the police. Go ahead, call them, Sugar told him, getting his voice very low. Then he moved a little closer to the doctor, and lifted his hand and ran his pointing finger lightly over the eye doctor's cheeks, then drew a line across his throat. The doctor became very compliant. Eyes getting soft and wet. The girl stopped hitting Sugarman and even the dog shut up. It was amazing what a discreet little threat could do. Sugarman had seen it in a movie somewhere. Some Mafia thing cooked up by a Hollywood nitwit. But it worked. The fingertip across the throat. Man, he'd have to keep that in the repertoire.

Sugarman probably wasn't going to get paid for the eye doctor case, which was fine, and he sure as hell wasn't getting paid for this one. Just doing it to help out his buddy. Thorn off on another pilgrimage. So it fell to Sugar to work the trenches, the boring stuff he was so good at. It worried him sometimes. Thorn, the action hero. Sugarman, the plodder. Not exactly the role he would've chosen. Though the fact was, he got into police work in the first place not to rev his heart, but to make a difference in the world. Help his fellow man. Dumb but true. Which, come to think of it, was a pretty good motto for Sugarman, an all-purpose rough-and-ready description of his character, the trajectory of his life. Dumb but true.

The manager of the Palm Air Towers was a twenty-something guy with purple hair the texture of straw. There were enough baubles hanging from the kid's right ear to start his own pawn shop. On his flat chest somebody had tattooed a butterfly that looked like it was only half finished. For good measure his right nipple was lanced by half a dozen silver studs. The guy wore black running shorts and quilted silver booties. Cold feet on an eighty-five-degree tropical night – some kind of health warning there.

Across the room the TV was tuned to a professional

wrestling match, and when the kid came to the apartment door to speak to Sugarman, his eyes never left the action.

'Peretti died. He drowned or something. It was in the paper.'

'I know that,' Sugarman said. 'I just wanted to see if he had any friends around here, people I might be able to ask a few questions.'

'Friends?'

It sounded like an alien concept to the kid.

The boy fingered one of his nipple studs while he stared at the TV. A blond muscleman bounced around the ring ranting at the audience and pounding on his chest like a chimp.

Sugarman considered trying the finger-across-the-throat thing to get the kid's attention, but he doubted it would achieve the right reaction. One good threat and this boy looked like he might swoon right into Sugarman's arms.

'Did Peretti hang out with anyone around here? You got any names?'

'Not around here, no.'

The blond wrestler was flanked by six bikini girls. Rough-looking ladies, the kind who grind up biker chicks and sprinkle them on their breakfast cereal.

'Hey, kid. You think you could give this your undivided for about ten seconds,' Sugar said. 'It might be important.'

A big, dark-haired man climbed into the ring and snuck up behind the blond guy and whacked him over the head with a folding chair. The apartment manager chuckled.

'His daughter lives in Palm Beach. Some rich bitch.'

'Peretti's daughter?'

'That's who we were talking about, right? Arnold Peretti, the dead guy.'

'That's right.'

'She came and took away all his stuff.'

'You have her address?'

The boy chuckled again as more men wielding folding chairs piled into the ring.

Sugarman reached out and put a finger on the boy's chin and steered his face around.

'You got the daughter's address?'

The boy looked at Sugar as if he'd just raised a folding chair over his head.

'Yeah, yeah,' the kid said. 'It's around here somewhere.'


Sugarman called Angela Peretti from a booth on Collins Avenue, apologized for bothering her so late, and asked if she'd talk to him. She didn't mind. He could come on over. She didn't sleep that much, not at night anyway. There was something weird about her voice, something a little drifty and unfocused, like maybe she was absorbed in the same wrestling match as the kid.

It took him an hour and a half to get to her place, a two-story French provincial house a block from

319

the ocean. The street was lit by dozens of security lights. Two in the morning and hardly a shadow to be seen.

She met him at the front door in her pajamas. V-neck top with red-and-green flower print, shorty bottoms that matched. She didn't seem particularly shy, standing barefoot out on the porch. She was in her early to mid-forties, with straight brown hair and gray eyes and a little ski jump nose. A tricky way of looking at you, quick, darty glances, then looking away at the trees or shrubs or dark sky. Like a plane strafing a target, zooming in, shooting a look, then gone.

'I'm sorry to bother you at such a late hour. Thanks for seeing me.'

'You're a shamus?'

'Not many people call me that, but yeah, I guess I am.'

She strafed him with another look, then fixed her eyes on the trunk of the oak in her front yard. The pleasant smell of the ocean was stronger up there than on Miami Beach. A lush, doughy aroma that, together with the untamable rumble of the surf, must have been a constant reminder of how precarious their perch on the edge of the continent was.

Angela stood beneath a set of halogen security lights and stared out at her broad front lawn. She had freckles on her face and arms and more freckles in the V of her pajamas. Sugar was fairly certain freckles covered the entire surface of Angela Peretti. Not that

320

he particularly wanted to find out. It was just idle speculation, something to do during the long pauses in their conversation.

'I'm sorry about your father's death.'

'He was an old man,' she said. 'Old men die. He was also a career criminal. In the kind of business he was in, he was lucky to have lived so long.'

'Still . . .'

'Are you working for the Braswells?'

She skimmed her eyes across his face, saw his surprise.

'I didn't think so. You don't look like the kind of people they hire.'

'And what do they look like?'

'Seedy,' she said. 'Lower life forms.'

She looked across the street at her neighbor, who had come out to stand on the front porch of his three-story Tudor mansion. The portly, white-haired man was staring openly at Sugarman. Probably the first time he'd ever seen an African American in his part of town. In Palm Beach the guys they brought in to polish their brass and pressure-clean the mildew off their imported tile had graduate degrees and all their shots and all their boosters and at least three ancestors from the *Mayflower*. Around there even the ivy got a background check before it was allowed to twine.

'You okay, Angela?' he called.

'Just fine, Vincent,' she called back.

'I heard voices,' he said. 'My bedroom, it's right here in front.'

'We'll try to keep it down,' Sugarman called to him.

He gave Sugarman a hard look, then about-faced and marched back inside, probably to call the riot squad.

'So you're a private dick, huh?'

Sugarman made himself breathe.

'I am.'

'You don't act like one. You act like a regular guy.'

'I'm one of those, too.'

She squinted at him, blinked, then looked back at her expensive landscaping.

'So who *are* you working for?'

'Good question. I guess I'm working for an old guy named Lawton Collins.'

'I know Lawton. You're a friend of his?'

'I met him once,' Sugarman said. 'But he makes a strong impression.'

'He has a debilitating memory impairment,' Angela said. 'Second stage, it could last for five, six more years just like that, or he could take a quick dive tomorrow, not be able to tie his shoes or feed himself.'

Sugarman nodded.

'He seemed fairly lucid to me. Half the time anyway.'

'Lawton and my dad were friends. My dad liked to spend time with Lawton. He said it was inspiring.'

'Well, he's run off somewhere,' Sugarman said. 'He's trying to track down Arnold's killer.'

'And you're trying to track him down.'

'That's right.'

'Is someone paying your fee?'

'This one's off the books,' Sugarman said.

'The police think Dad's death was accidental. But I don't buy that.'

'Lawton's convinced it was a murder. And he was there, an eye-witness.'

'What's your rate?'

Sugarman told her.

'Okay,' she said. 'I'll triple that, and I'll pay you a twenty-thousand-dollar bonus if you see to it that the entire Braswell family winds up in jail.'

Sugarman smiled.

'I'm afraid I couldn't do that.'

'My father provided very well for me. I've got a bundle.' She was speaking to the eastern quadrant of the sky.

'I'm sure you do, but I can't take your money.'

'Well, then I won't tell you anything. I'll just shut the door and leave you standing out here. See how long you last in the wilds of Palm Beach.'

Sugarman smiled. The woman had her chin in the air, showing the freckles on her throat, eyes on the sky like she was consulting the Big Dipper.

'You drive a hard bargain.'

'So are you in my employ now? You'll find out who killed my father?'

'Okay,' he said. 'Sure, why not? I'll try. But I can't promise who'll go to jail.'

'Okay, then. I guess the first order of business is to grill me.'

'I don't usually grill my clients. I reserve that for my suspects.'

'Don't you want to ask me anything?'

'All right,' Sugarman said. He was smiling. He couldn't help himself. This woman had an elfin mischief about her. 'Why do you think your father was murdered?'

'That's pretty general,' she said.

'I like to start general and work toward the specific.'

'Okay,' Angela said. She gave him a fleeting glance, then her eyes sailed away to the stars again. 'My dad knew something was very wrong in the Braswell family. And what he knew got him killed. If Lawton Collins knows the same thing my dad knew, then it could get him killed, too.'

'You know what that thing is?'

'Yes,' she said. 'I certainly do.'

'Is it about a ray gun?' Sugarman said. 'Airplane crashes?'

The woman stopped breathing and brought her eyes back from the heavens and gave Sugarman her full attention.

'You know about MicroDyne?'

'MicroDyne,' Sugarman said. 'I heard a little about it.'

'A.J. Braswell's company,' she said. 'He was the

324

founder. They have a plant out near the turnpike, west of town. They process computer parts. Coat microprocessors and chips and things like that with a special material A.J.'s son invented. It's a complicated process called spark plasma sintering. But A.J. doesn't run the company anymore. His daughter runs it now. Morgan Braswell. She's an evil bitch.'

She looked at him straight on.

'An evil, evil bitch,' Angela said.

She lifted her head a little as if overcome with pride for getting the awful truth out into the open.

'There's a man you should talk to. He's A.J.'s partner. His name is Jeb Shine.'

'What's he going to tell me?'

She took a breath. Sent her gaze out into the galaxies.

A shirtless man with a bald head and long fringe hair stepped out from behind the door. He had a long, pale face and brown eyes and a mournful mouth. He was wearing blue-and-white seersucker shorts and red tennis shoes with the laces undone. His chest was shapeless and his belly swelled over the waistband of his shorts. Angela looped an arm around his and tugged him out onto the porch.

'Jeb's been eavesdropping, haven't you, sweet pea?'

Jeb gave a curt nod.

'Jeb and I are engaged, Mr Sugarman. We met at a party a year ago and started talking and found out we had a lot in common. Isn't that right, Jeb?'

Jeb nodded again, his eyes on Sugarman's. Sugar

feeling a sag of disappointment; this woman, a complete stranger, lifting his spirits with her flirty looks, then out walks the slob boyfriend.

'You have something you want to tell me, Jeb?'

'Angela's doing a pretty good job. If she needs me to fill in any blanks, okay, I'm ready to do that.'

Angela Peretti blushed and lowered her eyes and peered out into the dark neighborhood, searching for eavesdroppers.

'What is it, Angela? If you have something to say, now's the time.'

She made several quick nods as if she'd consulted with the heavens and they'd given their approval.

'Jeb and I think they're doing things they shouldn't be doing.'

'What things?'

She inhaled through her nose and shook her head.

'Maybe I should come inside,' Sugar said.

'I called the Miami Police Department but they weren't interested. They said they'd send someone out to talk to me, but no one ever came.'

'Weren't interested in what?'

'The blueprints, schematic drawings. There's a whole box of stuff I found in Dad's apartment.'

'Blueprints of the ray gun?'

'Calling it a ray gun,' Angela said, 'that makes it sound like something from a cartoon show. But it's not. It's very real. Isn't it, Jeb?'

He nodded.

'And these blueprints, where did your father get them? From the Braswells?'

'That's right.'

'How'd he manage that? Something so valuable.'

'He had free passage on and off their boat. That's where he found them, on their fishing yacht.'

'What's the connection between your father and these people? Was he A.J.'s bookie or something? A fishing buddy?'

'The connection between my father and A.J. is blood.'

'I don't follow.'

Jeb shifted beside her. A housefly was tracking up his cheek but he didn't seem to mind.

'Blood,' she said. 'As in family.'

'You're related to the Braswells?'

'I'm not,' she said. 'But my older sister Darlene was married to A.J. Braswell.'

She fixed her eyes on a neatly pruned hibiscus bush.

'You and your sister, are you close?'

'Darlene's dead, Mr Sugarman. Ten years ago she hung herself in the attic of her house. She was one of them for seventeen years. That's what killed her. Being a Braswell.'

Sugarman looked at the same hibiscus bush that Angela was so absorbed in. It was a well-pruned bush. Healthy, with lots of double-wide blooms. A bush worth studying.

'Lawton described one of the guys on the boat,' said

Sugar. 'He said he was a blond kid with a sombrero. Is that anyone you're familiar with?'

Jeb muttered something under his breath.

'That's Johnny,' Angela said. 'Johnny Braswell, the baby of the family. All the Braswell IQ was siphoned off by the time Johnny was born.'

'Lawton said it was this Johnny character who cut Arnold's hand.'

She shut her eyes hard and bowed her head.

'Nice family,' Sugarman said. 'Kid slashes his own granddaddy.'

She wet her lips and looked directly at Sugarman.

'Know what's even more screwed up?'

'What?'

She let him have a long look at her eyes. Pretty and wide-set, long lashes and a sassy twinkle in there.

'My father,' she said, 'Mr Arnold Peretti, big-time underworld figure, bookie for the stars, he was also a doting grandfather. You should've seen him down on the floor at the Braswells' house, every Christmas, every birthday. Little Andy, and Morgan, and Johnny. He loved those kids. He loved them so much he could never see how totally fucked up they were. The most fucked-up little brats that ever slithered out from under a rock. That's who my father squandered his love on. Little shits like that.'

Thorn waited till Alex had settled in her bunk, pulled the blanket to her chin, said good night. He waited a little longer, staring up into the dark, listening to her breathing deepen, the first throaty flutters of sleep. Then he rose and tiptoed out onto the deck. It was well after midnight and the bar was closed, just a few late-night diners in their flowered clothes and deep tans stumbling back from the local restaurants.

He went for a walk across the grounds. A strong wind was whistling around the buildings and bending the palms. Fronds rattled and the smaller boats jostled in their slips.

He had noticed the dinghy earlier in the evening. It was a white rowboat, used to ferry hotel guests across the harbor to the isolated beach. It was knotted to a cleat near the dockmaster's shed. The shed was dark now, the dock empty. Throughout the marina men were dreaming of blue marlin rising to their lures.

Thorn stepped down into the dinghy and unlashed the line and pushed off. He banged the oars a little as he learned the right rhythm. By the time he was at the far end of the marina he was moving along nicely, a good even stroke, as stealthy as a dark wind.

He kept just beyond the halo of the marina lights, rowing out into the harbor, the black water glistening with gold. When he was past the final slip, he put the oars in the oarlocks and drifted thirty yards beyond the Braswells' yacht. He had an unobstructed view of it, sleek and white with a ghostly glow.

Lights burned in the narrow skylights of the two starboard cabins. He saw no one out on deck, no one moving behind the salon curtains. The current sloshed against the boulders on the far side of the harbor. Charcoal smoke was drifting in from one of the boats anchored beyond the mouth of the harbor. Someone having a late-night barbecue.

He was unarmed and undermanned. No way he could stage a successful raid on their boat. And not much chance he could sneak aboard unnoticed. There was a pistol-packing guard parked in the shadows. Though Thorn couldn't see him from his dinghy, he knew he was there. There was no way to tell what weapons the Braswells might have aboard.

It was foolish. It was absurd and risky to all involved. There were a hundred rational reasons why he should go back to the *Heart Pounder* and concentrate on Alexandra Collins's breathing, fall into the rhythms of her sleep. But he kept thinking of that airplane passenger in the track suit who'd had a seizure on the deck of the skiff. And the large woman who'd scooped him up and held him while he died, giving him some last comfort, some final moments of human contact. All of them had been safe and comfortable in their padded seats one minute, and tumbling from the sky the next. He kept seeing Lawton Collins, his wry, off-center smile.

Thorn lifted the oars, fit his hands to the grips, and rowed in from the dark, sliding toward the Braswells' yacht. Halyards tinkled and the water sighed around the pilings. He eased to within twenty yards, choosing his spot along the starboard cockpit. Step over to the dive platform and scale the transom, slip inside the salon, and pick his way through the dark, cabin by cabin, till he found the old man. If he was discovered, he'd use his fists if he couldn't find a heavy object along the way. It wasn't much of a plan, but it had rushed up from his gut and had taken such clear shape that it pushed away all doubt.

He coasted the last ten feet, slid the oars into the locks, and watched the big white hull come into reach. Another few seconds and he leaned out and touched her lustrous side, nudged his rowboat around her stern, cushioning the inevitable bump of wood against fiberglass.

He was easing up from his bench seat, in a half crouch, when a voice came from the dock nearby. Thorn went rigid. Holding the dinghy in place as it shifted and wobbled against the push of the tide.

It was Maurice, the Braswells' guard, who earlier in the evening had found Thorn less than amusing. He barked a warning. 'Halt.'

Thorn peered up into the dark expecting to see Maurice's humorless eyes, the dark barrel of his pistol. But there was no one there. And then another voice, out on the dock just a few feet away.

'It's just me, Maurice.'

And a mumbled response.

'Is everyone asleep?'

Maurice's reply was taken by the wind.

Thorn felt the shift of the boat as someone stepped aboard. Five feet away, the man crossed the cockpit and opened the salon door and closed it behind him. Thorn held himself in place. Maurice cleared his throat. He hawked up a wad of phlegm, and spat out into the water. A yard from Thorn's bow there was a small splash. Thorn watched the golden concentric ripples spread toward him.

Maurice dragged his chair across the wooden planks of the dock and sat down and lit a cigarette.

'Is everyone asleep?' the man had asked.

In that same detached voice Thorn had heard just the day before.

# 21

At dawn Thorn got two take-out coffees from the resort's large, airy restaurant, charged them to his slip, and was on his way back to the *Heart Pounder*, taking quick slurps of the dark, earthy stuff, when someone whistled from the pool deck.

'One of those for me?'

Sugarman sat at one of the stone picnic tables near the diving board. In a yellow polo shirt and blue jeans, sunglasses cocked up on his head.

Thorn came over, handed him a cup, and sat down across the table.

'They got flights this early?'

'If you know the right people.'

They sipped the coffee, Thorn looking out at the marina, the sun starting to shimmer on all that chrome and gold plate.

'You're hanging with some fancy-assed folks, Thorn.'

'But I'm trying hard to stay connected to my humble roots.'

'I'm sure these folks all worked diligently and earned each and every shiny doodad we see displayed before us. Pulled themselves up by their bootstraps, every one. The American way.'

'I suppose a few might have. Mostly it looks like a lot of lucky sperm.'

Thorn watched one of the smaller yachts edge forward from its slip. A deckhand smearing a rag over the tinted windows.

'What brings you all this way? Looking to catch a marlin?'

'Call me chickenshit but I prefer fish that are smaller than my boat.'

A sandpiper landed on the grassy fringe of the pool and poked its beak at a cocktail napkin.

'Did some digging last night,' Sugar said. 'Discovered some intriguing details about your buddies, the Braswells.'

'Yeah?'

'I spoke with a young man named Shine who's Braswell's partner in MicroDyne. He's decided he wants to blow the whistle on these nice folks.'

A group of ladies in pink-and-green golf clothes walked past, headed for the restaurant.

'From that stuff you read, you know the Braswells do military contract work. They got patent rights on a process they use to coat some exotic gizmos. Memory chips. Flashy high-tech doohickeys used in fighter jets and weapons systems. US Air Force is their number-one client. They use MicroDyne-treated chips in their fighters, missile guidance, all kinds of applications.'

'Coating? What kind of coating?'

'It's a metallurgical process the Braswell kid came up with when he was still in high school. Spark plasma sintering.'

'The one that died?'

'That one, yeah. Andy Braswell. It was his creation.'

'Must've been a brainy kid.'

'From what this guy Shine says, that's all the company has to offer, the kid's ideas. His notebooks. The sister is a business type, knows how to make the deals, market the product, but it was the brother who had the ideas.'

'What's it do, this plasma thing?'

'*Hardened* is the word they use. Hardened against nuclear blasts and the electromagnetic pulses that come after. The stuff Cappy told us about. They got the franchise on it. It's like a glaze that buffers the chips. Anybody wants a computer or a missile guidance system to stand up to a dose of electromagnetic energy, they need their chips coated with this shit. And they can only buy it from the Braswells.'

Thorn sipped his coffee. He watched the sandpiper moving through the grass, foraging among the cigarette butts and plastic cups.

'Hardened chips,' Thorn said. 'Getting ready for the Third World War.'

'The boy came up with the idea, showed it to his dad, but the old man didn't see much value in it. MicroDyne is making some kind of microprocessor at the time, doing okay. Not making a fortune or anything, but getting by. After the boy dies, the company starts floundering. Mother's hung herself, father's grieving, not paying attention to business. They're laying people off. Silicon Valley is kicking it up a notch and stealing all MicroDyne's contracts.'

Thorn watched a shirtless young man climb down into a white rowboat and push off from the pier.

'I read that part,' Thorn said. 'That's when Morgan comes home from college, looks around, finds a new direction for the company, pulls it out of the tailspin.'

Sugar nodded.

'Apparently what she found was her brother's notebooks,' Sugarman said. 'She comes up with this sintering idea, sells her dad on it, gets the plant converted, makes a couple of government deals, and away they go.'

Thorn watched a frigate bird hanging high over the harbor entrance.

'You with me so far?'

'So MicroDyne is coating all these doohickeys so they'll be safe against radiation pulses. Which means they have to test their product somehow, make sure they're doing it right.'

'Bingo,' Sugar said. 'They need some kind of a HERF gun.'

'So MicroDyne builds it?'

'No, no. Defense Department provides them with a little ray gun to simulate a nuclear pulse in a laboratory setting. It's just for testing, lots of safeguards. No way to steal the thing. Tamper with it, or even look at it funny, and the thing shuts down, alarms go off in the Pentagon.'

'But it's sitting there,' Thorn said. 'Inside their plant, so someone might be able to study the thing. Clone it maybe, offer it up for sale on the side.'

'There you go.'

'What about the battery problem? How do they make it portable?'

'Jeb Shine said Morgan's had them working on some new process, a few thousand times stronger than conventional batteries. That's what got him suspicious. MicroDyne doesn't do fuel-cell technology. They're like a hundred percent invested in this coating process.'

'Why?'

'Why what?'

'Why do it? Why risk your entire business like that, fooling around with something like this?'

'They're going broke,' Sugar said. 'End of the Cold War, budget cutbacks. The demand for this coating is dropping fast. They've got this one product, that's all. Somebody upstream from them closes up shop, stops building missile guidance systems, next

337

week MicroDyne feels the pinch. Jeb's been seeing it coming for a while. People standing around, the work's just not there to keep the plant going.'

A tall black man behind the shrubs cranked up a gasoline engine. Thorn watched him sling the contraption on his back and start blowing leaves off the sidewalk. They waited till he'd worked his way out of range.

'Sounds crazy to me, Sugar. What're they going to do? Set up an assembly line, start manufacturing ray guns? It's pretty hard to believe.'

'Yeah, same thing I was thinking. No way they can get away with something like that.'

Thorn swallowed the last of the coffee and watched the sandpiper rooting in the shaggy grass near a hedge. The sun was nearly up, a shaft of pink light cut through the bloom of golden red clouds that hung along the horizon like the ghostly remnants of exploded warheads.

'Peretti had blueprints of the HERF in his apartment,' Sugar said. 'Maybe they're selling the blueprints, let the terrorists take the risks of building the damn thing.'

Thorn watched as the frigate bird adjusted its wings slightly, caught a wind current, and swung a half mile to the east.

'No,' Thorn said. 'What if the idea is just to build one or two of these things, sell them along with the plans, just get a couple into circulation.'

'What? Like they're anarchists or something?'

'No, your company's losing money. You don't have enough cash coming in to keep your nice Palm Beach mansion up. You're looking for customers for the one product you've got. The military's cutting back. MicroDyne's got the peacetime blues. So what they do, they plant a seed. They get this HERF thing out into the world. All they need is one big event, unleash a little chaos. Then what's going to happen?'

Sugarman nodded.

'You got an evil mind, Thorn.'

Out in the marina, a man laughed and a woman screamed with pleasure.

'Everybody gets a good case of paranoia. The military, the police, everyone suddenly needs this plasma sintering bullshit. Plus, you'd have a lot of decent, law-abiding citizens clamoring for it. They don't want some drive-by terrorist to wipe out their hard drive, shut down their TV. If somebody had the market cornered, they'd pretty much be king of the hill. The next multibillionaires.'

'Set loose the virus with one hand, sell the vaccine with the other.'

'Root of all evil,' Thorn said. 'Like the preacher man says.'

'And that's what Lawton stumbled into.'

Thorn nodded.

'And crashing the planes?'

'To sell a new product, you got to show your buyer what it does. Right? That's what they were doing in the Everglades. That guy in the cowboy hat. He

339

was probably their buyer. They were showing off their merchandise. In fact, I bet that's what they had in the fish box they were bringing ashore. A HERF gun.'

Thorn looked over at the *ByteMe*, back at Sugarman.

'Jesus,' Sugar said. 'Killing hundreds of people as a goddamn sales pitch.'

'I've got to go, Sugar. Got to get Lawton off that damn boat.'

'Oh, yeah,' Sugar said. 'Cappy dug up something on that knife you pulled out of Lawton. Teensy company makes about ten a year. Some soldier of fortune mail-order business distributes them. Only one customer in Florida last year. Never guess who it is.'

'Johnny Braswell.'

Sugarman nodded solemnly.

'Bought all ten, eighteen hundred dollars apiece. Boy loves his blades.'

'Nothing we didn't surmise already.'

'One more thing,' Sugar said. 'Peretti's daughter, Darlene, married A.J. Braswell. Somehow Johnny, the youngest, he gets it into his head that because his granddaddy is a small-time bookie, that means the whole family is Mafia. So he sits around, watches all these gangster flicks, learns how he's supposed to act, all that bullshit slang, getting into knives 'cause he needs a signature or specialty. So there's Johnny, slicing off his own granddaddy's finger, tossing him overboard.'

'Just your ordinary all-American family.'

'Nest of vipers, Thorn. That's who you're mixed up with here. Nest of vipers.'

'Well, we can add another viper to the list.'

Thorn could hear his heart drumming in his ears.

'Yeah? Which viper is that?'

'Our friendly airline crash inspector. He snuck aboard the Braswells' boat last night. Seemed real familiar with the yachting set.'

'Aw shit,' Sugar said. He looked out at the marina, shaking his head. 'You should take a step back from this, Thorn. Call in the big people.'

'I can't, Sugar.'

'Christ, they got your name on the list. You went snooping around their factory, you stepped on some kind of trip wire. You've lost the element of surprise, Thorn. They're looking for you.'

'Yeah,' he said. 'And they're just about to find me.'

Jamie Wingo sat on the edge of Morgan's bed while she filed her nails. His hair was damp from the shower, a white towel knotted around his waist. Copper skin gleaming. Morgan was still in her shorty pajamas. The sheets and bedspread covered her lap. When he'd come in late last night, he'd slid under the covers beside her and touched her breast and kissed her ear. But she pushed him gently away, pleading a headache.

He didn't know it yet, but the sex part was finished.

For months now Morgan had gritted her teeth and measured out the exact erotic portion required to keep him hooked. But that was done.

Now he was looking at her gravely. There were fine white lines showing around his eyes. Dark veins branched at his temples. His skin was soft and sleek. His brown eyes had dark lights lurking in them. The kind of exotic good looks a lot of women might find alluring.

'I'm clean now,' he said. 'All freshened up.'

'I see that.'

He cocked his head and squinted at her.

'Morgan, what's going on? You call me, tell me to get over here, it's urgent. I drop everything, make excuses and come running. And then you push me away. What's bothering you, sweetheart?'

She looked up from her nails.

'I killed those two,' she said. 'Charlie Harrison and the girl. I shot them in my car.'

'I know, I know,' he said. 'Yes, that had to be hard.'

She could feel the boat taut on its mooring lines, rocking gently against the wake of the early fishing boats heading out into the dawn. The cabin was full of the mild blond light of early spring.

'But you needn't worry. Miami police don't have a clue. I've talked to Romano several times in the last few days. They're totally in the dark.'

'And Roy showed up. He was all huffy, threatening me, saying I'm not taking him seriously.'

He patted her knee through the bedspread.

'So you're stressed. Sure, this has been very difficult on you. Well, it just so happens I know an excellent stress reliever.'

She smoothed a ragged edge on her thumbnail.

'It's easy to be cavalier, Jamie, when you've managed to keep your own hands so clean.'

He eyed her for a moment, then reached out to touch her cheek with a finger.

'I'm in as deep as you are, Morgan.'

'Are you?'

'Very deep.'

'But you still haven't done your part, Jamie. You haven't convinced anyone about the HERF.'

'It's not as easy as I'd thought. No one wants to believe it. It's too radical. Too scary. They're looking for chafed wiring, nicks in the circuitry, all the usual suspects. The safety board is a very conservative bunch.'

'But that's your responsibility, Jamie. To make them believe. You haven't been doing a very good job of it.'

'Look, Morgan, next week they won't be able to keep their heads in the sand any longer. When we bring down the next one, I've decided I'm going to step up to the podium, look right in the camera, and I'll tell the world about the HERF, that it's out there. Oh, they'll try to discredit me. I'll be ridiculed. But no one will be able to ignore it anymore. It'll be huge, Morgan. A terrorist group with a frightening new weapon that no one can protect against. You can sell MicroDyne for a hundred times its value and walk away. It'll all be over and we'll be free.'

'Will that work? The direct approach.'

'I think it will, yes.'

'You thought the other approaches would work, too. But so far nothing has. How many planes do we have to bring down before you steer them in the right direction?'

'This will work, Morgan. Don't fret.'

'You keep saying that.'

He eased onto the bed and propped himself against the pillow next to her.

'What about the old man? Did you get anything out of him?'

'He's dotty,' she said. 'He doesn't remember where he put it.'

'But we really don't need that one, right? There's the new model.'

'Yes,' she said. 'The new one's at home in the attic. Better power cells. Twice the range. Minimal back flash. It'll work this time. A total meltdown. Cars, planes, power plants. Whatever we want.'

'Good, good.'

'You know,' she said. 'I really hate dealing with Roy. I hate being around him. Knowing he's going to get his hands on this thing. Mean bastard with some divine mandate. Going to wipe out all the blacks. Try to shut down the federal government, whatever he's going to do with it.'

'That's not our problem,' he said.

'Where the hell did you dig him up?' she said. 'How do you even know that kind of person?'

Wingo smiled.

'After every crash, the kooks come out, howling at the moon, trying to take credit, or putting out some theory about how the plane went down. A missile, a UFO. Roy was one of those. I got a hundred e-mails from him.'

'He makes my skin crawl. The man's truly evil.'

Wingo reached out, touched her cheek with a fingertip, ruffling the fuzz.

'I'm going to have to get back to Miami, darling. An hour or two, then I need to go.'

'What if you didn't go back?'

'What?'

'What if you disappeared, dropped out of sight?'

'What're you talking about? I can't do that.'

'But what would happen if you did?'

'I don't know what you're talking about, Morgan.'

'You've been telling people about the HERF.'

'Yes.'

'But they haven't listened to you. Apparently, they don't take you seriously.'

'Like I said, it's a hard sell. They're very conservative.'

'But if you disappeared, Jamie, what would they think then? Would your colleagues be more inclined to believe your claims? Might they think you'd been kidnapped, or perhaps even murdered by these people, these terrorists you were trying to warn them about?'

He shifted forward, turned his head slowly and studied her.

Morgan dug the point of the nail file into her thumb, watched her flesh whiten.

'You think I should disappear?'

'I think it might work. Yes, I do. I think it might.'

'I don't know, Morgan. It wasn't the plan.'

'I'd miss you,' she said. 'I'd miss you terribly.'

She turned to him, reached out her hand, cradled his cheek, and guided his lips to hers. His mouth softened and she felt him sinking away into the kiss.

She plunged the nail file into the side of his throat.

He jerked back, his eyes fastened to hers, lips puckering as if he meant to whistle a last tune.

She pulled it out, then plunged it in again. He gagged and grabbed for her hand but she was too quick, and drew it free and rammed it in a third time. His eyes held hers. They were foggy and perplexed as though he were about to ask a question, some final knotty problem that she could help him unravel.

He coughed and his left eye closed, then his right. Blood retched from his lips, spilled down his chin. He tottered briefly like some tall building whose foundation has been demolished, shock waves passing up through its length. Then he tumbled backwards against the sheets.

She drew a breath. Stared at his body. His eyelids quivered. There was a spasm in his right arm. A moment later, when he finally grew still, she leaned close and peered at this dark, silent man, at the silver stub of her nail file lodged below his Adam's apple, at the black thread of blood that coiled down the glossy flesh of his throat, staining her cheerful yellow sheets.

She lowered herself and pressed against him while his body was still warm. She lifted her head and rested it on his narrow chest, closed her eyes, and touched a fingertip lightly to his hairless nipple. So much like Andy's. Just that dusting of nearly invisible hair. She eased forward, flattening her ear against his left breast, and listened to the faint, final gurgles of his heart.

'Lover's quarrel?'

Johnny shut the cabin door behind him and stepped into the room.

Morgan sat up and yanked the sheet over Wingo's head.

'What're you doing in here?'

'I came to wake you. But I see you've already been up for a while. What'd he do, rub you the wrong way?'

'Get out of here, Johnny.'

'I never liked that guy. Never understood why we needed him.'

'We don't need him. Not anymore.'

'Just an empty suit, trying to hang out with the tough guys.'

Johnny paced across the cabin. He wore blue-and-white baggies and a white tank top, his sunglasses hanging around his neck. He spread his legs, and squared off in front of her as if presenting himself for inspection.

'"You kill a man, and that's not a pleasant thing to live with for the rest of your life."' A faint smile rose to his lips. 'I love Raymond Burr. He was much better at being bad than being good, don't you think? Kind of like me.'

'We have to get rid of this body, Johnny.'

'We can cut him up for bait.'

'I'm serious, Johnny. We need to get him out of here.'

Johnny broke his pose and stepped over to the bed and sat down at the edge. He reached out and touched Wingo's bare right foot.

'Were you unfaithful with this guy?'

Morgan stared at him, making an effort to keep the shock out of her face.

'What did you say?'

'Unfaithful,' said Johnny. 'Were you unfaithful with Wingo?'

Up on deck, her father started the big diesels. He revved them once, then cut them back to idle.

'That's the wrong word, Johnny. Unfaithful doesn't apply.'

'Unfaithful to Andy, I mean.'

Her lungs emptied and she struggled for a moment to refill them.

'What're you trying to say, Johnny?'

'You don't have to play games with me, Morgan. I knew about you two. I knew what was going on. Andy tried to hide it from me, but I knew.'

She opened her mouth but the words wouldn't form.

'He was kind of freaked out there at the end. He didn't know what to do.'

'He talked to you about me?'

'No, he never said a word. But I could tell. I knew Andy pretty good. I mean, I know I'm not the sharpest tack on the board, not smart in the way Andy was, or the way you are. But I knew Andy. I knew what he was going through.'

'What do you mean, he was freaked out?'

'Freaked out,' Johnny said. 'Mom came into the room, got in his face. She sent me outside, but I snuck back and pressed my ear to the door and heard the whole thing. She knew what was going on between you two. Man, was she pissed. That's when Briarwood came up.'

'Briarwood?'

'That girls' school in Vermont where they were going to send you, straighten you out. For delinquents, head cases, dopers.'

'They were going to send me away?'

'You mean I know something you don't? Wow, there's a first. Yeah, they were going to split you two up.'

'Keep Andy at home, send me away?'

'I guess they figured it was you that seduced him. It was, wasn't it? That's what I always thought.'

Morgan got down a breath. Let it out. Eased down another. Working hard to keep from shattering.

'You know, I always wondered about that, the way Andy died. Coming when it did right after Mom and him had their big talk. Like, if there was some connection. I mean, Andy taking three wraps like that on the leader wire, it wasn't something he would've done. He knew better than that. It just seemed weird, coming right at that moment. Him being so depressed.'

She looked across at Wingo's body beneath the sheet, felt the rumble of the diesels through the deck, the boat throbbing like some giant turning fork.

'You and Andy always reminded me of those two characters from *Double Indemnity*. Fred MacMurray and Barbara Stanwyck. You know what Edward G. Robinson said about them.'

The boat rocked gently from a passing wake.

'"They're stuck with each other and they've got to ride all the way to the end of the line. It's a one-way trip and the last stop is the cemetery."'

# 22

When Thorn got back to the boat with fresh coffees, Alexandra was barefoot, stretched out in the fighting chair, wearing one of Thorn's T-shirts, faded red with a logo from Snook's Bayside, a Key Largo restaurant. Riding dangerously low on her narrow hips was a pair of his old yellow gym shorts. The traveling clothes she'd packed were in the Jeep the police confiscated the night before. She wasn't about to try to reclaim them.

She hadn't slept well. Twice when he woke in the night Alex was padding around the tiny cabin, stepping in and out of the moonlight, making an aimless circuit. At dawn when he woke in the bunk across the cabin from her, she was snoring softly, face smushed in the pillow, her body in a tight tuck beneath the sheets. He studied her profile, the long, straight line of her nose, the angled cheekbones, a small sideburn brushing her ear. It was a strong face, Irish but with a whisper of Italian around the nose and eyes. As if some Roman nobleman was lurking in the tangle of her genes.

He watched her sleep for a minute, but when her snoring sputtered to a halt, he turned and headed outside.

Now as he stepped aboard, she yawned and stretched a sleepy arm toward the Styrofoam cups.

'One of those for me?'

He handed her one and she took a cautious taste.

'Cream, no sugar,' she said. 'You guessed right.'

'You have that cream-no-sugar quality.'

She looked at him, then stared down into her coffee.

'I'll take that as a fumbling compliment.'

'Exactly how I meant it,' Thorn said.

While she sipped, Thorn stood at the transom and surveyed the marina.

Up and down the docks engines were burbling, lines casting off, crew members wishing friends on adjacent boats good luck for the day's fishing. Today it was just recreational. But for a large part of the year these same guys competed intensely against each other in a variety of marlin tournaments with a great deal of cash at stake. Twenty-five-thousand-dollar entry fees, two to three million paid out to the winners. Side bets, calcuttas also in the millions. With a percentage of the boat's take often split among the crew, things could get fierce.

These boats were manned by blue-collar guys and owned by white-collar bosses, Harvard grads, Yalies, men who'd always finished at the top of their class, and didn't accept failure gracefully. As a result, many of these mates and captains bounced from boat to boat, moving up or down the pay scale as their reputations flourished or declined. He'd known a few of their kind. Far different from the deep-sea charter guys around the Keys. The charter crew's status wasn't measured by the trophy fish they brought in, but by how good they were at attracting repeat customers. A good catch was part of it, but not the only thing they were selling. Good sandwiches, good humor, patient instruction, and icy beer was often enough.

But these marlin guys were in another class. They were big-league pros. Their yearly wage was based on the size of the boat they crewed: captains got roughly a thousand dollars a foot, mates a little less. Not bad for prepping lures, checking the drag on the reels, keeping the heavy monofilament free of nicks, the boat scrubbed and polished, and for acting as lunchtime grill chef. Three, four thousand a month to stand at the transom and wire the fish. Early mornings, late nights, all day out in the sun, rough seas or smooth, a boy's life.

What made the good ones worth the price was the tournaments. Win even one category in the Bisbee

Black and Blue down in Cabo San Lucas, and the salaries were covered and the boat was tanked up for a full twelve months.

Considering they were such elite fishermen, there was nothing snooty about these guys. Their club was small and tight, but not restrictive. If you had the skills to bring giant blues back to the weigh station, it didn't matter if you were overeducated or undernourished, from Atlanta or Afghanistan, you could sit among them and share their smokes and drink their beers and partake in their late-night rituals.

For a season in his mid-twenties, Thorn had dabbled in their heady world. Second mate, then first on a fifty-five-foot Hatteras, the *Chupacabra*. But he quickly tired of the fishing, wearied of the team spirit, the obligatory camaraderie. He was too much of a loner for that kind of work. Too solitary to spend fifteen hours a day bumping shoulders with another twenty-year-old in a cockpit smaller than a motel bathroom. And the fishing itself was a long way from the kind he valued, stalking hair-trigger bonefish across the transparent water of the shoals, where fish and fisherman were on nearly equal terms. Fishing for marlin meant dragging bait for ten hours, replacing it from time to time, clearing the lines, making occasional adjustments to your pattern, but mainly you watched the baits hop and dive and skitter across the everlasting sea. Trance city. Zone-out time.

Hour upon identical hour, until finally, if you were good enough or had the gods on your side, there came that blinding explosion of fish and water, the cries, the screaming reel, and then the fight, sometimes tedious, sometimes quick, but more about brute strength and resolve and willpower than technical skill. A good marlin fisherman caught more fish than a bad one. But you could drop a sixty-year-old insurance sales-man with a paunch and weak knees and sloppy reflexes into the fighting chair and coach him step by step through the routine, and with the captain backing down on the fish at twenty knots, that giant blue fish would more often than not come floun-dering up to the transom. That was what finally turned Thorn away from the deep sea. Some sick-ening sense that he had participated in a ritual kill-ing. That he had aided and abetted men who were far less magnificent, far less powerful, and much less capable of beauty and grace than the animal they killed.

'You're not exactly Mr Communication this morn-ing.'

She had finished her coffee and dropped her cup in the trash bucket. Now she was standing with her arms crossed beneath her breasts, hugging herself against the early morning cool.

'I was off visiting my youth,' Thorn said.

'You did this, this kind of fishing?'

'Briefly,' he said.

'Couldn't cut it, huh?'

'Well, I wouldn't put it that way.'

'What way would you put it?'

He considered it for a moment, holding on to a painful grin.

'Okay, okay,' he said finally. 'I couldn't cut it, no.'

It won a tiny smile.

'Bored you, I bet.'

'Bored,' he said. 'And disgusted me sometimes.'

'I've never actually done it. But Dad talks about it a lot. Sounds too much like a bullfight to me. I've seen a couple of those. The big Hemingway spectacle. Bravery and honor and tragedy. A man stepping in the dangerous path of the bull. But come on. What kind of risk is it really? For every matador that gets gored, thousands of bulls die. Hell, it's probably more dangerous to work in a meat-packing plant.'

'You talk like a cop.'

'How's a cop talk?'

'Not much patience for bullshit.'

'And you have?'

Thorn shrugged.

'Hemingway still works for me.'

'I could have guessed.'

'Not his life,' Thorn said. 'All that barroom bullshit was sad. But some of the books stand up. The old guy alone in his boat catching that marlin, that's worth reading again from time to time.'

'He catches a fish and the sharks eat it before he gets it back. Sounds like existentialism one-oh-one. Sisyphus and his rock. Best thing about that book is, it's short.'

Thorn looked at her, then turned his eyes back to the busy marina.

'The old guy could've quit anytime, but he didn't. That's what I liked.'

'Tenacity,' she said. 'The pit bull approach. Clamp on, don't let go.'

'Steadfastness,' said Thorn. 'That's a better word.'

'You a college boy, Thorn?'

'Hardly.'

'Sometimes you talk like one.'

'Is that bad?'

Alex shrugged.

'I graduated,' she said. 'But I learned more in the first month of police work than in four years of school.'

Alexandra trained her eyes on the *ByteMe*. It was moored on the next dock at the very last slip. From Thorn's slip they could make out only the flybridge and the tuna tower rising above it.

'My dad's over there,' she said. 'On that boat with the goddamn guy who stabbed him, and I'm sitting here having coffee, shooting the shit.'

'Shooting the shit with a beach bum.'

'Okay,' she said. 'So I got it wrong.'

'And you don't even know for sure that Lawton's over there.'

'Johnny Braswell as much as told me last night.'

'You said he denied it.'

'He was lying.'

'You could tell that, just hearing his voice.'

'I know a lie when I hear it.'

'But we agreed,' Thorn said. 'We'd see if the plan works. If it doesn't, then we'll think of something else.'

'I'm giving it an hour,' she said. 'Not one minute longer.'

'I'm impatient, too. Sure, I want to go over there right now, try to muscle our way on board, use whatever force we have to. But even if they do have him, he might be on the boat, or they might have him somewhere else. In a motel room, a private house. He could be anywhere. We go rushing over there, and it fails, we're screwed.'

'I can't do this much longer, Thorn. Just sit here.'

Down the dock there was a stir, voices, murmurs. Thorn craned to his right and saw Farley Boissont in gray shorts and a tight black T-shirt striding down the dock. His muscles were freshly pumped and seemed to be lit by a quiet radiance from within. Wearing a pair of narrow wraparound sunglasses and bathed in the fresh morning sunlight, Farley resembled some kind of rough-hewn demigod, one of Poseidon's henchmen. All he needed was a three-pronged spear and strands of seaweed threaded in his hair. Beside him was a man a little older than Thorn with curly gray locks. He wore a white long-sleeved T-shirt and a pair of black running shorts. He was deeply tanned and barefoot and had a well-toned, athletic body, but walking next to Farley, he seemed almost scrawny.

The two of them helloed and nodded their way

down the dock, every eye following Farley's rolling gait. They halted behind the *Heart Pounder* and Farley asked for permission to come aboard.

Thorn waved him on, but the other man held back, staring at Thorn with depthless eyes.

'I'm A.J. Braswell,' he said.

'The name's Thorn, and this is Alexandra. You can come aboard if you like, or we can all get cricks in our necks looking up at you.'

He didn't register the remark. Just peered at Thorn's face, his eyes with a dull and empty shine, like a man so focused on his inner landscape that the world outside his body was a gray, one-dimensional place, not worth his best efforts. Thorn knew all too well about the haunted and the damned, their peculiar trances. The sun orbited their obsession, the galaxies arranged themselves in heavenly alignment around the object of their desire. They were all-powerful. They were nuts.

'I understand you encountered my fish.'

'Word travels fast.'

'Is it true?'

'We hooked a big blue with a silver cigar attached to its back. But it didn't have anybody's name on it.'

'That's my fish,' Braswell said.

'We had it up to the boat,' Thorn said. 'The swivel hit the rod tip, Farley was taking a wrap when the leader broke.'

'That's her, that's my fish.' His voice was so nearly

devoid of emotion it sounded as though it was piped up from some lost place inside him.

'Like I said, Mr Braswell, this fish didn't have anybody's name on it.'

'Farley told me it was over a thousand pounds.'

'Farley's being modest,' Thorn said. 'It was well over a thousand. Grand and a half, maybe more. Biggest damn blue I've ever seen.'

'Where was this?'

'Well, I don't know, Mr Braswell. I'd like to be neighborly, but it's just not in my nature to give away information of that sort.'

'It's the second time we've had that marlin on,' Farley said. 'I told Mr Braswell about that.'

Thorn smiled. Farley had the liar's gift, a pure heart and a simple delivery.

'It's true,' Thorn said. 'We caught her a few weeks ago out near the drop-off, and we've been hunting her ever since. Me and Farley believe we've got her figured out. At least well enough to jump her that second time. We're hoping the cliché is right and the third time's our charm.'

Braswell licked his lips. His shadowy stupor seemed to be lifting, eyes growing more alert, as if he'd just traveled a great distance in a short time and his mind was still a few steps behind his body, but gaining fast.

'Come on aboard, Mr Braswell,' Alexandra said. 'I'll go get you some coffee. Sounds like you boys have a few things to discuss.'

Thorn shot her a searching look. What kind of bullshit was this? He'd only been around her a few hours but he was fairly sure she wasn't the kind to defer to men. Nobody's coffee mistress.

She sent him a smile of sly innocence.

'It's okay, Thorn, don't worry. I'm not running off. I'll just get some coffee and be right back.'

When Alex was gone, A.J. came aboard. He paced the deck for a moment, then took an uneasy perch on the starboard gunwale. Farley sat on the transom. Thorn stayed on his feet.

'You've had two hook-ups on this same fish,' A.J. said. 'That's hard to believe.'

'Finding fish is an art,' Thorn said. 'And Farley here is the Monet of marlin.'

A.J. looked over at the big man.

'I'm well acquainted with Mr Boissont's reputation. I knew his father. Jelly was a very good man. Fine captain, fine guide.'

'Well, as I say, Farley's instincts, his knowledge of these waters, that's what led us to her a second time. On our next encounter, we're bringing that bad girl in. She'll be hanging up for all the world to see.'

'Do you know about the transmitter, that silver cigar you referred to?'

'We heard some dock gossip, yeah. You're tracking her via satellite. Like that fish has a little cell phone and it calls you up every once in a while.'

A.J. looked at Thorn more closely now, the last of the fog burning off, his eyes sharpening.

'Something like that,' he said.

'But it hasn't worked,' said Thorn.

A.J. Braswell rubbed the gray stubble on his cheek and looked out at the busy marina.

Behind Braswell a procession of clouds paraded along the horizon like pink floats trimmed with gold and saffron. In the west white stalky birds coasted out to sea for their daily rounds. Most of the big yachts were moving through the harbor now, mates yawning, making final adjustments to the lines, checking the giant lures. Gulls squealed near the resort's tiny beach and a heavyset man in a rubber bathing cap dove into the pool to begin his solitary laps. Looking around at such a place, it was possible to believe the earth would heal all its wounds and men of charity and good cheer would prevail. Spiced with honey and coconut, a warm breeze chimed in the outriggers and filled the lungs with optimism. In such weather, in such a place, even the most hard-bitten cynic might be tempted to grant forgiveness to his enemies and lay down his weapons and his anger forever. Fall to the ground in a benevolent swoon.

But not Thorn. Looking around the Abaco Beach Resort for the last few hours at all those magnificent yachts, the display of abundance and good health and all that shared passion for big-game fishing, was starting to piss him off. If this was all the wealthy folks could find to do with their accumulated good fortune, this nonstop show of gluttony and back-slapping bonhomie, then maybe it was time to storm the boardrooms and throw the buffoons out on the street. Let them test their favorite theory – that if the wealth were ever redistributed, the rich folks would reclaim their fortunes in no time through the same hard work and ingenuity that had led them to the top in the first place. Thorn would happily wager his last nickel on the Farley Boissonts of the world.

'Mr Thorn,' A.J. said. 'You're going to come fishing with me.'

'I'm sorry?'

'I mean no offense, Mr Thorn, but I look at your equipment, your boat, and yes, sure, it was fine for an earlier era. It would be fine now for pursuing most fish. But the marlin I'm seeking, as you've discovered yourself, requires more substantial gear. Tackle of the highest quality. A boat that is fast, maneuverable, and set up with the latest electronics. I hope I'm not insulting you, Mr Thorn.'

'I'm not insulted. Are you insulted, Farley?'

Farley gave Thorn a blank look.

'We'll join forces,' Braswell said. 'My science and your art.'

'Is that what you do, A.J., you co-opt your rivals?'

'I want to catch this fish, Mr Thorn. I've worked toward this end for the last ten years. If it's money you want, I am a wealthy man. You may set your price.'

Thorn sighed, continued his cramped pacing.

'We've been doing pretty well without you, Braswell.'

'Fifty thousand dollars,' he said. 'Fifty thousand for each of you if we get a hook-up. But I'm the one who sits in the chair. There's no compromise on that. I catch the fish.'

Thorn looked at Farley. Muscles moved beneath his shirt. Muscles squirmed in his face. A body like his was never at rest.

'Seventy-five thousand apiece,' Braswell said. 'But I catch the fish.'

Thorn came to a halt behind the fighting chair.

'I'll need to discuss it with my captain.'

'Certainly,' he said. 'Take you time. But we're missing some prime fishing weather. Waning moon, falling tide.'

Farley joined Thorn in the cabin. Out in the cockpit, Braswell slumped forward and turned his complete attention to his right palm as though he were trying to read his own grim fortune. Farley leaned against the galley wall. He brushed a dreadlock off his forehead and shook his head.

'Too damn easy, Thorn. It isn't feeling right to me.'

'We chummed the waters, he took the bait. What's not right?'

'I don't like it.'

'You don't trust him?'

'The man's gone off in his head. He's a crazy one, he is. No, I don't trust him.'

'He's invited us aboard his boat. That's where we want to be, Farley. That's the whole point.'

'Too easy, Thorn. Too damn easy.'

Thorn glanced over toward the *ByteMe*. She loomed

364

several feet above the adjacent boats, the chrome of her flybridge and tower glinting in the sunlight. A small red flag attached to the tuna tower trembled on its pole, then, as Thorn watched with stunned fascination, the flag suddenly lifted and stood out straight as if starched by the blast of a gale.

The concussion that followed a moment later fractured a side window in the *Heart Pounder*'s galley and threw Thorn forward against the edge of the butane stove. Another explosion followed in seconds and a scalding wind flooded the cabin.

Out on the deck A.J. stood gripping the starboard rail. Every boat in the marina was rocking in the choppy water. A ball of fire rose from the next dock, black smoke boiling into the heavens. There was another blast, and one more after that. The air shuddered and shook, and far away a woman's voice began to wail with the piercing horror of an air raid siren. More smoke darkened the sky, and from all around them came yelps of alarm, women shrieking, men barking orders at each other. The few boats left at the docks emptied; men lugged fire extinguishers onto the jetty, others stumbled outside with the drunken, stunned eyes of shell-shocked soldiers. This wasn't the battle they'd enlisted for.

Thorn jumped across to the dock.

'Hey, Thorn, hold on,' Farley yelled. 'It might not be over.'

But he was running, shouldering through the crowd on the dock, then racing down the sidewalk and cutting into the adjacent dock. Five boats were smoldering, their windows blasted out, charred wreckage. Patches of the water were aflame and the oxygen had been sucked from the air.

In the last slip the *ByteMe* pitched and swayed as if riding out a hurricane. Spiderweb cracks laced its side window and a shadow of soot covered its hull, but otherwise the big white boat appeared undamaged. There was no security guard in sight and no sign of Alexandra.

Thorn shifted to the right. Something on the edge of his field of vision had snagged his eye. He stepped to the edge of the dock, peered out through the flames, and after a moment of searching, he saw it, hovering inches below the rainbow sheen of gasoline and oil that coated the surface, the faded red of the Snook's Bayside T-shirt.

He took two steps and dove.

But when he surfaced, he was lost in the wilderness of smoke and fire and floating debris. As he treaded water, a hard shift in the morning breeze rose around him and began to push the closest bank of flames in his direction. It swept toward him across the dark water like a prairie fire feeding on brittle grass. The *whoosh* of heat stole his breath and drove him beneath the water. He kicked and breaststroked deeper, then twisted around to search for Alexandra in the murky cool. Yellow light flickered from above and lit the gloom just enough for him to glimpse her. Twenty yards to his left, her body, inert and ghostly, was drifting downward.

He spun around and dug through the water, flutter-kicked and churned his arms till he was beside her. He looped an arm across her chest, blew out the last trickle of air from his lungs, and whirled back toward the firestorm above.

Johnny threw open Morgan's cabin door.

'What the hell is this? The whole goddamn marina's blowing up.'

Morgan stood at her dresser looking into the mirror. Showing her brother nothing.

'That's Roy and his people, Johnny. They're letting us know what lengths they're willing to go to for the weapon.'

'Christ, we got to cast off, get the hell out of here, Morgan. You're just standing there.'

'So go topside, Johnny, and cast us off. We got Roy's message. Now we have a fish to catch.'

Don't ask him how he did it, but Lawton got the plastic cuffs off. He gnawed them for a while in the middle of the night but made no headway. He rubbed them against what looked like a sharp edge on the vanity, but it wasn't sharp after all.

Then somewhere shortly after daybreak they were gone. As if he'd dreamed them off. As if some power in his brain had shrunk his bones sufficiently so he could slip free.

He wanted to show someone. Maybe the fat blond boy who'd brought him a bandage and a glass of ice water and helped him drink it. Yeah, he wanted to show him. Johnny was his name. Very familiar, that boy. A face Lawton recognized and could put a name to, but he couldn't bring up the rest of the boy's file. He was sure it was in there, a rap sheet six feet long. He had that look about him. But his recollection of the boy was lost in the dense clouds, lost inside the smoke and haze that clogged the back reaches of his mind.

With his hands free, it only took a second to release the plastic tie around his ankles. He rubbed the blood back into his feet. Numb needles pricking the soles, jabbing the tender flesh of his toes.

He was just standing up, looking around the guest quarters, at the photograph of a marlin soaring from the sea hung on the wall beside the door, when the blast hurled him back against the bed. He lay there for a few minutes, groggy, wondering what part of this was dream, what part real. He hoped the real part included getting loose from the handcuffs. He hoped he could remember enough about what he'd done to duplicate it. He'd love to show the boy, Johnny, that he and Harry Houdini were cut from the same amazing cloth.

He lay there on the bunk for another minute, listening to the other explosions, feeling his ear thump with every squeeze of his heart. Johnny had cut his ear. He remembered that. He remembered the knife, its odd blade. But he didn't know why he'd been cut. There had been a good reason, but it escaped him now.

When he stood up the room was warmer. Much warmer. Hot almost, even though it was still early yet and he could feel the cool spray of air-conditioning blowing from the vent. But the room was hot and there was yelling and screaming outside and the boat was rocking. Lawton went to the slot of a window and pushed aside the curtain and looked out.

It was a war scene out there. Men with blackened faces and torn clothes and bloody gashes running without direction, men aiming their fire extinguishers and spewing white clouds of gas at the flames. The dock blown to pieces, pilings shattered. And on a section of the dock, not twenty yards away from Lawton, he watched as a rangy blond man climbed the wooden ladder that was mounted on a piling. He was soaking wet and he held with his free arm a girl with long black hair. A pretty woman with white skin. She had on a red T-shirt and yellow shorts, and the blond man laid her out on the dock and tipped her head back, pinched her nose and pressed his mouth to hers and blew into her, then pressed his hands against her chest, leaning his weight against her. He did this several times before a bubble of water broke from her lips, then a spew of foam and gooey fluid.

Lawton Collins stood at the window and watched the man saving the woman's life. The pretty, dark-haired young girl seemed so familiar. Someone's pretty daughter. He thought he knew her but wasn't sure. He'd had a wife once but he didn't know about children. Probably not. He felt too alone to be a father.

# 23

After her throat was clear and her lungs were working on their own, Thorn stretched her out flat on her back along a side dock. Her teeth clicked and a hard shiver rattled through her hands and arms. Thorn stood up, glanced around, spotted a broken cabin door on a sixty-foot Davis two slips away. The yacht was listing hard to starboard, its mooring lines taut, straining to hold the enormous weight of the sinking boat.

Thorn jumped aboard, poked out a panel of broken glass, unlocked the door, and stepped into the salon. The floor was submerged in half a foot of water. More water surged down the hallway into the staterooms. He was halfway across the salon, sloshing toward the companionway, when a loud crack sounded outside – one of the heavy lines giving way. The boat lurched and Thorn thumped a shinbone against the glass coffee table and almost went down.

He found his balance and continued wading through the knee-deep water into the master stateroom. Flinging open the locker door, he pawed through shelves but found only small bath towels. Then he turned to the bed, threw off the bedspread, and stripped off the two cashmere blankets.

He carried them in a bundle back to the salon and was almost to the door when a second mooring line popped and the yacht pitched hard to starboard, then the remaining lines snapped one after the other like a firing squad's barrage. He clambered out to the aft deck, lobbed the blankets up on the jetty, and hoisted himself onto the port gunwale. He teetered, caught himself, set his feet, then leaped across to the dock, and stood watching as the boat slipped under.

Alexandra's eyes were tightly shut. She'd crossed her arms over her chest, clasping herself against the trembling. Thorn pulled her arms apart and peeled her wet T-shirt up and tugged it over her head. Then he dragged off her gym shorts and lay the blankets over her and tucked them tight around her nakedness.

After a few moments her shivers gradually subsided, but her breathing was still ragged and her face ashen. Twice she tried to speak, but the effort made her wince and clench her eyes shut and sent her back into the semiconscious doze. Thorn gripped her hand and spoke to her in a calm voice, told her to hold on, it was going to be all right, she was fine, she'd gotten a little knock on the head, swallowed some water, but she was okay now, she was warming up, it would be fine, everything would be fine.

Down the dock, a young man cried out, his voice rising above the uproar. Thorn swung around and stared at the heavyset young man up on the flybridge of the *ByteMe*.

'It's pinging! It's pinging!' It was Johnny Braswell. He was fanning smoke from his face, leaning forward over the chrome rail. 'You hear me, Dad? It's pinging!'

The kid had on a white tank top and blue flowered baggies.

'It's moving, the ping is moving. Big Mother's on the surface.'

A few yards behind Thorn, Farley and A.J. were grunting as they dragged a large rectangle of fiberglass down the dock. It looked like it might be the T-top from an open fishing boat, probably blasted loose by one of the explosions. Straining mightily, the two of them brought it to the splintered edge of the dock and on the count of three heaved it across the gap. Then they set about nudging it and shifting it until it formed a makeshift bridge across the five-foot break between the landside dock and the section leading to the *ByteMe*.

'You coming, Thorn?' Farley called.

372

Behind him A.J. got a running start and bounced one foot on the fiberglass panel and sailed safely across to his side of the dock.

'I can't leave her. You go on.'

Braswell waited on the other side of the panel, hands on his hips. Wisps of black smoke sailed above his head. The air reeked of melting plastic and the woozy vapors of diesel fuel and high-test gasoline. Enough raw gasoline had seeped into the harbor to level half the island from the slightest spark.

Alexandra shifted her head against the planks. The boiled-egg lump disfiguring her left cheekbone was beginning to darken. It was now only a shadowy blue, but if Thorn knew his shiners, by evening that blue would darken to a glossy black and both her eyes would be swollen shut.

Otherwise she was unmarked, though her teeth still chattered, hands quaked. She was probably in shock, had a mild concussion, needed fluids, needed to get out of the sun and away from the billows of bitter smoke. From what he could see, there was a triage area being set up near the pool. The chaises were filled with customers, maids and gardeners in attendance, moving among the guests with trays of drinks and first-aid kits. As soon as Alex's breathing evened out, he'd carry her there.

Farley peeled off his sunglasses and glared at Thorn.

'What're you doing, man? This is our chance.'

'Go,' Thorn shouted. 'Go on. Catch that goddamn fish.'

373

Behind Farley, A.J. and Johnny were throwing off the lines. The exhaust bubbled hard. On the rear deck, Morgan Braswell stared at Thorn. She wore a baseball cap and sunglasses, but he could feel the sting of her look and see by the fierce set of her jaw that she had him in the crosshairs of her fury.

'Go with them, Thorn,' Alex murmured. 'I'll be okay.'

She squinted up at him for a half second, then shut her eyes.

'What happened to her?' Sugar dropped to one knee beside Thorn.

'Took a knock, swallowed some water, stayed under for a while.'

Sugarman glanced around at the fires and sinking vessels.

From the other side of the shattered dock Farley called out Thorn's name.

'They're pulling out, man. Let's move.'

'Go, Thorn,' Sugar said. 'I'll watch after the lady.'

Farley called out his name again.

Thorn pressed a quick kiss to Alexandra's forehead, then rose and sprinted down the dock, hurdled the fiberglass panel, hustled over to Farley, and as the *ByteMe* was separating from land, the two of them ran to the end of the dock and vaulted aboard.


Lawton stood at his cabin door and listened.

The boat was under way, the rumble of water and

the engines masking all human sounds. Once he'd gotten the cuffs off, he'd spent a few minutes poking around the guest cabin, but he found nothing that triggered any memories, so he decided to move on. He wanted to know where the hell he was and why. The handcuffs, this boat, these people, none of it made any sense. Like waking up inside someone else's bad dream.

Warily, he turned the handle and nudged the door open an inch. Enough to peek down the hall toward the stern. He could barely see through the dark-tinted door that led out to the sunny cockpit. Three shadowy men moving around out there. He squinted but couldn't make them out.

Lawton eased the door all the way open. Took one more good listen, but heard nothing, so he sucked down a breath and ducked across the narrow hall and opened the door and stepped inside the cabin.

Another stateroom. This one larger. Wall covering and curtains done in a man's colors, brown and burgundy and green. A half-full bottle of rum on the bedside table, a cell phone, a key ring, an empty glass. On the dresser was a brush with curly white hairs snagged in the bristles. Some nail clippers, an assortment of tiny bottles of aftershave that looked unopened. A room that gave little sign of its occupant's character.

Lawton had investigated enough cases, been in enough rooms, snooping through the possessions of the deceased or the suspected. He knew how trifling things could signal the hidden secrets of the heart. Magazines, postcards, geegaws on the shelves, items pinned to bulletin boards, trash in the waste can. But as Lawton made the rounds of this room, prowling through the drawers, peering under the furniture, he found none of those things. This was the room of a man without enthusiasms.

The only decoration in the cabin was a color snapshot in a tortoiseshell frame propped up on the dresser. Lawton picked it up and held it close. A blond boy and an older man stood to one side of a marlin that hung from a rope at a weigh station. The boy held a fishing pole and the dad had his arm around the boy's shoulder. They bore a clear resemblance to each other. Both of them with the same narrow face and deep-set eyes and the mop of curly blond hair. Both beaming into the camera, a proud moment. Father and son.

On the other side of the big dead marlin was a stumpy silver-haired man in thick glasses and a yellow polo shirt and khaki shorts that exposed his bandy legs. He had his arm around the waist of a dark-haired woman who had the same wide forehead and thin-lipped mouth as the silver-haired man.

Lawton took another quick look around the room, then marched into the small bath. He peeled off his smelly clothes, dropped them on the floor, and went into the shower stall and soaped himself clean. He dried off on a fluffy blue towel and went back into the stateroom and dug around in the clothes locker until he found an outfit he liked. Emerald green shorts with an elastic waistband and a white crewneck shirt made of silk.

He pulled them on, then combed his hair in front of the dresser mirror. When he was finished, he set down the hairbrush and picked up the photo again and gave it another look. The stumpy man was familiar. More than familiar. Lawton studied his clothes, his thick glasses, his bowed legs, his heavy gold jewelry. He walked over to the window and tilted the photograph so it caught more light. And then the name of the silver-haired man came to him. His friend, his dear friend.

'That was Andy, my son.'

Lawton turned and looked at the man standing behind him. It was one of the men from the photograph. Same rawboned body, same curly hair, only now the blond had faded to gray.

'And that other man is Arnold Peretti,' Lawton said.

'That's right,' the man said. 'You know Arnold?'

'He was a friend of mine.'

'Arnold's a good man.'

'He was a bookie,' Lawton said. 'I used to arrest him twice a year.'

'Is that right? So you're a police officer?'

'I'm retired. But at one time I was a damn good cop.'

The man nodded vacantly. Lawton took a longer

look at him. The man's bluish eyes were flat and blurry like somebody just coming out of anesthesia.

'This your room?' Lawton asked.

The man glanced around as though seeing the place for the first time.

'Yes,' he said. 'Yes, it is.'

'I'm Lawton Collins.'

He put out his hand and the man took it in his and gave it a single shake.

'A.J. Braswell.'

Lawton had seen eyes like his before. Guys who'd rotted away too long in solitary. Guys who'd taken one blow too many, one drink, one snort, one too many long looks into the empty spaces inside their head. And there were the scary ones, zombies who stayed in their rooms too long, dreaming, concocting a world that didn't exist. When they left their rooms one idea filled their brains, one course of action. Sometimes they brought a gun with them and used it in ways that made perfect sense, were completely reasonable, according to the zombie pledge of allegiance.

'You didn't know I was aboard your boat?'

'I try to stay out of my daughter's affairs,' Braswell said. 'I assume you're a guest of hers.'

'I don't know,' Lawton said. 'Truth is, I'm not sure why I'm here. I'm a little lost.'

He smiled and Braswell smiled back.

'Yes,' A.J. said. 'I know the feeling.'

'Are we acquaintances, you and me? Do we have a history?'

378

'No,' Braswell said. 'I don't believe so. I think we just met.'

'Where are we headed, do you know that?'

'We're chasing a marlin. The one that killed my boy, Andy.'

'Yeah, I've heard about that fish. Somewhere.'

A.J. was looking at the photograph again. Lawton looked along with him, a father and son, and on the other side of the fish, a father and daughter.

'I have a problem with my memory,' Lawton said. 'I get a little fuzzy. Can't seem to piece it all together. Things out of sequence, missing steps.'

Braswell nodded. 'There's a few things I wouldn't mind forgetting.'

'Oh, sure, you think that when you're young,' Lawton said. 'If you could just take a little scalpel and dig out those bad memories things will be better. Christ, I wish it worked that way. I'd buy a scalpel tomorrow.'

Braswell drifted over to a leather chair. He sat down and laid his arms along the arms like a pharaoh in his throne.

'So, A.J., are you involved in your kids' lives? Know what they're up to?'

'They're adults,' he said. 'They're free to come and go as they please.'

'Too bad you didn't do a better job raising them,' Lawton said. 'From what I can tell, you kind of dropped the ball.'

Braswell's eyes were fixed on Lawton, but they were still numb and flat.

'Maybe you were preoccupied,' Lawton said. 'They didn't matter that much to you.'

'Why are you talking to me this way? You don't even know me.'

'I have a daughter,' Lawton said. And as he heard the words leave his lips, he knew it was true. He saw her in his head. A chubby baby, a scrawny, anxious teenager, a fine-looking woman. The pages of a private picture album flashing past. 'Alexandra is her name. A nice girl. She takes care of me now. Watches over me, makes sure I don't wander off.'

Braswell nodded vaguely as if Lawton's words required careful analysis.

'I don't relish it,' Lawton said. 'Being a burden to the girl. I can be one hell of a cross to bear. I wish it were different, but there it is. An old man with a moth-eaten memory.'

Braswell's eyes turned inward and his right hand floated up from the armrest and cupped his temple for a moment, then swept back through his curly hair, fingers massaging his scalp.

When he spoke, his voice came from far away inside him. Lawton had heard that tone dozens of times over his long career, lawbreakers confessing their sins, a voice that was equal parts shame and bragging.

'I guess I'm something of a cross to bear myself.'

Lawton nodded but was silent. It's what you did when they were ready to talk. You stepped back, let them ramble, didn't try to steer them or you might wake them from their daydream.

'My daughter, Morgan,' he said. 'She dropped out of college and came home to work with me at the plant. And to help with Johnny. He was screwing up at school, flunking all his classes, in trouble with the law. Fights and drugs and drunkenness. I didn't know what to do. I was helpless. But when Morgan returned all that rowdiness stopped. She straightened him right out.'

'Well, if she did,' Lawton said, 'I don't believe he's stayed that way.'

Braswell didn't seem to hear.

'I'd lost my eldest son, then my wife. I felt like my guts had been scooped out. I had no reason to go on. But then Morgan came home and took charge. To tell the truth, I guess she's been acting as something of a nurse to me, too.'

'Thank God for daughters,' Lawton said. 'What would sick old men like us do without them?'

Lawton looked off at the small window, the foamy splash of the wake, the distant blue. They'd been under way for maybe an hour and now it felt like the engines were cutting back.

As Lawton was turning back to Braswell, the cabin door swung open and Morgan stepped into the room. She looked back and forth between the two men. A flush darkened her cheeks.

'We've arrived, Dad. We're right on top of the ping. It's time to fish.'

A.J. rose from the chair and gave Lawton another careful look.

'Will you join us, Lawton?'

From the doorway, Morgan said, 'I need to have a word with him first. You go on, Dad, entertain your guests. Lines are in the water. We'll be right there, won't we, Lawton?'

# 24

About a mile to the west across the flat span of sea, Thorn watched another white fishing boat heading toward a distant flock of circling birds. It was what any fisherman in his right mind would be doing, following the birds to a school of bait-fish where the large predators were likely to be congregating.

But as far as Thorn could tell there was no one on the *ByteMe* in his right mind. Including his own damn self, or else he'd be back in Key Largo clipping the last thread of a bonefish fly, fluffing its bristles. Or out in the backcountry, poling across the shimmering flats.

Thorn and Farley were perched atop white fiberglass fish boxes on either side of the cabin door. Farley with his arms across his bulky chest. Through his black wraparounds he stared out at the boiling wake, every few seconds swiveling his head from side to side to scan the unvarying blue, its flat surface marked only by a few yellow drifts of seaweed and waxy ambergris. Off to the south, the pillars of black smoke from the marina fire were breaking up, carried out to sea by the steady trade winds.

Johnny Braswell, running the boat from up on the flybridge, eased back on the throttle as they reached a seam in the coloration, passing from the faded cornflower blue to a shadowy rich sapphire.

'A drop-off?' Thorn said to Farley.

'Abaco Canyon.' He shrugged his heavy shoulders. 'Not the spot I would've picked, but what the hell.'

Johnny came down from the flybridge and lowered the outriggers and set the lines. He didn't look at either of them as he went about his work, doing it all with a cold, joyless efficiency. When the four lures were skipping nicely, he stood for a moment looking out at them, then climbed back to the controls.

Thorn slid down from the fish box. The salon door was shut and Johnny was up in the noisy breeze. Still, he lowered his voice.

'Well, here we go.'

'So what's the plan, Thorn?'

'Wish I knew.'

'Goddamn,' Farley said, 'I was afraid of that.'

'You got something against improvising?'

'I say we throw the whole bunch of them overboard, then take all the time we want checking over the boat, find that old man if he's here.'

'It has a certain appeal.'

'Better than sneaking around.'

'I was thinking we'd wait a while. See what exactly we're up against.'

'I can tell you right now what we're up against,' Farley said. 'Bunch of crazies.'

'Yeah, but we've got them outnumbered.'

'We do?'

'In the moral sense.'

Farley sniffed. He hadn't brought along his sense of humor.

'Never found being on the right side made a lot of difference.'

'What I was thinking,' Thorn said. 'When we raise a fish, things'll get busy, that's when I'll disappear, go look for Lawton.'

'Assuming we find a fish.'

Farley stared out at the skipping baits and at the endless sweep of blue.

'So, do your thing, Farley. Tune up your radar, this is when we need it.'

He looked at Thorn, showed his teeth, but it wasn't anything you could call a smile.

'If it were as simple as that, Thorn, I'd own a fleet of marlin boats.'

A.J. Braswell opened the salon door and stepped out in the sunshine.

'Any sign of her, boys?'

Thorn shook his head. Farley drew a breath and resumed his watch.

'Johnny!' Braswell called up to the flybridge. 'Anything on the screen?'

Young Braswell came to the lip of the bridge and leaned over the rail.

'We're sitting on the spot, Dad. Last ping came in two minutes ago. She's damn close.'

'Try circling.'

'Hey, Dad.' Johnny took off his sunglasses and let them dangle from the cord around his neck. 'What the hell we need these guys for?'

'They're our guests, Johnny.'

Johnny's grip on the chrome rail tightened.

'Be nice,' Thorn said. 'We're here to help you land this fish you can't seem to catch.'

'You don't think I know what you're doing here?'

Johnny settled his sunglasses back on his nose and jabbed them into place with his middle finger.

'I'm sorry,' A.J. said. 'I invited you along without consulting my children. It wasn't really fair of me.'

'It's your boat, right? You're the daddy. I'd say that puts you in charge.'

'If it were only that simple.'

'Why isn't it?'

'We've always fished as a team. That's why Johnny's upset.'

Farley grunted and stared out at the blue distance.

'Either you're boss or you're not,' he said, the sinews in his neck flexing as he spoke. 'Isn't no middle ground.'

Before he could answer, Morgan came out of the

cabin. Her sunglasses were propped up in her hair. She glanced at Farley, then trained her eyes on Thorn.

Braswell said, 'These are my guests, Morgan. I believe you already know Farley Boissont. Jelly's son.'

Her eyes were an intense blue and had a silver shine as if they were backed by tin foil. They seemed independent of the rest of her, more volatile, more severe, powered by some dangerous fuel that throbbed inside them. She wore a white T-shirt that hugged her body tightly, showed the pleasant swell of her breasts. The T-shirt was tucked into a pair of black bicycle tights that molded firmly over her narrow hips. The sum of her parts should have added up to a remarkable beauty, but those harsh, indifferent eyes undercut it all.

'Name's Thorn.'

'Yes, we meet again.'

Braswell stepped forward and laid a hand on his daughter's shoulder.

'You know this man?'

'We had a brief encounter last week. At the airplane crash.'

'The crash? You were there, Morgan? The one in the Everglades?'

'Oh, did I forget to tell you, Dad? Sorry. Yes, Johnny and I were out there fishing when the plane came down. Isn't that right, Mr Thorn?'

'That's one version.'

Braswell looked back and forth between his daughter and Thorn.

'Well, Thorn and Farley have had a couple of encounters with Big Mother. They're going to help us find her. They had her up to the boat twice.'

'Oh, really? And you believed that?'

Braswell gave Thorn an apologetic shrug.

Farley slid down from the fish box and stepped around Morgan and climbed up the ladder to the flybridge.

'Where do you think you're going?'

Farley stopped halfway up the ladder and looked down at her.

'Sooner we find that goddamn fish, sooner I can get the hell away from you people.'

They circled for an hour and got no more pings on the GPS screen.

Thorn joined Farley on the flybridge and they planted themselves on either side of Johnny at the control console. Before them on the long, sleek bow, a dinghy was lashed to the deck. An overpowered Zodiac with a fiberglass transom and stand-up steering console. Beyond the point of the bow, the featureless blue sea spread in all directions. No other boats, no birds, just a gentle two-foot swell.

Johnny steered the boat and mumbled to himself. Down in the cockpit, Braswell stared back at the skittering lures. He was slumped forward in the fighting chair, elbows on his knees like a ballplayer sulking on the bench. Morgan had stationed herself beside him, and every few seconds she turned and cut a look at Thorn.

As they passed again across the line between the light blue sea to the dark, bottomless depths, Thorn pressed his shoulder against Johnny and used his best conspiratorial voice.

'Hey, Johnny. Shot down any planes lately?'

The kid twisted back and gave Thorn an ugly sneer.

'I'm not talking to you, jingle-brain. I'm not talking to either of you. You don't belong here. You can just shut your yap, smart guy.'

'You and sis, you're quite a pair. Gunsel and Gretel, lost in the woods.'

'Fuck you, cheeseball.'

Thorn tapped a finger on the back of Johnny's bandaged hand.

'What happened to your thumb, kid? Been sucking on it too hard?'

Johnny jerked his shoulder away, but Farley was tight on his other side and the young man had nowhere to go.

'"Not only don't you have any scruples,"' Thorn said. '"You don't have any brains." *Detour*, 1945.'

Johnny turned and peered at him.

'What's wrong, pork rind?' Thorn said. 'You think you're the only person in the world ever saw a movie?'

'Okay, Johnny boy,' Farley said. 'Take it up to eleven knots.'

'What!'

'You heard me, boy. Bump it to eleven.'

'Eight's what we do. We were doing eight when we caught her last time; that's what we do, eight knots.'

'That's ten years ago,' Farley said. 'She's bigger now, faster. Likes a faster target. Take it to eleven.'

'Hey, who the fuck do you think you are?'

'You want to catch that fish, Johnny? Or spend the rest of your life chasing it? Do what Farley tells you.'

'I'm the captain of this goddamn vessel. I decide how fast we go.'

'Just because your hands are on the wheel, John boy, doesn't mean you're running the show.'

'Over there.' Farley was peering to the right. 'Hundred and twenty yards, that riffle.'

Farley's posture was straighter, eyes locked to water.

'I don't see anything,' Johnny said.

'Two o'clock,' Farley said. 'Eleven knots. Unless there's some reason you don't want this fucking fish.'

'I don't see what you're looking at.'

'Just do it,' Thorn said.

'Man, I don't know what you're seeing out there.' Johnny turned the wheel and nudged the throttle forward. 'I must have the wrong sunglasses.'

'Kid,' Farley said, 'you got the wrong eyes.'

Thorn turned and looked back at their wake, watched the big lures flitting across the surface, then diving a few inches below, leaving a trail of bubbles, then resurfacing for another brief ride across the sweet polished surface of the sea.

He was watching the back starboard lure when the dorsal fin rose and the long narrow bill knifed into view. It came so fast and the shadow was so large Thorn thought for a moment it was just a wishful mirage, a phantom rising from the depths of his reverie.

Then the outrigger popped and the slack belly in the line vanished.

'Fish on!' Braswell yelled. 'That's her, that's her.'

Johnny eased the throttle till the boat was almost dead in the water.

'It's big,' Farley said.

Thorn rubbed the sweat sting out of his eyes.

'Hell, it looks like a goddamn limousine.'

Down on deck, Braswell wrenched the rod out of the holder and fit the butt into the socket on his waist belt. Morgan reeled in the other lines and settled the rods back in their holders, then turned to her father, lowered his chair back and clipped the harness to the reel and eased it around her father's back. She cocked the chair back into place and both of them watched as the line whirled off the reel. Braswell fumbled with the drag, almost lost the rod as he braked down on the fish. Even from twenty feet away, Thorn saw the tremble in his hands.

Johnny had them in neutral, then slipped it into reverse, facing astern, his butt pressed to the console, steering by feel, trying to keep the fish directly behind them, but the slanting line moved from starboard to port and back again with amazing speed. Though the fish was already down in the heavy depths, it zigzagged so quickly it might have been gliding across the airy surface.

'Get down to the cockpit, Johnny,' Farley said. 'Make yourself useful.'

'Fuck that. I'm running the boat.'

'Maybe if we were catching a minnow, boy. But not this fish. Get down there, give your daddy water, rub his shoulders. Going to be a long afternoon.'


Face in the wind, Alexandra drew down breath after breath of fresh salt air, reviving slowly. By the time Sugarman had Thorn's old Chris-Craft a mile offshore, Alexandra's wooziness had mostly cleared. She could feel the puffiness growing around her left eye and a three-inch spike driving deeper and deeper into her temple with every breath. She was wearing a new set of Thorn's clothes. A black-and-white checked cowboy shirt with pearl snap buttons. A pair of old blue jeans shorts with frayed cutoff legs. She didn't remember selecting them or putting them on. A missing hour or two.

'You all right?' Sugarman gave her a quick look, then resumed his watch out the blurry windshield.

She told him she was going to be fine. It was nothing, she'd taken worse knocks playing with a litter of kittens. She said he should just keep steering the boat, keep his eyes sharp for the *ByteMe*.

'It's a big goddamn ocean,' he said.

And that's what echoed in her ears as the blood emptied from her head and she stumbled backwards, it's a big goddamn ocean, and bumped against the wooden side panel, a big goddamn ocean, and went down on the deck. Sprawling there, squinting up into the sun, watching the handsome black man bend down and scoop her up and carry her into the shadowy cabin and lay her out on the cot where Thorn slept the night before. Thorn's smell in the pillow. It's a big goddamn ocean. Breathing his earthy scent of sweat and suntan oil and fish and the musky undertone of sex. A smell she recalled only vaguely from her distant past. It's a big goddamn ocean, Sugarman said. Like they might never find the boat. Might never see her father alive again. Or Thorn. Whose smell she inhaled, like hay, or dry summer grasses, a pungent spice that filled her lungs and filled them again.

The boat was still grumbling along when she woke. Mouth dry, spike still hammering at her temple. She sat up slowly. A bolt of pain shutting her eyes for a moment. But she pressed her feet to the deck and pushed herself up and steadied herself against the bunk. She breathed in and out with great care, tried to keep herself erect. She was twelve feet tall and her head was full of helium. She was one of those giant balloons in the Macy's parade, unwieldy, anchored to the earth by a dozen cords handled by a band of drunks.

She stood in the center of the cabin, tugged to the left, then the right, forward and back. She looked out the narrow doorway and all she could see of Sugarman was his legs and his narrow waist. Steering that old boat, still searching for her father. Her father, Lawton Collins, who had been out of her sight for days. Never in the years that he'd been sick had they been separated this long. Never in all those years had she felt so hollow, so lost, so helpless.

With a hand against the cabin wall, she tottered forward into the narrow V-berth. Looking for the supply locker. A bottle of water was on her mind. Even if it was warm water, or hot. It didn't matter. So parched. Tongue pasted to the roof of her mouth.

She found the narrow locker door cut flush into the wood of the cabin wall. She thumbled back the latch and drew open the door. No water. Nothing but a large file box with a loose lid.

She shut the locker and turned away. Staggered briefly, caught herself. She moved down the narrow aisle, headed toward the sunlight. But she couldn't shake the feeling that she should go back, have another look. Not sure why, not sure what nagged at her. She stopped, stood there, dazed, head throbbing, and then a long sequence of connections fired off in her mind. A box, a box, a cardboard box.

She turned around, went back to the locker, opened it and pulled the lid off and looked inside. She drew a sharp breath, then put the lid back on and carried the box out to the deck and stood next to Sugarman cradling it in her arms. It weighed maybe twenty-five pounds. About the same as a portable television set.

'You okay?'

'Fine,' she said. 'Any luck?'

'Nothing yet,' he said. 'I've been on channel sixteen, monitoring the chatter. I put the word out, asked if anybody'd seen the *ByteMe*, but so far, nobody's come back. Mostly they're talking about the explosions at the marina.'

She scanned the horizon but saw nothing in any direction. An endless stretch of blue water, blue sky, stringy white clouds.

'We're heading south now. I heard someone on the radio mention another fishing grounds. The canyons.'

She nodded, shifted the box in her arms.

'What's that?'

'I found it below. I was looking for a bottle of water.'

Sugarman nudged the throttle forward, made a small adjustment in their course. Alexandra pulled off the lid and tilted the box in his direction.

He stared down into it for several moments, then looked into her eyes.

'Is that what I think it is?'

'Yeah,' she said. 'Dad must've hidden it the night he was at Thorn's.'

'Jesus, be careful,' Sugarman said. 'That could be dangerous.'

Alexandra peered down at the tangle of wires and the clear cells filled with colored fluids. It didn't look dangerous. It looked silly. It looked like a high school science project, a third runner-up in the half-assed terrorist division.

'Alex?'

She looked up at Sugarman. He was steering with one hand, the other reaching out for her as if he thought she was about to take another tumble.

'I'm fine,' she said. 'Don't worry about me.'

'I know I don't need to tell you,' said Sugar. 'But that thing is evidence in the murder of dozens of people.'

She nodded and settled the lid back in place. And turned around and set the box down in a corner of the cockpit. She stood next to Sugarman, staring out the windshield at the gentle rollers.

'You and Thorn,' she said. 'You're pretty good friends.'

She looked out at the empty blue.

'Since grade school,' Sugar said. 'Since forever.'

'Tell me about him,' she said. Eyes on the distance. Still smelling the pillow. The scent of his sweat.

'What do you want to know?'

'Whatever you think is relevant.'

'Relevant to what?'

She turned her head and let him have a good look at her face.

'Oh,' he said. 'I see.'

# 25

A.J. reeled in line and reeled in some more, then watched an hour's work fly off the reel in seconds. It was sweaty labor, hot and wordless. Grunting and lifting and cranking. Harnessed to the fighting chair, Braswell seemed to age a year each hour. His hands turning into cramped claws, muscles in spasm. Sweat tormenting his eyes.

Thorn knew the crushing ache in his shoulders and his lower back and quadriceps. Feet grinding against the deck for hours until his toes were blistered and bloody. Muscles stiffening, in revolt. A.J. was probably having the same silent conversation with himself that all big-game fishermen had sooner or later, a debate about hanging on, balancing the cost of his pain against the shame of defeat. Taking measured sips of the anger and hate that propelled him, that unreasoning, masochistic joy. It was mindless work. Connected to a creature who had only two reactions, attack or flee. It was, if you weighed it against mankind's vital concerns, trivial in the extreme. Mad and childish.

Hours and hours of agonizing immobility. Every act on display, every slump of shoulder, every groan and squirm and whimper. That old Cuban fisherman in his fictional boat had only himself to please, only his private demons to conquer. But A.J. Braswell had a larger audience, a more complicated one. More at stake in his struggle than simply proving his worth. This wasn't about fishing. This wasn't about any triumph of the spirit. It was the finale to a long sequence of calamities that had wrecked his family and everyone they had come into contact with. Instead of meaning, instead of love, the Braswells had this fish.

Thorn came down off the flybridge and sat on the gunwale and watched the fight up close. He spoke the customary encouraging words, the patter of solidarity. Every time he spoke, Morgan or Johnny glared at him as if he'd uttered a blasphemy, which of course he had. They were their own exclusive church, these three, their own holy trinity. They'd shared the same poisoned communion bowl for so long no one else could possibly know their pain or enter their hallowed sanctum.

Thorn smiled back at Morgan, deflecting her laser eyes as best he could. He was looking for his moment, sensing he only had one chance. And if it failed there would be no recourse but to do it Farley's way and take them head-on, toss each of them overboard and while they treaded water, proceed with a thorough search for Lawton.

The moment he chose was late in the afternoon, nine hours into the battle. The silence was grim, the sun only moments from setting the sea on fire. They might be locked in this contest all night. It might last all the next day or longer. There was no way to tell. Morgan looked exhausted. She had her head down, staring at a square of deck between her feet. Johnny stood close behind his father's chair looking out to the spot where the line entered the water. The giant blue had not shown herself again. She'd run steadily downward until nothing was left but the last few coils of line. The knot that held the line to the reel was only one layer away. One more run of even a few feet, a swish or two of her powerful hindquarters, and the game was over. A.J. Braswell was soggy with sweat and his arms looked limp and uncertain. Probably hallucinating, having some loony conversation with his marlin, bonding with her, a supernatural union.

Thorn eased to his feet, waited for a moment to see that no one had noticed, then stole across four feet of deck. Johnny still flanking his father, staring out to sea, Morgan watching her toe tap against the deck. Thorn opened the salon door and stepped inside. He was halfway across the cabin when the cold metal hooked around his neck. He stopped mid-step, and in the mirror wall behind the bar he saw the two of them frozen. The crook of the aluminum gaff curved around his throat. Morgan gripped the handle with both hands, the gaff's razor point pricking his flesh an inch below his Adam's apple, pressing so tight against his skin that if he sneezed he'd rip out his own larynx.

'You're not real smart, are you?'

Thorn slipped a breath past the pressure of the gaff. He managed a guttural noise. Holding still, seeing in the mirror a dribble of blood seeping from his throat.

'Did you think I wouldn't recognize you? Or what? I'd just say hello, oh my, what a coincidence, it's the hero from the plane crash. Is that what you thought?'

She tugged on the gaff and the blood began to stream in earnest.

'You came nosing around the plant the next day. I saw you on the security video. Then you're on my boat in the Bahamas. Tell me, Thorn. Give me a good reason why I shouldn't tear out your throat right now?'

He met her gaze in the mirror. Those shocking blue eyes were glazed by a crisp layer of frost. They professed a toughness that her mouth contradicted. Her lips were soft and uncertain, warped by a schoolgirl's shy discomfort. As if some part of her had been stunted long ago, and just below that crust of harsh indifference there was still a teenager who'd never overcome her unease around adults. A girl who had been banished from her childhood before she was ready. Thorn knew the look. He'd seen it more than once in his own face. A boy who was continually surprised to see the man he'd become.

'Have you ever thought, Morgan, that you might've been better off if you'd stayed in school, finished your degree, married a nice guy with patches on the elbows of his corduroy coat?'

'You don't know me. You don't know anything about me.'

'That's true,' he said. 'But I do know something about taking on more responsibility than you can handle. About cracking under the pressure. Trying to live up to some gold standard that's out of your reach. I know a few things.'

She tightened the gaff against his throat.

'I'm not cracking. I'm handling things fine.'

'Oh, yeah, you're doing great, Morgan. Just take a look around you, if you can see over the stack of bodies you've surrounded yourself with.'

'Who are you? What're you doing here?'

'Your dad and your brother,' Thorn said, 'do they reciprocate in any way? That's how it's supposed to work, you know? Give a little, take a little. But it doesn't look that way to me. Looks to me like those two are both full-time jobs. And you're working the night shift and the day shift just to keep up.'

Thorn felt the pressure of the gaff slacken.

'I can walk away any time I want. I'm here because

I want to be here. Nobody's forcing me to do anything. I'm a free woman.'

'I don't think so. I don't think any of your people are free.'

'What bullshit,' she said, but her heart wasn't in it.

'When somebody's drowning,' Thorn said, 'if you jump in and try to save them, you better be a damn good swimmer, because if you're not, the chances are pretty good they'll drag you down with them. That's been my experience.'

'Is that the best you can do? Can't think of another reason why I shouldn't tear your throat out?'

His eyes shifted to the scene behind her, a sudden burst of action in the cockpit.

'Oh, I can think of one.'

'Yeah?'

'Because,' Thorn said, 'your fish is coming up.'

Holding the pressure on his throat, she turned him to the door and saw what was happening.

'Go on. Move, goddamn you, move.'

Thorn pushed open the salon door and stepped outside. She pulled the gaff away and came up beside him.

A.J. Braswell was pumping furiously. As fast as his arms could move. The fish was rising with astonishing speed.

'Keep her astern, Farley,' Morgan called up to the flybridge. 'Do it.'

Braswell whirled the crank, his hand a blur. Line thickened on the reel.

Johnny spun around, shoved past Thorn, and hustled into the cabin. A second later he was back with a twelve-gauge shotgun. Holding it by the stock, he gave Thorn a humorless grin, then moved to the edge of the fighting chair.

'I'm cramping,' Braswell groaned. He writhed against the safety harness. He looked helplessly at Thorn, then twisted in the chair, muscles in spasm. 'I can't hold it anymore. I'm going to lose it.'

'You can do it, Dad. Hold on. You can do it.'

Braswell cried out and wrenched to his right. With his crabbed fingers he unsnapped the clips and thrust the rod at Thorn. Morgan screamed a curse.

The fish must have sensed the uncertain struggle up above and chose that moment to make a run. The reel ratcheted, line spinning free. With a moan, Braswell let go of the rod. Thorn snatched at it but it flew across the deck, clattered against the transom, and started to tumble overboard. Thorn lunged, seized it midair, and grappled for a hold, the fiberglass pole twisting and jerking like some electrified creature.

One-handed, he fumbled for a grip, finally got hold of the padded handle with his right hand, then clutched the forward grip in his left. He sucked down a breath, lifted himself upright, and levered the butt hard against his stomach. He leaned back and began to crank.

Beside him Braswell had slumped forward in his chair and was peering bleakly out at the water.

Johnny jammed the cool steel of the shotgun barrel against Thorn's cheek.

'Give me that rod, goddamn you. You're not part of this.'

Thorn lifted his elbow and brushed the barrel away, then bowed his back, flared his shoulders, and strained against the monstrous weight on his line. The fish reacted with another surge, catching Thorn off-balance.

He staggered forward, but managed to cock one foot up and brace it against the transom. He bent back, throwing all his weight against a fish that had to outweigh him by at least a thousand pounds. Thorn pulled back on the rod and reeled on the downstroke. Reeled and reeled some more.

'You bastard!' Morgan shrieked. 'You fucking bastard.'

Ten feet behind the boat the water humped as if somewhere down on the ocean floor a volcano had begun to erupt.

Thorn reclaimed the last of the line and his hands went still.

'Holy shit,' said Johnny.

As they watched, the dark blister on the water's surface doubled in width. Then in a white blast of seawater, the blue marlin exploded into view and soared into the air so close to the stern that any one of them might have reached out and touched her electric blue hide. The fish was lit up, her flesh glowing as if a switch had been thrown from deep

405

inside her molecules. Showing herself completely, her neon stripes, her dark scythe tail, her wild and furious eye.

Thorn watched as the fish stabbed her rapier at the sky, shook her head, and hung weightlessly before them as if she could suspend at will the gravitational laws. The marlin's glistening eye took them in, each in turn, and whatever reckoning she made seemed to infuriate that leviathan even more. She swiveled in the air, went on her side, and slammed back into the sea, a great belly flop that sent a flood of water over the transom and buckets of cold spray raining down from the sky.

Farley clambered down from the bridge and barked instructions to Thorn, telling him to reel, goddamn it, to tighten the drag, keep his rod tip up, turn that damn fish around before she had a chance to take a breath and flex her muscles again. He pulled on his glove and watched as Thorn cranked a dozen turns, watched as the double line emerged through the blue skin of the sea.

'That's my job,' Johnny said. 'I'm the wire man.'

Holding the shotgun one-handed, Johnny stepped forward, but Farley put his broad back to the boy, and Johnny had no choice but to watch helplessly as the black glistening bill appeared and the fish floundered and writhed.

Drenched by spray, Farley whipped off his sunglasses and tossed them away and leaned over the transom and snagged the wire in his hand and took a double wrap and hauled the fish close. Thorn watched the slabs of muscles in his arms and shoulders pump full of blood. The fish was massive. Larger than the great white shark that made such a stir in Islamorada a few years back, a world-record behemoth that hung at Bud and Mary's dock for twenty-four hours till every news organization in America had filmed it. But this was larger. Much larger.

On the marlin's back, the silver cigar-shaped pod glittered in the failing light. The steel hook that attached it to the marlin's gristly back had worked its way to the surface of the fish's hide. It was one good shake away from breaking free.

'Stand back,' Johnny said. He brought the butt of the shotgun to his shoulder. Aiming at the fish's eye.

'No, Johnny.'

Braswell rose from his chair. His shoulders were hunched in pain, his legs uncertain beneath him. He held his hand up, halting his son, and peered over the transom at the fish.

'We're not killing her.'

'Yes, we are. We're killing the motherfucker right now. This is it.'

Morgan picked up the flying gaff and stepped over to the transom and took her place beside Farley. He looked at her and shook his head.

'No gaff,' he said. 'I got her fine.'

But Thorn could see a pale light rising in his eyes, the strain already showing in the slightest of quivers in his neck and shoulders. Like the night before when he'd lifted the iron bar loaded with five hundred pounds from the rack on the bench press and held it aloft until his muscles were on the verge of failure.

Braswell stared at the fish, his mouth working as if he were carrying on a silent conversation with the monster, or perhaps mumbling a prayer on her behalf. The fish thrashed, but Farley held it in check.

'We're not killing her,' Braswell said.

'What!'

'Yes, we are, goddamn it,' Morgan said. 'Yes, we are.'

'No. We're letting her go. She did nothing wrong.'

'Nothing wrong! And what about Andy? What about Mom?'

Johnny was still sighting along the barrel, his aim fixed on the fish's right eye. The marlin lurched upward, slashing her sword just inches from Farley's ear. He heaved back, jerking the leader line upward to reinstate his authority, remind the fish that it was caught in an unyielding grip. The marlin's mouth opened and gulped down the treacherous air, and twisted defiantly, but Farley held fast.

'She was only trying to save herself. We got in the way. It was an accident, son. Bad bad luck. This is no monster. She's a creature that wants to be left alone. A force of nature.'

Morgan pulled her eyes from the fish and looked at her father.

'Force of nature! Then why the fuck have we been

out here, Dad, all these years? An accident? A fucking accident? Give me a goddamn break.'

Braswell looked at his daughter. She quieted her voice, brought it down to almost a whisper.

'You said this was the end, Dad. You said this would finish it.'

'I changed my mind, Morgan.'

They stared at each other for a short moment.

'Shoot it, Johnny,' she said. 'Kill the fucker once and for all.'

Braswell stepped in front of the shotgun.

'Put it down, Johnny,' Thorn said. 'Do what your daddy says.'

'You want this fish or not?' Farley asked casually. 'I'm not holding her much longer.'

'Just a second,' Braswell said. He kept his eyes on his son's, and put his hand on the barrel of the shotgun and nudged it downward until it was aimed at the deck between them. The boy's face went soft, his mouth stretching wide as if he meant to howl at the twilight. Braswell patted Johnny on the shoulder and stepped past him and went to the fish locker where Thorn had been sitting. He drew open the second drawer and pulled out another silver pod, longer and fatter than the one attached to the fish. Then he withdrew a stumpy harpoon from the same drawer and snapped the pod onto it, just behind the barbed tip.

'What the hell is that?'

'A new design,' he said, 'more durable battery, radio signal stronger. Better data collection.'

'Jesus, Dad.'

'No,' Morgan said. 'No way in hell are we doing that.'

'This isn't about you kids. This is what *I* want to do.'

'Oh, yeah? Not about us. It's about you. And there's a difference, Dad? The two things aren't the same thing? Now, all of a sudden you decide to do something like this all by yourself.'

'It's what I'm going to do, Morgan.'

'So you can follow that fish for the rest of your pathetic life? For what?'

'It's my decision, Morgan.'

Braswell stepped around the fighting chair and took a grip on the harpoon.

'Your decision,' she said. 'Like we can just go on our merry fucking ways? Are you crazy, you old bastard? I put my life on hold for the last ten years because of this goddamn fish. I sacrificed everything for you, your fucking company. And why? So you could stick another goddamn pod on this fish? No, sir. No way in hell.'

'It's a way to stay close,' Braswell said. 'To Andy. To your mother. A way to keep the connection alive.'

She looked at her father for a long moment, her face closing down, eyes losing their light. Her black hair fluttered wildly as if invisible bats were escaping from their roosts inside her skull. Behind her the sky was purpling, and overhead was a dense layer of corrugated clouds with gold beams breaking through tiny perforations like searchlights from on high.

'Kill him, Johnny. Kill the fucker.'

'Thorn,' Farley said. 'Could you take the shotgun out of circulation?'

'Sure thing.'

Farley's face gleamed with oily sweat. The fish was thrashing, using its last reserves to break free, but Farley kept his feet planted wide, his hand tight in the wire, and counteracted every move. But Thorn could see in his eyes that this was costing him dearly.

Thorn jammed the rod in the holder and came around the fighting chair.

'Shoot him, Johnny,' Morgan said. 'Shoot him now.'

'Who?'

He waved the gun at Thorn, then at his father.

'Shoot all of them,' she said. 'I don't give a shit.'

Braswell turned his back on his children and lifted the harpoon.

'Goddamn it, Johnny. Shoot him.'

Johnny swung the shotgun in a frantic arc, across the fish, his father, Farley.

On the far end of the arc, Thorn thrust forward and got a grip on the barrel and tore it from the boy's hands. It slipped from his hand and the gun clattered to the deck and Thorn stooped for it, taking a glimpse to his left as Braswell hammered the new pod into place, and then from the other side of the universe, Thorn saw a bright sparkle rocketing in, saw it too late, a microsecond, that's all, only enough time to shoot his right hand up in a feeble effort to deflect the blow, but missing by inches, the gaff crashing down on his ear, his temple. And the sparkle brightened inside his head. Setting off a string of flashes, red blooms of light, silent green explosions as Thorn tumbled to the deck, smacking his own fool head against the steel post of the fighting chair.

And from that position, on his back, on the floor of a steep-sided canyon, a mile away from the rim where sleepwalkers were speaking in slow-motion voices, electronically altered, Thorn watched Johnny raise the shotgun and watched its barrel and the butt kick against Johnny's shoulder. Watched Farley Boissont double over as if he'd taken a battering ram to the gut, and the barrel flared again, and the big black man with the dreadlocks and chiseled muscles bucked backwards over the transom, tearing the fishing line as he went.

The fish hung there a moment more, free of the torment of the line, surveying the spectacle with her cold, unblinking eye. Then she heaved a few inches upward and dropped back into the choppy sea.

A half second later Thorn felt the canyon floor drop away beneath him like an elevator plunging down its endless shaft, and finally finally finally he came to rest in a dark basement, dead but awake, seeing up through the long narrow shaft, in a square of light, the boy with the blond, stringy hair and the stupid hat and the chubby cheeks, slipping two more shells into the shotgun and saw that black steel eye coming down through the frame of brightness, down

412

and down until it pressed hot as a branding iron against his forehead and there was a sharp click and then he was no more. No Thorn. No noise. No pain. Just drifting in the black airless atmosphere. Falling through the pleasant layers of darkness, from black to blacker to blackest. And then a place that was black beyond all that.

'You hear that?'

'I did,' said Sugarman. 'Over there.'

He pointed, but Alexandra said, 'No, more to the south.'

And then a second explosion echoed across the miles of water.

'You're right,' Sugarman said. He took the compass heading, mashed the throttle down, and stared out at the last remnants of sunshine, a haunted sky full of bruised blue light, frigate birds floating through the high, thin atmosphere, like goblins feasting on the final moments of the day.

# 26

'Hey there, sleepyhead.'

Thorn opened his eyes. He had no arms and no legs. His body was floating in a vat of scalding oil.

'Welcome to the fiesta,' Lawton said. 'Me and you and this other guy.'

They were lying face to face on a king-sized bed. Thorn on his left side, Lawton lying on his right. One of Lawton's eyes was bruised and there was a knuckle-gash on his cheekbone. Thorn strained to sit up, but his body wouldn't cooperate. After a moment's rest, he managed to lift his head and briefly survey the situation.

Lawton was hog-tied with plastic cable ties and bungee cords and duct tape. Hands lashed behind his back with the binding around his wrists hooked to the cord that circled his ankles. He was arched backwards, his spine flexed against itself. Thorn assumed he was probably trussed up the same way. Which would explain why he couldn't feel his feet or hands. Just a numb ache.

'What other guy?' Thorn said. His voice sounded so far away he wasn't sure he'd spoken, maybe only imagined the words.

'Him,' Lawton said. And rolled onto his back so Thorn could peek across his belly at the man sprawled next to him. Naked and dead, with the silver butt of a blade protruding from his throat and blood scabbing his right eye, a deep slash on his cheek.

The old man rolled back and lifted his eyebrows.

'Not particularly sociable, this one.'

'Wingo,' Thorn said. 'The poor bastard.'

'Who's Wingo?'

'Never mind, Lawton. How are you doing?'

'Oh, I don't know. I been better, I guess. That damn girl sucker-punched me. Put me on my ass, almost knocked me out. A girl. Do you believe it?'

'She doesn't fight fair,' Thorn said.

He shifted on the bed, trying to ease the sharp pinch of the bindings on his wrist. But his new position only aggravated the pressure. Thorn winced and shut his eyes against the long, fat needle that hammered into the base of his spinal cord. He kept them shut and took a gulp of air. He listened to a high whine from deep in his inner ear. He didn't know how badly he was injured, and with his hands and legs bent behind him as they were, he wasn't going to find out soon.

When he opened his eyes again, Lawton Collins was hunched forward on the bed, kicking and squirming grimly. Huffing hard as he tried to wriggle free of his bonds. His face was red, his body contorting into an agonizing pose.

'Calm down, Lawton. Calm down. Relax.'

The old man ceased his struggle and went limp. Panting, he looked over at Thorn.

'I got free once already, but I'll be damned if I can remember how.'

'What happened to your ear? You're bleeding.'

'The kid cut me.'

'Johnny?'

'They were trying to make me tell them something, I forget what.'

Thorn lay still for a moment as images from the last hour trickled back. The colossal marlin, the new silver pod fixed to its back, Morgan's rage, the shotgun blasts, Farley blown backwards over the side. Thorn clenched his eyes shut and said a silent benediction. As if the gods ever listened to him, as if they ever listened to anyone. He said it nonetheless, a prayer of gratitude and respect for a decent man. A man who had tried his best to armor himself against the treacherous world. But no muscles could accomplish that. Thorn had learned long ago, there was no defense against people like the Braswells, only offense. Your own set of sharp teeth and claws and a vengeful thirst for blood.

Through the mattress, Thorn felt the throb of the

big diesels at low revolutions, just above idle. He imagined the happy family was having a powwow in the salon. If A.J. was still alive, he was probably trying to reassert his paternal authority. But from what Thorn had seen, the father didn't stand a chance in hell of winning back the esteem of those two feral children. Which meant that when their meeting broke up, the real fun would begin. Thorn assumed the only reason he was still alive was that Morgan did not yet know how much of her plot he was aware of, or whom else he'd confided in. Torture was in the offing. There would be a blade and there would be cutting.

'You don't believe me,' Lawton said. 'But I swear, I got out of these damn restraints before. I know I did.'

Thorn rolled over to face him.

'We're going to have to do this together,' Thorn said.

'I don't know. I usually work alone.'

'So do I,' Thorn said. 'But we're going to have to adjust.'

'What? I gnaw through your bracelets or you gnaw through mine?'

'Close,' Thorn said. 'I was thinking about that.'

He lifted his head and aimed his chin at Wingo.

'Oh, he's not going to help us. That man is in a state of rigor mortis.'

'I mean the blade.'

'What?'

'In his throat,' Thorn said. 'The blade in his throat.'

Lawton rolled onto his other shoulder and looked at the dead man, then rolled back.

'I think it's just a nail file,' he said.

'Well, it's more than we've got right now.'

'Yeah, sure,' Lawton said. 'But how the hell do we get it?'

'I'll do it,' said Thorn. 'Dead guys hardly ever bite back.'

Lawton scooted toward the foot of the bed. Even in the chill of the air-conditioning, he worked up a heavy sweat before he opened up enough space for Thorn to writhe the three feet to Wingo's side.

He didn't think about it. Didn't try to talk himself out of the squeamish reaction. He simply lowered his lips to Wingo's throat and clamped his front teeth on the half inch of steel and inch-by-inch tugged it loose from the cool, hardened flesh.

He spit it out on the pillow and examined it.

'Is it any good?' Lawton said.

'It'll have to be.'

'I'll cut you loose,' the old man said. 'I'm the trained escape artist. This is my area of expertise.'

Thorn tongued the nail file off the pillow and took the sharp, bloody end into his mouth. He shifted around on the white sheets until he was in Lawton's face.

'This is one for the books,' Lawton said. 'If it works, that is.'

Lawton brought his mouth close to Thorn's and

took the nail file in his lips, then worked it deeper until he had it clamped between his molars. Then he swiveled around to bring his face close to Thorn's bound wrists.

He spoke a few garbled words, dentist-chair talk.

'Lawton, we can discuss things later. Just cut the cords. Cut the hell out of them.'

But Lawton had to speak, and his muffled words finally came clear.

'Houdini,' he mumbled. 'Houdini would've loved this shit.'

Alexandra could see the faint lights, maybe a mile ahead through the increasing darkness.

'Is it them?'

'It's got to be,' said Sugarman.

'You wouldn't happen to have a gun, would you?'

Sugarman shook his head.

'Customs guys frown on tourists importing heat.'

'Great.'

'Hey, we got a ray gun. What else could we need?'

'Something that would draw a little blood.'

Sugarman looked at her.

She was gritting her teeth, a bitter smile that seemed to be holding back a sob.

'Stay cool, Alex. Your dad's okay.'

'You know that, do you?'

'Thorn's on the case. He'll look out for him.'

She sighed and mashed the heel of her hand to

the hollow between her breasts, grinding it against her sternum, trying to relieve the band that was tightening around her chest.

'What're we going to do, Sugar, when we get there?'

'Depends on what we find.'

'Unarmed like this, what can we do?'

'Throw the switch,' he said. 'Turn off their lights.'

She patted him on the back as if he'd made a weak joke.

'Yeah. Turn off their lights. That should put the fear of God in them.'


Lawton lifted his head to take a breath and Thorn twisted around to see him. A dribble of bright blood leaked from the corner of his mouth. Lawton shifted the nail file with his tongue and licked at the blood.

'Almost there,' he mumbled, then something else Thorn couldn't decode.

Lawton bent back to his work, sawing the file against an edge of the duct tape. All they needed was a tear and Thorn could do the rest. With just a nick in the edge of the tape he'd found he could rip it in half like a cotton sheet. They'd already cut away one section of tape and Thorn's hands were looser, feeling the first prickling sensations of life.

Out in the salon there was shouting. The family meeting getting ugly. Thorn could make out only a word here and there. Morgan's voice, Johnny's.

Either Papa was dead or speaking in muted tones. From the fragments he'd made out, he gathered they were still assigning blame, sorting out the guilt and responsibility for deaths past and deaths to come. Whining and upbraiding, the thrust and parry of a family who would never know the sweet relief of forgiveness.

'Shit,' Lawton said. 'I dropped it.'

'Where is it, Lawton?'

'On the floor. Here at the end of the bed. I see it.'

Without warning, Lawton rolled off the foot of the bed and flopped hard on the deck. He gasped. None of it was loud but the voices out in the salon went quiet.

Thorn wriggled over the side of the bed, let himself down as smoothly as he could, and squirmed quickly over to Lawton. The old man was trying unsuccessfully to pluck the nail file off the deck with his lips and tongue. While Thorn positioned himself and presented his bound hands, Lawton cursed and grumbled.

The big diesels notched up slowly, and the yacht's bow tipped up, then gradually settled back as the boat rose up on plane.

'Better move it, Lawton.'

Lawton fumed and muttered. His mouth stuffed with cotton and marbles. Thorn felt the old man's lips against his wrists, the jab of the nail file. Lawton's spittle and blood coated his flesh. With a grunt and a growl, he resumed the sawing. Faster now, while

421

Thorn strained against the fabric of the tape, his shoulders aching.

'There,' Lawton said.

He spit the nail file on the deck.

'I'm still caught,' said Thorn.

'Go up and down, your arms, pump them like pistons. There's only a little thread holding you.'

Thorn tried it and on the second pump, the duct tape broke apart.

There was a voice in the hall. It took Thorn a moment to recognize it, so different from how she'd sounded before. Morgan giving commands to her father.

'Keep moving. Go on. Move.'

A cold, rigid authority in her tone. The sound of someone holding a gun and damn well ready to use it.

Thorn brought his hands around, stretched his arms, worked the blood back into his fingers. He groped with the cable ties around his ankles, fumbled for precious seconds with the locking mechanisms. When he had them open, he snatched up the nail file and gouged several quick holes in the duct tape on Lawton's wrists, weakening it, then ripped it in two. He unknotted the bungee cords, unwrapped the several turns of duct tape, unlocked the cable ties. It took a minute, two minutes.

The voice in the hallway was gone.

He got to his feet. Lawton opened his mouth to speak, but Thorn put a quick finger to his lips. He moved to the edge of the door and waited. Lawton got to his feet and went into the small head and ran the water in the sink and used the toilet and flushed it. If that didn't bring them running, they could always try singing a verse of 'Twist and Shout.'

A second later Thorn heard the heavy clomp of someone running down the hallway. Even though he was prepared, when the door exploded he stumbled backwards and fell into the dresser. The shotgun blast had opened a fist-sized hole at eye level in the door.

Lawton came out of the head, rubbing his face in a towel.

'Cause for celebration,' he said. 'A feat worthy of the great Houdini himself.'

He took another step around the edge of the bathroom wall and Thorn hurled himself across the room and tackled Lawton around the waist and they tumbled back onto the bed as a second blast widened the first hole to the size of a cantaloupe. A spray of buckshot lashing his right leg, turning it hot and numb. He shoved Lawton across the bed.

'What the hell're you doing?'

Still clutching the nail file, Thorn put his hands against the man's bony chest and forced him into the crack between the mattress and the wall. Wingo was in the way, so Thorn wrenched the dead man's arm, pulled him aside, then crammed Lawton over the edge into the narrow space.

'I see you,' Johnny said through the hole in the

door. 'Nowhere to hide. Nowhere to run. Game's over. Time to go bye-bye, Tinkerbell.'

But the blasts must have bent the hinges off-center. The door moved a few inches, then stuck. Johnny leaned his shoulder against it and heaved, and the door screeched and started to move.

While he wrestled with the door, Thorn spun back and looped an arm around Wingo's waist and hauled him to his feet. A heavy corpse, stiffening. Thorn lugged him like a drunk toward the opening door, then got him moving, managing some good momentum by the time the door came open and Johnny stepped through smiling, lifting his shotgun. Wingo doing a last good deed, hurtling across the room, running interference for Thorn. Good old Wingo taking the blast in his face as Thorn followed a second later, staying low, his shoulder digging into the small of the dead man's back. Then letting him go and stepping out from behind him and uncorking a wide hooking arm, catching it around Johnny's throat, then slipping behind him, Johnny's neck in the crook of Thorn's arm. Thorn trying for an enraged second to tear the boy's head off.

But Johnny Braswell was one of those rubbery, strong young men. A kid who'd probably never spent a second in a gym, done nothing but work on a marlin boat to earn his strength, but that was enough, more than enough, because it was hiding there under the husk of fat and sloppiness, the power of honed muscles, a bullish, unmoving bulk. Thorn wrenched

424

backwards, tried to cut off Johnny's air, twisting hard and sagging his knees to bring all his weight against the boy's throat like some wrangler twisting a calf to the rodeo dirt.

Johnny didn't budge. He widened his stance and rode Thorn's grinding hold. Then when he sensed Thorn was weakening, about to change his angle of attack, Johnny swiveled to the side and wrenched the butt of the shotgun into Thorn's belly. The blow would've broken down a door, but it missed by inches, creased his ribs and knocked only half the breath from his lungs. Thorn staggered and dropped his hold. Something giving way inside his gut, some nameless organ whose function he didn't know. He heard a shrill whistle as he dragged down a breath.

Maybe those people trained in street fighting saw it all as a diagram. He'd heard that somewhere. That if you fought enough battles, then everything slowed down, got simpler. You saw with perfect clarity the geometry of punch and counterpunch, you feinted and dodged and suckered a less skilled opponent into your snare. But for Thorn it was all wild confusion. It was that way now and it always had been that way. He acted without subterfuge or strategy. If there was anything on his side at moments like that one, it was his simple creed. Inflict the most damage as fast as possible. Stay awake as long as you can.

He was only dimly aware of the nail file he'd palmed, that it had been riding in his hand through the mayhem. But as Johnny wheeled around, driving the heavy black barrel of the Remington toward the side of his head, and as Thorn ducked back out of its vicious arc, the nail file fit itself into his right hand as naturally as if he'd been facing off against switchblade punks all his life.

The shotgun clipped the edge of the door and threw Johnny off-balance for a half second, and as he was cocking his arms back to take a left-handed swing, Thorn seized the barrel and flung the shotgun across the cabin. It hit the wall next to the bed and clanged to the floor.

Thorn cocked his right fist and was measuring an uppercut to Johnny's jaw, when the kid whisked his hand by his belt and came up with a knife. Same kind as Thorn had pulled out of Lawton. Not for skinning rabbits, not for cleaning fingernails. Good for one thing only.

Johnny started to square off, take a stance, like they would play by some formal rules of knife fighting. But Thorn didn't wait for him to get set, he lunged at the boy, jabbed the nail file into the first available patch of flesh, which happened to be the side of Johnny's neck, and he pulled down and to the side and then back to the other side, ripping a ragged hole. Johnny gagged and stumbled backwards. He took a wild swipe at Thorn with that exotic blade, but Thorn blocked his wrist and deflected the blade downward. It nicked his shirt and left a warm trail across his right ribs.

Thorn continued to work the nail file back and

forth, esophagus and windpipe and Adam's apple, his hand slick with Johnny's blood.

Johnny bleated and his knife clattered to the floor.

That was the precise moment when Thorn could have stopped. Stepped away and let the boy fall on his back, but he didn't. He kept bulling forward, partly for Farley and Lawton, partly for the hundred strangers in a diving jet, but mainly for reasons of his own, because this was the only way he'd learned to handle rabid dogs. You didn't give in to human sympathy. You didn't weigh it all out on some delicate moral scale. You made sure the dog was dead and then you made sure he was even deader than that.

Thorn dug the nail file back and forth in the boy's neck, through the hot gristle, the meaty layers, shoving him backwards until Johnny thumped against the wardrobe, his butt riding up onto the counter-top. The boy gurgled like a newborn at his mother's breast, his eyes rolling inward. Behind him the wardrobe mirror shined. Thorn looked past the dying boy at the creature reflected in the glass. Killer caught in the act. Blood smeared across Thorn's mouth and cheeks as if he'd eaten a pie without his hands. Blood seeped from Johnny's artery, coating Thorn's arm. A look on Thorn's face he didn't recognize. A look he'd never seen on any human face.

# 27

Morgan heard the shots coming from down below. Johnny executing Thorn and the old man as instructed. She would've left the flybridge, gone down to supervise, hold his hand, make sure the klutz didn't screw it up, killing two men who were bound up head-to-toe, but she was a little preoccupied at the moment, watching another boat approaching across the dark water. From the spread of its running lights, it looked like a small fishing boat, which meant she could almost certainly outrun it if it came to that. But now she wanted to know who it was that kept changing their course each time she changed hers. Dogging her, now getting even more aggressive, on a heading that would cross her bow in only a minute or two.

So she didn't go down below to oversee her little

brother. She kept her eyes on the boat, watching it drawing closer. Coming from her starboard, which gave it the right of way if you wanted to get technical, but she didn't think the rules of the sea were going to apply to this situation. She didn't think any rules were going to apply. She just had that feeling.

'Try both of them at once,' Sugarman said. 'Both buttons.'

'My father's on that boat. And Thorn.'

'Your father wear a pacemaker?'

'No.'

'So what're you worried about? It didn't kill anybody at Neon Leon's. It just shut off the power. That's what you said.'

'You sure about this?'

'I'm not sure about any damn thing. But hey, we gotta do something quick. They make a run, we're screwed.'

So, Alexandra shifted the cone, directing it toward the *ByteMe*, and took a deep breath and pressed both buttons. The device hummed. Quiet as a small electric shaver, then a few seconds later she felt a sharp tingle in her sinuses, a sudden rush of electrons or neurons or some damn thing flashing up her spinal cord. That could've been the electromagnetic pulse, or just a jolt of her own adrenaline.

Even though she hadn't been to Mass in twenty years and had long ago lost hope that God was watching every sparrow as closely as she once believed, still, at that moment, as another throb brightened her nerve endings, Alex said a few silent words of thanksgiving.


In the mirror Thorn watched Lawton crawl back onto the bed.

He caught Thorn's eyes. Thorn starting to feel the buckshot smoldering in his leg, and the sting that swiped across his right ribs.

'I think you can stop now,' Lawton said. 'Looks like the boy's finished.'

Thorn nodded. He let go of the nail file. Let his arms fall to his sides. The bones had turned to iron. He might never lift them again.

'So, tell me,' Lawton said. 'You done that a lot, kill guys with your bare hands?'

Thorn stepped away from the dead man. Johnny's chin slumped forward, pressing against his chest, long blond hair falling around his face.

Thorn looked at Lawton.

'Not for a while,' he said.

'Could've fooled me,' the old man said. 'Could've fooled the hell out of me.'

And a second later, Thorn was still looking at Lawton, trying to find something to say, when the lights went off and the big diesels shut down.

\*　　\*　　\*

'Mother of God,' Sugar said. 'The damn thing works.'

'There's a couple of lights still on,' Alex said. 'Up on the bow.'

'Well, it works ninety percent.'

Alex said, 'Now what?'

'We give them a good ram.'

'What?'

'Hit them broadside, knock them senseless.'

'What's that accomplish, Sugar?'

'I don't know. Maybe it's all Thorn will need to change the balance of power in there. Shake things up; in the chaos, we come aboard, take over.'

'Damn risky,' she said. 'A lot of unknowns.'

'At this point, what isn't risky? Safe thing is to call for help on the radio, sit out here all night till somebody comes. But I don't know how safe that is for Lawton and Thorn.'

'Can this old barge take the hit?'

'Thorn spent the last couple of months replanking the hull. All new wood, like iron.'

She looked out at the dark. Shaking her head.

'Okay, okay,' she said. 'Ram 'em. Ram the hell out of them.'

'Aye, aye.'

Sugar eased the throttle forward, got the engine revving, five knots, ten, the pleasant acceleration, fifteen, rising up to plane, the sweet night air, lush and tropical and freshened by its long trip across the open ocean, twenty knots now, and then a little more, twenty-two, twenty-three, nice cruising speed, that big engine not straining at all, the rush of water off the bow, the white foam behind them glowing in the moonlight.

He aimed at the yacht's bow, going to give them a glancing blow. Despite his words to Alexandra, and though he trusted Thorn's workmanship, Sugar knew when their wood hull bashed against the Braswells' reinforced fiberglass at this speed, chances were good they'd crack something structural, almost certainly start taking on water. Then it was just a matter of how big the leak was versus the efficiency of Thorn's bilge pump.

Alexandra leaned close, spoke through the bluster.

'You sure about this, Sugar? You're sure?'

He nodded. Though he wasn't sure, not at all.

'Hold on,' he said. 'This isn't going to be pretty.'

They were a hundred yards out, no sign of movement on the boat. Not even a flashlight, just a couple of lights burning up on the flybridge and the top deck. Could be a ghost ship for all he knew. Everyone dead or dying. Could be anything. He didn't let himself consider it. Just kept his eye on the dark profile of the hull, closing faster now, fifty yards, forty. The moonlight giving the water a ghostly look, golden white glaze, like some eerie frost.

Thirty yards out, he picked his spot, three feet back of the point of the bow.

'Hold on.'

Twenty yards, then ten, that's when he heard the outboard motor roar and saw the stern lights moving off behind the bow, heading north. He had to blink to make sure it was real. A dinghy bouncing across the dark sea. And he jerked the wheel hard to starboard, hard, hard, but still not quick enough. He watched the big black shape looming now, bigger than it seemed before, enormous. A goddamn freighter. What was he thinking, ramming a boat like that?

They clipped the edge of the hull, Sugar cringing at the scream and crunch of the surfaces colliding, a piece breaking off the *Heart Pounder*, a chunk of chrome flying off into the night. The jolt sent Alex toppling into him, knocking him away from the wheel, the old Chris-Craft heeling over, still going full speed, but now listing hard. Crashes in the galley, broken glass, pots, skillets. A fishing rod tumbled across the cockpit deck. Sugarman had one hand on the wheel and was pulling himself upright, with an arm looped around Alex to keep her from going overboard. Noticing in that second how raw-boned strong she was, feeling that strength as she pushed away, grabbed hold of a chrome handle and hauled herself up.

'I guess we didn't fry everything,' he said.

'I guess not.'

Off-balance, wedged sideways against the cockpit wall, Sugar corrected the wheel. Doing it slowly, pulling back on the throttle at the same time, drawing them out of their tilt. When the boat was under control, he pushed himself erect, flattened the throttle, giving chase.

For half a mile he trailed the zigzagging dinghy across the black sea, long enough to know it was useless. It was skipping along at fifty knots, a third again as fast as their top end. As it pulled away, Sugar fixed Thorn's handheld spotlight on the boat, managed to still its shudder long enough to see only one person aboard. Dark hair fluttering in the moonlight.

Sugar swung around in a wide arc and headed back toward the yacht, using the spotlight to locate it in the shadows. They came alongside, Sugarman cutting the engines, idling up, putting their starboard hull against the port of the *ByteMe*. Alex went up on the bow and got the lines ready. Sugarman inching closer, squinting at the dark boat, feeling suddenly exposed.

The familiar voice came from the shadowy cockpit.

'That you?'

'Yeah, it's me, Thorn. It's me. You okay?'

Thorn said he was fine. Everything was fine, except they lost Farley Boissont.

'And Dad?' Alexandra's voice was stony, bracing herself for the worst.

'A couple of nicks, nothing serious.'

Something splashed out in the dark water, then it splashed again. Overhead the sky was immense, more stars than Sugar had ever seen.

Alexandra tossed the lines across to Thorn and he leaned his weight against them and hauled the boats close. He hung a couple of white bumpers overboard and the boats snugged tight against them. He made the lines fast, then came back to the cockpit and put out a hand, and Alexandra gave him hers and stepped up to the taller gunwale.

'Thorn killed a guy.' Lawton stood beside the fighting chair. 'He killed Johnny Braswell. I watched the whole mess. But it was self-defense all the way. Johnny had a twelve-gauge, Thorn had a nail file.'

Sugarman chuckled.

'Even odds for Thorn.'

Lawton stood beside the chair waiting for Alexandra, waiting with his arms slack at his side in the moonlight, watching as she hopped down from the gunwale and took two steps and pulled him into an embrace and hugged him hard. Then after a minute or two, she stepped back and held him at arms' length, wiped her eyes and peered into his face.

'Your ear,' she said.

'Punk cut off my earlobe,' Lawton said. 'Wouldn't you know. There goes my earring.'

Sugarman stepped aboard.

'And the father?'

Thorn said he was lying down in his stateroom. Doing okay but not saying much.

'Man's in shock,' Lawton said. 'Just found out what a piss-poor job he'd done raising those kids.'

Alexandra put her arm around Lawton's back.

'Speaking of piss-poor,' Thorn said. 'That was some kind of thump you gave us, Sugar. You didn't dent my boat, did you?'

'Little ding. Nothing you can't fix, Thorn. Doesn't seem to be taking on any water.'

'We should get back,' Thorn said. 'Notify people. Stop Morgan from getting off the island. Turn Braswell over to the cops.'

'I don't think you need to worry about Morgan,' Sugar said. 'The HERF was on board your boat the whole time. That's how we turned off your lights.'

'What if there's another one?' Thorn said.

'It's not our problem,' Sugar said. 'We're done.'

Sugarman took a seat on the transom.

'Banks,' said Lawton. 'That's what I'd do. I'd turn off their alarms and help myself. Go down the street, one by one, load up my sack. Buy me a big boat, sail around the world.'

'It's not our problem,' Alex said. 'This is FBI, CIA, anti-terrorist people. It's what those boys live for. This is way out of our league.'

'We'll need to give statements,' Sugar said. 'But beyond that, I think we're free and clear.'

'Well, good,' Lawton said. 'Then we can stay over here in the islands, do a little marlin fishing.'

Everyone was silent, looking around in the glow from the *Heart Pounder*'s lights.

'Damn right,' Thorn said. 'We're here in marlin paradise. Let's put some meat on the deck.'

# 28

Saturday morning, April twenty-ninth, Thorn woke before dawn and went out on the porch with his coffee. The pink buffalo was staring at Blackwater Sound, watching it brighten, then begin to turn silver. The buffalo seemed fascinated by the way the light seeped through the bay, spreading below the surface like a thousand underground rivers of molten lava. Thorn watched along with the pink buffalo as the silver turned to tin and then quickly dulled to a series of increasingly darker greens. Not that transparent blue of the Bahamas, but beautiful in its own way.

Thorn sipped his coffee and listened to her move around inside the house. She was clinking in the cupboard, rejecting the mug Thorn laid out for her, choosing her own, stirring in the half-and-half.

Down on the *Heart Pounder* he could see Lawton stretching his arms. Father and daughter on the same circadian cycle, sharing that biological connection. And lots of others, too, that he'd noticed. Similar handwriting, little tics and gestures, the cadence of their talk. He wondered if they noticed it. Wondered if that's how it was with every parent and child. Nobody as free as they liked to believe, just a helpless bundle of inherited traits. Even Thorn, an adopted kid who never knew his parents. Still, doing things he couldn't control, destined to repeat the behaviors of people he'd never met. Which, when he considered it, was a lucky thing. His one way of getting to know them, by being himself, doing what their genes whispered in his ear.

He stared out at the bay and watched the green turn deeper, richer. Listened to the toilet flush, the scuff of her leather sandals on the wood floor. He could smell her coming, the quiet scent of late-blooming jasmine, a subtle change in the force field. Feeling that lift in his pulse that he'd forgotten, that he'd thought he was too old for, or too jaded. He'd been afraid that one too many women in his past had dulled his longing.

Then the screen door yawned as she came outside, and the slap of it behind her. He wanted to swing around and see her standing there. He wanted to sweep her up and carry her back to the mattress where they'd fit together so naturally, so instantly. Without a lot of talk, even in the afterglow, both of them panting, sweaty, even then, when talk was okay, even expected, they hadn't felt the need. Just lay there in the silence, barely touching, but closer than he'd been to anyone in years.

But Thorn held still. Didn't want to scare her with his intensity. She sat down beside him on the picnic bench. She sipped her coffee. Cream, no sugar. She lay her hand on top of his hand, scratched the skin lightly with a nail. The pink buffalo kept her vigil, guardian of whimsy, god of all large, unfathomable beasts, as if she were gazing out across the vast pasturelands searching for her mate, the other pink buffalo who would some day come thundering across the whitecaps of the bay and in a cloud of dust would halt beside her and nuzzle her and begin to recount his adventures.

'Is he up?'

'For a few minutes. Same as you.'

She cleared her throat. Cut a glance his way, then returned to the bay.

'You feeling anxious?'

'About what?' he said, trying for nonchalance, but hearing the edge in his voice.

She thumped an admonishing finger against the back of his hand.

'No, I'm not worried,' Thorn said. 'I've never seen so many federal agents swarming in one place.'

'They should shut down the airport.'

'They can't do that.'

'Yeah, yeah. The panic. Worried the press will find out. Still it seems like the prudent thing to me. What I would do if I were in charge.'

'Thank God you're not.'

'Why?'

'You wouldn't be here, you'd be up in Miami.'

She patted Thorn's hand again.

'They'll catch her,' he said. 'She's out of control. It'll be over by lunch.'

'I turned my cell phone off. I don't want to know. I just want to be here, be with you and Dad. I can read about it in the paper next week.'

'Maybe we'll take the boat somewhere, go over to the ten thousand islands, poke around the oyster beds. Stay overnight, count the constellations.'

'The three of us.'

'Of course.'

'He likes you. He never liked Stan, my husband. He hasn't liked any of the men in my life until you.'

'It's the boyish grin.'

'You take him fishing,' she said. 'None of the men in my life knew the first thing about it.'

They looked out at the bay some more. A boat passed. It was going slow, a Mako with a family of four and a dog. Everybody was talking at once.

'There's a gun in your bedside table, Thorn. Did you know that?'

'You were snooping.'

'I'm a cop. I can't help it.'

'Sugar let me borrow it. Just until Morgan's caught.'

She looked at him for a moment, then nodded.

'Maybe I should call Dan Romano, check in, see how things are going.'

He looked out at the cloudy sky, at the sun spearing through the chinks.

'If that's what you want.'

Lawton was walking down the dock, headed for the house. He had on his favorite outfit. Blue sleeveless T-shirt and yellow Bermuda shorts. He stopped and studied the pink buffalo. He bent down and got eye to eye with her and said something to the beast, then he straightened up and came up the lawn and up the stairs. Everyone exchanged good-mornings.

'Got any eggs?' Lawton said. 'I was thinking about a cheese omelette. Or pancakes would work, too. Even better, how about both together? And bacon, I love bacon. I know it's no good for you, but at my age, what the hell?'

'I've got a full larder, Lawton. You name it, we'll whip it up.'

Thorn got up and followed him into the house. Lawton went over to the refrigerator and started hauling things out. At the kitchen window, Thorn looked out at Alexandra. She was standing in a corner of the porch, her cell phone to her ear, her head bowed, shoulders hunched over as if she were trying to duck a bullet that she saw streaking out of the sky.


Morgan spent the week in a motel on Biscayne Boulevard near downtown Miami, watching the hookers come and go. Hearing the johns through the thin walls, their groans, their baby talk. She got her hair

441

colored. Now she was blond. She bought bright new clothes in a Cuban department store, pink horn-rimmed sunglasses. She used the last of her cash and charged nothing on plastic because they'd trace her instantly. She knew they were looking, knew the whole thing was exposed, even though there was nothing on TV or in the papers. They had to know. She could feel it, the weird barometric pressure shifting in her gut. And she knew who was to blame. The same one who killed Johnny. The asshole who'd wormed his way into their lives and corrupted everything.

With the last of her money she bought a pistol. A pawn shop on Biscayne sold her a .38 Colt with a box of shells, no questions, no wait. She stayed in her room at the Sinbad Motel and aimed the pistol at herself in the tarnished mirror. Her hand was steady, never wavered. She emptied the cylinder, aimed at the mirror, and squeezed the trigger and didn't flinch when the hammer hit. Aiming at herself. Killing the weird blond girl in the mirror, over and over.

On Saturday morning before dawn, she drove up to Palm Beach, parked five blocks from the house and took a route through the neighbors' backyards. She didn't think they'd have her father staked out. But she was careful anyway. Coming down an alley that connected her street with the two adjacent ones.

There was an FPL van parked a block away from her house, but nobody working on the lines. And she saw a man in an upstairs window across the street. He was looking through a narrow part in the curtain, smoking a cigarette. Not Mrs Schaffer, the old lady who lived there. And she doubted the cigarette man was a visiting relation.

She moved down the alley, bush to bush, and ducked into an enclosure of wood lattice that shielded a neighbor's garbage cans. The Waste Management truck came at seven-fifteen. In twenty years the truck was hardly ever late. When the skinny black man jumped down off the back and started for the cans across the alley, Morgan slipped around the front of the truck and cut through the hedge and entered the Braswells' yard.

All views were cut off from both directions. If the cigarette man was watching, he saw only the rear of the garbage truck. If the FPL crew had their binoculars out, they saw only its side. She used her key and was inside the house in seconds.

Her father was in his study. He was wearing striped pajamas. He sat at his desk staring into the computer screen. He'd logged onto the site that relayed his satellite information and he was staring at the screen, a nautical chart that showed a sprinkle of islands. Looked to Morgan like the Virgins. A blue ping was pulsing below the largest island. Big Mother was making good time, headed somewhere fast.

She stood behind him for several minutes and watched him staring at his screen. Finally he sighed, sensing her presence, and he swiveled around and looked at her. He looked at the gun in her hand, then back at her eyes.

He held her eyes for a long time before bowing his head.

'I deserve this,' he said. 'It's all been my fault.'

'You're right, Dad. You're absolutely right.'

He looked back up.

'I shut down after it happened. After losing them, I simply shut down.'

'You did, yes. You shut down.'

'And you had to figure out everything on your own. Without a father, a mother. You had to struggle with it all by yourself. No guidance.'

'I did okay,' she said.

He shook his head.

'Johnny's dead.'

'I know he is.' She raised the gun but didn't point it at him. The garbage truck would come down the alley on the other side of the house in a minute and it would use its crusher, very loud, fifteen to twenty seconds. She'd heard it from her bedroom window every Saturday morning since she was a girl. Waking her up as it compacted the garbage from their street.

'They're looking for you.'

'I know.'

'A great many people. There's no escape from this, Morgan.'

'Don't be so sure.'

'What're you planning to do, shoot me?'

'I left something in the attic I needed to get. And I wanted to see you one more time. That's all.'

'I'm sorry, Morgan. I wish I could say something, make it all better.'

She shook her head. She was feeling fine. Amazingly clearheaded. Seeing her father for the first time. A man who had been unprepared for the cruelty that befell him. Just like everyone else. No one was ready. Even though they had to know it was coming. It was always coming.

'You can't fix this, Dad. Maybe you could have fixed it back then, but you didn't and now it's too late. The family is finished. We're all gone now. Andy, Mom, Johnny. Now you and me. We're gone, too.'

'Do you need anything, Morgan? Money? Food?'

She smiled.

'I needed something once,' she said. 'But not now. I've learned to do without it.'

She heard the truck rumbling around the corner, headed down the alley.

'Andy's death, you know, that wasn't an accident.'

'What?'

'You were going to split us up. Mother told him you were going to send me away to school.'

Her father absorbed her words slowly.

'We talked about it. I remember that.'

'Ship me away and keep Andy at home. Like I was some spiderwoman. Some pet you could discard.'

'What do you mean, it wasn't an accident?'

'Andy and I,' she said. 'We loved each other.'

Her father peered at her.

'We loved each other in every way.'

Her father lowered his eyes and studied the floor at her feet.

'It was beautiful, joyous. I didn't feel guilty about it.'

He looked up, shaking his head. His eyes shining.

'Andy's death was an accident, Morgan. A terrible accident.'

'No, it wasn't. Andy was smarter than that. He never made mistakes. He took an extra wrap on purpose. He wanted to die.'

'No,' her father said. 'No.'

'That's what he did,' she said. 'A grand exit. Such a romantic.'

Out in the alley the garbage truck's brakes squealed. She heard one of the men whoop at the driver, then the clatter of cans on the pavement.

'But that's not why I'm here, Dad. All that's over and done.'

The color had drained from his face.

'You invited those men aboard our boat, Dad. Why did you do that?'

He wiped the dampness from his eyes.

'Morgan,' he said as if trying to stir her awake. 'Morgan.'

'That wasn't right, Dad. We were still a family. We were damaged, we had our faults, sure, but we were still a family. A unit. And you violated that, Dad. You invited that asshole aboard. He was there to destroy us and you fell for it and let him onto our boat. And look what he did, he killed Johnny. He killed my brother.'

She aimed the pistol at her father's chest.

Her father stood up and raised his right hand toward her as if he meant to touch her cheek, wipe away her tears, wrap her in his arms, give her the hug he'd neglected to give her before. But the bullet knocked him back into his chair. Outside in the alley, the garbage truck was compressing its rubbish. She shot him a second time. Two in the heart. The second slug swiveled him around until he was half facing his computer screen again.

She stood there for a moment watching his last moments leak out of him. On the screen, the blue ping was blinking. Big Mother was on the move.

# 29

Thorn went to the Yellow Bait House, bought three dozen live shrimp. Now Lawton was using them to catch mangrove snappers. The fish were only eight, nine inches long, not keepers, but Lawton didn't mind. He'd catch one, hold it up for Alex and Thorn to admire, then gently release it. He wore a wide-brimmed straw hat, something Casey had left behind, with a yellow-and-pink ribbon that dangled down his back. He cast like a pro, sending out his baited hook with an easy flick. Thorn was impressed. Excellent motor skills.

It was nearly noon and Alexandra stood at the bedroom door giving Thorn a look. She'd peeled off her shorts and unbuttoned her blue workshirt, showing a few inches of white skin from her navel to her throat. She still wore her black bikini panties. He finished washing the last breakfast plate, put it in the rack, and went over to her.

'He'll be okay?'

'He's fishing,' she said. 'He's in heaven.'

She took his hand and guided him into the bedroom and shut the door. She took off the workshirt and lay down on the sheets and watched him undress. When he was naked he came over to the bed and slid in beside her. She looked into his eyes for a few seconds, then took hold of his chin and guided his lips to hers. They found the fit, relaxing, opening to each other. Going away, the border between them melting. The kiss lasting for minutes, a delicate give-and-take. Alex now the aggressor, easing up on an elbow, pressing down on him, then lifting up and straddling his waist, sliding down till she was flat against him, beginning a slow grind. Thorn cooperating, bending his injured leg out of the way, giving her a better angle as she worked against him, raising him until he fit between the V of her legs, sliding up and down against her silk panties. No hurry to tug them off, to fit him inside. No hurry to end this teasing warm-up. They both knew it was going further than that. It already had and it would again and it would again after that. No need to say it out loud, no need to do anything but lie there and kiss her hungry mouth and lift his hips and press and stroke.

After a while, she broke the hold, slid away to his

449

side, ran her hand across his stomach, around the tender perimeter of the bandage where Johnny had sliced him. A pause. Both of them had been on the verge of the wild part, losing control. But she wanted a break, wanted to draw back, say something. He could feel it coming as she coiled the hair around his navel.

'Yes?'

She nestled closer.

'When you wrapped me in that blanket, Thorn, was that really necessary? Stripping off my clothes like that.'

'I thought it was.'

'You looked at me, didn't you? Lying there naked, shivering.'

'I might have. Briefly.'

'Nobody's ever done that before.'

'Looked at you naked?'

She gave the coil of hair a sharp tug.

'You know what I mean. Saved my life.'

'Oh, that,' he said. 'Just part of the full-service package.'

'I want to thank you, Thorn.'

'You've already done that.'

'I'd like to do it again.'

'Well, if that's how you feel. Sure, go ahead, thank me.'

She tugged the coil again.

'How do you feel about Lawton?'

'I like him,' Thorn said. 'I like him very much.'

'He's like a child,' she said. 'If he makes a new friend and that friend deserts him, it can be crushing.'

'I'm not a deserter.'

'Yes,' she said. 'I didn't think you were.'

'He's a good man. He's funny sometimes. All that Houdini stuff.'

'Funny's only part of it.'

'I know. Funny and sad. But at least the funny is there.'

'It's not easy, Thorn, watching it happen. It's not easy at all.'

'You seem to be handling it.'

'He likes you,' she said. 'You shouldn't let it spook you if he starts thinking you're his son. Something like that.'

'I don't spook easy.'

'You can be funny, too, Thorn. I lied when I said you weren't. The way you were when the SWAT team was here. Pretending they were room service.'

'My heart was about to explode,' he said.

'How's it feeling now?'

Thorn smiled.

'Rich and full.'

He rolled onto his right shoulder and kissed her temple. He kissed along her hairline. He brushed his lips against her eyebrows. His hand was touching her breasts and she was making a noise in her throat, like a mourning dove in the late afternoon, settling in for the night. It was one of her noises, one of the early ones. Purr, coo, growl, the bird sounds and the dangerous animal sounds. He liked them all. The entire range from the first huffs to the anguished cries at the end. She reached out for him and gripped him gently and moved her hand up and down his length, then explored with a delicate fingertip the tender rim.

The start of another journey. Heading off along a pleasant winding road that disappeared a little way ahead into the trees. Part of the excitement was not knowing where the road led, how long it was. Maybe to the other side of the earth this time. All the way around the globe. He hoped so. He always hoped so.


'That's it? Stalling cars? I'm supposed to be impressed with that?'

Roy scowled at her. The aluminum case at his feet bounced against the fiberglass deck.

Morgan kept the skiff moving. Twenty knots, a half mile off shore. The HERF was strapped down on the bow, aimed at US 1, the narrow strip that connected the mainland to Key Largo and points beyond. Water on both sides, nowhere to turn around. Shut down that road, it wouldn't be long before traffic was backed up for twenty miles in both directions.

She smiled at Roy. He was wearing a black silk shirt and the same tight jeans he always wore. Boat shoes this time, a white cowboy hat with a leather band. He was shaking his head.

'Think about it, Roy. Think about the possibilities.'

'What possibilities? Invest in a wrecker company, get rich towing cars I've stalled with a million-dollar gun. Take a long goddamn time to make back my investment towing fucking cars, missy.'

'I hate that missy shit.'

Roy glanced at her, then looked back at the highway. Nothing was moving over there. A few cars had plowed into each other when they lost their power steering, their power brakes, their batteries. Cruising along at seventy and all at once they've got nothing. Not as dramatic as airplanes falling from the sky, but it fit her plan. Nothing moving in or out of the Keys. Cell phones fried.

'Is this all you've got?' Roy said.

She heard it coming, the *whap* of its rotors, the growing roar. She looked back to the north and saw it following the curve of the highway, hovering low. The inevitable TV chopper, Channel 7, the sensational station, always first on the scene. The one with the reporters who stooped down over the blood and dabbed a finger in it and held it up still fresh for the folks at home to see.

'Okay,' Roy said. 'Now this is better.'

Morgan unlashed the HERF from the bow and turned it on its side so the cone was pointing upward. She waited for the chopper to work its way down the row of stalled cars, all those people standing out on the shoulder waving up as if a rescue basket would lower and take them on their busy way. The chopper was less than five hundred feet as it passed over them.

Morgan pressed the two buttons and stepped back behind the console. In the lab she'd almost eliminated the back flash, but there still had to be some. No telling what the long-term medical effects might be, all that electromagnetic energy passing through the body over and over. As if long-term effects still mattered.

The helicopter's noisy engine shut down and the gawky bird tumbled, nose first, onto the highway. Screams from the people in their stalled cars, then the *whoosh* of the fireball reached them, rocking the boat and blowing off Roy's hat. It tumbled overboard and he yelled at her to go fetch it before it sank, it was his goddamn pride and joy, his favorite Stetson. So she turned the Whaler and skimmed over to where the hat floated right side up and Roy bent over the side and scooped it out and turned around, slinging water from the hat and looking for a half second at Morgan before he saw the pistol in her hand.

'You do that and you're dead, missy. You won't last till sunset.'

'That's plenty long enough,' she said.

Roy took two shots in the stomach and was still standing. Tough old Texan. A third shot took off the top left quadrant of his skull and sent him sprawling backwards over the side.

A minute or two later, she was reloading when the second chopper came, this one from Metro-Dade police. She set the loaded pistol on the console and went over to the HERF to wait for the chopper to move into range.

'Something's wrong.'

Lawton was standing in the doorway of the bedroom.

Thorn opened his eyes and lifted his head off the pillow.

'What is it, Dad?'

Alex held the sheet over her breasts. Her father turned his eyes to the living room.

'I don't know,' he said. 'But something's wrong. Something changed.'

'He's right,' Thorn said. 'I hear it.'

'Hear what?'

'There's no hum.'

'What?'

'It's quiet out there. Saturday, there's always a ton of traffic. Half of Miami down here getting drunk. But not today, the highway's quiet.'

'I don't hear anything different,' she said.

Thorn sat up. He walked naked over to his shorts, picked them off the floor, and stepped into them. He grabbed his white T-shirt and he and Lawton went out on the porch. Alex joined them a minute later, carrying her cell phone.

'Nothing,' Thorn said. 'Everything's shut down.'

While Thorn pulled on his T-shirt, Alexandra went to the railing that faced Blackwater Sound. She dialed a number and listened for a few moments, then said, 'Dan, hey, it's Alex.'

She listened for several minutes, then said, 'Yeah, I will. Yeah, yeah. Don't worry. Thorn's here. We're safe. Everything's quiet.'

She hung up and set the phone on the picnic table.

'Two helicopters shot down over the eighteen-mile strip. US 1 backed up from Homestead to Islamorada. A forty-mile-long parking lot. We're cut off, Thorn. Stranded. They're keeping the choppers grounded. Too risky. Boats, that's all they're using. Coast Guard, Marine patrol, they're out looking for her. She shot her father early this morning. Braswell's dead.'

'She's coming here,' said Thorn.

Alexandra lifted her eyes and looked out at the shimmer of the bay.

'I know,' she said. 'We should get ready.'

Thorn went back inside for his shoes. Alex joined him a minute later.

'Just that one gun?'

'I didn't want that one, but Sugar insisted.'

'We should call him. He could help.'

'He's up in Miami, visiting his daughters.'

She nodded. Slipping into her sandals. While Thorn searched for his boat shoes, she went out on the porch. A second later she yelped.

He hustled outside, a shoe on his right foot, his left bare.

'Dad,' she said. 'I told him to wait right here.'

Thorn leaned over the rail, peered down at the shoreline.

'He's fishing. He's working his way down the rocks, behind those mangroves. It's okay. I'll get him.'

Then he saw the Boston Whaler idling along the coastline, a blond woman at the wheel.

'Get the gun,' he said. 'I'll get Lawton.'


Morgan had to stop a couple of times before she found anyone who knew where Thorn lived. Finally a guy at the gas docks at Jewfish Creek pointed out the spot on her chart.

'Wood house, up on stilts, shingle roof, all surrounded by woods.'

'Thanks,' she said.

He leaned against the gas pump, smiling at her.

'Thorn's always had good taste in broads.'

If she hadn't wanted to save her ammunition, she would have left the asshole in flames.

Now, as she approached the house from the north, easing past a jet ski rental place, a waterfront restaurant, she saw the house in its own little cove. Rustic as hell. A jungle on either side of it, nice cushion between it and the three-story mansion to its south and the condos to its north.

Morgan felt fine. Never better. The slate clean, starting fresh. New lungs, new eyes, heart full of promise. She had a half million dollars at her feet. Endless possibilities. Just this one chore before she headed off across the water, found a new place. Gave herself a new name, a new beginning. It felt damn good. Killing her father. Killing Roy. Free of all that. It felt wonderful. She knew it wasn't supposed to. She wasn't so out of touch that she didn't realize that. But there it was. She felt so free, so light. That must be what salvation was. Grace. You broke loose of your sins, you transcended. You shattered the bonds. That's how she felt. Liberated, emancipated. Fantastic.

Just this one last little task and she was gone.

'I got something,' Lawton said. 'I thought I was just hooked on the bottom but this is a fish. This is a big damn fish.'

Thorn cut his bare foot on one of the jagged limestone chunks. He sucked down a breath and hobbled over to Lawton. The old man was leaning his weight against the tug on his line.

Twenty yards out the Whaler was still idling. The girl with blond hair was smiling at him. He saw the glint of the pistol lying on the console.

'It's a grouper,' Lawton said. 'Or maybe a nurse shark. I don't know. It hasn't shown itself. Doesn't feel much like a shark though.'

'Yeah,' Thorn said. 'There's a grouper hole right there. Right where you are. She took your bait and went back inside. She's going to try to break the line against the limestone.'

'Devious goddamn fish,' Lawton said. 'I'm going to give her some slack, see what she does.'

'Good plan,' Thorn said.

He cut a look back at the house, but didn't see Alexandra anywhere.

Thirty feet down the shore, Morgan eased her bow up to the rocky bank, gave it some throttle and ran aground. Blocking his way back to the house. Nowhere to run in the other direction, with a thick stand of mangroves running all the way to the waterline.

She had on pink shorts and a yellow jersey underneath a neon blue Hawaiian shirt. The pistol was in her right hand. Not trying to hide it.

'And yet again we meet,' she said. Coming closer, a little wary now that he hadn't tried to flee. 'Houdini and his assistant. Putting on another show.'

Lawton's reel started to spin, the grouper confused, making a run. Over the years Thorn had hooked it a half dozen times but never landed it. Always going back in the hole, sawing the line in two. Must have a lip full of rusty hooks. A wily fish, but somehow Lawton had managed to fool it.

Thorn stepped away from the old man, facing Morgan. Nothing in his peripheral vision, no sign of Alex. A quick stab of worry that Morgan was working a double-team, someone outflanking them from the highway side.

He took another step away from Lawton, trying for as much separation as possible. The old man was intent on his fish, working it, fiddling with the drag, cursing, talking to it.

'You killed my brother,' she said as if it amused her. 'You killed Johnny. You tore his throat open.'

'I understand you've been fairly busy yourself.'

She smiled. Pulled off her sunglasses and pitched them into the water.

'Yes, it's true. I've been severing a few of my ties.'

'A new beginning,' Thorn said. 'Like that's possible.'

'Oh, it's possible.'

'Dye your hair. Easy as that.'

'Damn right it is. Cut the knot in one swipe. Born again.'

'I don't know,' Thorn said. 'Bullshitting yourself is one thing, bullshitting God might be a little tougher.'

Lawton was cranking the fish in. It flopped once, splashed. But it didn't break Morgan's concentration. She raised the pistol and sighted on Thorn's chest.

She was about to say something more when a pistol shot flared and a chunk of limestone at Morgan's feet blasted away and sprayed the water. She lurched backwards, but kept her aim solidly on Thorn.

'Hey,' Lawton said. 'Cut the horseplay. There's some serious fishing going on here.'

Alex shouted from thirty feet away.

'Drop it, Morgan, or you're finished.'

Alexandra stood beside the pink buffalo, using both hands to aim Sugarman's pistol. She was taking small steps forward.

'Last chance,' Alex said. 'Drop it now.'

Morgan waited. Alexandra came closer, holding her aim steady.

'Good-bye, Thorn,' Morgan said.

She whirled and dropped to one knee and fired. Pink plaster flew off the buffalo's mane. Her second shot hit home. Alexandra crumpled sideways into the grass as Thorn dove onto Morgan's back, wrenched the pistol from her hands, and clubbed her skull, once, twice, feeling her go soft beneath him, raising the pistol again, then catching himself. He dropped his hold on her and stood up and slung the pistol into the shallows. Blood was darkening her blond hair. She wasn't dead, but she wasn't going to be awake for a long while.

He ran across the rocky ground and fell to his knees beside Alexandra.

Her eyes were open. The slug had torn through the outer edge of her thigh. He ripped off his shirt and knotted it tight against the blood flow.

Alex gave him a faint grin.

'Here we are again,' she said.

'Save it,' he said. 'I'm taking you to the hospital.'

'Not going to undress me this time?'

'Later,' he said. 'I'll do it over and over. I promise.'

'Good,' she said. 'I like it when you undress me.'

He pulled her up in his arms and held her for a moment, both of them watching as Lawton hauled the grouper up from the shallows. The old man bent down and scooped up the fish and turned around, holding up his silver prize with both hands.

'This one's a keeper,' he yelled.

He was walking up the bank, smiling. A happy old man.

'Damn right it is,' Thorn said. 'Damn right.'